ON WINGS OF DARK MAGIC—

A shrill keening filled the air, rising swiftly in intensity, and suddenly they appeared—gargoyles, those creatures out of nightmare visions, the ancient guardians of Horlach's gate!

Leathery, scabrous wings beating violently, the creatures smote wildly with talons, teeth, and barbed tails. The Venturers blurred in a vision of fury. Swords struck, rebounded.

As one of the creatures flew at me, I could sense Kaedric choosing his first victim. Yet even as his sorcerous fires ate at the gargoyle's heart, I felt a terrifying foreboding of doom, a fear all too soon confirmed as Kaedric's spell was turned against all of us by Horlach's sorcerous trap. . . .

FIRE GET

Cheryl J. Franklin

DAW BOOKS, INC.
DONALD A. WOLLHEIM, PUBLISHER
1633 Broadway, New York, NY 10019

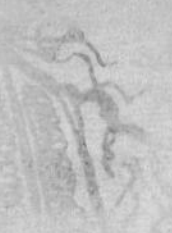

Cover art by Tim Hildebrandt.

DAW Book Collectors No. 726

To Dr. Walter S. Cascell, who
always understood so much more than
communication engineering,
but never quite mastered levitation

First Printing, November 1987

3 4 5 6 7 8 9

PRINTED IN THE U.S.A.

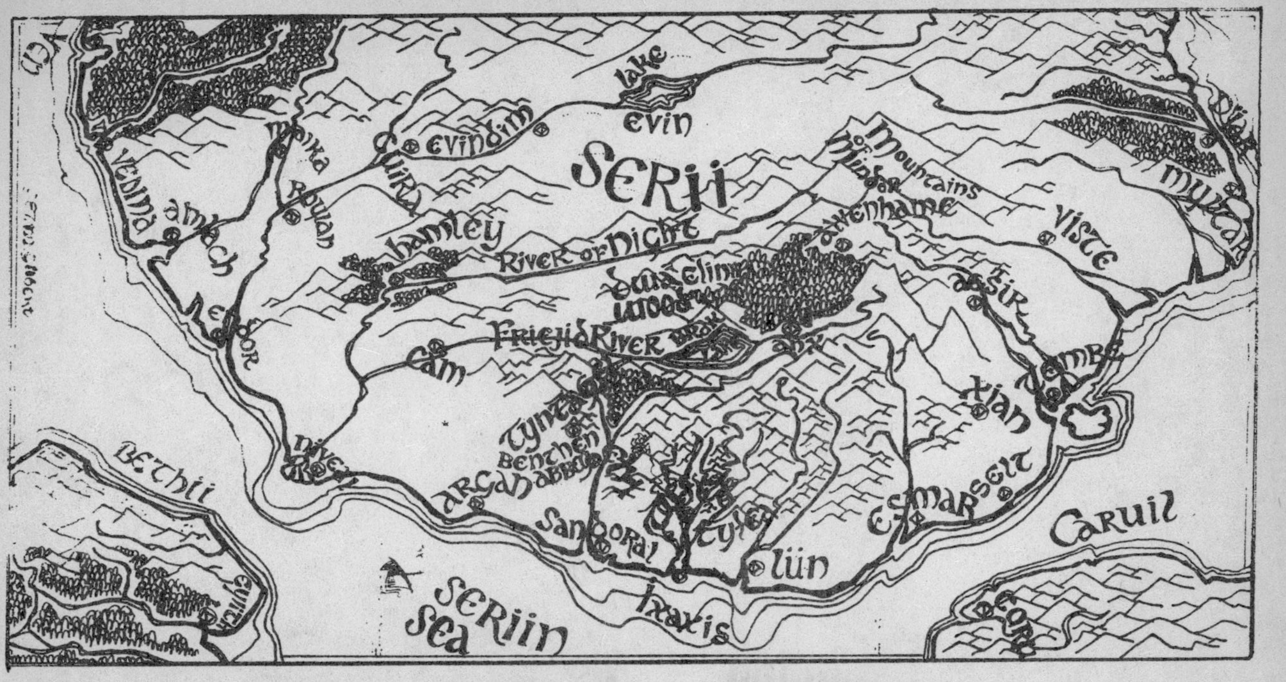
SERII
Evin
Lake
Evindim
Guira
Hamley
River of Night
Mountains of Mindar
Viste
Mystar
Cam
Friejid River
Wood
Tyne
Benthen
Argan Abbey
Sandoral
Niven
Ledor
Vedina
Amlach
Royan
Xian
Esmar
Selt
Lün
Tyler
Ixaxis
Seriin Sea
Caruil
Bethii
Eyith

I. THE SPARK

Chapter 1

Year of Serii—8983
Ixaxis, Serii

The ferry approached. The priest who waited at the dock had watched it journey the breadth of the narrow strait. The dawn was chill, but the clouds were high, and the island loomed sharply in the midst of the choppy sea. Occasionally, the priest darted a brief glance at the dark, incurious boy who squatted near the dock's land-edge. The boy was small and excessively thin; he tossed a glinting dagger from hand to hand with idle expertise.

Churning water tossed the ferry roughly against the dock. The dock shook, and the priest jerked to regain his footing. The dour ferryman placidly secured his craft.

A short woman, bundled against the damp, disembarked, pulling a limp scarf from graying, disheveled curls. Disgruntled, she muttered, "I despise boats." She stared coldly at the priest. "I did not think members of your calling cared to associate personally with our guild."

The priest answered evenly, "I bring you a candidate."

"Would you then sacrifice a member of your flock to us? That is what your sort calls heresy, is it not?"

"No calling is immune from folly," said the priest. "I recognize the difference between those who might follow my vocation and one who must follow yours." He gestured toward the boy, who maintained a sullen disregard of the conferees.

The woman frowned disapprovingly at both the boy

and the wickedly honed blade he sported. "Have I been dragged across the sea at this appalling hour to salvage an unsavory urchin? Your letter indicated life-threatening urgency, not some holy man's mission of charity." She grimaced with distaste. "What makes you think this mudlark has the makings of a wizard?"

The priest answered very softly. "He destroyed the city of Ven."

"Ven was destroyed by fire."

"Ven was destroyed by this boy's anger."

The woman looked sharply at the priest. She turned a pensive gaze upon the boy and walked deliberately across the dock. The boy did not acknowledge her. "I am Mistress Marga," she said. "What is your name, boy?"

The knife spun from the boy's hand. He caught it deftly, held it before him, and studied the blade closely. He looked up at the wizardess and studied her with the same emotionless intensity he had bestowed upon the knife.

The woman returned the boy's stare, noting with greater interest the startling impact of clear blue eyes as cold as frost looming in the emaciated face. They seemed to penetrate deeply and with purpose instead of shying from her as expected of a lad of such wretched background. She shivered, absurdly uneasy for one who could cow the highest Lords of Serii.

The boy rose abruptly to his feet, and she realized how very young he was to be so hard. Deliberately disparaging, she said, "The priest seems to think you have sorcerer's blood in you. Did you concoct that fable to avoid religious conversion?" As the boy did not answer, she continued caustically. "It was a novel but foolish deception." She turned away from the boy and began the return walk to the waiting ferry.

The priest warily watched both wizardess and boy. The boy closed his eyes tightly, clenching his fingers around the dagger as he pointed it toward the woman's back. The woman stopped, and the priest smiled slightly at the brief shock displayed on the wizardess' countenance. The woman turned again to the boy, who lowered his arm, seemingly against his will, and dropped the knife to the rocky earth. The boy's eyes pursued the knife. He regarded the wizardess from lowered lids.

"It appears you were right, priest," said the wizardess thoughtfully. "He is a revert. Does he know his parents?"

"Only his mother, and she is dead."

"A pity," said the woman. "Both his parents must have been latents."

The priest nodded vague comprehension. "Will you take him then?"

"As your letter so aptly stated, priest, we have little choice. A Power like that is far too dangerous to let grow untrained. Yes, we will take him. I think you have brought me far more trouble than a miserably early morning boat ride." She called to the boy. "I am cold and hungry for my breakfast, and I do not intend to wait for you all day." She acknowledged the priest curtly, "Father Medwyn," and marched determinedly to the ferry.

With a slow, peculiarly graceful act of caution, the boy recovered his dagger. He hesitated, then crossed to the priest and paused. The holy man raised his hand in blessing. The boy neither spoke nor varied expression, but he waited until the priest had completed the prayer before stepping lightly onto the rocking ferry.

The ferryman released his craft and maneuvered it into the returning current. The priest watched the ferry as it journeyed back to the island which owned it. He saw it meet the far shore, though he could no longer discern its passengers. He seemed disappointed, as if some expected event had not transpired entirely as he had hoped, but he smiled ruefully and began to turn away.

A light beamed across the water, and the priest raised his eyes. It was a clear and golden beam, and it sped from the far dock to the water at the feet of the priest. The priest smiled broadly. "Thank you, my son," he whispered.

Chapter 2

The cliffs were steep and chalky. They crumbled at the gentlest touch, and their shards littered the narrow beach. They gave the island an insubstantial semblance which was deceptive. The chalk coated the island in filmy layers, but the foundations were built of solid adamant.

The ferryman had not lingered at the dusty white beach. He had deposited his passengers and continued toward the cove which lay on the island's leeward side. The craft bobbed and disappeared around a bend of unkindly shore.

"Come along, boy," commanded Mistress Marga. She walked with assurance toward the cliff and seemed to vanish within a fold of rock. The boy watched quietly. Since debarking, he had made only a single move, a slight shrug which had sent lightning across the channel he had just traversed. He had frowned then, as if regretting an impulsive gesture.

He crossed the rough sand carefully, suspiciously studying the cliffs which dominated his view of the legendary island. He stared closely at the wrinkled steps which had been carved from the stone. There was a smooth plane of darker rock beside them. He stepped through it.

Mistress Marga faced him. She nodded slightly at his appearance, but she gave no other sign of acknowledgment. She had bypassed the simpler tests which she had planned, choosing instead the difficulty of the unexpected. She had known full wizards to take the stairs regularly without ever noting the door embedded in energy's illusions. She wished for a moment that she had allowed the boy to precede her. The hint her disappearance gave might have been unnecessary, and now she would not know. She reminded herself not to underestimate the boy's Power on the basis of his origins. Not every major Power had risen from the ranks of Serii's nobility.

She led the boy through the gently luminous lower halls of Ixaxis. The ways were seldom traveled; few students knew of their existence, for very few recent students had descried the spell-hidden entrance. The Powers of Ixaxis had waned since Ceallagh's days.

Mistress Marga opened the wrought-gold doors of a small cubicle and waited for the boy to join her. The boy stiffened. The wizardess observed the hesitation which might have signaled fear, and she filed the reaction carefully in her mind. The boy entered, but he remained tensely defensive from the moment she closed the doors until their reopening in the Ixaxin school's lower storage chamber. She could feel his Power waiting, and she gathered her own Power, an act of caution which she knew her fellow instructors would deride as absurd.

"This way, boy," she ordered. She knew the name by which the priest had called him, but she would not use it until the boy gave it. The priest—she had disregarded most of his letter as superstitious exaggeration. She would reread it with greater respect.

The boy was absorbing the abundance of wonders in his new surroundings, and Marga slowed slightly to allow his observations. He would be questioned later to discover their extent and perspective. He could not have known much of art or any fine craftsmanship in the slums of Ven.

She took him directly to the Headmaster's office, and bid him wait in the tiny entry. The boy was guarded there from any possibility of escaping, and she thought he knew it. Such perception ought to have been impossible without extensive training.

"He is a major Power, Vald," argued Marga to the white-haired Headmaster. "He would totally disrupt a novice class."

"Really, Marga, it is unlikely he can even read. How can we possibly place him at a senior level? It would be utterly unfair to him—as well as to the other students who have worked toward that status for years."

"Senior status is not a matter of prestige. It is a gauge of developed Power, and some of our students could bear a reminder of that distinction."

"I am sorry, Marga," said Master Vald with finality. "He goes into the novice class. When he is ready for advancement, he may petition for the testing like any other student."

"At least meet with him."

Master Vald sighed. Mistress Marga could be a very difficult and obstinate woman, but she was a gifted teacher. "Very well, Marga. Bring the boy here, but please recall that I have a class to teach in a few minutes."

"Did I ever forget a class, Vald?"

"Not one of your own."

Marga sniffed. She opened the office door and beckoned to the boy, who appeared not to have moved at all. "This is Master Veld. He is the Headmaster. He will direct your studies according to your capacity and development."

"What is your name, boy?" asked Master Vald, and the boy gave no answer. Master Vald looked at Marga with considerable exasperation. "There is little purpose in your coming here, boy, if you do not intend to answer the simplest question. To be accepted for full Ixaxis training is a high honor. If you prefer not to accept our teaching, we shall bind your Power and return you to the life you left. Now, do you wish to be schooled with us?"

For a breath's moment, there was no response, and Mistress Marga grimly wondered what Master Vald would do if no answer came. She knew that the implied threat of returning the boy was hollow. They could not bind a major Power. They must train or eliminate, while they were still able, any Power which threatened Serii. That was the life and purpose of

Ixaxis, but the mandated alternative to training had been unnecessary for millennia.

The boy's clear blue eyes narrowed in an inspection too knowing for an ignorant slum-child. He is proud, this boy, thought Master Vald with disapproval. "I wish to be schooled, Master Vald," said the boy in a careful emulation of Master Vald's clipped accent.

Days ago he knew only the incomprehensible Ven patois, thought Marga. It is remarkable that he even understands us, but already he has begun to copy us. I told Father Medwyn that he was a revert. I only half believed it, but he is; he truly is. He has the Power, the intelligence, the tenacity of life of a Sorcerer King. Lords help us if he has as well their unscrupulous, egotistical cruelty.

"Very well, boy," said Master Vald, "we shall accept you as an Ixaxin novice. Mistress Marga will take you to the Hall of Novitiates."

"Master Vald," acknowledged Marga with the half-bow of Ixaxin respect. She disagreed with the Headmaster's placement of the boy, but Master Vald had handled the interview well. The boy did not demur from following Mistress Marga in either bow or exit from the Headmaster's office.

"This is Hrgh, boy," said Marga. "He is one of our senior students, and he will be your class proctor."

Hrgh smiled as engagingly and insincerely as only a Dolr'han of Liin could manage. He was not allowed to use his title as long as he was a student, but no one could mistake the finely chiseled features and the perfect self-assurance of Serii's highest House. "You are from Ven?" asked Hrgh, and his voice was a smoothly perfect instrument of charm befitting the heir of Liin.

The younger boy stiffened very slightly at the question, and he granted it only a minimal nod. Marga grunted. The boy was determined to be difficult; perhaps Master Vald was correct in keeping him with the novitiate. "Explain our rules to him, Hrgh," said Marga. "Assign him quarters and a student's robe, and introduce him to his instructor."

"I know the proper sequence, Mistress Marga," returned Hrgh with a touch of condescension.

"As you know the proper respect due a scholar," rebuked Marga. Arrogance was a Dolr'han failing, and Marga enjoyed reminding the young Lord Hrgh that Ixaxin status was a function of merit rather than family birthright. Sorcerous Power was inherited, but its correct application demanded incessant work. Marga reconsidered: it will be difficult to teach that lesson to this boy of Ven who does so much without effort. She noted then that the boy was displeased by her censure of Hrgh. So, he is still vulnerable to certain types of Power, she thought with sharpened interest.

"You did not complete the introductions, Mistress Marga," said Hrgh in a grudgingly deferential tone.

"The boy has given us no name, Hrgh," responded Marga. She felt some reluctance over leaving the boy in Hrgh's care, but Hrgh was very capable. Hrgh was the strongest Power they had, though he was still some years away from scholar status. Marga closed the door behind her and felt the release of a flood of pent up tension of which she had been unaware. This waif shall not succeed in frightening me again, she asserted, and because she was Marga, her resolve became fact.

That old woman has no sense of her station, thought Hrgh, and look at this miserable specimen she has brought me: a nameless slum dweller. "As you give no name," said Hrgh indifferently, "I shall call you Venkarel. That means Ven-no-name in the ancient language of Liin. You are cognizant of Liin, I trust."

The boy looked uncertain. It made an ordinary child of him for the moment. He shook his head, and his dark hair fell across his crystalline eyes.

"You are not a very communicative sort, are you?" demanded Hrgh. "Liin is only the First House of Serii and the wealthiest, most influential domain in the Seriin Alliance."

"The King lives in Tulea," proffered the boy tentatively.

"You do speak. How comforting. I naturally exclude His Majesty from comparison. However, I must say that Tulea is only one city rather than a true domain. I cannot expect you to appreciate the difference, of course, but I assure you that Liin has no peer. These will be your quarters." Hrgh opened the shuttered door of a stark room which was little more than an alcove in the warren of the novices' dormitory. Hrgh pressed his hand to a recess where a lock would normally be found. The recess began to glow with pale gold. "I have marked it: Venkarel. It will be your place of sleep and your place of study during your years in the novitiate. You will eat in the common area with the other novices."

"Where are they?" asked the boy with his first show of interest.

"At class, of course. This is a school."

"Why are you not at class?"

"I am senior level, you impertinent serf, and novices do not question the higher ranks."

The boy dropped his lids lower over his blue eyes. "I am sorry, my lord Dolr'han," he said very humbly, but there was a flash of Power which Hrgh did not detect.

"We do not use titles here," said Hrgh, but the boy's servility pleased him. Hrgh did not consider the incongruity of a boy who knew nothing of Liin recognizing Liin's ruling family and its heir. Hrgh did not consider the strangeness of his own decision to cultivate this boy, this Venkarel, as a member of a Dolr'han's select group of followers.

Chapter 3

The Venkarel sat alone in his assigned room. He wore the gray robe of an Ixaxin student, and there were books on his desk: elementary texts which were his to read. He had mastered these and others in the library's privacy, but he would not yet admit to greater knowledge than his instructor had demanded. The other novices bemoaned the weight of work, but the Venkarel distrusted their complaints. This learning was so simple; these people appeared to give so many things without demand for payment. The Venkarel suspected entrapment, though he had not defined its form. He trusted none of these people save Hrgh. The Venkarel did not himself understand why he made this exception, but he did not question it yet; Hrgh had ensorcelled him well.

The Venkarel had learned survival in the slums of Ven, and his teachers had not been gentle. He knew the ways of treachery. He knew no other way to live. He had followed the priest, because only the priest had dared come to him after the terrible fire, the fire which had eaten his world. He had followed, because he had not known how to live in a world suddenly bereft of enemies. He felt comfortable here, though this place was very strange, because here he could find enemies again. He thought he understood the rules. The strong survived, though strength was measured differently on Ixaxis. Here, he was strong.

The Venkarel had categorized his fellow novices as either conspirators in deception or idiots. He had known their kind: Deev and Ag had been the same. The Venkarel regretted the comparison as he thought of it, for it recalled the blood, the fire and the madness.

Hrgh was the only Ixaxin who had gained any measure of the Venkarel's confidence. Hrgh was the only member of senior level whom the Venkarel had met. The Venkarel's conclusion seemed to him as obvious as Zerus' essential postulates of wizardry, which the Venkarel had recently learned: it was clearly necessary to become a member of the senior level.

"What is this?" demanded Master Vald, reluctantly focusing his eyes on yet another of the seemingly endless documents which crossed his desk. He stared at the latest for only a moment. "Master Helmar," remonstrated the Headmaster, "This is a student's test paper. I am not here to review individual examinations."

Master Helmar shuffled unhappily. He was a timid man who little resembled the common conception of a wizard. "I thought you might wish to see this one, sir," he said hesitantly. "It is—not usual."

With a sigh of irritated contempt for underconfident instructors who distrusted their own judgments, Master Vald gave the paper his attention. His eyes narrowed. "These results indicate a perfect score."

"Yes, Master Vald." Master Helmar continued apologetically, "I have tried to discover an error in my assessment, sir, or some irregularity in the boy's responses."

"There is no such thing as cheating on an Ixaxin test, Master Helmar. You know that," mused Vald, distracted now from the chronically uncomfortable instructor. The test results certainly appeared authentic. "I thought we had no strong candidates for senior level this term? How did this student's progress escape notice?"

"He seemed ordinary, sir."

"Helmar, I have never known a perfect score to be accomplished before. This student is clearly not ordinary. I hope you have not misjudged your other pupils so badly."

"He was in my class only three weeks, sir," responded Helmar defensively. "I had little time to gauge his abilities properly."

Master Vald stiffened, and his Power flared into the instinctive shield against danger. "What is this boy's name?" asked Vald cautiously.

Master Helmar answered with equal care, "He is called Venkarel, sir."

"Indeed." Master Vald was not pleased. Marga would gloat. "Send for Mistress Marga, Helmar. Tell her we have a new student for her senior level class." She has shown such fascination with the boy, thought Vald sourly; let her try to manage him.

Mistress Marga enjoyed her small triumph over the Headmaster. It was pleasing to have one's judgment vindicated, and it did not hurt one's standing either. Naturally, Marga did not reveal that she had herself questioned her initial assessment of the Venkarel's abilities. The boy's performance in the novice class had been far from outstanding. Marga had begun to doubt her instincts, but the Venkarel was her student now, and she could substantiate her first analysis. She was pleased, but she was greatly disturbed.

When he was aware of observation, the Venkarel held closely to the average pace of the other seniors. In the private sessions, Marga worked the Venkarel more severely than any other pupil of her long career, though she did not reveal how far and fast she pushed him, lest the boy realize how he was betraying himself. His advancement to senior level had accrued little notice because he was not a novice long enough to be known. He had begun to gain some acceptance because he seemed harmlessly mediocre and Hrgh approved of him. Perhaps acceptance was his only purpose in deception; it would be a common enough motive.

Still, pondered Marga uneasily, he does not try to cultivate friends. It is as if he plays a game against us, and only he knows the rules. I must teach him Ceallagh's laws of restraint before he grows beyond me. I have never had a more urgent task, for he learns so quickly on his own. He sees and remembers everything. I must mold him, or we will have another Horlach, and we have no Ceallagh and Tul to defeat him. I must make an Ixaxin of him.

How did they hold him so long in Ven? Father Medwyn said he was a slave; no wonder the boy rebelled. Lord Gides dur Ven deserved death for allowing such depth of crime to grow in his domain, but his folly cost many innocents as well. The boy's Power must have been dormant until the day of fire, or the cost might have been even greater. Thank the lords that the priest had sense enough to bring the boy to us.

I am nearly tempted to ask the priest to come here again. The Venkarel gave some trust to Father Medwyn, whereas he has given none to us. No, the boy does follow Hrgh. Most of the students do; it is the Dolr'han Power, and it is potent. Perhaps I ought to be glad that any of us can influence the Venkarel. I just wish it were another. Hrgh is so fully a Dolr'han. He expects to replace Alobar as Infortiare in a few years, though he knows the Lord of Ixaxis cannot also be the Lord of Liin. Hrgh will not like to learn what I intend for the Venkarel.

Marga extinguished the oil lamp beside her desk; Ixaxis had older lamps which gave cleaner light, but she disliked using that which she could never understand. The moon struck the waves below her window. She wished uselessly that the present Infortiare were a stronger man or at least a stronger wizard. She wished that she might call him from Tulea. An Infortiare ought certainly to be strong enough to remain Ixaxin after less than a century in the King's castle, but Alobar had become Tulean and wholly mortal in his perspective. He has even grown old, she thought, though he has known fewer years than I have. He is a kind, old man, and he is useless to us.

A single wizardess ought not try to decide the future of Serii without her liege's will or knowledge. If I am wrong, if the boy is truly no more than a minor sorcerer made precocious by life-threatening circumstances, then I shall look the fool. I shall lose my status and any chance at a seat on the Ixaxin Council, and I shall have nothing. As a wizardess who has acted independently of her liege lord, I may find my Power bound from me as well.

Marga began to pace, then seated herself with deliberation. Ruing the Venkarel's appearance in her previously well-ordered life achieved nothing. The Venkarel was an aberration, and she would have preferred that he not exist; but he had come, and she could only do as she deemed necessary. She knew that she was tampering with Ceallagh's laws, with the King's will, and with the age-old stability of Serii and her world. That was the problem with aberrations: they were contagious. Marga knew that the Venkerel would make of her an aberration as well, but she would teach him to the limits of her capacity and his. She twisted the fine gold chain which marked her as an Ixaxin scholar, and she did that which she had not done since the vicar of Cuira drove her father from the church on the basis of Marga's Power: she prayed.

II. THE TINDER

Chapter 1

Year of Serii—8988
Ixaxis, Serii

The young man with the grass-stained tunic twisted her fingers with his broad hand. "Dad and Ma are at their duties, and the cottage is empty this hour, Ericka," he said coaxingly.

"Quietly, Jhobl," answered Ericka, a young woman whose attractions did not extend above her neck. "The children will hear you."

"I thought you said they never listened to you."

"They are my charges, Jhobl. I cannot just leave them when I wish."

"They play in their own garden, Ericka, and they will be the happier to be without a watchdog for a while. They get little enough time to enjoy themselves as children ought." Jhobl planted a surreptitious kiss on Ericka's neck, and she giggled her delight. "Let them play their games," wheedled Jhobl with another kiss, "while we play ours."

The amorous pair started guiltily when the little girl approached. She was a tiny, solemn thing with hair a shade of gold just shy of white and gray eyes too large for her face. "I cannot find Dayn, Mistress Ericka," she said.

The governess dropped her arms from Jhobl hurriedly, straightening herself into something of a dignified demeanor. She assumed her most authoritative manner. "Now, Rhianna, he was here only a moment ago. Were you not playing together?" she asked patiently.

"Yes, Mistress Ericka."

"And what were you playing at?"

"Dayn hid from me, and I was to search for him."

"Then, Rhianna, it would be unfair of me to find him for you. You know how your father feels about fairness."

"It is not cheating to ask for help," protested the little girl seriously.

"Do not argue with me, Rhianna," said Ericka sternly.

"Yes, Mistress Ericka," said the child again.

"Very well then. Finish your game honestly, and do not come back here until you have done so."

"Yes, Mistress Ericka." The little girl looked troubled, but she curtsied carefully and returned to her search.

"That should take care of them for an hour at least," said Jhobl admiringly, "since the little Lord Dayn will not want to be found. You are a clever one, Ericka." The woman smiled with satisfaction at his praise.

The two of them started toward the neat brick cottage which housed the head gardener of Tyntagel Keep and his family. Ericka stopped suddenly and looked back at the grove of oaks to which she had consigned her charges. "Nothing will happen to them," said Jhobl heartily. "Come along, and quit worrying."

Ericka creased her brow as she responded, "Dayn will be all right, I suppose."

"And so will Rhianna. She is a tough little thing, after all."

Ericka shook her head as she answered, "As if I did not know it. A swat sends other children into tears, but I could nearly kill that one, and she would take no notice."

"Then what bothers you, Ericka?" demanded Jhobl with burgeoning exasperation. He had worked long at this conquest of Mistress Ericka, and he did not enjoy delaying for His Lordship's offspring.

"She is up to something," answered the woman slowly.

"Children are always up to something, Ericka, but they survive it."

"She is not an ordinary child, Jhobl."

"Just what does that mean? You think she is another such as her mother?"

"Jhobl!" exclaimed Ericka with shock. "You should not even say such things in jest."

"Well, is that not what you meant?"

"I never did!" protested Ericka vehemently. Jhobl smiled winningly, and Ericka relaxed. "You are a one," she chided with restored good humor. "All right, I suppose old Baerod's get can tend to themselves a while." Jhobl laughed with her, and she yielded to his insistence, following him through the cottage gate.

Beneath the mottled, oaken canopy they had left, a very small girl watched the day grow darker. She had tired of the game her brother played at her expense, and she was frightened of being alone. She feared her governess almost as much as she feared her father, so she would not leave the wood until her brother had been found. Frantically, she wondered where he hid, thrusting her thoughts against the trees. The leaves sighed in the gathering dusk.

"You could not have seen me, Rani," argued a very displeased young boy moments later, still dubious of his sister's ability to discover his fine hiding place. "I was much too high in the tree. You watched me hide," he accused.

"I did not," protested his sister.

"You did. You cheated, and I shall tell Mistress Ericka."

"It is not cheating to ask for help," insisted the little girl uncertainly.

"There was no one here to help, you stupid baby." The boy grumbled, "Why did I have to have a stupid baby sister anyway?"

Relieved that her brother had not contradicted her view of the game's rules, the little girl continued stubbornly, "I asked the oak, and she told me where you were."

Her brother looked at her with exasperation. He

started to sneer at his sister's set face. His dark eyes grew wide. "You used sorcery," he whispered with dawning horror. His voice grew louder with panic. "You *are* a sorceress. Get away from me!" he shouted. He pushed the little girl, and she fell, bewildered. She was only four and not yet learned in Tyntagellian prejudice. Her brother was seven; he raced to his father's keep to report the abomination he had found. Lord Dayn did not play with his younger sister again.

Chapter 2

Year of Serii—9001

The tutor was a pale man with the flaccid, boneless appearance of inactivity. His brow bulged and rose to a balding dome. His colorless eyes were prominent above an insignificant nose. He shifted stiffly, moving his hands as does one who is insecure in his position.

The girl whom he addressed was young, but she was old enough to discomfit the pallid tutor for more cause than the whispered stories about her heritage. She had known many other tutors, and her gaze could invariably rob the pale man of his assurance. She made him sense that she had heard all that he could tell her many times.

"Even the least daughter of Tyntagel's Lord must attend the responsibility of her position, Lady Rhianna," said the tutor in his high, irregular drone. "You are accorded the rights befitting a member of a Seriin First House. Your father, Lord Baerod," the tutor stumbled over the name, "expects that you duly uphold the honor of that privilege. You should serve the more gladly, knowing that you are a burden to him."

The girl, whose hair was fallow silk, studied her tutor with deep, gray eyes. She knew that the pale man lacked the strength to hold his position long. He creaked with anxiety each time he lectured her, and her father did not tolerate such inadequate behavior. She returned to her desk with a fluid motion; her tutor watched, and his head jerked nervously after her, following the sunlight's dance across the girl's frail form. He felt, as always, peculiarly awed by her obedience of his command.

The dark and ugly woman who occupied the classroom corner observed the man's reaction with disapproval. She fingered a talisman, a twisted thing which might once have been a living creature, and glared at the girl with venomous hatred. The woman resolved to bespeak the girl's father that night and recommend the tutor's dismissal.

Chapter 3

Year of Serii—9007

"She is past old enough, Baerod," insisted Lady Altha. "If you do not arrange her marriage soon, it will be admission to all of Serii that you consider your daughter a sorceress."

The Lord of Tyntagel rhythmically tapped the finger on which the onyx signet of his station glinted. He was infuriated with his cousin, and he scowled. No wonder the Esmarians returned her so promptly after her husband's death, he thought; her tongue could sear a wizard. But she is right in this. I cannot pretend that Rhianna is fully mortal if I refuse to see her properly wedded.

"She would bear children," he argued, more to himself than to his cousin, "and they would perpetuate her Power."

Lady Altha wagged her bony head. "Not necessarily. She is your daughter as well as Eleni's. Why you had to take up with that Alvenhamish witch, I shall never understand. You already had three children from Darya, and there were countless suitable women if you felt you had to wed again. You could hardly have made a worse choice, short of marrying an Ixaxin."

"That is enough, Altha," ordered Lord Baerod fiercely, and Lady Altha grew petulantly silent. Altha manages the household well, thought Baerod, but at times she is as much trouble as Rhianna.

Tyntagel's liege lord paced the length of his darkly paneled office. Lady Altha is correct: Rhianna is a liability. Lord Brant has already approached me, and I cannot postpone an answer indefinitely. If I approve her betrothal to Brant's son, I shall be defying Seriin law, because Rhianna is unquestionably a sorceress. If I admit that Rhianna is a sorceress, I shall be admitting guilt of keeping her from Ixaxin testing, and the Infortiare will strip me of my authority. If I refuse to arrange her marriage out of deference to Ceallagh's ancient laws, I shall be making a mockery of all I have done and said against Ixaxin rule. Brant will never join our effort to depose the Infortiare if I admit that I fear my own daughter's Power. I can contribute little to our effort if I lose Tyntagel.

Our need for allies is immediate. Venkarel is already restoring the old Ixaxin authority with the King, and we must stop him before we have another Horlach in our midst. We need every weapon we can muster, and we are so unprepared. We were so sure that Hrgh would replace Alobar. Who could have guessed that Ixaxis had raised such a devil as Venkarel? Who would have imagined that even Ixaxis could be so mad as to let a revert live? We were lazy, and now we must fight against time. We must stop Venkarel before he realizes his ambitions, before King Astorn becomes fully the Infortiare's puppet, before we are bowed again beneath a Sorcerer King. We must stir every force of mortal Serii against Ixaxis before it is too late.

We have lost Hrgh, but he was always a tainted tool. Lord Borgor is doing well in Tulea; as Adjutant, he may be able to keep the King's Council from Venkarel's grasp, and Borgor's wife has much influence with the royal family. We have warned the other members of the Seriin Alliance. Our agents are spreading throughout Serii. We must enlist all true Lords of Serii—even those whose kin are Ixaxins—if we are to counter the Lord of Ixaxis.

We must be ready to combat Venkarel when he returns from Ardasia. We have little more than a year in which to prepare. He is foolish to leave Tulea at such a time, but he makes too few mistakes. We must not hesitate to use his absence from the court. We must be united against him before he returns.

Rhianna is a liability, but she can gain us Lord Brant and Niveal. Brant will ask few questions about her; he will be glad of any dowried bride for a son who battered his first wife to death. If we delay the actual marriage, Brant will be too deeply involved in our cause to leave us when he realizes what Rhianna is. Tyntagel will lose Niveal's trade, but we shall have Niveal's aid against Venkarel. Perhaps I can negotiate with Morgh Dolr'han for compensating trade arrangements; Liin has as much at stake in this war as I have.

"Send a missive to Niveal, Master Evram," commanded the Lord of Tyntagel. "Inform Lord Brant that I should like to discuss further his suggestion regarding alliance of our Houses. Invite him to Tyntagel at his earliest convenience."

"Yes, my lord," answered the young man with deference, but Master Evram's eyes were worried.

Chapter 4

Shadows fell heavily across the forest rim, and the weathered castle stone glowed with the burnished gold of dusk. From beneath my darkling oaks, I could see the keep clearly, but I fancied it a distant thing, like an etching in a frame. It held that ordered world in which I had no proper part, though it had been my home for all the years of my life.

The dark of spring's slow evening deepened. Above me misty stars appeared, shy precursors of bejeweled night. I had tarried overlong outside the keep; I would merit the scathing bite of censure for my tardy return. I laughed silently, and a mouse scurried in startlement. My father could impart very real reprisals for disobedience, but he seldom accorded me his direct attention. And I no longer feared scolding from any lesser authority, not after years of daily lectures from family and tutors alike.

Interminable education had successfully impressed upon me the duties of my position. The obligations of obedience never waned, but my formal schooling had ended. The end of my studies came unexpectedly, though I had been educated to an extent which amounted to absurdity for a Seriin noblewoman, and the sudden conclusion left me dangling uncertainly. I had detested Master Chiarge, my final tutor, though he had displayed no more callous cruelty or excess than his numerous predecessors, but I almost rued his departure now, a month removed from him in memory. Freedom of time let me realize my dearth of future plans.

It was an empty feeling which clutched me, a void which refused to be filled by the normal concerns of a

Seriin noblewoman. I could match my sister's skills in those arts, such as needlecraft and music, considered requisite for any nobleman's wife, but few visitors to my father's keep approved of sorcerous blood. I had been educated more fully than either of my brothers, though they would each occupy governing positions in which the knowledge might better be applied. I had amassed considerable quantities of useless lore (I could recite a thousand years of rulers for every country in the Seriin Alliance), but the haphazard learning of a peasant child would have served me more practically. The indefinite duties of a patrician spinster had replaced the relentless regimen which my father had heretofore dictated, and I needed to believe that a more active design awaited me.

The oak beside me reached deeply into the earth, exuding a more substantial reality than thoughts of my present circumstances. His spirit calmed the uncertain tenor of my mind, and I leaned against his bole in contentment. The blight which had threatened him was fully cleansed from leaf and limb, and I knew I had wrought one thing well during this otherwise useless period of freedom.

My mother had named me for the legendary Lady of Dwaelin Wood. I had often wondered if my mother's Power had told her that I would bear Rhianna's gift to heal and hold the wild things of the land, or if she merely chose a name common among her people. I could bespeak and understand the simpler lives. It was the trait which had estranged me from my own kind.

I scarcely remembered any camaraderie with a member of my own family. My brother Dayn, always the least intolerant of my kin, had once given me a measure of grudging, childish friendship. I was four years old, and he had thought me brave, for I did not cry at the expertly inflicted thrashings bestowed by our governess, Mistress Ericka. His approval was as marginal as one might expect of a boy afflicted by his younger sister's perpetual company. Even that little had lasted only a season.

Mistress Ericka was the only governess I had shared with any of my siblings. After her dismissal, a new governess had arrived, but I was not among her charges. A hard-faced nurse of solid peasant stock appeared to tend me and guard the other children from me. I never heard the nurse's name, for she was a superstitious woman; she wore about her neck a prominent amulet of rancid tallow and animal hide such as demons purportedly shun. There were other governesses and tutors for my education, but the nameless nurse had watched me almost incessantly until a year ago, when she had vanished as wordlessly as she had come.

I had disliked the eternal suspicion which had covered that nurse's face like a mask, but she had been a fixture no more annoying than summer midges. By the time I realized that my virtual imprisonment was unusual, I had accepted it. My father had proscribed Ixaxis testing for me, but I learned that his decision defied Seriin law only after I had been taught to abhor the Power which Ixaxis schooling would have fostered in me. My father's overriding hatred of wizards, their Ixaxin guild, and their Lord, the Infortiare, had produced odd gaps in my education, but I had no ambition to become a wizardess. A legion of tutors had instructed me to distrust Ixaxis, to despise the Infortiare, and to loathe my own abilities. Having once, years ago, suggested that the contributions of Lord Ceallagh dur Ixaxis to the foundations of Serii equaled those of King Tul, I was unlikely ever to repeat the crime; the memory of cold porridge and daily beatings for a month did not fade quickly. I acknowledged Tyntagellian histories with all their obvious gaps and inconsistencies, because it was my liege-father's will that I do so.

The last remembrance of sunlight left the sky, and the keep spread darkly against the planes of evening's violet hills. The keep was a squat and angular structure which had grown by haphazard, boxy appendages for too many centuries. It might have been lovely once, the two original towers lifting the eyes from the central structure to the proud, distant heights of the

Mountains of Mindar; the greatest loveliness remaining rose from the groves of oaks which huddled near the keep's encircling walls. Only the oaks had withstood the warping of Tyntagel dreams into iron of stark contour. Dour Tyntagel prospered, but my father's rule held nothing of dreams.

I sank my heart and mind into the warmth of the oak, my great friend who had stood a sturdy bastion for so many lifetimes of mage and mortal both, hoping to forfend a fit of that familiar bitterness which had hovered too closely of late. I thought forcibly of my sister, Yldana, who had wed Lord Amgor dur Amlach and gone with him to the King's court in Tulea. I thought of my brother Balev, who occupied himself in the exalted matters appropriate to the heir of Tyntagel; his spiritless, tedious wife, Nadira, had recently borne him a second daughter of exemplary normalcy. Dayn served presently as a captain in King Astorn's army, and in a year he would assume the dynastic functions of his rank.

Envy in my soul had long ago grown stale and sere. I could not conform to my family's pattern, but I could walk in the Tyntagel woods in companionship with the gentle ones therein. I could not rue the gift which gave me such friends. I faced the evening wryly receptive. I had stayed the dragons of despondency for another day. I plucked persistent leaves from my long tweed skirts and sought the bare earth path to my father's gate.

Chapter 5

I hastened, belatedly concerned by the certainty of repercussions if I were discovered in my late return to the keep. I had allowed just sufficient time to assume some delicately impractical dinner attire and the aspect, which fooled no one, of a decorous lady who had whiled away the afternoon in suitable passivity. Intently contemplating my possible punishment, I failed to notice Evram's approach.

"You have been avoiding me, Rani," he called. I had nearly reached the isolated stairs which led to the keep's back passages, and I debated whether I could attain them before Evram reached me. He anticipated me, as he often did, crossing to me in a bound and pinning me with his arm.

"Let me go, Evram," I pleaded. "I shall be late as it is."

"A few more moments will not harm, or does the lady of Tyntagel grow too grand to associate with her father's secretary?"

"Your status in this keep outshines my own, Master Evram. It is you who risk contamination by speaking to the Tyntagel sorceress."

Evram reached his fingers to the nape of my neck in a soft caress. He whispered reassuringly, "You are not a sorceress, Rani. I shall not believe it of you, whatever others may say."

"I am my mother's child, Evram, and I must go." I tried to pull free gently.

"Only if you promise to meet me after supper."

"You know that I cannot. I must read to my great-aunt until she tires of it, and by then you will be home and the keep will be locked against you."

"Lady Retl has the grippe, and she will want no company tonight. We may not have another such opportunity. Meet me in the garden house, Rani."

His hand moved tentatively, and I moved decisively away from him. "I thought you had agreed not to think of me thus, Evram."

"I agreed to give you time, but I shall not wait like Nimal until your father has wed you to some Seriin lord whom you do not love."

I answered austerely, for kinder words would not dissuade Evram. "You are presumptuous, Master Evram." He released me, for the force of my denial hurt him. I had never before used the voice of my rank against him. "I am sorry, Evram," I said sincerely.

"You are Lord Baerod's daughter after all," returned Evram bitterly. It was a cruelly knowing insult; I had upset Evram badly. He gave me a stiffly formal bow. "I have behaved improperly, my lady," he said with excessive, hollow contrition. "Please accept my apology."

He did not raise his face to me, and I spoke to his chestnut brown hair. "In the future, Master Evram, I trust you will recall that I *am* your liege's daughter." He darted at me an unhappy glance which I refused to acknowledge. I breathed a sigh of sympathy only when he had gone. Evram felt betrayed. I had rejoiced once that Evram did not shun me for my sorcery, but I had sorrowfully concluded that stubborn illusion was the true recipient of his love. Evram refused to connect me with what he considered an irredeemable sin; he refused to believe that I could speak with a tree.

I concentrated more firmly on passing unnoticed through the maze of corridors which I had trod for years. An uneasy aspect of my tainted abilities, evading notice was a gift I used seldom and guiltily. I attained my room without further interruption, but I touched my chamber door to find disquiet, familiar and inescapable. There is no privacy in Tyntagel Keep, I thought ruefully. I turned my face toward the worn, silver tile floor in resignation. Lady Altha's presence in my somber chamber did not augur well for me. She disliked me intensely and only grudgingly accepted me in what she viewed as her personal domain.

Lady Altha's sharp profile, an uncomfortable medley of prominent nose and jutting chin, promised malevolence with every angle of taut rigidity. She whirled toward me, emitting the peculiar crackle of a flounce of stiffened black silk and crinoline. Her dull umber eyes reflected neither light nor kindly emotion. I ought to have grown immune to her tirades; I bore them better than most by dint of practice, but the heat of her tongue could still occasionally wound me.

Lady Altha sputtered in her haste to express disgust. "You have no more responsibility in you than a selfish child, Rhianna. You might at least show consideration for your father, whose absurdly excessive generosity toward you defies all bounds of sense. The debt you owe that saintly man is altogether unrepayable. How you have the nerve to keep him waiting astonishes me. It will not establish a favorable first impression for Lord Brant, I assure you. Do quit dawdling, and try to present yourself decently. You look as if you have been wallowing with the swine—or the swineherd." The hard-packed Tyntagel soil on which I had sat did not cling, and the swineherd was a boy of ten who shook as if palsied each time he saw me near. Lady Altha was not exhibiting her best vituperative form. I could only conclude that my father had perturbed her with a rare imperative.

She thrust at me an extravagant gown of pale gray sea-silk, finely embroidered and fitted, and I accepted it with meek dismay. Warily silent, I fumbled with laces and clasps meant to enclose my sister's more substantial frame. I recalled certain of Evram's words from an alarming new perspective.

Lady Altha maintained her shrill scoldings as she draped me with an absurd excess of pearls and silver filigree, berating me as usual for circumstances I did not control. "You have no concept of your duties, Rhianna. By your age, Yldana had received offers from every significant House of Serii—including Liin. It takes more than a First House heritage to attract a Dolr'han." I restrained a reminder that the extolled Lord of Liin had conspicuously omitted the rite of marriage from his offers to my sister. "If you had only inherited a little more from your father!" grumbled Lady Altha disparagingly.

Lady Altha's diatribe did not waver as she swept me from my room; our footsteps beat aching echoes in my ears. "You might show some gratitude for your father's considerable efforts. Niveal is an important House, and Lord Grisk has a very promising future, despite those ridiculous stories about Lady Tilla's death. Personally, I cannot imagine why Lord Brant would consider you for his son. You are scarcely a prize, even with the substantial dowry your father has offered and the influence of a First House lineage as your portion. Your father's labors must have been monumental." Lady Altha gave me a last inspection, a despairing shake of her head, and a muttered sigh of exasperation before she thrust me through the arching portal of my father's hall of office.

It was a vast room with dark oaken vaults and sparse, severe furnishings. It was the hall of Tyntagel Keep which outsiders most often encountered, and it did not cast a promising light on Tyntagellian hospitality. Tyntagel acknowledged an emphatic allegiance to King Astorn and a fierce pride in having likewise served Serii since the reign of King Tul, but we had grown socially isolated from Serii's myriad of other peoples, and not just because of the forbidding mountains and canyons that surrounded us.

I knew such terror at entering my father's office that my very blood and marrow seemed to crawl. I entered with that appearance of icy calm which alone bespeaks me as my father's child. My feet tapped evenly across the marble. I walked directly, straying not even by glance, to the cluster of straight-backed chairs which constituted my father's sole concession to visitors' comforts.

I curtsied, a deep if marginally willing obeisance. "Your pardon, my Lord Father, for my tardy arrival. I regret my inability to have obeyed your summons more promptly." I spoke the words precisely, but my mind was furiously fitting to the lanky, white-haired man seated at my father's side the name which Lady Altha had supplied: Brant, Lord of Niveal.

"We shall assess your absence later, Rhianna," answered my father bleakly. "We have more salient matters to discuss at present." Black eyes flashed dire displeasure, but my father's tones flowed with formal courtesy before our guest. "As you may be aware," he continued smoothly. "Lord Brant's second son, Lord Grisk, recently suffered the loss of his chosen wife. The grievous bereavement proved compensatingly fortuitous, since Lady Tilla had produced no heirs in three years of marriage. Lord Grisk will wait the customary year before remarrying; the necessary agreements for your betrothal, however, may be established in advance without impropriety."

"Hamley cannot alone fill all the cradles of Seriin nobility," interrupted Lord Brant in raspy tones of pleasure at his uninspired witticism. "And by-blows only serve to fill a wench's purse." My disciplined father allowed himself only a brief closure of eyes against Lord Brant's coarsely distasteful practicality; Niveal's proffered bonding evidently entailed much value. Lord Brant croaked with impolitic humor, "Tilla was a pretty thing, but delicate beauties make better mistresses than wives. I ought never to have let Grisk sway my choice the first time. Pick a wife for strength, I told him; pleasure is easily found." Niveal's ruling lord laughed heartily.

My father tented his fingers carefully. The quavering light from the amber sconces struck the black onyx of his signet. "You will be wed at year's end following Lord Grisk's mourning, Rhianna," said my father crisply. "The marriage will take place in Tulea, since Lord Grisk currently represents his father and Niveal on the King's Council. You will depart for Tulea with the next spring's first caravan."

With a modicum of asperity which I wryly recognized as injudicious, I remarked, "I must gratefully assume, my Lord Father, that it was my antithetical semblance to the lovely Lady Tilla which first recommended me as a suitable bride for Niveal's matrimonial prodigy. Naturally, my heritage imparts its own special value."

Lord Brant obliviously deflected the storm of my father's anger. "I trust, Baerod, that the girl is stronger than she appears. She has a rather spindly look about her. It would not do to have another as brittle as the last."

My father rhythmically tapped the finger on which his signet shone, a certain sign of his rage. His placid response testified impressively to the level of his self-control. "Rhianna may appear fragile," he said persuasively, "but even her brothers, whom you know to be strong men both, cannot surpass her claim to endurance of health."

"I suppose appearance would be misleading in a sorceress' brat," mused Lord Brant. He tugged at his lapels, garish brocade offenses on an otherwise innocuous velvet coat. "The girl did not inherit her mother's other tendencies, I trust?" he asked bluntly. I cringed at thought of kinship with a man so tactlessly blind to his counterpart's notorious point of sensitivity.

My father glanced at me bitterly. "Rhianna has scarcely more actual Power than I have." Lord Brant nodded approval of the response. I could have cited a legion of dissenters to my father's affirmation, but I did not press myself to give argument under the circumstances. My audience with the Lord of Tyntagel had ended. I would receive no further words, no verbal picture of my intended husband, and certainly no request for my opinion. A clock chimed dolorously as my father dismissed me.

I closed the oaken door and leaned against it heavily, wishing that the wood still held the reassuring pulse of life. My father had refused to apprise Ixaxis of a potential wizardess, but that he would further discard law and tradition in ordering a sorceress to unwilling marriage appalled and shocked me. I realized now that Evram had attempted an indirect warning, but I had gauged his hints by his own refusal to believe me a sorceress. That my father, who too well comprehended the truth, would disregard it was a contingency I had never considered. I could not argue with my liege's command, and I could not comply. I needed another choice; I needed words of calm advice. Evram might listen, but I could not expect him to counter any order my father might give. My father was Lord of Tyntagel, Evram's liege and my own. It was my father's right and duty to command our lives. Momentarily pushed beyond the bounds of sanity, I careened into the only course I could accept.

Chapter 6

Having never previously contemplated rebellion, the plans which I formulated in the ensuing panic-laced hour lacked much in rational substance. I could think only of the trees, my Tyntagel oaks who had never betrayed me. I only wished that I might lose myself among them, discarding duty and its concomitant suffering.

My liege-father's world had used me badly, and there was a forgotten forest not so many leagues from Tyntagel. The heart of the ancient realms of the Sorcerer Kings had been deserted, save for Alvenhame, since the fall of Horlach. They lay northeast of Tyntagel, and the Dwaelin Wood lay still among them. I opened *A Geographical History of Ancient Serii* and stared at the words:

> "During the early years of the Sorcerer Kings' Era, the tract of land known as the Dwaelin Wood was the domain of a lesser Sorceress Queen who used the name Rhianna. Her province lay in the botanical sciences, an area of research which in her later years absorbed her full attention. The human element apparently did not interest her, an aberration which probably preserved her from the covetous designs of her fellow sorcerers, who were at that time obsessed with the conquest and subjugation of mortal realms.
>
> "Rhianna's history is of note chiefly because of its antiquity. Rhianna belonged to the third generation of sorcerers. She is one of the earliest sorceresses of whom any specific history remains, since most records of the early sorcerers were

obliterated in their long, mutual struggles for supremacy. Horlach's origins preceded her, but not even names can be definitely associated with other sorcerers prior to the seventeenth generation and the clan of Marbruk.

"Rhianna did not partake of the policies of territorial expansion popular among most of the Sorcerer Kings, but she was equally notorious in her inhospitality to visitors. She eliminated trespassers in her realm as brutally as Horlach did, though she occasionally made exception for individuals she considered of value to her experiments. She imported seedlings and soil samples from throughout the ancient world, and those who brought them to her were generally well repaid, if they survived the sorceress' characteristically erratic temper.

"Rhianna's Dwaelin Wood was by all accounts a remarkable, living artwork. Those who did survive encounters with Rhianna acknowledged universally that her domain had no equal for beauty in its natural form. After her death, the Dwaelin Wood gradually returned to a state of wilderness, but Rhianna's impact persists to this day in the hybrids of her creation."

My nerves shrieked to escape my liege-father's will without delay, but I clung to colder caution; a preprandial disappearance would draw needlessly prompt attention to my intent. I joined the household as silently, as calmly as ever did a lady of that House, and I took my appointed place at the long, narrow table. The chairs which customarily separated me from Lady Altha had been removed; Lady Retl supped in her room, and Dayn patrolled against brigands, guarding the northern reach from Hamley to Lake Evin. Balev, heir and dark foil to our father's fierce iron gray, conversed with Lord Brant. Nadira, her red-gold hair tightly curled, minced primly to the seat between her husband and Niveal's Lord.

Those cousins who closely served my father entered:

Lord Denor, tall, gray-haired and cadaverous beside his smug and lumpish wife, Lady Wylla; Lord Lachren with Lady Havia, the pair of them too haughty and affected to take notice of me though I sat across from them. My elderly great-uncle, Lord Praetor, arrived in typically querulous mood. He sat beside me and began, as he invariably did, to accuse me of maliciously crowding him.

They chattered normally, their voices discordant against the musicians' softly throbbing lutes. My family observed no change within me. They could not doubt my compliance with my liege's command, for the way of rebellion had been lost with Serii's birth. Not one among my kin had ever sought to learn to read my moods, as I had theirs.

I must have eaten, for I drew no comment, but I could never recall any portion of that meal. When at last my father's rising signaled dismissal, I rose and followed Lady Altha, but I lingered in the dim corner of the upper hall while my family dispersed. I stared at the flickering candles with fixed calm, and I waited.

When an hour of silence had wrapped the keep in chimeric calm, I moved cautiously toward the kitchens. A few indistinct murmurs spilled from the servants' rooms adjacent to the narrow ways I walked, but the access to the pantry which I sought was clear. I gathered journey cakes, flint, a knife, and potent herbs. When I had completed my pilfering, I crept up the steep back stairs to my room.

An owl screeched against the night, but the keep had grown still with sleep. I donned an often patched skirt and tunic, topped them with a heavy woolen cloak, and gathered my chosen supplies into a coarse twill bag. The garments I selected had once belonged to a governess of congenial disposition and regrettably short tenure. Had my family remarked them, they would long ago have been discarded as ill-suited to a lady of high rank, but the things were durable and far more serviceable than the finer garb I possessed. Few critical eyes would espy me in such an outfit.

I took little, for I owned nothing. My father held

first title to all the possessions of Tyntagel, and he had never troubled to gift me with anything but my sister's excess. I carefully stowed in their case the pearls which I had worn at supper; I wished no accusation of thievery to follow me. I cast a single glance at my room: the gilt ceiling chased with a tortuous, abstract design which had given me many childhood nightmares; the bed curtained with musty, stifling draperies of burgundy velvet; and the cold, unyielding floor inset with rose marble of unimaginative geometric pattern. The room held memories, but few were good. I locked fast the gilt-encrusted door behind me, a gesture less purposeful than symbolic.

It was absurdly easy to desert my life's home. I knew every back stair and hidden alcove. I knew the trees too well to be daunted by the purportedly impregnable inner wall which encompassed Tyntagel Keep. The outer wall was a more formidable barrier, for it had been built to withstand the flow of madness following Horlach's demise, but I thought myself a shadow and passed before the guards unseen. No Ixaxin wizardess was I. Still, I knew a few small tricks, and the Power which condemned me would suffice for my escape. I dashed to shelter under the forest eave as if pursued by all the hideous gargoyles of Horlach's creation, bidding mental farewells to my precious oaks.

I did experience qualms at the prospect of deliberately tapping my sorcerous Power, but I rationalized determinedly against my Tyntagellian training. The Infortiare was Serii's highest ranking subject, and Ixaxis was heeded throughout the Alliance. The first Infortiare, Lord Ceallagh, had yielded the crown of Serii to the mortal Tul with the understanding that Ixaxis would restrict its own rule to ensuring the honorable application of sorcery. I refused to recall my father's contention that Lord Venkarel sought to restore sorcerous autocracy. I concentrated on the belief that Serii as a whole did not share Tyntagel's prejudice against the bearers of Power. Tyntagel abhorred sorcery, disavowed the influence of wizardry, but supported a kingship and kingdom founded by Ixaxin intervention. The dichotomy had always disturbed me; now, I savored it.

I moved with such haste as I was able to maintain, stumbling through the night up the rocky, weed-held tracks across Tyntagel's treacherous boreal rim. There existed no proper roads through the mountainous barricade of Tyntagel's northern boundary, but Mindar's hills held many passes for a single traveler: steep, narrow and winding ways. The trees and shrubs guided my steps from harm, for I should otherwise have stumbled again and again. Taut nerves denied me sleep for three days after my precipitous departure, and the leagues of my treason stretched behind me.

If my father were to keep the disgrace and my escape at all hidden, it would be many days before discreet searchers could eliminate the most likely, southern routes. Such trackers as would eventually descry the proper path would not overtake more than faded traces of my passing. I did not need to travel quickly; I need only endure.

The hills of Tyntagel's north marked a drastic change of clime and contour with their ridges. The lush southern slopes I knew; the northern tracks were hard and dry, robbed of soil and moisture by the wind which swept endlessly from the barren plains. There were rivulets, trickles of water cradled between the rocks, fingers of springs which fell from moister heights, but they were paltry things compared to the water-rich Tyntagel streams. Such water as touched the northeastern front of Mindar's lesser heights had worn narrow paths through glassy rock. Of growth and life, the lands were largely barren, defying even sorcerous empathy to find better sustenance than the plain meal cakes I carried.

I turned northeasterly to travel across terrain increasingly rugged but less devoid of life. I merely skirted the Mountains of Mindar, but even the least of their abundant, jagged peaks and treacherous scarps are not kind to unwary strangers. It was a lonely land and a strange one, but the first days' desolation gradually yielded to a more serious season of spring. My progress east brought glimpses of the ancient valleys, the heights of King Horlach's erstwhile domain and the verdure of Rhianna's gardens. I curled each night in comfortless, rocky hollows, but nearby trees gave me solace.

My life did not resettle graciously. As I calmed from my initial, panicked flight, guilt drove sly talons into me as I gradually realized what I had wrought. A Seriin lady of a First House, albeit less pampered than most of my class, I had in an evening discarded all that I had ever known. The world at large was not my father's park that I ought to greet it blithely and familiarly, as visions of the Dwaelin Wood too readily inclined me to do. A most trepid adventuress, my aspirations demanded much of Dwaelin Wood.

Chapter 7

If I had heeded the advice of Seriin history, I would have held obediently to my liege's dictates. I would never have trespassed on the shunned lands. There was cause for the desertion of those rich domains. The example of Alvenhame might have warned me: I knew that the people of Alvenhame incessantly recruited mercenaries to patrol their borders. I knew that brigands roamed the old domains unfettered by Seriin law, because there were reportedly older evils that patrolled better than any King's soldier. I knew that predators such as dyrcats throve in the lands north of Tyntagel, though they were found nowhere else in our world.

I could guide a dyrcat's mind. I could evade the brigands as I had evaded the guards of Tyntagel. I hated the guilt of my flight, and I did not savor the losses it incurred, but I did not initially fear. I had never believed in the ineradicable impact of the Sorcerer Kings. I began to learn.

I felt the darkness of oily evil before my eyes beheld its source. It was Brak Lake; I knew the name from many atlases, and I knew its history. Sorcerer King Horlach had coveted the land and the people who lived beside the thriving lake in an era long past. Horlach had wrung the hope from the people, and he had wracked the rich life from the teeming waters. The lake should have shimmered with activity, but it had been stained to a lifeless void which spoke more damningly of sorcerous Power than all the texts of my father's keep.

I wished for Evram's comforting kindness or even Lady Altha's spite. The few trees struggling to survive near Brak Lake were stunted not only in their limbs but in their souls as well. I reached to them as I would to the woods of Tyntagel, but no soft answers did I find. The spirits were within my touch, but they would not respond, and I did not press them. I could cure a tree of blight but not of madness.

I shivered, ragged with icy exhaustion and fear. Brak Lake was the stuff of dark legends. It lay as far beyond my understanding as the Sorcerer King Horlach himself. I felt condemned by my own paltry Power and was desperate to reach Dwaelin Wood. Brak Lake gave me warning, but I did not heed it.

When I first sensed the Dwaelin Wood, my eagerness fanned hope within me. Under the spell of my wishful thoughts, I became almost blissful, despite my ceaseless fatigue and the recognition of my losses. Only one note jarred: having expected to find no dwelling-place of man so near the forgotten realms, the burg I discerned beyond the Friejid River disturbed me. A league from its walls, I could feel the breath of it spilling unsavory air. With every instinct warning me to avoid the place, I carefully detoured around it. Any lingering fear, I banished with the thought that even the lawless reportedly shunned Dwaelin Wood.

For that night I refused to dwell on matters grave and bleak. There was a meadow at my feet; a gently rolling slope, it led from a steep, stark hillside to lush and thriving verdure. The granite boulder sheltering me was covered with emerald, mossy growth. Frail golden blossoms dusted the craggy sides and spilled across my grassy bed. The evening was cool, but spring had come to keep the winter at bay. Dwaelin Wood spread before me, and I rejoiced.

I had never held hope for freedom in my old life. I'd spent too many hollow years knowing only my father's iron walls and will. A priest I once heard speak gave rise to a briefly cherished notion that I might one day escape, but the pathway of faith had been forbidden me because of my sorcery. Near Dwaelin Wood, I felt that I had found that hope again.

I needed hope in any form. By flight, I had forsaken duty to my liege. I had confounded his agreements with Niveal, for my father could not indefinitely conceal my absence from Lord Brant. My sire would see my act as a maliciously conceived rebellion designed to denigrate his noble name. It was a crime of betrayal, and I knew it too well.

Two sparrows lit upon a dusty twig, rousing me from dangerous reverie. Their tiny thoughts were filled with flirting and the finding of choice seeds: familiar things and balm to a troubled heart. The solemn strangeness eased.

Chapter 8

Year of Serii—9000
Tyntagel, Serii

"The rose silk is adequate," drawled the young woman who clearly commanded the attention of the room. "But this," she added with a sniff of distaste for a bolt of pale blue, "is impossible."

"Lady Yldana," pleaded the unhappy merchant, "You did request its making. It was a very expensive investment, which I financed only on the understanding of your assured purchase."

"Your financial woes do not concern me, Master Thesto," said the woman with a pout of displeasure. "I could not possibly wear anything so dreadful."

Master Thesto turned ashen, torn between his great loss of invested gold and the troublesome customer whom he very much wished to cultivate. He searched the room for allies but found few candidates. The Lord of Tyntagel showed no interest; he was rapt in a study of his own, having attended only to humor his eldest daughter. The old peasant woman wrapped in hideous talismans caused Master Thesto to shudder, and he hastened his survey onward to the old woman's charge, where he paused with a gleam of inspiration. Master Thesto was still a stranger to Tyntagel.

He smiled as winningly as his oily face allowed. "Perhaps it would suit the Lady Rhianna," he suggested hopefully. The pale gold girl whom he addressed looked at him with startlement.

Lady Yldana frowned at the merchant, and he cringed

as he realized that he had erred, though he knew not how seriously he had jeopardized his hard-won standing as a vendor to the ruling family of Tyntagel. His abjection saved him; Lady Yldana laughed, her humor now piqued. "What an inspired idea, Master Thesto," she mocked. "That faded pallor does rather resemble Rhianna's coloring. They merit one another. Buy the lot, Alhda," she added to a servant, who returned to her mistress a nod of humble compliance.

Yldana smiled at her sister's downturned eyes. "Are you not pleased, Rhianna?" When her sister did not respond, Yldana tutted, "Surely you are not concerned by the loss of any beau who sees you in Master Thesto's dreadful creation? Dear little sister, you have no beaux to be bothered by it. Is it not an inspired arrangement?" She shed delighted radiance upon the room. The Lord of Tyntagel nodded absent agreement with his dark-haired daughter's whim. The face of Master Thesto reflected a man too bewildered to be pleased by the solution of his dilemma.

Year of Serii—9007
Dwaelin Wood, Serii

As a child I used to watch my sister, so secure in her hold of our father's heart and mind. It had always seemed to me that Yldana owned without effort the gift of molding her surroundings to her whim. Her beauty was indomitable, but it was a quality less simple than flawlessness of feature which graced my sister. I could not, as I watched her in our youngest days, imagine any circumstance finding Yldana in less than perfect control. Yet in my initial days in Dwaelin Wood, I often wondered how Yldana would have fared beneath the ancient intertwining limbs, whose leaves whispered enmity with every dry and papery word.

Very different from my precious friends in the dells of Tyntagel, the giants of Dwaelin Wood bred uneasy fears, contagion from their own suspicious lot. Age had brewed in a bitter cauldron the lost beauties of Rhianna's domain, and my pretty dreams were quickly consumed. The Dwaelin Wood hated, and it used its harted cannily. The trees tolerated my presence with disdainful resignation, because I greeted them with my mind, and they knew I harbored no intent to harm. They had outlived every history Serii could recall. I was a dust-mote in their view; I was a transitory thing.

I had not found the haven I sought, but still my days in Dwaelin Wood passed gracefully at first. I had no strict preceptor waiting to strike me at a hinted lapse of concentration. I had no need to fear the next summons to my father's office, wondering what new infractions I had wrought and what punishment I should incur. I need not tremble because I had perhaps forgotten some duty to my kin. There were no sidelong glances of suspicion as I walked, no superstitious whispers to surround me like a net. The Dwaelin Wood misliked me, but it was impartial distaste for all humanity, a distinction which made Dwaelin Wood significantly easier to bear.

I had found a cavern, a welcome gift to one accustomed to a roof of substantial stone. I had entered the cavern eagerly, for the disturbances of too many recent, restless nights lurked fresh in my memory. It was the feral odor which recalled caution, though the strength of life-force ought to have rung warning within me. My eyes could determine nothing in the dimness, but the sound of breathing came from more than the gentle wind. I retreated carefully, hoping that the dyrcat's languor would outweigh curiosity.

I stared upward through the tightly meshed leaves of aloof giants; Dwaelin Wood's incessant duskiness would soon bow to true night. When I slept beneath an open sky, I felt a vulnerable sense of unease. But Dwaelin's relentless canopy had not lessened my yearning for night-shelter.

I tried to set aside the mingled nervousness and unnatural, almost voluptuous euphoria which the prospect of using my treacherous Power stirred in me; a dyrcat owned Power of its own, enough to stun its prey, enough perhaps to overcome a minor sorceress. I was tired and made impatient by disappointment, else I might have merely sought a safer shelter. Without considering my full intent, I retraced my steps to the cavern entrance.

The dyrcat had awakened, or my Power had made me more able to perceive his watchful regard. He crouched, awaiting me, his sinuous tail twitching very slightly, his golden eyes irresistibly brilliant. He was an enormous specimen, fully as long as a tall man's height, and his silken, shadow-colored fur cloaked the rippling sinews of a prosperous hunter. I met his gaze, and I reached for his mind.

The tantalizing scent of prey, the eagerness for blood spurting fresh between great, fanged jaws: the violence of the dyrcat's instincts shook me. I had seldom touched the mind of any creature more deadly than a hunt-hound, and I little liked the frenzied sensation of seeing myself as a succulent meal. The dyrcat clenched his muscles to spring, commanding me to abide and submit. I turned the thought against him, and it was he who could not move. Bewilderment invaded the killer's feverish passions, and I used his confusion to lighten the burden of my strained mental hold.

I struck fire from a flint and set it to a candle. The dyrcat blinked and dropped his head like a startled kitten. I circled him at a distance, exploring his lair; nothing gentle lurked in the vicious consciousness which struggled in him, locked from action by my own will. The cavern was vaster than I had hoped. Broken stalactites and rust-colored stains suggested that it had not always been so dry a refuge, but any moisture had long ago left it. The limestone network intrigued me with its castles and curtains, especially where it sequestered a tiny portion of the cavern with an access far too narrow for a dyrcat's frame. Within the sanctum stirred a draft, yielded by a crevice from deep and winding earth-wrapped ways; the draft reduced the dyrcat's musky scent to a tolerable annoyance.

However sable sleek and splendid, a dyrcat is not one whom I would ordinarily select as neighbor, but known danger can from unknown grant reprieve. Brigands and the hints of ancient evil at Brak Lake posed sufficient menace to warrant precaution. Yet even as I claimed the inner cavern, I felt no great certainty that the dyrcat would be so readily controlled a second time.

I released my grip on the dyrcat with a certain wariness, but, to my relief, the dyrcat seemed at least as leery of me. He tested his returned mobility, spared the cave in which I cowered some suspicious glances, and thenceforth accorded me only watchful circumspection. I never trusted his disinterest sufficiently to pass within easy reach of his huge, curved claws, but I did eventually grow less frantically restrictive in the holds I exerted over him. We eyed each other cautiously, the dyrcat and I, but necessity bred a grudging tolerance.

Furnished with a carefully gathered bed of bracken, my dim dwelling was no more austere than many a chamber of my father's keep, and I found its character in many ways more desirable. Though crudely hewn, my cavern was securely private as no castle's room would be. I derived the boom of nearly absolute protection not only from my dubious neighbor, the dyrcat, but also from the aged trees. No one entered Dwaelin Wood unnoticed by its leafy denizens. Their perceptions granted me warning; their choice of paranoic solitude ensured my sanctuary.

I persistently affirmed that even a stark and hungry life offered better comfort than any Niveallan existence. Had I been cleverer in the ways of bending favor, I might have avoided both contingencies, but I could not emulate Yldana. Her gifts gave her the human world. Mine gave only survival, a quality which did not greatly enhance the charm of a noblewoman, a species supposedly too fragile for any exertion greater than a courtly dance.

Mere survival demanded too little of me, and I lacked even a tithe from my father's library to make any solitude bearable. I, who had always been content to be alone, learned from Dwaelin Wood what suffering true loneliness could bring. Melancholy pondering began to plague me, and I gained no solacc from my surroundings. Despite the variety of flora in the vicinity of my chosen dwelling, study of unresponsive life was an insufficient substitute for acrid memory. The dyrcat discouraged other animals; I could hardly seek rapport with dyrcat-prey while maintaining even a scant link with the savage dyrcat himself.

In desperation, I stretched my Power toward those in whom the dyrcat had no interest. I found a blossom of a deep blue sheen as luminous as the polished metal of a warrior's bright sword; it flourished on a vine of cunning persistence and lush beauty. I could not doubt that it owed life to my namesake, for its thoughts burned more clearly than many mammals', but it shunned me. The tantalizing brevity of rapport augmented my frustration, until I was nearly mad with hurt and aggravation. I threw my Power and my soul into the grasp of Dwaelin Wood, and that voracious essence absorbed me.

I did not dream nor think beyond the day, each one of which was like the next and the previous. I had tied thick wrappings around my mind, and I did not notice time's passage. Blossoms died, and green faded to summer's tired hue. Summer waned, but I did not recognize the difference, noticing nothing beyond my tiny world of food and sleep and simple studies of my home territory. I was not a lady of Tyntagel; I was a creature of the Dwaelin Wood who knew no other life—until one day as I was gathering columbine, I saw the Venturers.

They had camped beside a clear and leaping rill. There were three men: two were rough and knife-edged warriors indistinguishable from others whom I had seen pass. I might have disregarded those two, evading them as I had the others who had strayed through Dwaelin's grasp. I might have ignored them all, had I not heard the third man speak.

Language, I had forgotten; it stretched itself along old paths within my mind. "How could you have dwelt in Alvenhame for two years without sampling Alvenhamish brandy, Master Hamar?" The man spoke tauntingly. He was handsome; Yldana would have sought his sole attention. With that thought, I realized: I have a sister; I am Rhianna dur Tyntagel, and I have lost four months to the Dwaelin Wood.

"Alvenhame does not pay its soldiers so well as that, Master Ineuil," growled the larger of the warrior pair.

The handsome man grinned. "There are ways of remedying that circumstance," he said suggestively.

"That is why we are here," said the third member of the party. He stammered in a harsh accent which nearly defeated my newly awakened comprehension.

"So you are," mused Master Ineuil. He was fairer in coloring than the Tyntagel norm, but I could detect in his aspect no flaw more serious than a vague suspicion of indolence. He bore a sword but no armor, nor was his visage scarred as those of the professional soldiers he accompanied. "Venture can be a highly profitable trade."

"You have already recruited us, Master Ineuil," said the first warrior. "You need not continue to parade the benefits of our choice." The warrior stood and stretched the thews of his arms; he was undoubtedly the largest man I had ever seen.

"I merely make conversation, Master Hamar," answered Master Ineuil blandly. "We could return to a discussion of Alvenhamish brandy, if you prefer."

"Which only you have sampled," muttered Master Hamar.

"Or perhaps Master Gart could regale us with some morsels of personal history," suggested Master Ineuil cheerfully. He turned his face expectantly to the shorter of the two warriors, a grizzled man whose features were as blunt and knobby as an aged oak and as ruddy as mahogany.

"I am not much for story-telling, Master Ineuil," responded Master Gart shyly.

"A scintillating fellow like you?" scoffed Master Ineuil. "You must have scores of romantic conquests to recount." It was an unlikely accusation, given the most cursory inspection of Master Gart.

"Leave him be," warned Master Hamar to the impudent Master Ineuil, "or I may test those sword skills we discussed on you."

"He meant no harm, Hamar," interposed Master Gart.

"Certainly not!" exclaimed Master Ineuil with widened green eyes. "I have only respect for both of you. Should I have otherwise selected you two out of all Alvenhame's mercenaries?"

Master Hamar, only partially mollified, said, "I hope you fight better than you lie, Master Ineuil."

"My talents are manifold, I assure you," answered the fair man with excessive solemnity.

He would have proceeded, but Master Hamar grunted, "No more tales of your exploits, Master Ineuil. We have already heard your opinions of Bethii, Pithlii, Ardasia, and Mahl, not to mention your extended discussions of Serii's diversity of trollops. We have had no quiet since we joined with you, and I am past ready for a rest from talk."

"That is not a very sociable attitude, Master Hamar," commented Master Ineuil, but he did allow the conversation to lapse.

I had listened with a shameless fascination. Venturers had become less common than in Serii's early days, and I had encountered only one other prior to that day in Dwaelin Wood. There had once existed, in that era after Horlach's defeat, both more cause and more incentive for the Venture calling. I had studied the strictures of Venture, the artifice created by Lord Ceallagh to cleanse a newly freed Serii of King Horlach's more hazardous mementos. The first Infortiare had designed the Venture concept to give hope to those in need of a new beginning, but a Venture was only to be undertaken for a truly important cause, and the Venture code was strict. A pledged Venturer could not leave his quest until it was fulfilled, not though years passed and age thinned the hopes of youth. Release could be granted by the Venture Leader, whose rule over his party was absolute, but reprieve was seldom offered save for direst infirmity; the Venture Leader must justify any release to the Infortiare himself. The rewards of Venture might be great, but the risks grew accordingly.

A man had once arrived in Tyntagel, the grayest, thinnest man whom I had ever seen. He was the last survivor of a Venturing band, enslaved by a vow he had made thirty years before to follow a hopeless path. He ought to have been bitter, I had thought. Yldana had derided the folly of his self-imposed affliction; Balev and Dayn had proclaimed the man a certain criminal deserving of any suffering he accrued. The stringy little man in shabby clothes had looked at my brothers, Tyntagel's proud young lordlings, at Yldana already womanly in figure and hypnotic in her effect, and he had smiled with gentle eyes in which laughter danced.

I never knew the nature of the quest nor why he came to Tyntagel. Whence he journeyed and where he later went were shrouded from my knowing, but I had in cameo fashion glimpsed a man whose purpose gave him life. Perhaps he was flotsam in an absolute sense, but he mattered and he knew his worth.

After four months in Dwaelin Wood, I was sufficiently lost and lonely, riven even from the harsh stability of my father's dominance, to have followed an Ardasian trader to Caruil. If I could have borne to dwell lifelong in silent contemplation of the Dwaelin Wood's ways, I might have found some shade of contentment in the end, but if loneliness grants any boon, it is the gift of freedom. The Venturers had unwittingly brought my latent restlessness to light.

Even the thought of pursuing the trio I had encountered was at least as mad as my initial flight from Tyntagel. I knew nothing of the Venture goal; I knew nothing of the three sworn unto it, save that they were strong and secure even amid the chorus of enmity ringing against them from every tree and leaf, and I had seen no other trespassers display like confidence. I lacked the courage to bespeak the men, fleeing instead to my small shelter as if the Venturers could offer me harm though they could not even detect me. Still, I kept their presence in my mind.

Even as I did battle with myself, I gathered my few possessions, bestowing a blessing upon the stony hollow which had served me well. I had discarded my familiar life once; this second upheaval was easier by far. The dyrcat would be glad at my departure, and he would not be alone in his relief.

Chapter 9

For some few days, unseen and silent, I trailed the Venturers' twisted path. In my cowardice, I observed them from the shadows, unknown to them save as a rustle of sighing wind. I did not fear them physically; I had learned enough of shadow-weaving in my Dwaelin stay to make evasion simple, and they did seem to be men with some measure of honor. It was a derisive refusal of my offer to join them that I feared. I chided myself for my procrastination, but I could not summon sufficient nerve to risk a confrontation.

Still, I eavesdropped fervently, striving to fathom the motive of the Venturers. They spoke sparingly, almost cryptically, of their quest, confounding both my curiosity and my expectations. I did gain a cautious respect for their skills, and I realized that these Venturers were very far removed from the impoverished visitor to Tyntagel.

They formed an odd trio: only Master Gart at all resembled my preconceptions of a suitable Venturer. Master Ineuil was too undefinable: a chiaroscuro of contrasts. Master Hamar was too filled with anger, hating the world's greater part and suspect of the rest; in Master Gart he seemed to have some faith, but hard, I suspected, had been the earning. The warrior pair evinced the camaraderie of long acquaintance, but toward him they called Ineuil they displayed a marked reserve. The restraint was not reciprocated, but Master Ineuil, I thought (more rightly than I knew), was one whose easy manner revealed little of honest sentiment.

Gart was the steady one, quick of hand but much slower of wit than the effervescent master Ineuil, who loved to taunt him. Master Gart, even of temper and reliable, muted Master Hamar's outbursts like sound cotton wool. The ravages of a warrior's lot had deprived Master Gart of half an ear. Stolid stability wreathed Master Gart, and I found him likable, though his appeal was rather akin to that of a friendly mastiff.

I could not find any like appeal in Master Hamar. His unreasonable sullenness nearly discouraged my interest in the Venture a dozen times, though it was easy to appreciate his value to such a cause. Master Hamar's was the simple force of massive strength. I saw him lift from the trio's path a fallen limb of enormous substance and weight, and it caused him no apparent whit of effort. He sparred frequently with Master Gart, and each played his weapon skillfully. It seemed to me a dangerous game with potent arms, but no serious blood was drawn. Both were expert, and each knew the other's measure well.

Master Ineuil, the rogue who loved to banter (he often pursued a monologue if no audience would cooperate), fitted the role of Venturer least of all. He seemed uncommonly literate for a mercenary, yet freely extolled the rewards of judicious thievery. He appeared to be widely traveled, as were the others, but Master Ineuil's accounts betrayed a familiarity with a circle of affluence far exceeding a successful mercenary's comfortable prosperity. I might have named him thief; he broadly hinted as much, and Master Hamar often gave him the label. But a thief whose larceny results in significant wealth does not assume a Venture's rigors. Master Ineuil possessed a scoundrel's perspective, a courtier's tongue, and (by his own declaration) too much charm for his own good. I could not adequately explain him.

The three were strangers to me, but I trailed them faithfully from Dwaelin Wood, mentally fashioning them into the main fixtures of the narrow world I had inflicted upon myself. The Dwaelin Wood sped them on their way, since their goal was departure for the village Anx. The name of their destination was not familiar to me, but the most likely prospect for its location did not please me greatly. I had espied one settlement along Dwaelin Wood's southern border. To anticipate the existence of another would prod coincidence overly far.

When I could no longer pretend that the Venturers intended any more palatable goal, I sat upon a granite block and engaged myself in serious debate. I had no reason to follow the Venturers, but I had quite as little reason for any other course of action. I had grown confident in my ability to shield myself from view, and entering Anx would not bind me irrevocably to a Venture. A dram of curiosity added its weight; I rose and ran to trail the Venturers into Anx on a dry summer evening.

The field was sere grass which crackled as we crossed it. The soil was stony and brittle, though the Friejid River tossed the glare of summer light nearby. The leaden wall rose sheer before us, and there were men at the gate who bore arms of deadly uniformity. The men wore many coats and colors, and they eyed the Venturers carefully. The Venturers returned these gazes with a confidence I envied. I trailed the Venturers closely through the studded steel gate, feeling more secure in the three men's proximity. Two strides beyond the wall, the air was thickly yellow, and I turned around to justify my senses, for I had seen no change of atmosphere until I stepped within it.

A sudden pulsation of black netting rose from the soil inches before me. It soared above me, circling over me, and covered the city. As I stared, a small brown sparrow, unwilling trespasser, flew at the barrier and fell, a sorrowful mass of fused and blackened feathers. Some of the men near the gate laughed and pointed. A skeletal creature which might have been a man crawled from the lee of the wall, snatched the fallen bird and tore at it with his teeth. The watchers laughed more heartily.

The Venturers had nearly escaped me in my distraction. They were entering an alleyway which exuded a vile stench. Ineuil made an uncomplimentary allusion to sewer-raised rabble, but he kept his comments short and subdued. A heavy grunt oozed from the smoky haze, and blood spattered the ground as a man slumped against a dirty building. His murderer ransacked his belongings, while onlookers walked indifferently away.

"Anx has lost none of its charm," said Ineuil carelessly.

"Nor its contempt for the unwary, Master Thief," answered Hamar. "Look to yourself and not to the dead."

The Venturers spoke little after that exchange. They fought once but briefly, dispatching a trio of attackers who sprang upon them from a crumbled doorway. "It is fortunate that Anxians seldom cooperate well," commented Ineuil as he wiped and sheathed his bloodied sword.

We spiraled through the vicious, layered city, each stratum of which had been built on the bones of more ancient, sunken structures. The upper layers were most heavily trafficked, but they had crumbled in places, and the Venturers took occasional stairs to the lower flame-lit tunnels, weaving between moldering edifices until clear upper passages could be found. There was death everywhere around me, and it was greeted imperturbably as a natural phenomenon by those I saw. I had seen death before, having too often tended the sorely ill to have avoided it, but I had never witnessed callous murder. It surrounded me in Anx. I should have minded the slayings more had the victims not seemed as foul as the predators.

The Venturers took lodging within an Anxian inn, the likes of which would pale the meanest hovel of ill-repute in Tyntagel to seeming gentle splendor. Loud curses rang from it, filth encrusted it, and the creatures who filled it were the lowest villains. In the first minutes following the Venturers' arrival, I witnessed two murders, one rape and at least a dozen thefts. It was a busy and prosperous inn.

The Venturers supped together in the common room, but with nightfall they separated. Ineuil, in company with a woman of incredibly crimson hair, climbed the stairs to the room which he had taken. Gart and Hamar joined a sallow man who boasted an unsurpassed knowledge of local gambling establishments; the three of them strutted out the inn's door, and I remained, forlornly confused, a prim ghost in the midst of vile chaos.

I passed the night in the common room, evading sleep lest my shield of shadow fail and the Venturers escape me. With dawn, I hoped the Venturers would take their leave of Anx, but morning passed and they did not even emerge from their respective chambers. By the hour of their evening appearance, I was wholly weary and disgusted with their choice of lodgings. I followed them hopefully to another inn where they merely drank and took their dubious pleasures as they had done the previous night. The woman who accompanied Ineuil the second night was a buxom brunette.

I would have left the city then, my interest in the Venturers vanquished by the unwholesome air of Anx. I could have passed the outer barricade of Anx as I had done on entering; I had become more shadow than substance. It was the web of force which daunted me, the web which had destroyed a tiny sparrow, the web which completely encompassed the city. Tyntagellian lore decried such imprisoning barriers of energies perpetuated by sorcery, though the secret of their creation had mercifully been lost with the fall of the Sorcerer Kings. The simpler versions prevented unwanted traffic either one way or both; the more complex systems eliminated the interloper. To those who lacked the requisite key, all accounts acknowledged the barriers impregnable.

Reft of viable alternatives, I dwelt in Anx, cowering in attics or other, lesser holes. It was neither a comfortable existence nor a secure one, for I knew myself vulnerable to the first Anxian who might find me. The weak and unwary did not long survive in Anx's maw; their discarded corpses fed a pyre in the city's central square. It was the vile stench and smoke of that fire which perpetually polluted the air, but the citizens disregarded the atmosphere as completely as they did the unfortunate contributors to its source. There were always new victims, for Anx held wealth for the greedy and freedom for the iniquitous.

I could travel freely within Anx, so long as I maintained my somewhat ghostly status. It was an odd sensation, intoxicating in its way to one so otherwise helpless among Anx's murderous crew. Had I possessed their prevalent penchant for larceny, I could readily have established a highly profitable career. I grew quite adept at stealing meals. I might as easily have taken costlier items without qualms toward the disreputable owners whose right to such goods were as dubious as mine. The notion was mildly entertaining, though it hardly consoled me for my imprisonment within the city. All the wealth of Serii, Bethii and Mahl, a considerable percentage of which seemed destined to materialize in Anx, offered little enticement to a captive specter.

It was remarkably disconcerting to walk the world entirely unperceived by one's fellow beings, however distasteful those beings might be. The trees of Dwaelin had known my presence; I had no like reassurance in Anx. I played foolish pranks to assert my continued existence in the world. To steal a gambler's drink and trade it with another's provoked strong reaction among the violent tempers of Anx. I found it perversely comforting to realize that the Lady Rhianna an Baerod yn Eleni dur Tyntagel had at least retained her ability to irritate.

I watched those who regularly trafficked to and from the city, though it meant trespassing in territory which terrified me. Each trafficker bore a key: a disc of pewter hue, smooth as moonlight and covered by a tracery of ebon lines. Each key permitted passage of one traveler alone, and only once could it be used, for passage returned it to its source. I tried to steal one, but they were more closely guarded than any mundane treasure. The keys were sold for enormous price and distributed just prior to the purchaser's departure from a central cache, itself impenetrably barriered. Whatever ruffian band (currently a renegade crew of Caruillan pirates) controlled the single central key could command the city and virtually inexhaustible wealth. The privilege tended to be transitory; there was always a new band, larger or stronger than the last.

I had tried my new skills at thieving, but I could not steal a key. I could have stolen the price, but I dared not reveal myself long enough to make the purchase. For all my searching for a method of escape, I remained entrapped.

I returned to shadow the Venturers in simple hope that they, who had in a manner brought me, might lead me from the cage. Any latent craving for human company I might have felt in Dwaelin Wood had diminished rapidly under the influence of Anx, but desperation for departure's means gave me a far stronger motive. I trailed them again, but the Venturers had settled themselves as if for a long stay. Masters Gart and Hamar fought incessantly when they did not drink or gamble, calmly dispatching those who sought to rob them and maiming many an injudicious instigator of petty quarrels. Ineuil's sword did not idle, but he appeared more cheerfully determined to sample every moderately attractive harlot in the town. I was naive, and the behavior shocked me; yet, as I compared the Venturers to others whom I saw in Anx, I could not wholly condemn them. The Venturers did not inflict meaningless brutalities as did the other inmates of the town; they wrought no harm maliciously, though their obvious abilities instilled in jealous Anxian moguls a careful and cunning respect. The Venturers puzzled and annoyed me with their lingering: indulgence in the plentiful vices of Anx constituted an unlikely quest. Being personally eager to exit Anx and having little else to occupy my mind, I wondered irritably what the Venturers awaited. Despite their steady attendance to Anxian pleasures, there was a measure of impatience in all three men.

I came near to bespeaking them, but I had formulated no fit words of approach. The Venturers would quite reasonably doubt the intentions of a fleeing lady of Tyntagel in the unlikely ambience of a thieves' burg. I had concocted a more palatably appropriate history, one which would possibly justify my interest in a Venture, but I was still loathe to assume a sorceress' cloak with such feeble abilities as I possessed.

Little enough did I know of sorcery, formal study of which had been anathema in Tyntagel. I knew the tales perverted by Tyntagellian prejudice. I knew that sorcerous practitioners' Power ranged from the trickery of mere charlatans to the unimaginable gifts of the Infortiare. As for the gauging of such abilities, I could not even assess my own. I had known from the moment I chose to trail the Venturers that it was sorcery I must exploit to join them, but I took no comfort from this decision.

III. THE SPARK (PART 2)

Year of Serii—9003
Liin Keep, Liin, Serii

"Even you cannot challenge the decision of the Ixaxin Council, Hrgh," implored Lord Arineuil earnestly. "I like their choice no better than you do, but this is not the way to combat it."

"I am challenging Venkarel—not the Ixaxin Council," declared Lord Hrgh Dolr'han with the full, regal confidence of his birthright. "Venkarel has deluded the Council, thanks to that besotted old woman, Marga, but there can be no deception in a true trial of Power. I am the Infortiare in the eyes of Serii. Mine is the strongest Power of our time. I *will be* the Lord of Ixaxis."

"Then let the King decree it, Hrgh. The King's Council is even now pressing Ixaxin to reconsider its selection. Let them complete what they have begun, and you will be Infortiare without need for this farce of challenge."

"Farce?" demanded Lord Hrgh fiercely. "Arineuil, I want all Serii to know that I am Infortiare by right of Power. I want Ixaxis to know, and I want Venkarel to know." Hrgh's silver eyes grew feverishly bright. "I befriended that treacherous scrub, Arineuil. I will not see him take that which is mine. I will not see him use Serii as he used me."

Lord Arineuil shook his head with exasperation. "He is using you still, Hrgh. If he defeats you in this trial of Power, the King himself will be unable to depose him."

Lord Hrgh regarded his friend with contempt. "You

actually believe his lies and trickery. Arineuil, I know Venkarel."

"And I do not?" retorted Lord Arineuil dur Ven. "Venkarel decimated my family's domain before he even began his wizard's training. You will not defeat him, Hrgh."

"I know my Power, Lord Arineuil, and I am a Dolr'han."

"You are a man blinded by arrogance."

"And you, Arineuil, are an impertinent fool."

"Venkarel will defeat you, Hrgh," insisted Arineuil wearily.

"Then curry *his* favor," sneered Hrgh, "instead of wasting my time." Lord Hrgh stomped from the room, a richly golden hall of the fabulous Liin Keep.

Lord Arineuil watched his friend with frustrated anger. "You are the fool, Hrgh. Venkarel will defeat you, if only because you underestimate him. He will conquer you, and there will be no one left who can defy him."

Something dark laughed unheard.

IV. THE KINDLING

Chapter 1

Year of Serii—9007
Anx, Serii

Hindsight often strips illusion from the truth, but the chaos of my final full day in Anx long defied my paths of reason. The answers which I thought I sought, I found. Never had more confusion of emotion burned my mind.

I rose that day at dawn. It was a somber time, but such slanting early light as crept through mountain passes could better penetrate the smoky shroud which hovered over Anx than later, stronger daylight, which yielded only a yellowing stain. Beyond the window cracks of my attic domain, I saw a whispered hint of rose suffuse the sky. Beyond my black-webbed cage loveliness still lived.

A severed shriek pierced gentle thoughts. Anx inflicted unpleasant punishment on those who dared relax their guard. I shook the dust from my draggled skirts, a poor substitute for a proper cleaning. I stepped gingerly down the treacherous stairs of the building which currently claimed the title of inn, dodged sleeping forms huddled in the lower halls, appropriated the remnants of a loaf of bread, and quietly passed outside. There was a crumbled ledge on which some yellow lichens grew; aside from man, those lichens alone made willing home in Anx. As nearly mindless as living things could be, no better comrades had I found of late than those pitiful symbionts.

I gnawed the gritty bread, a sorry substance, poorly leavened and impure. I had thrown away so much of life that I no longer knew what lay beyond my hand's reach. I gazed upon the western gate of Anx as if my sight alone could bear me beyond the imprisoning veil. I wore a glum mood when I observed that most contradictory Venturer, Master Ineuil, who, since his arrival in Anx, had not hitherto shown himself before midday. He, too, scanned the western gate, and more restless did he seem than I had previously beheld him.

I roamed the city aimlessly throughout the morning, but always when I strayed near the western gate I found Master Ineuil waiting and watching. Once I came upon him as Masters Hamar and Gart approached his side. The three conferred briefly. Hamar gestured impatiently toward the gate; Gart glowered. Ineuil shook his head irritably, turning his back in curt dismissal. Gart and Hamar continued on their way with no good humor.

Not until dusk did I find Master Ineuil absent from his point of vigil. The oddness of his behavior had revived my curiosity. For want of better goal, I resolved to investigate the Venturers' evening occupations, though I expected no extraordinary discoveries. I began my search idly, peering into all the sordid holes which the three had recently frequented. I sought them from inn to tavern, until the hour grew late and my interest devolved into mere obstinacy. I explored every odd pocket, persistently hunting through even the most noisome quarters. With keening nerves, I searched the alley haunts of murderers, the hives of wretches too cunning to die but too weak to prosper, and the bars and brothels of the veriest villains. Whether by chance or by a force more needful and obscure, I finally discovered a darksome tavern hidden beneath the snarl of the city's more trafficked strata.

A sign, begrimed to near illegibility, proclaimed the tavern's name to be Ceallagh's Crown. The tavern's sour ambience defied any connection to that conqueror of King Horlach, and I smiled wryly at the irony. I was mildly impressed that any Anxian had considered honoring history's hero, but the inappropriate application of his name typified the Anxian mentality. Lord Ceallagh had established Serii's governing duality of

King and Infortiare by rejecting kingship and its crown. I refused to credit any Anxian with the subtlety of sarcasm.

Ceallagh's Crown boasted a few rough tables and was dimly lit by a single, flickering lamp near the entrance. The tavern keeper appeared no more sullen than others of his kind. The filth and stench were not excessive by the standards of Anx. Considering its environs, Ceallagh's Crown appeared to be a reasonably wholesome establishment.

As I crossed the tavern's threshold, I summarily revised my opinion of Ceallagh's Crown. As sudden and intense as the impact of a blinding flame to the dark-accustomed eye, a sudden flaring attacked that part of me which understood the trees, and I reeled beneath a wave of bitter pain.

With breathtaking abruptness, the fire vanished. The tavern resumed its ordinary appearance. The few customers speaking softly amongst themselves betrayed no evidence of disturbed awareness. No sign existed of any aberration, save the echo of a dully beating rhythm which drummed still within my veins. Suddenly I feared that madness had evoked the terrible burning in my blood. Had I lost my understanding of reality within Tyntagel's gray stone walls? Was all that I thought had passed only the product of delirium?

Suddenly I saw the trio I sought. The lamp which should have burned near them had been shattered, and a hazy darkness shrouded the corner in which they sat. I had not previously seen the two men who accompanied the Venturers. One of the unfamiliar pair was a small man, gray-haired and robed in priestly garb. I found a clergyman's presence incredible in those surroundings, but it was the other of the pair who attracted my attention, though for no cause as obvious as a holy calling. The second stranger occupied the corner chair, flanked by Gart and Hamar on one side, Ineuil and the priest on the other. He was dark of hair, angular and excessively lean, and he wore a cloak of severest black at odds with Anx's gaudy norm, making him difficult to perceive clearly in the lightless room. His eyes glinted with the pale, frozen blue of winter's ice, and from dark depths he watched me. His eyes pinned me, a frightened butterfly beating frantic, helpless wings. I wrapped myself more tightly in the shadows of the room, hoping desperately that coincidence alone bound that sharp, cold inspection of me.

Bleak humor twitched the corner of an uncompromising mouth, set in a face too carefully controlled to contain any softness of purpose. It was not at all comfortable to find laughing at me a man to whom I ought to have been entirely beyond detection. I wanted to escape his gaze, but I feared to leave even more than I feared to remain. My ability to elude notice was my only hope of preservation in a singularly hazardous environment. If I remained for other reason than attempting to extract an explanation of his perception, I did not acknowledge it at the time. I breathed deeply to still my trembling and drew near the table where the Venturers had assembled.

The three whom I had followed leaned forward to catch the quiet words of the gray-haired priest. I listened closely, stilling my pulse to read the silence. "The Taormin is a powerful instrument, too potent for any mortal's hand, however well-intentioned."

"If it grants such enormous Power," asked Master Ineuil sardonically, "how do you suggest we approach and take it? After exerting such effort to acquire the thing himself, Hrgh is not about to relinquish it at our request. Do the brethren of Benthen Abbey profess some special knowledge of the trinket which they have guarded so long?"

"We should not be so foolish as to seek such knowlege, Master Ineuil," chided the priest. With a pause and a glance at Gart and Hamar, the priest elaborated, "The Taormin is one of the few relics of the evil days still in existence, and it implacably resists destruction. We of the Abbey have been its custodians, its jailers in a very real sense, for untold ages, though few among us have understood the nature of that which we guarded. None of us knows more of it than that which I have just told you. Our calling denies the sort of Power the Taormin gives; that is why it was originally given into our keeping, and that is why the abbacy of Benthen is a deceptive honor. Hrgh's ambition blinds him to the danger he courts. The longer he holds it, the more secure the Taormin's grasp of his mind will be."

"It is not we who have delayed matters so long," muttered Hamar ungraciously.

The cold-eyed one had not ceased to study me, but now he turned a quizzical eyebrow to Hamar and spoke. "I comprehend the inherent urgency of the situation far more clearly than do you, Master Hamar. Any delays were entirely unavoidable. If you think that I have treated the matter too lightly, let me reassure you: I should not be here at all were the potential dangers not vastly more serious than even Abbot Medwyn appreciates."

"You are enormously reassuring, Kaedric," said Ineuil sarcastically.

"I am pleased that you find me so," countered the one called Kaedric sharply. "According to every known account, the Taormin binds to itself those who use it as surely as it is itself bound to the heinous image of its late master. I am not particularly eager to contend with Hrgh, but he is a far more palatable hazard than that which he may unwittingly release." The speaker exchanged an unfathomable glance with Master Ineuil and leaned back in his rough chair with the exaggerated ease of a confident predator. "I do not think you would care to encounter either obstacle without my assistance."

Gart grumbled an unintelligible comment. Hamar glowered, sullenly unresponsive. The priest shifted uncomfortably, watching Kaedric with concern. Master Ineuil looked amused, but he clenched his hands more tightly than before.

Abbot Medwyn broke the ominous silence, selecting his words with obvious care. "Alone of us, Master Kaedric is equipped to counter Hrgh. I called this Venture against Master Kaedric's intention to pursue the Taormin alone. I have not wavered in my reasoning: the world has many dangers and many means through which to counter them. I freely acknowledge, however, the incomparable value of Master Kaedric's expertise in a matter of this sort. I have named him Venture Leader, and I shall follow him. Any who would join us shall obey his word as law until the Venture's end. Agree, or go your ways now."

Stillness ensued until Ineuil responded. "We knew and accepted the Venture's terms before we journeyed here, Abbot. You have few enough followers as it is; very few are mad enough to follow one wizard into another's lair, however crucial the cause or substantial the reward. Do not tempt those who do support you into desertion."

"So be it," decreed Master Kaedric. The cold blue eyes returned to me as he continued, "The Venture is called and we are oath-bound unto it. I suggest that we acquaint ourselves with our rapt audience before proceeding further."

His comment elicited some bewilderment from the other Venturers and roused terror in me. Master Ineuil recovered first, remarking speculatively, "So I was right about the shadow. I thought I felt it in Dwaelin Wood, but my talent for that sort of thing is small."

Kaedric's gaze mocked me, his derision perversely strengthening me with angry defiance, though I had never shuddered more acutely before my father's direst temper. I summoned my sire's stark calm, since my maternal gifts had forsaken me. I willed release of my insubstantial cloak and, unshielded, stepped into the dusky light of Ceallagh's Crown. Master Ineuil laughed, Master Gart snorted, and Master Hamar sneered in disgust. The abbot covered a startled smile and darted a puzzled glance at Master Kaedric, who continued to regard me without expression.

Master Ineuil inclined his head toward me, remarking, "Had I suspected the loveliness of our shadow, I should have been less concerned with eluding her and more determined to seek closer acquaintance."

A flush of embarrassment threatened me; I was unaccustomed to receiving pretty speeches even in mockery. Master Kaedric commented dryly, "Having displayed such keen interest in our business, perhaps the lady will condescend to share with us her name and purpose."

Since I so clearly merited the allegation of guilty intrusion, my anger immediately directed itself toward my accuser. It was quite unjust of me but useful, since it reinforced my nerve. "My name is Rani," I said calmly, avoiding a precise truth which might connect me with a nobly born lady of Tyntagel. "I should like to join your Venture," I continued, gratified by the astonishment my words caused while at the same time horrified as I realized what I had offered.

Master Ineuil appeared to find my declaration exquisitely humorous, but Master Kaedric remained unresponsive. I wished the light were better, that I might more easily read the implacable planes of the wizard's face. The wizard inquired soberly, "And what skill, Mistress Rani, do you offer as aid to our quest?"

I answered with far more surety than I felt, "I have some ability as a sorceress. Obviously, I could not have survived long in Anx without a certain measure of Power." Having launched myself on rash impulse I had no intention of retreating.

Master Kaedric answered idly, "The blindness of the many will not avail you where we are bound."

"I have other gifts," I responded coldly. "If your Venture is vital, can you justifiably reject any proffered assistance?"

"A demon's aid is not a boon," snarled Hamar with disgust, reminding me of my Great-Uncle Praetor with his chronically unpleasant disposition.

"She does not much look like a demon to me," drawled Ineuil contemplatively. "On the other hand," he added with an uncharitable inspection of my tired raiment, "She does not appear to be a very prosperous sorceress."

"Power does not discriminate between pauper's robes and prince's silks, as you of all people ought to have realized by now, Master Ineuil," answered Master

Kaedric harshly, darting forth an unexpected flash of fierce anger, the first emotion he had shown.

Master Ineuil's green eyes narrowed, but he shrugged and grinned. "She obviously does have other gifts which I personally find infinitely more intriguing."

"She brings trouble," said Master Hamar menacingly, and the warrior giant rose to threaten me. Master Gart, who had so far observed the proceedings in silent detachment, grabbed futilely at Hamar's arm, as Hamar clenched his powerful fingers on my shoulder. I winced, but I made no struggle for release; it would have availed nothing. I hoped that Master Hamar wished to cow me rather than inflict serious harm, although Master Kaedric had already intimidated me so greatly as to make Master Hamar's endeavor superfluous.

"Sit down, Hamar. We do not need the notoriety of a public spectacle," suggested Master Kaedric calmly, but his quiet words effected that which Gart's force had not. Hamar released me, reluctantly obeying the cool voice with its tones of authority. Master Kaedric continued without pause, considering me with deceptive mildness, "The only traits which Mistress Rani has so far exhibited are impetuousity and foolhardiness, which characteristics unfortunately do not constitute capital crimes. If she endangers us, I shall eliminate her myself." The impersonal promise frightened me a great deal more than Hamar's violent demonstration.

Master Kaedric's words subdued the warrior's explosive temper, though Master Hamar continued to eye me with suspicion, and Master Gart watched Hamar closely. The priest, Abbot Medwyn, suddenly seemed fascinated by the table boards. Master Ineuil leaned back with an unreadable grimace. The tavern keeper and a few remaining customers occupied themselves with their own affairs; Ceallagh's Crown would sanction violence as indifferently as any other Anxian establishment.

With a glance at Master Kaedric, Abbot Medwyn intervened. "Mistress Rani," said the abbot kindly, "we appreciate your offer of aid, but ours is not a mission to be lightly assumed. I carry a share of Master Kaedric's responsibility for the safety of the Venture members, and I cannot condone your impulsive offer."

"Sir Abbot, my offer is sincere," I retorted very bravely for one ready to expire from fear. "That it may be impulsive and unwisely offered does not mitigate the value of my help. You would gauge the measure of my worth of you? There is no tree nor flower, no bird nor other small one of this world with whom I cannot speak. The gift is not so illustrious as skills which others of your party may bring, but it has merit." I was making rather free assumptions regarding the goals and limitations of those to whom I spoke.

"I say let her join us," inserted Ineuil cheerfully. "None of us truly knows what dangers we face. As Master Kaedric so gently reminds us, our chiefly needed attribute is sorcery." Master Ineuil grinned at me with rather excessive familiarity, an impertinence hardly complainable under the circumstances.

"She already causes argument," groaned Hamar dolefully. "A woman on a Venture!"

To my considerable surprise, Master Gart came to my support. "Women have often Ventured, Hamar. A sorceress belongs not to the common sort of your knowing."

"Mistress Rani could prove useful," drawled Ineuil, the perfect polish of his speech more noticeable by contrast with Master Gart's. "She has already trailed us from Dwaelin Wood to Anx, the one no more kindly disposed than the other toward incautious trespass. Southern Dwaelin is not a place in which *I* should care to linger alone."

"We are not heading for the Dwaelin Wood," commented Master Kaedric. "Its selective hospitality bears little relevance in Mindar's passes."

I answered him quickly, hoping to forestall another spate of objections to my person, "Even darkest passes are not devoid of those lesser voices which it is often well to heed. I seek no profit of your Venture; I wish no burden of my welfare bestowed upon you." I hesitated, recalling a nuance of Venture law recounted by that long ago wanderer through my father's land. The Venture Leader's cold eyes probed me, and I tore my gaze from them with an effort which grew painful. I spoke to the abbot, a far less disquieting audience. I plunged myself into insane commitment. "Sir Abbot, I offer to serve your Venture without demands. So long as I uphold the Venture law, you cannot refuse my aid."

"Mistress Rani understands Venture law well," piped Ineuil mischievously. "She cannot be forbidden from our ranks on the basis of hazard to her person, if she accepts the hazard freely. I, for one, rejoice in our good fortune."

Abbot Medwyn glanced uncertainly at Master Kaedric. The wizard watched me fixedly, but he acidly remarked, "When one calls a Venture, one cannot quibble with its inconveniences. You would not have me go alone, Medwyn." Inserting a dark look at the irrepressibly grinning Ineuil, Master Kaedric continued, "I should not stand in the way of such a marked determination as Mistress Rani's, but it would be remiss of me to omit a pertinent caveat. I have sown death before, and I shall not hesitate to sacrifice life again for this Venture's cause. The acceptance of Venture binding-without-demands frees the Venture Leader of any responsibility for the claimant's welfare. Be assured, Mistress Rani, that my attention to Venture law will be no less punctilious than your own."

I met his stare, which pierced to heart's blood. His eyes are cold, I thought, only because they hold no slightest touch of green or gold or amber to counter the pallid blue. It is a physical oddity, attractive as such, and it tells nothing of temperament or trait. It should not hold me; he could not bind me by a gaze. I could walk from the tavern now and leave him to fading memory. There would arise another route from Anx; perhaps Master Ineuil or Master Gart would buy me a key if I stole the price. I need not follow this wizard, a man more dangerous than any Anxian cutthroat.

Abbot Medwyn said softly, alternately contemplating Master Kaedric and myself from a well of old regret which I could not credit to my own plight, "Mistress Rani, you are forcing us to contribute to your destruction. Please, reconsider your offer."

I answered very coolly, "I am quite satisfied with the conditions of the binding as they stand." Oddly enough, it was true. At the last affirmation of my unlikely decision, even my doubt had ebbed to leave me remote and empty. I certainly did not court the solicitude of these strangers, having known only indifferent contempt from my own kin. The concept of danger was too distant to trouble me, and I felt a breath of purpose which defied the fear the wizard roused in me.

"We reserved departure keys only for five," interrupted Hamar, persistently determined to thwart me. "It is late now to obtain another by morning. Are we to lose another day because this street-witch insists on joining us? I warrant all she wants is a departure key anyway." I squirmed inwardly; Master Hamar came uncomfortably near to the truth.

Reasoning in a tone of bland innocence, Master Ineuil insisted, "Hamar, even you cannot deny that there exist far easier ways for a comely young woman to obtain an Anxian departure key than enlisting in a Venture." Master Hamar laughed, but he did cease his objections. I studiously avoided blushing; if I were to play the role of intrepid adventuress, I could scarcely afford the misplaced sensibilities of a sheltered Tyntagellian maiden.

Gart offered helpfully, "Perhaps she has a key already," and expectant looks of varying sympathies met me.

"I have no key," I confessed awkwardly, "but I can supply the price."

Master Kaedric, an unlikely savior, terminated the discussion with an impatient gesture. "Departure keys are the least of our concerns. If we are to leave at dawn, we ought not spend the night in pointless debate. Meet at the eastern gate." He rose, unfurling his narrow height from the tavern's close corner. He was nearly as tall as Master Hamar, though the wizard was very much leaner. He loomed over me as he passed, giving me a momentary, dispassionate glance. He flicked a substantial spate of gleaming coins at the tavern keeper in parting; on the scale of Anxian bribes, it was a mildly impressive sum.

With the Venture Leader's departure, the sustaining energies of defiance and fear fled from me. I was suddenly too drained and exhausted to care for anything but sleep's blessed release. I did not even realize that I had again engulfed myself in shadow, until Master Ineuil bowed sweepingly in my general direction, saying, "If you are yet with us, fair Shadow Lady, then let me bid thee a pleasant repose. I do hope you will honor us with your more substantial presence in the morning. I find it difficult to confer meaningfully with a ghost." Master Hamar commented on the speech with a stream of imaginative invective which perturbed Master Ineuil not at all. I did not wait to hear more, glad even of the smoky stink of Anxian air after the tavern's stifling miasma.

I had found the key to my cage, but its price was strange and dear. I had sworn blind obedience to an unwilling and enigmatic leader who avowed he would not hesitate to see me murdered. I had no clear concept of the nature of the obligations I had assumed. At the least, I should be constrained to share the company of four men of very dubious gentility and a priest who appeared unlikely to adopt the role of proper chaperon. That the prospect would have horrified any of my transitory governesses, served only slightly to console me.

I was utterly frightened, knowing how tentative was the Power which I had offered to the Venture's cause. Yet I still anticipated the morning with a rare eagerness which I could in no way justify. I fell asleep reciting every name of folly I knew.

Chapter 2

Morning neared slowly; its frosty gray gave hint of the coming winter, though autumn had barely begun. I awoke shivering but grateful for the brisk air which fed my energies. In the lesser dark of predawn, I gathered my few possessions and moved quietly down the stairs. I had maintained a precautionary supply of foodstuffs, albeit through methods unorthodox for a young lady of scrupulous upbringing. I headed directly for the eastern gate, snatching a hurried and meager breakfast en route. My state of mind was not conducive to a hearty appetite.

Like so many Seriin cities of ancient origin, the plan of Anx followed a series of concentric circles pierced by spokes of major roads. Though marred by later layers, Anx remained largely symmetrical, but of the eleven roads which emanated from its hub, only the northern five had been maintained beyond the city's central district. The eastern gate crossed the road which was least traveled of the five, for it led into the inhospitable realms of the Mountains of Mindar.

I arrived at the gate early, moving swiftly through deserted streets. Not even the token Anxian guards were evident that chill morning. A single figure stood before the barrier I hoped to cross. The man was dimly visible; yet, he was unmistakably the Venture Leader, Master Kaedric.

Reluctant to share that solitary vigil, I lingered in the alleyways to await the rest of the company. I was not so distant, I suspected, that Master Kaedric's uncomfortably acute perceptions would be genuinely defeated. I trusted rather that his distaste for me would lead him to ignore me, physical separation merely easing the task. I selected a convenient wall to which some traces of plaster tenaciously clung, propped myself against it, and watched for the remaining Venturers.

Idle waiting breeds anxiety, but it was not long before Masters Gart and Hamar made their appearance. Abbot Medwyn arrived very soon thereafter. I tarried briefly, suffering some last qualms. A pallid, timid wraith, I joined the four men. Engrossed in their own preparations and discussions, they gave me no apparent notice. I was still uncertain as to whether they would indeed supply my escape from Anx. I stood awkwardly beside the group, imbued with a feeling of displacement. I studied the stained and sandy soil with a care of attention it did not merit.

Master Ineuil arrived last and unabashedly late, though the sun had yet to lift above the city's smoky pall. He called out an airy greeting, firmly directed toward me. "Exquisite lady, if you but knew how greatly I dreaded to find you had forsaken us, you would surely weep in pity of the desperate night I have spent." I had observed Master Ineuil quite long enough to assess accurately the degree of his desperation. I took appropriately little stock in his flattery, but I responded with a smile, despite myself cheered by the small attention.

Master Hamar muttered unpleasantly, "If Master Ineuil managed to remember the departure keys amid his suffering, perhaps we can get on our way."

Ineuil shook his head plaintively. "Master Hamar, you are a man of no faith. You ought to take lessons in the subject from the good Abbot Medwyn here. I, fortunately, require no such instruction. My faith is so supremely developed that I do not even question our Venture Leader's ability to make five keys suffice for six people. I trust you are suitably impressed by my piety."

"You are a conscienceless heathen, Ineuil," rebuked the abbot mildly.

"Master Ineuil might impress me more," suggested Master Kaedric dryly, "if he offered to pass the barrier keyless himself. It is he who is so singularly enchanted with Mistress Rani."

Master Ineuil chuckled mirthlessly. "You would enjoy that, Kaedric. It would revive fond childhood memories, no doubt." Abbot Medwyn shook his head, while Gart and Hamar exchanged dubious stares in echo of my own puzzlement.

"Distribute the keys," demanded Master Kaedric curtly.

Ineuil murmured blandly, "As Our Leader commands," and handed keys to Abbot Medwyn, Gart and Hamar. Ineuil seemed to weigh the last two keys, each wrapped in a gaudy silken fragment of antiquity. That which his left hand held he gave to me. The protecting fabric fell free in my hand. The disc revealed glowed subtly silver, its smooth surface fiercely cold. Almost immediately, the surface warmed, and the characteristic tracery of black appeared.

I raised my head just as Abbot Medwyn, key held high before him, vanished through the web. Gart and Hamar were already lost to sight. Ineuil still studied the key he held; Kaedric examined the barrier. Each ignored the other outwardly, but one of them hated, and I could not determine which or what. I feared for both of them without knowing why, and I nearly yielded the precious key in my hand so as to alleviate that angry, inexplicable tension.

Instead I grasped my key before me as Abbot Medwyn had done. I breathed a silent plea, closed my eyes, and stepped through the wall of my prison. Beyond a slight disorientation, I felt only the flight of the key from my hand. I opened my eyes, turning to verify my escape. The enclosing net of Anx was nowhere evident, though I carefully scanned the space where I knew it to exist. The air rippled vaguely as Master Ineuil penetrated the wall; the disc he bore shimmered and disappeared. The Venture Leader joined us beyond the deadly barricade with an admirable nonchalance for one who had carried no protective key.

"If you did not need a key, Kaedric," said Ineuil,

"You might have told me before I wasted the price." He added with a gallant flourish, "Not to sound ungracious to Mistress Rani."

"If you can wade through a stream, Master Ineuil, why would you ever bother with a bridge?" The wizard spoke scathingly, and his ice-blue eyes held anger. There is deadly bitterness between these two, I thought, and I wondered what manner of man I had so rashly agreed to follow. Watching Hamar exchange cryptic whispers with Gart, I decided I was not alone in my uneasy conclusions.

Chapter 3

I felt a very ragtag piece of chaff on my first day from Anx, but freedom from the loathsome hole made the morning hours glorious. I followed the Venturers absently, caring only that the sky above me shone clear blue once again. I was free of Anx, free of my father's rule, and free of the aimless solitude to which rebellion had led me. The Venture carried me, and I rejoined to feel again a focus of allegiance. Only when we turned to climb from the gently sloping valley into the mountains themselves did the demands of the enforced march begin to claw at my pleasure.

The road from the eastern gate of Anx dwindled quickly into a primitive path, ill-defined and uneven. My glance strayed northward to the black-green stain of Dwaelin Wood, a wistful tingle briefly reminding me of my discarded fantasy of Rhianna's realm renewed. We journeyed southeast along the foothills' edge, but the highest and most awesome of the Mindar peaks, menacing bastions with long and jagged shadows, loomed above us. My increasing aversion to the lofty passes did not derive from any lack of grandeur; the view sprawled in as majestic a beauty as any vista I had ever seen, dwindling the heights of Tyntagel's horizons into paltry hillocks. I could have enjoyed the view keenly from a less intimate perspective.

I stumbled over a rough stone, painfully recalled from inattentiveness. I had again fallen behind the others, and I hurried to narrow the gap. My normal stride could not match the pace set by Master Kaedric, but I knew better than to protest. Interloper that I was, I could scarcely complain about unchivalrous behavior.

As we trod a level stretch of path in midmorning, Master Ineuil dropped back to bespeak me. "What brought a lovely sorceress to live in the Dwaelin Wood?" he asked curiously.

I answered tersely, shy of individual conversation with this confident rogue whom I had for some time studied unseen, "I am fond of trees."

"Dwaelin Wood does have enough of those." Master Ineuil regarded me doubtfully and shook his head. "What a dismal waste of a comely woman. Mind you, I have known women who ought to be consigned to a lightless corner, but you, Mistress Rani, are not among them."

"I think you cannot be very selective to say so, but it is a kind compliment and I thank you."

"Truth is easy praise: shall I earn gratitude for calling the iris the eye of heaven?" he demanded lavishly. With bland disregard for accuracy, he added, "The thanks I merit are from the world for having extracted you from hiding." He emphasized his words by reaching his arm about me in a more than comradely fashion.

I was severely flustered but determined not to show it. Master Ineuil's interest might have pleased me under other circumstances, but the thought of spending an indefinite term of Venture fending off his advances alarmed me. "Have you not enjoyed enough conquests of late?" I asked with asperity as I stepped away from him.

"Mistress Rani, you have been observing me in Anx as well as Dwaelin Wood! I never had a woman join a Venture for me before. It is a rather stimulating approach. We must arrange some privacy to further the idea."

"I shall dislike to disappoint you, Master Ineuil," I began.

He interrupted me volubly, "If you tell me that you did not join the Venture for my irresistibly appealing company, I shall be utterly devastated, and my agony will land squarely upon your conscience. You will impart disservice to yourself and to the Venture, and that would not be in keeping with your Venture oath."

"You have a fascinating perspective on Venture code, but I doubt that Abbot Medwyn would support it," I said with more hope than belief.

"Holy men have such limited notions," complained Ineuil piteously. He had let his arm drop willingly, but he still walked closer to me than I found comfortable.

Master Kaedric glanced back at us. Cold eyes appraising, he called to Ineuil, and the fair-haired scoundrel left my side with a grimace and a shrug. The Venture Leader murmured to him some words I could not hear, and I walked alone for the remainder of the day. Master Ineuil cast me a few bright grins over his shoulder, but he did not defy the obvious decree of Master Kaedric.

Master Kaedric gave no more direct indication that he knew I followed his troop, but Master Ineuil was not the only one he warned away from me. Master Gart paused once with a shy consideration to aid me up a treacherous incline, but Master Kaedric's immediate censure of the action made any further courtesies unlikely. Master Gart's unexpected and incongruous kindness pleased me rather more than Ineuil's insincere praise, but I held no quarrel with the Venture Leader's relentless policy. I had known myself unwelcome from the outset, and if I were ostracized from the company proper, I should not need to learn as quickly their individual ways; nor should I risk revealing myself. As the day lengthened, however, and my struggle to keep Master Kaedric's pace grew more daunting, I did begin to wonder what Venture-sworn duties would entail upon a Venturess deserted by her fellows.

* * *

We had traveled with minimal halts more vertical miles than I liked to consider, and I had lost count of the repetitive ridges which now separated us from Anx. The miles did not daunt the professional soldiers, Hamar and Gart, and Ineuil complained only of boredom. The venerable abbot did not complain at all, but his steps began to falter near evening, a weakening for which I silently thanked him. The forbidding Master Kaedric displayed a concern for the holy man as for no other among us.

The Venturers speedily made camp with no need for any aid from me. Even Master Ineuil executed his tasks with silent intensity, no frivolous jocularity in evidence that night. The chosen site did not inspire cheer: towering, ashen crags on three sides and a spindly pine were the sole relief from stony stringency. I established myself near the pine, somewhat removed from the rest of the party; ancient and weary, the tree's serene tenacity solaced my ragged nerves.

I would have gladly assisted the others, but Master Kaedric's terse commands assured me that my feeble efforts only interfered. So, pursuing the voiceless whispers of the wild, I wandered from the camp to gather such produce as the vicinity offered: angelica, burdock and monarda I added to my own herbal stores; I amassed truffles and sweet apples as a timid offering.

Other foraging than mine had stocked the Venturers' larder, but the Venturers appeared to be more practical than imaginative in their acquisitions. I dropped my contribution before the fire where they gathered. Abbot Medwyn, at least, seemed pleased by the addition to the meal.

I was not so entranced by the eating of charred rabbit that I would ask to join the men in supper, especially when I had felt the buck's death cry, but the fire tempted me sorely. My woolen cloak was warm but did not cover me completely. I debated only a moment. The cold did not suffice to overcome that most worthless commodity, pride. I withdrew wordlessly from the circle of warmth and ate my few bites of

Anxian cheese in the solitary company of the tired pine, which at least did not despise me.

I was nearly asleep, yielding mindlessly to my exhaustion, when I received the first recognition of my status as a Venturess: Master Gart summoned me to a sentry shift. I winced at thought of my lost sleep. I had safely passed many nights relying solely on the warning of the wild things, but no danger more heinous than my father's trackers had sought me. I had brought the Venture duties on myself; the thought gave me little consolation. Rubbing tired eyes, I followed Master Gart to the fire. At least I should for a while enjoy warmth.

The Venture Leader was delineating to Abbot Medwyn a scheme of rotational guard duty which I privately considered pointless. I did not even try to pursue the logic of the thing, though its careful complexities might have intrigued me in days of more monotonous Tyntagel tutelage. I heeded the points of immediate interest, resolving to face each duty as it arose. For the first night, Master Gart and I should take initial watch; Ineuil and Hamar would assume the second, and Master Kaedric with Abbot Medwyn would see the night to its end. I sighed and forced myself more fully awake. It would be another three hours before I could seek sleep, and the prospect depressed me.

Had the night brought an army of Caruillan raiders leaping from the dark and brandishing swords, I doubt I could have roused sufficiently to give the warning. Fortunately, my first night as sentry passed quietly. A single curious predator impinged upon my awareness, and he was wary enough to avoid a near approach.

Master Gart studiously polished his blade, though any whisper of wind brought him stiffly alert. I watched the puckered scars scattered across his blunt hands as he honed his sword. It was a guardsman's weapon, the hilt embossed with the worn crest of an unfamiliar House.

"Did you serve that household?" I asked with a nod at the blazoned metal.

Gart smiled shyly. "From the day I could hold a weapon until my thirtieth year. My parents and my sister serve it still."

"Why did you leave?" I asked, genuinely curious. Few family guardsmen left that secure service for a mercenary's uncertain destiny.

"His Lordship cannot support all of his servants' children," said Gart a bit defensively, and I thought the answer had the air of a tired quote. The parting had been accepted with obedient grace, but it had not been welcomed.

"I do not recognize the crest. Is it a Seriin House?" I asked to distract him from his memories of regret.

"It belongs to the House of Coprak dur Sashchlya of Mahl," responded Gart proudly. It was not the name of any major holding, but it might have been Tul dur Tulea for the glow of importance which Gart accorded it. I decided that Lord Coprak had been a fool to dispense with such a persistently loyal adherent, but I bowed my head as if suitably impressed.

"Do you know Master Hamar from Mahl, then?" I asked.

"Hamar is Caruillan," answered Gart. He added hurriedly, "But he does not hold with piracy. He was fleeing the agents of Blood-Talon Cor when I met him in Pithlii. Seven of them were attacking him when we met. I beheaded two of the scum, and Hamar and I have fought together ever since." Gart grinned fondly. I blinked, baffled for a response. The piratical King Cor of Caruil and his murderous affairs were very remote from my frame of reference.

Neither Gart nor I excelled at conversation in such total absence of common perspective, but we lapsed into a surprisingly comfortable silence. I might have been an ordinary daughter of a keep, seated at my father's own gate, the grizzled warrior at my side a retainer whom I had known from birth. The Venture and its ancillary duty of nightwatch began to seem less onerous, but I was no less glad to see the shift end.

* * *

I awoke to the throbbing protest of muscles driven too strenuously on the previous day. I rose awkwardly, hobbling painfully as I tried to coax my abused legs into motion. The camp was astir; I left it to lave icy water into sleep-filled eyes as hastily as stiff muscles would permit. I half expected to find that the Venturers had departed when I returned.

The day progressed at winter's pace, awful with the tedium of discomfort. My previous difficulty in matching the Venturers' speed was magnified tenfold, and Master Kaedric's edict against me held wholly unbroken. I ached and bit back tears of frustration and hurt. The Venturers paused at midday, but I feared to sit overlong lest I be unable to coerce my body again into movement. I spent the time resentfully watching the men enjoy their ease and resolving that I should not again let pride keep me from sharing any meager luxuries available: the warmth of a fire or the sustenance of a substantial meal. I should not again yield the greatest portion of my provender to men who neither needed it nor even gave any thanks for it. If twilight ever came again, as I had begun to think unlikely, I determined that I should have a proper supper and a pot of primrose tea, coat my most miserable limbs with wintergreen liniment, and let the trees do my guarding for me.

With every trudging step, I asked myself how I could have brought myself to such a pass, my initial, overwhelming joy at escaping Anx long since vanquished by physical discomfort. I lacked the requisite will for a hermit's life, as my brief stint in Dwaelin Wood had too ably proven. The years spent in study at my father's house no longer seemed so dreary a life, but by running away, I had surely eradicated that as a possibility. The traditional destiny of marriage might have made an acceptable life had it not implied constraint still more rigid than my father's rule; I lacked the perspective to be by nature a suitable wife to any proper Seriin lord, and I could not wish to commit to a life of meek, obedient and mindless hypocrisy. I knew no trade, save for the marginal one of sorceress. With no great glee, I cycled to the conclusion that Venturing was perhaps not the worst of roles for me.

The day did end, of course, though by midafternoon I had perforce retreated in mind to that distant corner out of which my claims to endurance rose. I moved rigidly and automatically, but I did not lose sight of the Venturers. By evening, I felt a mean-spirited dearth of charity toward them, which fortified my nerve if not my good sense. When the camp had been settled for supper, I approached the fireside where the men were gathered. Master Kaedric was quite engrossed in scribbling odd symbols in the sandy soil with the tip of a highly polished dagger. The other men chatted idly as they dined on a stew of twice-charred meat and some assorted tubers which I had collected during the day. The trees whispered, and I took strength. I served myself and seated myself carefully. Not one of the Venturers protested. Master Ineuil looked from the abstracted Venture Leader to me and winked broadly. Abbot Medwyn shared my tea. It had been remarkably easy.

Another first shift as sentry, which I thought a less equitable arrangement than Master Kaedric's abstruse scheme ought to have produced, again deferred my sleep. Forbidden from rest and painfully stiff, I was not a particularly sociable companion, even solaced by food and warmth. The prospect of fending Master Ineuil's irrelevant and suggestive prattle through my current blur of fatigue did not lighten my mood. I winced as I sat beside him, my legs reluctant to bend according to my wish.

Master Ineuil tutted and wagged his head. "One might almost suspect, Mistress Rani, that the privilege of my company does not entice you so much as your slumber."

"Your perception is keen," I answered less graciously than I might had my legs and spirit ached less feverishly.

He sighed heavily. "How shall we ever extend our

relationship if you insist on disliking me?" he asked wistfully.

His regret sounded deeply sincere: I nearly protested with admission of inability actually to dislike him. I stopped the words, reminding myself of the lessons of observation. I felt wryly flattered, but I had no intention of becoming another conquest. My answer turned sardonic. "Under the circumstances, we seem destined to a certain furtherance of acquaintance, like it or otherwise."

"Only if we use our time together to greatest effect. The travails of travel do not optimize conversational opportunity. Aside from which, my lovely sorceress, our Venture Leader is tediously determined to keep us apart. You cannot have failed to perceive the heinous nature of his scheme of rotational guard duty?" Master Ineuil's tone of horror was quite affecting, as was the innocent widening of his leaf-green eyes. "You and I, lovely Sorceress Rani, shall not again share a sentry shift for over a week."

With a notable lack of sympathy, I suggested, "The only heinous aspect to Master Kaedric's scheme is its monumental complexity. If you have deciphered it sufficiently to predict beyond a week, I am indeed impressed."

Master Ineuil beamed, his green eyes glinting delight. "We progress already, dear sorceress. I have impressed you." He leaned closer to me, his voice sinking to a throaty whisper. "Our lives are linked by fate, my Rani. We were bound when you stepped from the shadow into my life."

The man was quite impossible. He had spouted a very similar speech at least a dozen times in Anx, and it sounded all the more ridiculous now that I was the recipient. "Really," was my only comment.

He straightened, dropping the pose of seducer with uncomplimentary alacrity. "A bit much? You are right, of course. Excessive exposure to the Anxian environment has deprived me of subtlety. I shall endeavor to improve." His conversation veered abruptly. "Regarding a less innocuous purveyor of subtlety: I do hope

Our Leader's disdain for chivalry does not prejudice you against the rest of us. Kaedric can be excessively difficult, but it is generally prudent to heed his stronger stances."

"I did rather force myself upon the Venture," I conceded weakly, resisting the temptation to glance toward the dark huddles where the other Venture members slept.

"A fortuitous circumstance for me, fair sorceress, though I am not quite sure just why you did it." Ineuil eyed me curiously. "I wonder if you know how much of a risk you take in countering our Master Kaedric."

"I had not really considered the matter," I lied.

"You ought never to underestimate a wizard, my Rani. The most insignificant of actions can mask monsters. Ixaxin training is partly to blame; it breeds tortuous thinking. But those who seek the training think oddly to begin."

"You imply that Master Kaedric was trained on Ixaxis. He is a full wizard then." I was ingenuously intrigued, though the revelation merely confirmed the obvious.

Master Ineuil disregarded my comments, though I was sure he heard them well enough. He pursued his own thoughts airily. "Complexity can marvelously disguise simple truths: consider Kaedric's infamous scheme of watch. It ensures that each pair of us six shares duty at least one sixth of the time, and the number of turns at each shift is evenly distributed among us through a thirty-six day cycle. Each of us, however, is paired with precisely one other Venturer exactly one-third of the time, weighting the shifts rather substantially. The emphasized pairings are notable: Kaedric with Gart, myself with Hamar, and you with Abbot Medwyn. Do you not find it fascinating?"

"Hardly," I answered with what I hoped was a quelling lack of enthusiasm. I did not want to contemplate Master Kaedric; the wizard had already lodged too firmly in my mind.

Master Ineuil remained undaunted. "You are not intrigued by the fact that our Venture Leader has concentrated the two (if you will forgive me) apparently weakest members of the party? It tells me that Kaedric sees more in either you or Abbot Medwyn than might be expected, and I think I know the abbot well enough to discount him for the stronger role in this case."

"It tells me that your logic is as convoluted as Master Kaedric's."

"My lovely one, you are unkind. Kaedric delights in twisting puzzles to obscure purposes. My interest lies solely in the motivational reasoning of a man I am sworn to follow for the nonce."

I nodded vaguely, determinedly refusing greater interest. Without encouragement, Master Ineuil's prattle grew less consequential, though it persisted for most of the three hours. I began to appreciate Hamar's protest against incessant talk. Exhaustion gradually frayed my attention to the point of ignoring my fellow sentry. I struggled just enough to heed the trees and to force my eyes to retain their focus, but energy to squander in absorbing the erratic irrelevancies of Master Ineuil's chatter departed me. I remembered, however, and pondered, when at last I had earned my rest, the thought that Master Kaedric might not consider me as entirely insignificant to the Venture as he pretended. Master Ineuil's speculations refused to be dislodged; he had activated in me an irrationally insistent interest of my own in Master Kaedric's mode of reasoning.

Chapter 4

I had lived a thoroughly ordered life until my rebellion against my father's choice, and the Venture had restored a comfortable dearth of freedom which revived in me old habits of study. I began to sort the Venturers into niches in my mind, as if I were matching stockings rather than men of mutable dispositions. Swayed by my own conclusions, my theories of these men became my reality. I did not presume any claim to friendship with the five, but the Venturers of my visions grew familiar, and my history held few fonder human connections to dislodge them.

These were hard, disparate men, alike only in acceptance of cruel beauty or fair cruelty. Gart persisted in shy reticence; Hamar glowered in silent distrust. Abbot Medwyn was a man who combined in rare counterpoint faith with placid pragmatism; he barely spoke to me, though he could be quite gregarious with the others. Ineuil talked endlessly, but he very seldom conversed, and nonsense dominated his speech. Kaedric's reserve was unyielding. Each man told me astonishingly little.

It was by Gart that I felt most nearly accepted, despite Master Ineuil's persistent effluence of praise. That Gart's attitude toward me suggested the timid deference of a vassal toward his Lady did nothing to promote companionship, however. Master Gart belonged to that most class-conscious breed of peasantry to whom the least measure of literacy bespeaks authority. Only with his long companion, Hamar, was he entirely at ease; the two of them proudly proclaimed a common heritage of low birth.

I could not doubt the depth of friendship between

Hamar and Gart, but I could not fathom it. Hamar suffered perpetual anger, the sort which rises from festered sorrow, and it did not make him pleasant company. I pitied Hamar for the pain which obviously goaded him, but my sympathy ebbed with proximity. Restrained by soldierly discipline, he had not openly threatened me since Anx, but his hatred blared forth at me. The dour features of his bald head stiffened at every sighting of me; his suspicious glare pursued me as certainly as the wardings of the old peasant woman who had held my childhood in strict custody. It was not the Tyntagellian sort of prejudice which filled Hamar, for it did not extend to Master Kaedric, but it was no less pervasive. Watch duty with Master Hamar was a grueling ordeal of mutual distrust.

Abbot Medwyn accorded me little more confidence than did Hamar. The abbot was vastly more tolerant of sorcery than any priest of my prior acquaintance, but he would speak to me only sparingly. He did not hide his disapproval of my presence. He took his Venture very seriously, and he viewed my jointure as irresponsible whim. He was not chronically somber as are so many of his years and calling; Ineuil drew as much laughter as censure from the abbot, and the laughter showed less reluctance in the issuance. But the Abbot of Benthen Abbey bore a heavy weight of worry where the Venture was concerned.

Master Ineuil still defied my efforts to categorize satisfactorily. Apparently a very capable warrior when necessity could overcome indolence, he lightly professed himself to be both trickster and thief, and his eclectic education had not excluded a sampling of the mage's art, though his actual Power was more minimal than my own. He clearly enjoyed the role of irresponsible scapegrace, but I began to suspect a very shrewd manipulator hid behind the pose.

There remained the Venture Leader, the wizard who effected minor wonders with casual indifference: lighting a fire with a glance or exploding a nutshell rather than cracking it in the ordinary way. If I had ever visualized a Sorcerer King, his aspect would have much resembled Master Kaedric; any staunch Tyntagellian would have placed him immediately. Saturnine and cynical, remotely merciless and coldly impersonal, he fulfilled the very image of the remorseless men and women who had tyrannized the ancient world. I had been taught to despise wizards. I wished I could despise Master Kaedric half as much as I feared him.

Chapter 5

Whether by misfortune or some malicious humor of the Venture Leader, my first watch, my first solitary confrontation with Master Kaedric was scheduled for the night's final shift. Nervous fear forbade me more than fitful sleep as I counted the hours before me. I surrendered to insomnia's inevitable victory when the second shift was little more than half over. I arose, intending to give benefit of those elusive minutes of sleep to Abbot Medwyn or Master Gart. Too late for unobserved retreat, I found Master Kaedric surveying the nightscape alone.

"You will regret your lack of rest, Mistress Rani," he murmured with disinterest.

I answered tartly, too afflicted with nervousness to restrain my tongue. "By your own words, Venture Leader, my well-being concerns myself alone. The prospect of lost sleep does not seem to have deterred you."

"Ineuil's injudicious wit is contaminating you. It is not an endearing characteristic."

"I have never believed in hypocritical propitiation," I said, achieving an admirably scathing tone which doubtless failed to hide my reluctance to approach the wizard closely.

"An admirable policy, but a hazardous one if

misallocated. Do you intend to assume sentry duty, or were you planning a surreptitious exit from our Venture? I shall willingly release you from your oath."

It was a weighty and generous offer, though the Venture Leader would unquestionably prefer to see me go. I had been freed from Anx; I could pursue my own path unencumbered. Instead of making such a sensible choice, I responded loftily, "I may yet be of use to you, Master Kaedric."

He shrugged indifference. "Then you may as well take your post. Or perhaps you see better through basalt." He acknowledged the overhang which slanted across the entrance to the cave wherein we had made camp. I had welcomed the shelter earlier, for the rain fell softly outside, and the cave was dry and warmly defended against the wind. I had not considered how close to Kaedric I would have to stay because of the narrow access.

I braced myself with the thought that an adept wizard could bespell me quite as well from five feet as from five inches, if he were so inclined. I could hardly expect to contribute anything to the Venture if I were going to be daunted by the prospect of sitting near the Venture Leader. I was stubbornly determined to be of value; it may have been a form of atonement for my dereliction of filial duty. I seated myself with what grace I could manage, taking excessive care to avoid any wisp of contact with the Venture Leader.

He leaned against a fold of polished rock siding, long legs drawn close and crossed after the manner of street dwellers. His cloak was rough, and his fingers tugged restlessly at the collar. He had walked in the rain, for the sheen of it caused his thick hair to cling tightly to itself rather than to stray errantly as was its wont. Ineuil was the more handsome, for Master Kaedric's lines had been drawn too acutely, but the wizard had a graceful strength and eyes which were inescapable.

The rain fell, dimpling the pool which had gathered beyond the cavern access. I watched it carefully. I reached for the thoughts of the trees, but my mind was too troubled to hold the contact long. The dark, cloud-filled sky roiled before me, for the cave opened onto a ledge which had been lifted boldly from the mountain's smooth skin of soil. The clouds thinned, and an aureole of hidden moonlight softened them, but the world a few paces from my face remained a blurred and featureless shadow. I drew my feet more tightly beneath me to keep them from the splatter of the rain, and I clasped my arms about me firmly for warmth.

I spoke randomly, my throat tight with discomfort. "Am I so predictable that you dismissed both Abbot Medwyn and Master Gart in anticipation of my early arrival?"

"I felt the need for some solitary contemplation."

"I should be pleased to leave you to it, Master Kaedric."

"I never doubted that," he responded dryly, a hush above the rain. He added with his distinctive precision, an exactitude of enunciation which seemed to shield another accent, "But a Venture Leader ought to know something of his followers, and you do appear boundlessly determined to follow." An odd sensation of sitting/standing, meeting the gaze of wintry/fiery eyes in both a gloomy cave and a glittering emptiness tantalized me. Kaedric asked quietly, "What drives you so confoundedly to pursue this quest? Our goal means nothing to you. I doubt you could even tell me what it is."

I answered faintly, "I was not aware that a Venturer's motives demanded scrutiny," hoping that the Venture Leader would desist from questioning me as I tried to consolidate the doubling of image through which I saw him.

"Some degree of explanation could ease your position. Master Hamar, for example, considers you a dubious ally indeed. He distrusts women in any case, and your mysterious appearance among us does little to calm his suspicions."

"It is difficult to defend against irrational prejudice."

"Granted. But you must admit that you are an atypical Venturess, Mistress Rani."

"Then I have found a Venture well suited to me," I retorted.

"Others among us have strong motives regarding the Venture goal itself, a factor which compensates for much that would be otherwise unlikely." An arrhythmic rustle from a ragged copse below us drew his attention. The veil between the images I saw of him thinned. I listened closely to the whisper of fading leaves; something breathed in the rainy night. The air constricted around it heatedly. A darkness slipped beyond dead rock, and I lost the thing's touch.

Kaedric relaxed imperceptibly, releasing the thought which had lashed our watcher into flight. I could feel the pulse of the wizard's Power, a singularly disconcerting sensation which disturbed me far more than the prospect of any nearby prowlers. Unreasonably embarrassed, I blushed as if discovered in some intimate secret.

I found clear blue eyes assessing me curiously. "You are not only an unlikely Venturess, Mistress Rani. You are a very singular sorceress as well."

I disliked the direction the conversation was taking toward my sorcerous claims. "There was something in the copse which the trees found unfamiliar," I countered unnecessarily.

"That 'something' has been studying us for some hours, but for the moment it seems to have accepted my suggestion to depart. Our observer did not distress you; I did. For an apparently educated sorceress, you react remarkably like some credulous child equating wizardry with atrocity."

"I am not fond of sorcery, Master Kaedric, but that makes me no less a sorceress," I stated sharply, wondering helplessly what form of ignorance I had betrayed.

"I am not questioning the existence of your Power," remarked Master Kaedric evenly. He regarded me with a keen attention which I refused to confront. "Your doubt of my ability to recognize it does intrigue me, however. Is it my Power or your own which you question, I wonder?"

"Since you persist in denying my value to the Venture, it should hardly surprise you if I suspected you of a lack of perception," I answered haughtily, speaking rudely out of a sudden suspicion that I could thereby best dispel the Venture Leader's interest.

For some moments, he kept silent. He watched the night, but I felt him studying me closely. Rain touched the earth in a delicate patter. The whispers of the woods had dimmed, lost in the glare of the Power beside me. I tried to reach the mind of an owl, but I could not sufficiently escape the man.

"If you were a whit less transparently ingenuous," he said after the minutes had stretched achingly, "I should doubt you as fervently as does Master Hamar, despite the rather reliable evidence of my perceptions."

I straightened deliberately, forcing my eyes to meet those of the Venture Leader, the clear blue mirrorlike in reflected fire-glow. I repeated stiffly, "I may yet be of use to you, Master Kaedric."

"That is a paltry reason to risk life and soul."

"It suffices me, for I do not risk so much." I continued more bitterly than I had intended, "Durability takes no more account of worth than does the gift of Power."

"Power respects nothing," stated Kaedric flatly. "But even a wizard is bound by a physical shell. Are you so certain of your 'durability' that you would care to test it against a full wizard's Power?" He whispered dangerously, "Are you so sure that you would care to test your strength against me, for instance? With the Taormin in his hands, Hrgh's Power may not be so different from mine. You ought to know what that kind of Power can inflict before you taunt it."

The beat of his Power grew as he spoke, pounding through me until it began to rule the throb of my heart and lifeblood. The rhythm shifted, and the pulsation burned. "Have you ever seen a man afire from within?" demanded Master Kaedric softly. His words held a fever-bright intensity which was almost seductive. "The skin begins to shrivel as the moisture leaves it, and the eyes wither. He cannot scream aloud, for the fire steals his voice. He falls and writhes, but the flame cannot be extinguished, because his own life energy turns inward to help consume its host. It is not a death I should recommend. Is that what you wish to face, Mistress Rani?"

"We each face what we must, Master Kaedric," I answered firmly, trying to deny the tightening pain. I had dreaded Master Kaedric's dissuasion so deeply that its unpleasant arrival actually eased my fear. After the years of my father's tutelage, I could distinguish sincere attack from intimidation, even when the weapon wore a radically different guise. The Venture Leader controlled his Power carefully; I found myself certain that he would cause me no more serious harm now than he had in the Anxian tavern, and the game he played annoyed me.

He ceased his onslaught. An ill-fortuned rodent cried death as the talons of the owl tore its flesh. The mingled hunger and suffering pierced me more deeply for the rawness of my wracked senses. I clenched my arms tightly in misery, forced on myself a rigid control, and spoke with angry hauteur. "You remind me, Master Kaedric, of a bully who tortures small creatures so as to reassure himself of his own superiority."

Kaedric watched me a moment closely, then turned away and commented, "I have roused terror in far more stalwart individuals than yourself, Mistress Rani, but the reaction is not generally an urge to provoke me further. I do find your behavior a trifle eccentric." He startled me with soft laughter, and he grinned fleetingly, for a brief instant disarmingly approachable. "If you detect any unnatural disturbances around us, I trust you will inform me," he continued. "You do appear to be highly empathic toward certain life forms. With brigands and less palatable foes roaming these mountains, no warning system can be too complete."

I glanced perplexedly at the man beside me, seeking evidence of mockery. Impenetrable reserve resumed, he studied the cloud-covered sky. A lock of velvet-black hair obscured his eyes from my sidelong view, and the smooth, hard line of his jaw revealed nothing.

Chapter 6

The next days followed closely the pattern of those first, save that my aches turned dully permanent and my feet turned raw with blisters. The gray and rocky way we trod changed minimally, but the verdant carpet of Dwaelin Wood seemed to withdraw ever farther below us. A few tenacious pines and the scions of a hardy breed of lusterless shrub clung to barren stone. An occasional bird or skittering rodent would acknowledge me briefly, but they were cautious of the company I kept. I understood their wariness; comprehension did not console me for loss of their companionship.

We traveled for another fortnight before the validity of Master Kaedric's cautionings became manifest. We had departed from the established trail to reach our goal in the heart of the Mountains of Mindar. The way had grown steadily more difficult and unpredictable, but this should hopefully deter the marauding bands which so frequently preyed upon each other in the relatively halcyon lowlands. Ineuil and Gart had one night reported the approach of a pair of would-be robbers, but the glint of polished steel had sufficed to discourage the interlopers. Whatever creature had watched us at the cavern camp had not appeared again. Anx had fallen miles behind us, and my mind had grown easier in the far more peaceful wilderness.

Our rate of progress had deteriorated, impeded by sliding rocks and thorny shrubs. Retraced steps abraded tempers. Both Gart and Hamar freely cursed every uncooperative stone; Ineuil darted verbal barbs with indiscriminate liberality; Abbot Medwyn grew unwontedly quiet, save for some suppressed mutterings of a less than pious air. Kaedric grew grimmer, scowled often, and spoke scarcely at all. My own lot having improved significantly from the first, unnecessarily ghastly days beyond Anx, I savored a slightly vindicative sense of justice in the current distress of my companions.

We had been following the third in a series of narrow, apparently unassailable canyons for over an hour. The last ended, as had the others, at the base of a daunting arete. As he had done twice before, Kaedric climbed the accessible base of the barricade, examining its crevices for a means to mount or circumvent the obstacle. I mentally applauded his indomitable persistence, but I did not follow the others to the canyon's end. I was confident that they would soon return as they had come. I sat on a boulder to wait, massaging my right ankle, for I had wrenched it earlier in the day.

I let my mind roam to my surroundings. A few birds pecked grubs from a rotting log. A mouse snatched a seed with greedy glee. A cluster of columbine touched tentative roots to a stony crack. I pictured my sister's horrified distaste for my present circumstances, my brothers' disapproval of my fellow journeyers, and my father's angry disdain. Lady Altha would have shrieked very shrilly of the improprieties of my surroundings. By now, the plans for my journey to Tulea would have been well advanced; I should have been suffering the attentions of a dozen dressmakers in preparation for my presentation to Lord Grisk dur Niveal. I sighed, content despite soreness and fatigue.

The sun warmed me, and I became for the instant heartily glad of the Venture I had chosen to pursue. Master Kaedric did accuse me justly: I had only the dimmest notion of our goal. I enjoyed the Venture as a surreal interlude, detached from any reality I understood. I did not fret at the delays which racked the others, because I had forgotten the future and the past.

Suddenly daydreams, bruised toes and aching muscles were all forgotten. The wild things, leafed and furred and feathered, cried resounding terror. I think I screamed in echo, but I never heard my own cry. I heard an ominous twang, saw a feathered shaft strike the stone a breath away from Kaedric, felt the rush of hurtling arrows as the Venturers scrambled for cover. I willed myself less than a shadow in starlight, pressed flat against the cliff, and prayed that stony solidity might protect me.

I could see Hamar's hunched shoulder protruding from cover, but the other Venturers had vanished from my view. I scanned the opposite heights for the source of the attack; I found a hollow and a solid, hidden ridge. I felt the force of willful violence now, a score of murderous predators gloating on the effectiveness of their trap. They had grown silent following the initial flurry of assault. They awaited some betraying movement from their quarry, and they were patient with the self-confidence of assured success. They outnumbered us badly, and they held as well the advantage of position. I breathed raggedly; dust had caught in my throat, and tears gathered as I stifled a cough.

The air rose, distorted, from the canyon, and the cool clarity of autumn warped into currents of summer-hot heat. The scene before me had subtly shifted. The atmosphere suffocated; the cliff face against which I leaned turned searing. The heat above me became yet more intense. Clattering stones and scattered oaths signified an unwilling departure of the attackers.

Master Kaedric reappeared, leaping deftly down an inadequate stair of boulders to the level of the sand. With an imperious gesture, he summoned the other Venturers and waved them toward the canyon egress. I merged with them as they reached me, still enshadowed by my fear, in time to hear Kaedric whisper sharply to the party, "A slight scorch will not long deter our friends from pursuit. We need a more defensible position, preferably one less riddled with well-armed thieves."

"There was a place not far back which might suit," offered Ineuil after a moment's consideration. Kaedric nodded approval, and Ineuil added irritably, "You nearly cooked us back there, O Venture Leader. Could you be a little more selective in your next attack?"

Kaedric answered distractedly, "Next time I shall be pleased to practice on you, Master Ineuil." Gart shouted warning as an enormous ruffian in greasy furs and motley bits of rust-flecked armor leaped before us. I jumped back, feeling exceptionally useless, as Hamar parried a weighty axe blow. From pocked cliffs before and above us, a dozen more of the brigands appeared. The constricted space between the canyon walls prevented them from reaping full advantage of their greater numbers, but the same feature of landscape held us firmly caged.

The thieves jeered and taunted, aware of their advantages and apparently undaunted by their brief setback at the canyon's end. Even the downing of several of their own by the swords of Hamar, Gart and Ineuil did not seem to deter them. The villains now visible on the upper ledge, a group more prosperously attired than their fellows in the forefront of the attack, cheered the carnage below them as if enjoying a highly entertaining spectacle. The delight of the men remote from the fray—and at least one woman whom I could see beside them—ebbed considerably when a knife spun from Kaedric's hand to catch the neck of one of their number. The injured man sagged, blood spattering freely over his tasteless finery; his fellows retreated to safer cover, leaving him to howl his death. The robber band had underestimated their prey.

I had tended wounds in Tyntagel, eased a soldier's death, and cleansed the stump of a farmer's leg severed to prevent the spread of black infection. I had not known the dreadful wrack of deliberate killing; the spread of death in that nameless canyon furthered the education begun in Anx. Blood-drenched earth and dismembered, dying men sent me reeling with nausea. That those who suffered were both my enemies and murderous thieves did not alleviate my horror. Masters Gart and Hamar tallied their victims with emotionless zeal; Ineuil mocked his prey, darted deadly, agile thrusts, and danced away from steely retaliation. Shadowed as I was amid the hail of blows, I nearly lost a hand to one of Ineuil's fluid brandishes.

Kaedric stood guard before a calm but very somber Abbot Medwyn. Save for that first knife cast, the Venture Leader had used no obvious weapon. The brigands did not approach the remote pair. Though Kaedric gazed afar as if oblivious, at his feet an unbloodied corpse shriveled, pallid and mindlessly contorted.

More attackers joined the battle, and the Venturers slew less easily. With a shouted command in a vaguely recognizable Mahlite dialect, Kaedric consigned the abbot's defense to Master Gart and climbed to a rough outcrop just below the bandits' ledge. His position made him a prominent target, but none of our assailants seemed inclined to press him, however much their chiefs (safely ensconced behind stout barricades of boulders) might urge it.

The glances of the brigands began to stray uncertainly to the man silhouetted against the beige and umber strata. I watched him also: I could feel around me all the life-beats save his, which should have pulsed most potently. Though clearly visible, Master Kaedric's withdrawal was far more complete than mine. The air around him rippled slowly, faster, searingly bright. Spirals shivered, fire flew, and a reedy wail of agony rose from the canyon walls. Some of the brigands fell; others scrambled madly. Swords and axes, pikes and daggers dropped forgotten, rattling dismally. A shrill scream seemed to tear sound from the very stone and cast it at reverberating mountain walls.

The fallen men blackened and burned to curling cinders. A few men struggled and crawled blindly, even as their flesh fused and melted from bones already crumbling. Ineuil began to seek the lingerers, ending their torment with quick sword thrusts; Gart and Hamar joined him in his task, and Abbot Medwyn knelt to pray above the dying. I saw Kaedric, and his eyes had filled with fire, though it may have been an image visible to me alone. I shut my own eyes tightly but could not seal away the sounds and scents. The slaughter filled my mind, until I was nearly as mad as the thieves who begged to die.

Chapter 7

When my mind cleared, miles had been lost. I followed Abbot Medwyn docilely, trailing the other Venturers and treading carefully along the ridge which had previously daunted our efforts to reach it. A wisp of smoke and a glimpse of leaping flame marked the battlefield behind us. I averted my eyes from the site of carnage and from the dark figure of the man who led us.

"Are you returned to us, Mistress Rani?" asked Abbot Medwyn solicitously.

I gazed blankly a moment at the robed man who walked beside me, then answered heavily, "Thank you, Abbot, I am quite recovered now."

"I am most pleased to hear it. Sorcerous self-healing still disconcerts me." He loosed the cowl from his head as he nodded. He continued briskly, "I may need to raid your herbal stores this evening. Master Hamar took a slash across the ribs: not a deep wound, but it may infect."

"I have myrrh and echinacea."

"Between us we have a rather satisfactory pharmacopoeia, Mistress Rani. Would you also have some yellow jessamine?"

Uncomprehendingly, I responded, "Yellow jessamine is a bit beyond my abilities, Sir Abbot. That is a rather odd request for a soldier's wounds."

"Kaedric does not wage ordinary war," he answered, and my memory-wracked soul agreed with a shudder.

Abbot Medwyn looked troubled. "Ixaxins use yellow jessamine as a restorative after intensive energy expenditure. Kaedric dislikes the practice, but it has just occurred to me that the herb might be of value. Well, I ought to have thought of it before I left the Abbey." He raise his eyes to me and smiled. "Are you surprised that a priest has studied wizards' lore?"

"I suppose I ought to be surprised at nothing just now; my emotions are worn raw. But, yes, I find it strange." I continued heatedly, "I find it strange that you, a holy man, traffic with anyone who works such destruction as Master Kaedric has done. I find it strange that you can still show such concern for him. I realize that he saved our lives, but surely even murderous thieves do not deserve such death as that. How can you condone it?"

"I do not condone it, nor, I think, does Kaedric. I only dimly understand it, and that little has taken many years, much patience, and a large measure of friendship. As you are a sorceress, the reasons should be more clear to you, but I suppose your Power is nearly as far from Kaedric's as mine. Be thankful for that lack, Mistress Rani. There is no comfort in a gift of that magnitude." Personally I found little comfort in Abbot Medwyn's explanations but I did not speak more. My own prejudice haunted me enough.

We halted early that night, though we traveled several miles before a suitably defensible site could be found. Exhaustion's palpable presence gripped us. We had no sooner established camp than Master Kaedric wordlessly left us. Abbot Medwyn moved his arm slightly in the traditional plea of protection, murmured a soft prayer, and returned to the tending of Hamar's wound.

"I hope you pray for the unfortunates whom Our Leader has yet to meet," scoffed Ineuil. "Those we left are a little past salvation." He winced as the cold astringency of the salve which I was applying to his arm penetrated.

Gart issued a disgruntled chuckle, and Hamar grumbled, "I never mind a few added scars, but I like to feel some purpose in their earning. We might as well have stayed in Anx. This Venture is one wizard and four bits of extraneous baggage." With a scowl at me, he added, "And a fifth bit which is most extraneous of all."

"Kaedric is notoriously effective," commented Ineuil acidly. "But he could have saved us all some trouble by exercising a shade more promptitude." He winced again. "Mistress Rani's gentle ministrations do brighten the situation, however." Hamar snorted in disgust.

"None of you knows whereof you speak," chided Abbot Medwyn, "if you believe that Kaedric does not need us. It is for Kaedric that I pray."

"You may as well pray for the devil, Abbot," said Ineuil. "The two are not such distant kin." His acrid comment received no argument. Even Abbot Medwyn merely bowed his head more diligently to his task.

I shared the second watch that night with Master Ineuil. Irritating though he could often be, I felt easier on that occasion for the distraction he provided. "Fair Mistress Rani, do you not think my wounds deserve some further care?" he asked very seriously. He extended his finely muscled forearm for my inspection. "I feel some definite concern for this one."

Humoring him, I examined the gash; it was a shallow score, probably uncomfortable but clean. "I doubt your survival hangs in the balance, Master Ineuil."

"I shall arrange a more needful injury if it will gain me your tender ministrations."

"The exchange seems scarcely equitable," I responded, provoked to laughter despite myself and the day's memories. My mirth shattered as a long firelight-cast shadow crossed me.

"You have always had the most inconvenient sense of timing, Kaedric," said Ineuil sourly. "Do you never sleep?"

"Do you never tire of testing me?" snapped the wizard with an abrupt and angry clenching of his long fingers. The two men measured each other, and Ineuil gave a brief, humorless laugh.

"Just once, Kaedric, I should like to be able to meet

you on a par. In fact, I should like to see anyone meet you in a truly even contest."

"There is no such thing as a truly even contest in this world," said Kaedric mockingly. "Someone inevitably loses." The wizard turned to me. "Mistress Rani, you share a certain rapport with creatures of the wild. How well can you control the exchange of information?"

I answered him reluctantly, as if reciting by rote a lesson to one of my more daunting and demanding tutors, "Most life forms communicate on a level of primary emotions. I can impart more complex messages, but the effectiveness of the reception depends upon the individual's mode of thinking. If the pattern is sufficiently similar to my own, I can generally emulate it and force comprehension."

"We require a guide. I suggest that you make an effort to find one." The cold-eyed wizard spun immediately away, striding determinedly toward the darkness. He had allowed me no opportunity to demur.

"Welcome to the Venture, Mistress Rani," gibed Ineuil. "You wanted to be useful, I believe."

Frustration tensed me, inadequacy clawing my heart. Take care what you wish, Rhianna, especially in a wizard's hearing. "Master Ineuil, I do not even know our destination. How can I possibly convey instructions to a guide?"

"A sorceress should never permit impossibilities to daunt her," he scolded. "Witness Our Leader's example. However, in this circumstance, perhaps you would permit a mere, primitive mortal to help. We are headed for the castle of the late and unlamented Sorcerer King Horlach, though I rather think that time has reduced the castle to a few moldy, underground chambers. I cannot imagine why Hrgh would choose to inhabit the beastly ruin—he used to be inordinately fastidious—but I apparently misjudged him in a number of ways."

"You know the man we seek?" I asked, unreasonably startled.

"So I thought, but I underestimated his ambition."

"And one should never underestimate a wizard," I said slowly, remembering Ineuil's previous warning.

"Nor the ambition of a Dolr'han dur Liin. I was guilty on both accounts."

"Lord Hrgh Dolr'han dur Liin," I voiced mechanically.

The young jet-haired woman emerged from the carriage, resplendent in emerald velvet and soft ermine. She greeted her dour father with a light embrace and a teasingly secretive smile. She tossed an irritated order at a laggardly servitor and took her father's arm as they entered the looming keep. The keep was gray, and its Lord was iron, but the raven-haired daughter shed warm brilliance on both. Neither father nor daughter observed the pale-haired girl who watched them from the upper stair.

"You look well, Yldana," said the middle-aged woman who greeted the noble Lord and his daughter in the great hall of Tyntagel Keep. "Did you journey smoothly?"

The young woman negligently dropped her cloak in a servant's hands as she answered, "The journey was odious, as always, Lady Altha." Smiling again, she added, "But my stay in Tulea was very satisfactory."

"You found Lord Amgor's kin to your liking?" asked Lord Baerod with a proud inspection of his beautiful daughter.

Yldana gave a slight shrug. "They are Amlachians, Father, and Amgor adores me. Amgor was a bit of a bore about it all, actually. However, Amgor may not be the only Seriin lord aspiring to a match with Tyntagel." She tilted her head and regarded her father through long lashes. "I do think Lord Hrgh Dolr'han took quite an interest in me, as well."

Lady Altha's flat brown eyes nearly gleamed. "The heir of Liin! Baerod, imagine it: your daughter the Lady of Liin."

The expression of the Lord of Tyntagel had grown stoic. "Lord Hrgh is a wizard, Yldana," he said tonelessly.

A faint frown flickered across the young woman's face. "I did not say that I intended to marry him, father." Her enthusiasm returned. "But he is charming and very handsome."

"And he is a Dolr'han, Baerod," added Lady Altha firmly. Lord Baerod glared at his cousin, and Lady Altha bit back her praise of Liin, saying only, "One must make allowances for a Dolr'han."

Yldana wheedled coaxingly, "Lord Hrgh is not like other wizards, Father. I know that you will approve him when you meet. Uncle Dhavod did."

"You have not invited Lord Hrgh here?" demanded Lord Baerod, but his words were not harsh.

Yldana gave a horrified moue. "Father, I would not. Hrgh has not spoken to me formally, as yet." She twirled in a delicate dance across the parquet as she headed for the stair. "But if he were to request permission to visit, I could hardly refuse, could I, Father? One does not say no to a Dolr'han!" She tossed a kiss to her father from the banister. She brushed past her younger sister. "Should you not be at study of something, Rhianna?" she murmured disinterestedly as she passed.

"Welcome home, Yldana," answered the younger girl wryly.

"Baerod," insisted Lady Altha sternly, "Liin is the wealthiest domain in Serii. You could not deny that to Yldana."

Lord Baerod spoke grimly. "Lord Hrgh may well relinquish the heirship of Liin if Alobar dies."

"Then you would be father-in-law to the Infortiare, and you could work directly against Ixaxis instead of playing these fruitless games of yours."

"You wag your tongue too freely, Altha," said Tyntagel's Lord. His cousin was silenced, but she smirked complacently at his back.

The Dolr'han request for Yldana's hand never arrived. Yldana had shielded her disappointment, citing the impossibility of taking a wizard for husband. It was a transparent ploy. The Dolr'han mystique, strongly abetted by Liin's wealth, could have easily surmounted the force of even Tyntagellian prejudice.

Lord Alobar had died little more than a year later, when Yldana was already affianced to Lord Amgor. No one had doubted that Lord Hrgh Dolr'han dur Liin would replace Alobar as Infortiare. Lord Hrgh had actually yielded his heirdom to his younger brother, Lord Gorng, in anticipation of the Ixaxin Council's official announcement. Hrgh's renunciation proved premature: Ixaxis selected the unknown Venkarel over the paragon of Liin.

Lord Hrgh and most of Serii had roared with the outrage of injustice, and Lord Hrgh had challenged Lord Venkarel to a contest of Power. To the stunned elation of Hrgh's supporters, Lord Venkarel accepted Hrgh's challenge. Shock encompassed Serii when the Dolr'han was defeated. Yldana, who cared nothing for the politics involved, had cheered the defeat of the man who had spurned her. It was the only time I ever heard our father reproach her severely.

I began to theorize aloud. "When Lord Hrgh could not become Infortiare by his own Power, he sought another means. He stole this thing, the Taormin, so as to oust Lord Venkarel." Ineuil raised an eyebrow but did not contradict me. I shook my head. "But surely Lord Hrgh cannot expect Ixaxis to accept him as Infortiare under such conditions."

"In theory, the Taormin could exterminate Ixaxis and everything else we know—if anyone knew how to use it. It was the secret of Horlach's success over his competitors, and the Ixaxins are not what they were when Ceallagh led them in Horlach's defeat. However, I doubt that Hrgh has thought beyond trouncing Venkarel. Overconfidence and hatred of Venkarel drove Hrgh to tackle the Taormin. If it were not such a stupid move, I might laud it."

"You supported Lord Hrgh's challenge."

"I supported Hrgh—not his insane challenge. I certainly did not support Venkarel," hissed Ineuil with abrupt vehemence. "Venkarel is a coldblooded, calculating bastard who happens to have more Power in his fingertip than any other wizard or wizardess born of the past hundred generations. The challenge was a farce from its issuance."

"Lord Hrgh evidently thought otherwise."

"Hrgh could not accept the fact that a whore's son could ever better a Dolr'han. The tragic irony was that popular demand would have persuaded Ixaxis to replace Venkarel in a short time. Venkarel's selection was a marginal thing at best."

"Until the challenge sealed it."

Ineuil nodded thoughtfully. "Venkarel felled a Dolr'han with all of Tulea as witness, and there could be no further question as to Venkarel's superiority of Power. By Ceallagh's laws, the strongest wizard at the time of selection is Infortiare. Hrgh's punishment was far worse than official banishment from Tulea and Ixaxis; nothing can recompense a Dolr'han for loss of pride."

"You still prefer Lord Hrgh to Lord Venkarel, but you have joined a Venture which favors Lord Venkarel over Lord Hrgh."

"I personally despise Venkarel, but he is as clever as a fiend and certainly far more knowledgeable about wizardry than I. If Venkarel fears the Taormin, then Hrgh's attempt to use it is suicidal insanity."

"Lord Venkarel must have his own followers. Why employ someone who hates him?"

"The challenge was in some ways an expensive indulgence on Venkarel's part as well as on Hrgh's. The feelings against Ixaxis have been mounting steadily ever since."

"Is that an answer?" I asked. Ineuil shrugged. I digested his previous spate of information. "Master Kaedric directly serves Lord Venkarel," I concluded.

After a moment's pause, Ineuil answered, "Unquestionably." He cocked his head, "I must remember not to underestimate sorceresses either."

Chapter 8

I woke myself in the early dawn so as to essay compliance with the wizard's pointed suggestion to seek a guide. Somnolent night still cloaked many of the Mountains' tenants, but I issued wisps of thought to test each tentative touch. I could quickly eliminate those of stationary or overly sedentary habit, as well as those unable to maintain a steady focus of mind. Less surely, I discarded those whose gentle timidity I dared not risk to Master Kaedric's menacing presence. I nearly despaired before I found the one I sought.

When the stars faded fully, I rose and crossed to the wizard. Deliberately, I emulated that austere formality which he could so eloquently project, as I said, "I have found a guide, Venture Leader. We shall proceed according to your command." I was fey with success, intoxicated by the distant touch of the Nighthawk, and still enough myself to delight in the quick, startled flicker of Master Kaedric's eyes. I was only marginally aware of Master Gart's curious stare.

I should have been less eager to comply with the Venture Leader's wishes had I realized the means by which he would command his Venture's guide; I had yet to learn the lesson which Ineuil consistently reiterated. The wizard channeled his instructions to the Nighthawk directly into my mind, and the shock shattered my precarious control. My own panic at Master Kaedric's touch nearly exceeded that of the bird, and, together, the Nighthawk and I fled the mental flame on wings which beat through the dashing winds.

We were unfettered by leaden limbs, and the tortured lands could not hinder our flight. The Mountains of Mindar extended to the ends of our universe, their minutiae clear to our sight. We soared and darted, rushing upward to plummet swiftly through roaring air, veering from impact a breath away from earth.

Pain gripped my arms, and my unsteady legs supported me again on the barren rock of the Venturers' camp. Long fingers, brutally tight, encircled my wrists. I debated desperately the odds of escaping those hard, slender digits, but Master Kaedric abruptly released me. I rubbed my wrists with grateful relief.

"Your Power exceeds your control to a dangerous degree, Mistress Rani," said Kaedric coldly. "I trust you managed to absorb the sense of our goal, at least." I returned the wizard's stare, uneasily aware that my new certainty of destination was not of my own devising. The bitter flavor of decayed Power formed an unmistakable lodestone to Horlach's ruined home, and Master Kaedric had implanted the cognizance of it within me. "We must retrace the last mile," I said in answer.

The Nighthawk's aid speeded our passage considerably. Each night I gathered the image of local geography from my nocturnal partner and conveyed it to Master Kaedric in the morning. Practice enabled me to transfer the visions to a terrestrial frame of reference without effort, though the first few days had kept me wavering with disorientation. Such obstacles as escaped the Nighthawk's aerial view were few and minor. We encountered no further human intervention; the few survivors (whom Master Kaedric asserted did exist) of our prior contest had evidently spread the warning.

Master Kaedric had developed the habit of departing each evening from the rest of the company. Never social, he had grown yet more aloof since the attack in the canyon. Abbot Medwyn fretted at the Venture Leader's absences, but even the abbot conversed more freely when Kaedric was gone from us.

The moon was rising, but it was timid still of the waning sunlight. The fire crept along the scarred bark of an old log, trying to blaze into warmth. The two men coaxed the flame that it might be ready for the return of their companions. They were disparate men, oddly united.

Ineuil asked with dark, bleak insistence, "Why did you call this Venture, Abbot?"

Abbot Medwyn retorted with uncharacteristic sharpness, "Why did you join it, Ineuil?"

"You know why I joined it," snapped Ineuil. "Hrgh must be stopped in his madness, but I would rather not see Hrgh left to *him*." Ineuil jerked his head toward the wooded path which Kaedric had earlier taken. "Gart and Hamar joined in honest intent to aid your Venture, because they did not know whom they would need to serve. Mistress Rani's reasons are suspiciously obscure, but yours are the more so. You have favored that damned wizard for years, even defying your church on his behalf, but you know what he is as well as I do. He does not need us to aid him in recovering the Taormin; if it can be done, he can do it alone. So why are we here, Abbot? Is this another Ixaxin game?"

Shaking his gray head adamantly, Abbot Medwyn replied, "Whatever you may believe, Ineuil, I called this Venture because I deemed that in this Kaedric wished help, though he would never ask it. When I told him that Hrgh had taken the Taormin, he was afraid, Ineuil. I had not otherwise seen true fear in him during all the years that I have known him."

Ineuil pursed his lips and contemplated the holy man. "That might increase my respect for the Taormin. It does not tell me how we who are not heir to the Immortals' gifts can contribute to the recovery of the thing."

"Tul aided Ceallagh."

"Did he?" demanded Ineuil. Abbot Medwyn stiffened slightly at the blasphemy of doubt. "Oh, I know the story well enough," continued Ineuil impatiently, "And I much prefer to serve a mortal kingship rather than an Ixaxin thearchy. But I never understood just what Tul did that was so outstanding in the battle against Horlach. Ceallagh led the attack. Ceallagh defeated Horlach—with some help from the Ixaxin Circle. Tul generously accepted the glory of kingship. Explain to me, Abbot, how the great Tul contributed to the foundations of Seriin freedom, and perhaps I shall find a clue to the role you expect us to take."

Abbot Medwyn waited for Ineuil to complete his outburst. When Ineuil halted expectantly, the abbot said simply, "Tul maintained Ceallagh's humanity."

Ineuil pondered the abbot for several moments. He finally said in a velvet voice, "You do not assign easy tasks, Abbot Medwyn."

"It is a task at which I have long labored myself."

"Are you his friend or his conscience, Abbot Medwyn?" asked Ineuil carefully.

Abbot Medwyn gave a slight, unhappy shrug. "The two may well be the same." He turned his eyes upward to the moon's growing glow. "I feared him the day I met him, a half-starved waif amid the ashes of a dying city. I had no greater love for sorcery than others of my church, but he was a boy in desperate need, and I had no choice but to help him. I have not regretted it, but I have never ceased to fear his Power."

"You are not alone in that," said Ineuil with a grimace.

Abbot Medwyn smiled wanly. "No. I think even his fellow Ixaxins fear him. What must it be like to be instantly feared by everyone you meet?"

"Do not try to stir any pity for him in me, Abbot," said Ineuil darkly.

The abbot sighed. "You have little cause to love him, I know. He would not welcome—nor even understand—pity in any case, but it does seem a lonely life."

"Ixaxins have each other. If you are so concerned for him, why did you deliberately omit other wizards from this Venture?"

Abbot Medwyn shifted uncomfortably. "I do not

understand wizards, Ineuil, but they seem to interact unpredictably with their own kind." The abbot frowned. "They cooperate in the ordered Circles of Ixaxis, but they suffer still the characteristic which kept the Sorcerer Kings in constant conflict. The Infortiare is the only Lord of Serii who traditionally retains no retinue in Tulea, and I think that there is reason for that custom."

"Abbot Medwyn," remarked Ineuil cynically, "I think you distrust Kaedric as much as I do."

"I distrust what he has the potential to become. With the added influence of the Taormin. . . ." Abbot Medwyn left the sentence dangling. "Until that infernal challenge, Hrgh was far more sanely 'mortal' than Kaedric has ever been."

"I certainly shall not argue that point. You are a devious man, Abbot Medwyn. You called this Venture so as to surround Kaedric with enough 'mortal' influence to counter his darker instincts when we find Hrgh and the Taormin. Is that why our sorceress' presence displeases you so?"

"My efforts to dissuade Mistress Rani were not altogether on her behalf," admitted the abbot slowly.

Ineuil mused, "Mistress Rani seems unlikely to affect Kaedric in any respect, since he disdains to acknowledge her." Abbot Medwyn did not answer, and Ineuil persisted pointedly, "Or do you think Our Leader shows her a trifle too much contempt? She is only a minor sorceress, of course, but Kaedric has always tended toward inverted snobberies, if anything."

Abbot Medwyn weighed his answer as he spoke. "I think Kaedric fears to contaminate her, which only enhances my concern."

"She is rather an innocent, but she seems well enough able to care for herself."

"Ineuil, you have at times felt Kaedric's Power as I have. It is a very disturbing sensation even to one who is essentially immune to sorcerous exchange."

"So Mistress Rani endangers herself by accompanying us; that is not a novel notion. I cannot believe that a minor sorceress could present a reciprocal hazard to Our Leader." A rustle announced Master Hamar. "I fear, Abbot Medwyn, that you will never appear upon my roster of great chefs," said Ineuil, transitioning to innocuous topics without hesitation.

Chapter 9

My isolated state had not diminished with the passing days of Venture, but the Nighthawk's tenuous acceptance cheered my spirit. As the days of rapport extended, the Nighthawk came to know me and to greet me after his fashion. He led us much deeper into the Mountains' grip than his traditional territory allowed, a strongly generous act of trust which shamed me, because I should have forced his sacrifice, albeit reluctantly, had Master Kaedric so demanded.

Reliant on my little Nighthawk for companionship as well as guidance, I felt sorely rent by his desertion. He departed abruptly, his joyous antics in the waning night breaking into a desperate dart for his homeland. No cajolery would return him; no pleading would he heed. The distance stretched between us, and the surety of contact ebbed. I could have forced him back to me, but I could not bear the hurt of his struggle against my bond. With more regret than I had spared for my lifetime's home, I let fall the tie between us.

I informed Master Kaedric tersely of the loss. Expecting displeasure and orders to seek a substitute, I found his indifference grating; I wondered acridly if my Nighthawk's selfless aid had been of so little value. The wizard said only, "Horlach's influence still unsettles the neighborhood. Our path henceforth should be fairly clear." He dismissed me from his notice, fixedly studying a narrow cleft which we would likely near by nightfall. I watched for a moment the wind-rippled cloak of a man who was utterly removed from my understanding. I resolved never to fall into the trap of sympathy for him; then, I wondered why the notion even occurred to me.

We reached the narrow pass with late afternoon. Red stone walls loomed above us, blocking from view the nether trail, which I had seen angle downward from the Nighthawk's vantage. Just prior to his desertion, the Nighthawk's gaze had chanced across a verdant dell beyond the twisted pass. I hoped that we might find the wood by eventide, for the prolonged confinement in a realm of sterile stone chafed my soul severely.

The paucity of native voices did not strike me until we entered the cleft itself. Those lives which I could feel all rose behind me; from beyond the lengthy passage came nothing. I wondered if the green oasis were illusion born of my own craving, but the detail of its recollected image dissuaded me. I became uneasy, nervous of confinement between the towering escarpment walls, anxious to escape their clutch, but fearful of the silence beyond.

My disquiet eclipsed normal reluctance, and I hastened forward to gain the wizard's side. Ineuil raised a brow, but he moved to let me pass without comment. The Venture Leader looked down at me with mild surprise, and I steeled myself to bespeak him. I whispered, for I hesitated to disturb the echoes unnecessarily. "The area we are approaching is wrong, Master Kaedric."

He inquired tonelessly, "Is that a navigational opinion or an aesthetic judgment?"

"The direction is correct, but I ought to detect something beyond this fissure. I saw—the Nighthawk saw—a wooded hollow not far ahead. I cannot sense it."

Kaedric slowed his pace minutely. "That was where the bird left you?" he asked.

"He saw the dell, but he never reached it." The

wizard frowned, and his consideration of my words appeased my pride but did nothing to ease my tension.

"I wish I could reassure you, Mistress Rani, but Horlach's legacy persists in uncomfortable ways. You have at least reassured me that my own nerves have not yet grown fully unreliable."

I shook my head, more to dispel the thought that Master Kaedric shared my uneasiness than to disagree. "Yet you intend to continue on this route?" I asked.

"Would you prefer to spend the night in this unnatural corridor? We have come too far to return before dark." I could only continue to shake my head helplessly, and Kaedric nearly smiled, but it was not a mirthful expression. "Whatever awaits us must be faced eventually," he said. "Perhaps I am become claustrophobic, but I prefer to proceed without delay. If you have a persuasive alternative, I am not adverse to hearing it."

"We might be better for some rest," I offered tentatively, but it was procrastination, and I knew it as well as did the man beside me.

Kaedric did halt us long enough for a vote. The party chose to continue, but we moved more cautiously. The Venture Leader's unprecedented willingness to defer to the concensus of opinion quenched any levity among us.

The trail began its descent. Red stone turned black at the passage's end, smooth obsidian pillars marking the terminus as if it were a gate of doom. "Your guide has dismal taste, Mistress Rani," complained Ineuil. "Remind me not to let you choose our next place of assignation."

"It is the entrance to Horlach's estate," said Kaedric soberly. "Horlach was not notoriously sympathetic to the wishes of amorists."

Kaedric passed through the pillars, and in a moment we had all joined him. The land looked little different from that which we had left on entering the corridor, barren rock and dusty gravel comprising the bulk of the scenery. Mountains' shadow had held it obscurely dark until we stood within the exiting alcove's midst. I felt foolish over my fears. Though I still could not sense the lives of the green hollow I now could see, the scent of distant blossoms reached me and somewhat salved my distress.

A shrill keening filled the air, rising without direction and growing quickly to stark intensity. A sour wind struck me, and I discovered the justification of my concern. The gargoyles appeared, the ancient guardians of Horlach's gate. I had read their description, and for a space of seconds I could only stare at them, disavowing their existence in my own time and space.

Leathery, scabrous wings beating violently, the creatures smote wildly with talons, teeth and barbed tails. Their bodies were bloated, taut membranes encrusted with livid veins. The Venturers blurred in a vision of fury. Swords struck, rebounded. One sword blow pierced its target, puncturing the monster and deflating it with a rush of yellow ichor. Red blood mingled with the viscous, oily issue; the gargoyle had raked Gart's back in its fall.

I had shadowed, but one of the beasts flew directly at me, unhampered by my effort to hide. It tore at the flesh of my upraised arm, craning its maw toward the blood it drew. The vile thing repulsed me; its stench choked me; but I stretched my mind to restrain it in the only defense I knew. I had thought the dyrcat unsettling, but the gargoyle of Horlach spawned horror. With effort, I could hold my attacker a pace away from me, but I could do no more to influence it, nor could I in any way aid my fellow travelers.

Ineuil, Gart and Hamar slashed fiercely, and the ichor flowed, spreading across the ground in slimy puddles. Such damage as the Venturers wrought slowed the attack but did not halt it. Hamar lopped the head from one gargoyle only to find the body as menacing as before. The gargoyles could be downed, but there appeared to be no way to kill them short of total butchery. I could see Abbot Medwyn beating randomly at the creatures with his staff; his efforts seemed no less effective than the sword thrusts. The gargoyles persisted in slow dominance.

I sensed it immediately when Kaedric chose a victim: the creature I was containing shared its counterpart's knowledge. The gargoyles evinced no dismay at the flame eating their comrade's heart; the prospect stimulated them to eager frenzy. I felt a foreboding which Master Kaedric evidently shared, for he abruptly curtailed his assault, but the process of destruction proceeded on its own momentum. Inner fluids boiling, the gargoyle exploded in a scattering of scorching gobbets. A few tiny particles hit me, though I stood farthest from the source, and they delved through fabric and clung to skin. I could feel the sharp bite of acid pinpricks which would not be dislodged. They etched trails of remorseless burning. Horlach's guardians had been well designed to discourage sorcerous attack.

I scanned the Venturers with little hope. Hamar had slowed, his prior wound reopened and bleeding now profusely. A hurtling gargoyle knocked Gart to the stained earth as I watched. Kaedric snatched Gart's sword and used it to ward the gargoyles from the soldier's immobile form. The wizard wielded the sword like one more accustomed to the closeness of dagger play; I felt irrelevant surprise that he had ever bothered to hone a blade skill at all. Already, the wizard had modified his Power's attack to a slower, more effective form. I did not doubt that the wizard would preserve his own life against even Horlach's gargoyles; I did begin to despair that the Venture Leader's Power would extend that preservation to the rest of us.

Ineuil's shoulder had been badly torn. Even Kaedric had been marked; beading scratches crossed his finely boned hands. Abbot Medwyn, curiously enough, showed fewest ravages of all. His long staff struck his assailants most often on their whipping tails, but those gargoyles about him had begun to grow sluggish in their movements.

My grip on my attacker weakened, and others of its kind began to hover nearer. I let go my futile shadowing, and my hold firmed again to preserve me. Soon, however, another gargoyle swept before me, focusing on me murky orange eyes of spite which waited for the inevitable failure of my Power. I comprehended my poor, lost Nighthawk's panic as I watched defenselessly; jagged talons ripped my arm from wrist to neck.

I sank hopelessly to the blood-spattered earth. The gargoyle which had raked me churned the dust about me with its beating wings. Abbot Medwyn's staff struck the thing's tail heavily above the daggered tip, and the gargoyle crumpled in slow, almost dignified defeat. I heard the abbot cry aloud his elated discovery of the creatures' weakness, and I considered the unpriestly nature of the shouted advice as I tumbled into oblivion.

I revived marginally to see Ineuil fell a last remaining gargoyle by severing its whipping tail at the base. Kaedric and Hamar gathered Gart between them. Ineuil limped heavily on a flesh-shredded leg. Abbot Medwyn collected his pack and my own, dropped mine wearily, and beckoned me to follow. I dragged myself in his wake, reclaiming my supplies with a struggle. A sorely tattered band, we stumbled down the incline to the valley of green. By a crystal rill bedecked with bejeweled fern, I slumped exhausted.

Chapter 10

My eyes opened to a sun-blessed view of leafy boughs and cerulean sky. Reassured, I let my eyelids droop once more. I greeted the trees, and they responded warmly. It puzzled me that I did not know these ash and alder; I thought I knew each tree of Tyntagel. The oddity did not concern me greatly; no more than did the prospect of my father's anger when he learned that his daughter had slept in the grove like a common vagabond.

"At last my sorceress awakes," said Ineuil, recalling me to the present. "But if she does not soon reopen her lovely eyes, I shall take drastic steps to assure myself of her recovery. Perhaps a kiss—such always seems effective in romantic sagas."

"If you try it, Master Ineuil, I shall give you over to a dyrcat I know, and he has a most unpleasant temperament," I answered lazily, reluctant yet to relinquish my drowsy peace.

"I remember now why I have never pursued sorceresses. Perhaps I shall leave you to Kaedric after all. It would serve him right."

"Where is Master Kaedric?" I asked, suddenly awake.

"Wandering somewhere conveniently distant, I hope. Abbot Medwyn is over that way a bit," he said with a vague wave of his arm, "ladling some ghastly broth into Hamar and Gart. I, fortunately, have been declared cured and no longer in need of such unpalatable measures."

"How long have I slept?"

"Three days and nights, by my reckoning, though I confess I lost some time myself. Those ugly beasties apparently list poisoned fangs among their attractions. Abbot Medwyn has had a busy time of it, tending us all."

"I must offer help to him," I said briskly, shaking dust from my skirts and observing a need for serious mending before long. My arm, which had been laid open by the gargoyle, had sealed with only a trace of a scar. I felt astonishingly well. "Will you direct me, Master Ineuil, or shall I find the camp myself?"

"You are a singleminded wench," sighed Ineuil. "Very well, I shall direct you, but I think your choice displays a lack of discernment. I appreciate your company far more than will those you seek to aid."

"I did not join this Venture to amuse you, Master Ineuil."

"The fact did not escape my notice. There should be a law against beautiful women who have no trace of romance in their souls."

"What did you say about never pursuing a sorceress? I do believe you would flirt with any woman you met, be she blushing maiden or toothless hag."

"At least credit me with some selectivity. I am actually quite particular as to the women I cultivate."

"When you are granted unlimited choices," I amended.

"Quantity does help, I admit. But I promise you, Mistress Rani, if some day I find you in the midst of Serii's fairest, I shall still seek your company over the rest. And I trust that you will regret every aspersion you have cast upon my character." Ineuil pointed at a clearing dimly visible through the trees. "Our temporary home lies yonder. You may detect the aroma of the abbot's brew: rather reminiscent of moldering eggs, I think."

"It is pungent. How did I manage to escape its benefits until now?"

"Kaedric's idea it was, though I wish I could take credit for the results. Our Leader insisted that your ailments would be best served by solitary repose. Abbot Medwyn patched your more obvious wounds and trusted the rest to wizard's judgment." I could not protest Master Kaedric's cavalier abandonment in light of the successful outcome, but I was pleased to maintain annoyance with the Venture Leader on any pretext. I did dislike the thought of having spent three days in isolated oblivion amid a Sorcerer King's haunted domain.

We found the clearing deserted, though Abbot Medwyn's despised tonic simmered above a low fire. Ineuil led me to a shallow cave hidden beneath a curtain of fern. The light diffused through leafy green lent a strange distortion of color, but the wanness of Master Gart was due to a more serious cause. Abbot Medwyn bent beside him, inspecting Gart's bandaged brow and the puckered streaks which spread to the warrior's jaw. Hamar cut short a joke—a stale and most improper one which I had heard my brothers tell—as I entered, and his broad grin turned sullen and suspicious. Gart, however, brightened.

"Master Ineuil," warned the abbot, "if you have

awakened Mistress Rani prematurely, you had best look to your excuses before Kaedric returns."

"Why does everyone doubt my intentions?" bemoaned Ineuil. "Having Mistress Rani's own interests in mind, I appointed myself the guardian of her recovery—a position which Our Leader neglected to fill—and I receive nothing but ingratitude and censure. This situation could become entirely demoralizing." He stalked from the cavern, flicking a dangling fern from his path.

"Sir Abbot, I awoke quite on my own," I protested. "Please do not blame Master Ineuil on that account."

"He has plenty of other accounts for blame," quipped Gart with an effort. His wounds stiffened his face, but he managed a lopsided smile.

"Do hold still, Master Gart," scolded Abbot Medwyn, readjusting a dressing on Gart's neck which I had not previously seen. "If I did not censure Master Ineuil regularly, Mistress Rani, he might be forced to realize that he is not nearly as irredeemable as he pretends, and the prospect would devastate him."

"If you please, Abbot," interrupted Hamar. "I could heal a lot faster if this woman would leave us to some peace." Abbot Medwyn frowned, and Hamar continued, "Did no one notice that the gargoyles heeded only her? Even Master Kaedric could not control them so well. Does no one else find that an unlikely circumstance? Mistress Rani's Power seems to be peculiarly constrained to her own welfare—and perhaps that of Lord Hrgh Dolr'han. Lord Hrgh's supporters do include a number of ladies, I have heard, and this wandering sorceress is a mite too knowledgable for my taste. Were you disappointed that the gargoyles did not finish us, mistress, or are you just playing with us until your liege lord comes?"

"I am not your enemy, Master Hamar," I retorted, shaken less by Hamar's outrageous allegations than by the lack of protest from Abbot Medwyn and Master Gart. "If you have need of me, Abbot Medwyn, I shall be no more distant than the rill."

My contentment dissipated, I strayed farther than I

had indicated to Abbot Medwyn. I sought forgetfulness in the hearts of the woodland dwellers, for there was an ease of security in this place, but Hamar's words rankled. The grain of truth in his accusations could easily coat the whole with credibility, but it was too late to be honest about my name and origin, even had I wished it. I could sympathize with Ineuil's protest of injustice.

I encountered Ineuil near the glade where I had awakened. He was engrossed in casting seed cases in a pond. He scowled at me terribly, saying, "If you have come to make amends with me, Mistress Rani, you may as well return whence you came. I am not yet done sulking."

"Master Ineuil," I demanded, "do you concur with Master Hamar's assessment of me as villainess?" I was sincerely anxious for the answer, though I was unsure why I had developed such a concern for the Venturers' opinion.

Ineuil promptly dropped his querulous pose. "Hamar has been at you again, has he? You ought not to mind him so much, Rani. He has been venting his anger on the feminine gender for years because of some Caruillan woman who once treated him foully. There is no personal malice involved. Anyway, one cannot generally please everyone, and four out of five is an admirable average."

"You vastly exaggerate my popularity, but I appreciate the lie. I am sorry if I seemed ungrateful for your attention earlier."

"You really are depressed," he said sympathetically. "Come, sit and tell me your woes. We shall console each other from the doldrums, which are probably just an after-effect of the gargoyles' poison. What nonsense did Hamar spout at you?"

I sat as commanded, wanting very much to be consoled. "He suggested that I served Lord Hrgh and conspired toward the gargoyles' attack."

"You would have to be a rather incompetent spy to perpetrate an attack which harmed you as much as any other. Is that all that concerns you?"

"Abbot Medwyn and Master Gart seem to share his suspicions."

"I find that difficult to believe."

Hesitantly, I whispered, "I have not been entirely truthful as to my personal history."

"I had not noticed that you even gave one, but we are none of us in a position to quibble with that sort of deception."

I looked at him curiously. "No, I suppose you are not." Ineuil had always seemed misplaced in a Venture, and he admitted to acquaintance with Lord Hrgh. Master Kaedric's solitary wandering could easily foster sinister implications to a mind so inclined, and it was not difficult to credit the wizard with devious motives. "Master Hamar knows none of you save Master Gart," I said, feeling perversely better for the thought.

"We are a dubious lot, all of us, so you may as well accept the stigma of association and expect to find yourself suspected of wicked schemes. Proper young Seriin women do not join Ventures, do not travel the countryside unchaperoned, and certainly do not practice sorcery (not openly, at least)."

"Having committed so many improprieties, I ought to be a jaded sophisticate by now. Instead, I come seeking reassurance like a toddler with a skinned knee." I smiled at him somewhat shyly. "You are kind to give it to me. I am not very practiced in the art of friendship; I am not sure I know how to return it well."

"You are making me feel like a cad. Mistress Rani, I always have ulterior motives. I think we had better return to the camp before I utterly disillusion you." He smiled at me almost sadly, and I thought it the sincerest gesture I had seen him make.

We walked under autumn's green and golden boughs, and I finally concluded that the besotted women of Anx had more cause for their choice of favorite than fair features and sly charm. Ineuil was blatantly faithless, but he could instill the delight of self-contentment through his attention. Naiveté abetted my feelings; no man save Evram had ever courted me, and Evram's image had already faded from my mind. I certainly did not count Lord Grisk, my deserted bridegroom, as a suitor. Ineuil did not prate extravagant tributes that afternoon. He was more silent, more clearly troubled, and I liked him far better than I had thought I ever should.

The Venture party remained in the dell for another two weeks, awaiting the return of Master Gart's strength. We should have waited longer had Master Gart's remarkable constitution not so well supported the abbot's cures. I passed much of the time with Ineuil, listening to his tales of far lands and fabulous escapades. Half of his stories glared obviously false; the others glimmered with doubtful excess; but they entertained. Master Kaedric had declared our dell to be a haven of security, a boon of the land's ancient tenants to counter the bane of the gargoyles at the gate. None of us wished to disbelieve the wizard's assertion.

I saw Master Kaedric only once in all those days. I came upon him in the wood; he studied the ripples of a stream as they danced across their flowing mirror. He held in his hand a gold medallion of intricate design suspended on a fine gold chain, and he moved it restlessly so that its reflection in the water returned white flame. He did not look up at me, but he stilled his hand and clutched the gold from my sight with an intensity of subjugated violence. He vanished from my mind, leaving a gaping cold where subdued fire had been. He wore a dangerous mood, and I escaped him hastily.

Chapter 11

It was difficult to leave the vale and reinvade the desolation which surrounded it, but Abbot Medwyn's potions having restored Master Gart, Master Kaedric returned to us impatient for departure. The leaving affected me oddly; I seemed to awaken from a many-months' dream and find myself, the once sheltered lady of Tyntagel, on the verge of a battlefield which soon would run with disaster. Beyond the dale and its soothing assurance of tree and flower, a mounting trepidation began to haunt me with nightmarish chimeras of gargoyles, slaughtered brigands, and concocted visions of a man whom my sister had once adored and a wizard whom I feared to fathom.

Dust swirled beneath my feet. The sky was gray with heavy clouds, but no moisture had reached the powdery earth. Blue clay and black mica striated the ocher stone which seemed to grow from the path, a startling contrast in color alien to Tyntagellian geology. I clasped my cloak tightly against the chill.

A week's span from the healing glen, Hamar, who had been journeying several paces ahead, halted and stared at the sheer mountain face before him. The path widened where he stood, and cracked planes of white stone gave evidence of crumbled paving. On the broad cliff which had drawn Hamar's attention, black bands of metallic sheen framed a precisely inset door. The surface of the door had been marred by the years and vandals, but delicate traceries hinted at a wonder of workmanship.

"Another legacy of old King Horlach?" suggested Ineuil.

Kaedric did not answer but approached the door

and gingerly positioned his fingers on a faintly etched diadem. The surface shimmered slightly, the patterns became clearer. Kaedric traced the length of a spiral, and a section of the door receded from a rather orthodox lock and hasp.

"Have you retained your flair for unsolicited entrance, Master Ineuil?" asked Kaedric.

"I would not relinquish such a useful skill, but I am not particularly eager to exercise it here. Horlach's surviving unpleasantries may not be restricted to his gatekeepers."

"We are seeking Horlach's dwellings, unless you have suddenly reinterpreted Hrgh's words to you," said Kaedric sardonically. "This could be an alternate access."

The dark man and the fair exchanged a look which held no fondness. Kaedric stepped back, and Ineuil bent to examine the lock. Moments later, the door smoothly swung wide.

"By the privilege of your rank, Venture Leader," said Ineuil with a mocking bow, "yours is the honor of entering first."

Kaedric twisted his lips in a dangerous smile. He took a torch from his pack, ignited it with a glance, and entered the dark recess. Abbot Medwyn followed him closely; the rest of us lagged only briefly.

A massive chamber burned as bright as moonlight with reflections of Kaedric's torch. I caught my breath in awe, nearly colliding with Gart in my distraction. Only the square of dim sunlight from the doorway broke the illusion of a perfect sphere, polished floor mirroring a ceiling of lucent tapestries. Wrought of delicate inlays, a garden bore glowing azure and yellow-gold blossoms on vines which spun to a crystalline midnight sky. Snowy water lilies clustered at our feet; our own reflections wavered in translucent depths.

"No gargoyles and no Lord Hrgh," sighed the practical Gart.

"Gart, you have no sense of artistic appreciation," said Ineuil.

"He is correct, however," said Kaedric solemnly.

"My hopes are proven as groundless as Master Ineuil's concern."

"Evening is near. We could make camp here," suggested Hamar.

"I should rather not accept Horlach's hospitality unnecessarily, despite the exquisiteness of the accommodations," answered Kaedric.

"Nimal's home was never Horlach's," protested Abbot Medwyn.

"You are a romantic, Medwyn," remarked Kaedric tolerantly. "If Nimal of Castor did exist, he was entirely Horlach's tool—gifted but abysmally corrupt. If this was his home, it is as tainted as any other of Horlach's possessions."

"Nimal of Castor," mused Ineuil. "As I recall, he was a sculptor who killed his ladylove and then spent the rest of his life slaving for Horlach in misguided atonement. I do not recollect any stories about his home."

"It was the home he built for the Lady Varina dur Castor," said Abbot Medwyn. "He surpassed all his other efforts in its creation, but it was never used."

"He loved the Lady Varina, the youngest daughter of his liege lord," I remembered softly, "And she returned his love, but she obeyed the dictates of her father and wed a man of her own rank. Nimal perceived the act as betrayal and slew her."

Abbot Medwyn nodded. "He built a home for her, unable to believe in the death which he had caused. Some versions of the legend say that Varina's spirit forgave Nimal his brief madness and awaits him in the hall he built for her, until such time as Nimal forgives himself and joins her."

"And some say that Lady Varina offended King Horlach," interjected Master Kaedric, "inspiring Nimal to play the paid assassin, destroying a woman who loved and trusted him, so as to reap a very lucrative commission."

"I find the versions of both the romantic and the cynic unbearably depressing," said Ineuil. He added to the room at large, "With all due apologies to any lingering ghosts, participation in this accursed Venture depresses me quite enough." He strolled out of the door.

I could not impugn Ineuil's assessment of the melancholy saga, but it was a story I had always perversely cherished. Abbot Medwyn's rendition accorded with the one I preferred to accept. Though thought of Lady Varina's selfless observation of duty now pricked me with guilt, I still felt most clearly the Lady's unembittered hope amid the pathos.

Rapt with introspection, I scarcely noticed that I had picked up Varina's stone. I thrust it deep within my pocket and did not rediscover it until late evening. Smoothly whorled and milky white, the stone extolled the same miraculous workmanship as the chamber we had found. As glowed the chamber's stars, so the gem's soft radiance spread fragile firelight across my fingers. I felt an empathy with the stone, which was an unlikely fancy; I could not envision my besotted Evram in the role of the intense artisan, Nimal, and I had singularly failed to comply with duty according to Varina's example. I found Kaedric regarding me oddly. Defensively, I clutched my find, shielding it from view as he had previously hidden a medallion of gold from me.

"I did not intend to snatch it from you," said Kaedric slowly. "The Lady gifts whom she will."

"I thought you disbelieved such legends, Master Kaedric," I said, strangely struck by the wizard's incongruous comment. "Your rendition of the story earlier hardly accords with a generous specter."

"I dispute the heroism of a man who murdered the woman he purportedly loved. I meant no disparagement of the Lady Varina. Her boundless devotion has always awed me." With the causticness to which I had grown more accustomed, Kaedric proceeded, "Does that admission fail to conform to your preconceptions of a wizard's perfect lack of mortal feeling? Forgive me, I shall endeavor to maintain a more circumspect profile."

"Master Kaedric," I answered carefully, "I have never

met a wizard before. I can only gauge a wizard's perspective by the references I know."

"You were never tested as a potential wizardess," he stated flatly.

"No." I elaborated with imperfect honesty, "My Power is very restricted in its nature." I omitted mentioning that my father would have forbidden me the opportunity of such testing had I held the Power of Ceallagh.

"Power may be potent though it is not broad in kind. You are strong enough to have held a gargoyle." He tilted his head as he spoke, and firelight caught the momentarily revealed gold of the chain concealed about his neck.

"I do not create fires with my mind," I returned a little brusquely.

Kaedric answered with brittle glass tones, "Do not use me in judgment of all Ixaxins." His vision had turned beyond me, and I thought I felt a thousand people cry.

Warm with discomfiture despite the evening chill, I forced a neutral tone. "On which side of the Ixaxin norm do you fall, Master Kaedric?" I clung tightly to cool nacre.

His steady, cold gaze returned to me. He responded sardonically, "So far as I can discern, I am very much the worst of the extant species."

"You exclude the Infortiare—and Lord Hrgh," I whispered, not knowing why I felt the need to lower my voice. The other Venturers seemed to have retreated to some small, unreal world very far away from us two.

"No," answered Kaedric, as I had known he would. I pressed Varina's stone tightly to still my disquiet.

The rain, which for days had threatened us, at last fulfilled its intent. Torrents turned the clinging dust to clay which only grudgingly relinquished my every step. Cold and wholly wretched, I recalled warm evenings at the hearthside in Tyntagel with a wistfulness which ignored the less pleasant aspects of the remembered times. Even a night's rest brought scant relief. The minimal shelter of an exposed cliffside made sleep elusive at best. Hamar often glared at me accusingly, as if to blame me for the ire of the elements which impeded our progress. In my drenched and bedraggled condition, I presented a singularly unprepossessing candidate for the minion of a Dolr'han. I thought bleakly that if Master Hamar could detect in my pitiful mien more of menace than of rabbity fear, he had a gift of imagination unsurpassed in history.

Trudging in endless misery, head bowed before whipping rain and sleet, my mind and body grew numb to the surrounding world. Days blurred into dreary nights, and I walked in a dripping cloud, mechanically following the shadowy shapes before me. The stinging which spattered my hand only slowly penetrated my private fog. I brushed at the hand absently, but a network of crimson beads dotted my skin. Rain streaked the blood, and I recognized the cause with a sigh. Trackers from the northern moors of Tyntagel often complained of the pestilence of tsiljieks. Less tenacious kin of leeches, tsiljieks presented no real danger, but I found their presence unpleasantly appropriate to the dismal shards of Horlach's domain. I wrapped my scarf more protectively about my head, striving determinedly to ignore the spreading prickle of punctured arms and ankles.

The tsiljieks did not plague us alone. Eely tendons writhed unseen in the mud and periodically snatched at unwary feet. Gart persistently tried to capture one. He never succeeded, and I was just as glad. The tsiljieks, the unseen serpents and the reek of decay had united in my mind to discourage our trespass, and I had no wish to give further form to our foe.

The rain ebbed at length, yielding to the icy pall of winter. The terrain grew hard, frozen and slick. Mud, affixed to my skirts, dragged at my steps. Silver-white rime dusted stone and limbs of winter-sleeping shrubs, and the wilds were silent to my mind. The season of stillness had begun its soft intrusion, and Tyntagel oaks were miles and months lost. I watched the five men and felt alone.

Chapter 12

Newborn snow cloaked that morning, my last as a Venturess. It was the new year's first day, and it entered gently. The cold had increased, but I had slept soundly, and the stark wintry beauty revived my flagging spirits. The Mountains of Mindar towered above us and around us, freed at last of confining clouds and splendid in their dominance. We did not travel long beneath their spell that morning. Amid a shattered tumble of finely wrought stone, the arched entrance to Horlach's subterranean palace still stood in somber invitation.

They came from under, over, through the stony, pock-marked ruins: near-men, once-men. Their leprous flesh clung in tattered strings to twisted limbs. From rims of blood-colored pulp peered appallingly human eyes. Horlach had infected them, and they could not die. Hacked and hewn by the Venturers, they could not use their strength effectively, but even dismembered pieces continued their writhing attack. The anguish of eons tore my soul with barbed claws. The things cried in my mind, sibilant proof that these had been Sorcerer Kings and Queens, conquered by Horlach and condemned by their own inability to forsake life.

Royal limbs littered the snow. An undead queen grabbed a severed hand and pressed it to the stump of her arm; the flesh melted, fused and joined under the gaze of her warped Power. She jerked a sword from an undead torso and rushed at Hamar with a rapturous whine. Hamar countered her blow easily and severed her body at the waist with a sword-swipe of enormous force. Hamar grinned as he slashed at her dangling breasts; he laughed at her now feeble efforts to wield her sword against him. He turned to another attacker and forgot her.

The undead fought with potent blades of fear and dread, yet I found them pathetic. Their physical efforts could not compete with the agile strength of live opponents, their Power could focus only on extending their own tormented existences, and they were too mindless even to know that they battled to protect a Sorcerer King who had been vanquished millennia ago. Gart and Hamar fought the pitiful guards with the same zeal as in their Anxian competitions, an enthusiasm of sport which they had not shown against living opponents. The exhilaration of the two warriors sickened me more than the creatures they destroyed. It revealed the depths of Hamar's bitterness, roused by legitimate female prey, and such hatred ought never to be unfettered; I understood that Gart merely empathized with his friend's rare delight, but I would never again be able to see Gart unclouded by that grisly conflict. The shy warrior of Mahl, who had in a manner charmed me, ceased from that moment to exist in my mind.

We reached the arch, and Ineuil exercised his skill on the rusty lock of an iron gate. The grate of reluctant metal told his success. Kaedric called to Gart and Hamar. With a final lunge, Gart tumbled through the gate. Hamar delayed, continuing to savor the torment of another fallen sorcerer Queen. Kaedric called again, insistently now. Hamar turned from his victim reluctantly and did not initially see the arm which reached for him. He sliced it free with a curse, momentarily distracted. The mangled queen reassembled her stringy strength and with her other arm drove her sword through Hamar's back. The warrior looked puzzled. He fell, and the deathless swarmed upon him, but I knew he was already beyond knowing.

Gart screamed denial. The rare sport had turned as viciously real and as sorcerously evil as Horlach's memory. Gart raised his sword and poised to leap against the murderers of his friend. "Leave them," commanded

Kaedric sternly. Gart struggled against the Venture Leader's will, but the warrior could not but join us beyond the gate, bidden by implacable eyes of blue ice and the Power within them. Ineuil slammed fast the gate, sealing us from all but a faint filtering of the sun.

"Bloody, pious Ixaxin," growled Gart unevenly, leaning against the crumbling wall and glaring at Kaedric with fixed hatred. Gart's anger had mastered his stutter: "You spend our lives like copper kelni on your sorcerers' quarrels, and you do not even care enough to see if Hamar lives."

"Hamar is dead, Gart," said Ineuil wearily.

Gart spared Ineuil a look of venom. "And you pander for them, Master Ineuil." Gart returned to Kaedric. "You may live for a dozen of my lifespans, Master Kaedric, and you may be able to destroy Serii with a thought, but you are no more human than those mindless monsters outside and certainly no more worthy."

"Kindly save the moralizing for a more opportune occasion, Master Gart," commented Kaedric coldly. "As a warrior, you ought to be more seasoned to death than to bewail it this way." The wizard was inspecting the dark corridor leading from the alcove in which we stood. "Hrgh has apparently renewed a portion of the lighting system," he said, dismissing any concern over the loss of one of his followers. A dim, unwholesome glow snaked down the visible hall. Kaedric entered the corridor purposefully.

Abbot Medwyn regarded the Venture Leader's back with pained distaste. Ineuil said soberly, "Your purpose in Venture fails, Abbot Medwyn."

The abbot frowned mournfully and took Gart by the arm. "There is nothing more we can do here, Gart," said the abbot. "We must continue." The warrior complied meekly, his furor spent, his eyes tortured.

I trailed the solemn and diminished company through a labyrinth of dark passages. The lighting was sporadic and capricious, and the footing was often treacherous. The Venture Leader led us without pause down the long and broken stairs, and we followed him, using the touch of cold walls where other guidance failed. We pressed deeply into the mountain. I counted six hundred and thirty steps before I stopped trying to keep track. The granular texture of eroded walls sanded the skin from my fingers, but it lent a measure of security in the darker regions. At one wholly lightless point, a glutinous smear, quivering and repellant to the touch, encouraged me to rely more heavily on other than the tactile sense. Though I disliked doing it, I found that I could sense Master Kaedric quite clearly with a modicum of concentration, and the discovery did smooth my progress.

The ages had not treated kindly the palatial residence of the mightiest Sorcerer King. Throughout the lower levels, we encountered very few chambers of any residual glory; none compared with the cavern of Nimal, though much of Nimal's artistry must once have graced Horlach's castle as well. I grew increasingly doubtful that Lord Hrgh could have made of the ruins any retreat acceptable to a Dolr'han dur Liin.

We passed at length beneath a pillared arch, and found ourselves treading on a black marble floor. Silver mist suspended sourceless above us emitted a light unlike the bilious glow of the other halls. The mist illuminated, but it also concealed. Only when we stood at the hall's end, did the next chamber grow clear to view. The room gleamed brightly gold, unmeasurably vast, and mirror-burnished. The spell-cast curtain which surrounded it refracted images and confused the eye. I could see clearly only the emblem repeated on every facet: infinity's symbol entwined with the initial of Horlach, the crest of a Sorcerer King.

I heard the voice before I saw the man: a voice of persuasive refinement which befitted a lord of Serii's First House. "You disappoint me, Arineuil," said Lord Hrgh with the sorrow of trust betrayed. "You least of all did I expect to see surrender to the Venkarel. Even if our long friendship could not withstand his Power, I should have thought the memory of your murdered kin would have preserved you from his tainted alliance."

Woodenly, Ineuil responded, "I have not forgotten

the atrocities of the past, Hrgh, but if my concern for you could not outweigh a futile vendetta, then I should indeed be no true friend."

"So," sighed Lord Hrgh. "He has convinced you that he preserves my welfare by your aid." The curtain across the portal dissipated, and I saw the noble lord of Liin, and he was indeed as fair to see as any prince of legend. Solemn gray eyes regarded Ineuil from a strongly molded face of classic design. A narrow circlet of gold bound auburn hair, and golden raiment added to the aureole of majesty. Enthroned upon a time-worn bench, Lord Hrgh Dolr'han dur Liin could well have been a king giving judgment on his vassals. I knew whence Yldana's yearning for Lord Hrgh had grown, but despite the Power and compassion flowing from the shining man, I felt a chill.

Lord Hrgh spoke again, and his voice rang proudly, tragically. "You have been clever, Venkarel. The good Abbot Medwyn you ensorcelled long ago, and now you take my greatest friend and ally. Did you tell them of the Taormin? Did you tell them that I took it to preserve it from your grasp?"

"I have no need for the Taormin, Hrgh. But if I did wish to take and use it, the decision would not be subject to your veto. I am the Infortiare, Hrgh. I did not seek the post which you so coveted, but that choice belonged to neither of us."

"You err, Venkarel," said Hrgh. "You defeated me once by trickery, but I shall not repeat my incautious faith in the honor of an upstart scrub. Dismiss your followers, Venkarel. I would not see these misguided innocents further victimized."

Watching and listening I felt myself to be viewing a history which had passed long before my birth. Abbot Medwyn chanted a toneless benediction, closely watching Master Gart the while. Gart's loyalties at that moment must certainly have merited the abbot's question, but the warrior stood stoic and still. Ineuil had turned away from the proceedings, wrapped in his own despondent conflict.

I studied Kaedric, a hard, dark silhouette, thin and

worn. The golden Lord Hrgh made a far more credible picture of Serii's highest Lord. Kaedric advanced through the portal, and the curtain which had vanished flared again, blurring the two opponents.

"Pray well, Abbot Medwyn," said Lord Hrgh. "The soul of Lord Venkarel bears a heavy burden of iniquity." I felt the bolt of Power which Hrgh flung against Kaedric; the sensation came dimly distant through the shield of the translucent curtain. Kaedric parried it easily.

"You have grown lazy, Hrgh," said Kaedric. "Any Ixaxin novice could strike more cleanly."

"Do not lecture me on a subject I mastered while you slept in the sties of Ven," shouted Lord Hrgh angrily. I heard Kaedric form a mirthless laugh and stop it aborning. The ever-shifting curtain froze to clarity. Lord Hrgh with a smile of sly cunning brought forth from his robes a pod of amber filigree which glowed with milky yellow light. The color warmed and whirled; it ran to Hrgh, engulfing his face and his hands. Fire sprang from Kaedric, brilliant blue and tightly focused. It struck Hrgh but swirled about him and sank into the brightening pod. The energy of the Dolr'han flared outward, the yellow light expanding in a fiery sphere. Streaks of burning darkness filled it. Across the marble floor spread a smoldering trail of sulfureous ash. The yellow light touched Kaedric and shattered in a shower of blinding sparks. Then the room became flame, blue-hot and burning umber, and the only vision I had came as fire in my mind.

The voice of Lord Hrgh crackled with Power. "Submit to me, Venkarel. You cannot defeat the Lord of the Taormin." I heard Ineuil cry out to Hrgh. A virulent bolt shot from the hand of the Lord of Liin, and Ineuil crumpled. "Thus shall I crush you also, Venkarel, unless you accept my rightful dominion."

"You will not use me as you have used Hrgh," answered Kaedric.

"Bravo, Lord Venkarel. You recognize your true foe. You will make an admirable tool, far better than this feeble fool who fancied himself a sorcerer. It is a pity to damage you as I must. This era of yours seems to lack any other Powers of interest." The darkness in the yellow fire redoubled, and blue dimmed to pale silver-gray as Kaedric suffered the blow of the Sorcerer King.

If I had thought, I would have fled. Nothing held me, unnoticed as I was where I clung to the carven wall. Kaedric had called me impetuous and foolish. As I had touched an ailing oak of Tyntagel, I reached out my will to Kaedric, Venkarel, and I restored him.

I screamed at the corrosion of fire which filled me. Shock at my intervention stemmed the battle for a pulsing instant. The darkness twisted within Lord Hrgh Dolr'han recoiled, then burst forth in anxious seeking for the intruder. In that moment of distraction, Kaedric's Power swirled anew. Locked in a realm of charred anguish, I knew relief as the darkness left its search for me and turned again to its attacker.

I drew within me Kaedric's pain, though I felt my own blood boiling. I no longer tried to help him: I could not block the channel which I had opened. My strength seeped from me, and all my memories were lost in a maelstrom of flame and horror, ageless death and the countless victims of a timeless hunger. Identities shifted, distorted and merged, a confusion of sorcerers, wizards and madmen, wicked, woeful and wise men whose destinies crossed in the Taormin. Tides swelled, pulsed and tried to tear apart the tangle, even as the Taormin sought to swallow us in its grasp. Three of us fought, resisted and reinforced the shatterer: Horlach, Kaedric and Rhianna. As a splinter of glass flies free from a broken whole, I spun from infinity to unconsciousness.

[illegible]

[illegible] I would have [illegible] I [illegible] was [illegible] [illegible] [illegible] that [illegible] [illegible] [illegible] [illegible].

[illegible] I could not think the [illegible] [illegible] [illegible] [illegible].

V. THE FIRE

Chapter 1

Year of Serii—9008
Benthen Abbey, Serii

The blanket was coarse, the pillow hard, but the smooth linen smelled of fresh spring herbs. I stretched lazy muscles and opened eyes heavy lidded with long sleep. Focus came unwillingly: white-washed walls, beam-crossed ceiling, a dark wood bench polished by age. Pale sunlight fell from a large embrasure overlooking the pallet on which I lay.

An effort to rise brought a wave of dizziness. I fell back to the cot, weak and spent, daunted in the endeavor to review my surroundings better. I considered the strong beams above me and concluded that sleep enticed me more than exploration.

I drifted into a somnolent state which was not quite sleep, and the world therein was afire. The flesh melted from me in blackened streams, leaving me raw and vulnerable and lost. I thrust my spirit forward and opened my eyes. Placid brown eyes returned my gaze from a round, beatific face. The face smiled, so I smiled in response.

The cherub moved away, gathered an armful of linens from the dark wood bench, and left the room through a narrow doorway. An elderly man took her place beside me; a rough brown cowl covered his head. I beat at my sluggish mind and found a name which seemed to fit him. "Abbot Medwyn," I whispered, enormously pleased by my own cleverness.

I slept and woke and gained with each awakening a little more of strength and surety. The fire dreams became less fierce, though they did not fully leave me.

The cherub often returned to tend me; Abbot Medwyn came less frequently. Neither spoke aloud, though they conveyed some thoughts by simple gestures.

From the window of my cell, I could view a portion of the abbey gardens: orderly rows of budding beans and marrows carefully tended by silent figures in dull brown robes. I watched their labors in the gentle sunlight, and I was very glad when my cherub gave me a robe of my own and led me to work beside the peaceful, diligent gardeners. Each man and woman kept to silence, and I gave no thought to another way after my single whispering of Abbot Medwyn's name. I learned the few signs by which to make known the nominal needs of simple living. I strengthened slowly, and I grew to health.

The garden stalks burgeoned; blossoms furled their lacy fingers and brought forth their swelling fruits. I watched the dawns with the abbey sisters in the silence of morning prayer. I came to know the bells which called us. I knew the sisters with whom I lived by their eyes and their clever hands, but they were nameless, as was I.

I was contented. Our abbot was gentle and good. We worked long, but we had laughter, though we had no words. Only the troubling of my sleep concerned me still; in sleep, I was alone and unsolaced. With the night-fire and fear came a myriad of shattered fragments: great oaks, gray walls, and eyes of blue ice. I began to see visions of Abbot Medwyn in grimmer settings than the pale of Benthen Abbey, and none would give me comfort in this one question. As the weeks of halcyon springtime passed, the faces of my dreams began to dominate as well my waking hours, and I clung to the peaceful present with increasing desperation.

Evening of a day of storm: an hour had distanced the thundrous rumbles which echoed in the abbey halls. Lightning's ferocious crackle had filled the afternoon, but only the intermittent glare of distant glory touched Benthen Abbey now. The violence of the storm had stirred my inner dreams to frenzy, and I worked with frantic energy to exorcise my restless specters.

Abbot Medwyn summoned me as I completed the polishing of a row of dedicatory plaques. I followed him to his office, second foremost of the rooms which faced the abbey gates and separated the men's halls from the women's. He closed the door and bade me sit upon one of the two straight-backed chairs.

Abbot Medwyn contemplated me over interlaced fingers. "You have been with us for nearly four months, Rhianna," he said. The sound of speech startled me, but response in kind seemed suitable.

"I can recall no more than half that time. I must have been very ill."

"You needed much healing, Rhianna, but you have recovered your strength of body. Your brother, Lord Dayn, has come to take you home to Tyntagel."

For Abbot Medwyn's sake, I tried to understand. I tried to remember a brother and a home outside the abbey. "Is it very far?" I asked.

Shaking his head, Abbot Medwyn pushed a parcel toward me. "These things are yours, Rhianna."

Gingerly, I pulled aside the fold of linen wrapping: a woolen skirt, a cloak and tunic, worn and heavily patched; amid them, a stone of a curious milky-white. I clasped the stone slowly and let my fingers trace the polished whorls. I heard the distant thunder, and the seconds passed. Memory heeded my summons reluctantly. Each fragment of its return eroded my illusory peace. I continued to hope that Abbot Medwyn might dismiss me before my shell of healing serenity cracked, but he did not relent.

"As you fell," said Abbot Medwyn, "Kaedric took the Taormin from Lord Hrgh, who fled into Horlach's maze with a tormented cry quite inconsistent with his previous poise. Kaedric transported us here. He used the Taormin; ask me not how. I wish he had not used the foul device, but it did preserve your life and Ineuil's as well against a questionable alternative."

"You sent for my brother. How much has he been told of how I came here?"

"We sent word to your family only that you were ill and under our care. Kaedric told me your name and kinship before he left."

I did not remark the plainness of the latter comment to my mind. I had acquired new memories along with my own: seemingly senseless images, but I knew them to include Ixaxis and Ven. I presumed without much happiness that the man from whom the images came had accrued some share of my history in exchange.

"I ought to see Dayn. My brothers do dislike waiting." I searched the abbot's eyes. "If I asked to remain here in the abbey, I think you would refuse me. Have I been so unsatisfactory an oblate?"

"I should welcome you to our order, Rhianna, if you truly wished the vows and were not already committed to another path."

"My father has committed me to marriage against my choice."

Abbot Medwyn blinked. "It was not of marriage that I spoke, though that estate does conflict with our vows. Benthen Abbey may not accept a practitioner of wizardry."

"I am not a wizardess, Abbot Medwyn."

"The Infortiare disagrees. Your brother is in the anteroom."

I regarded the door which led to the outermost chamber of the abbey, the anteroom which was reserved for occasional visitors. I pictured my brother pacing in distaste for his current duty. Poor Dayn always incurred the undesirable tasks which Balev and our father shunned.

I had not seen Dayn for nearly two years; that last meeting had consisted of a single formal dinner held during his brief soldier's leave in Tyntagel Keep. He had looked very fine in the crimson uniform of a royal officer, but he had already talked eagerly of the end of his term of service. He wore nobleman's finery now, though an empty scabbard hung at his side; he reached abortively for the missing sword, as if its unaccustomed absence (abbey rules forbade the gear of warfare) distressed him. Poor Dayn—he needed no further unhappiness beyond the prospect of seeing me again. He had not faced me squarely during the twenty years since some leap of logic, intuition, or the sudden coalescence of scattered observations gave him recognition of my sorcerous nature. At six years of age, Dayn had seen in me what no one else had dared observe. I wondered how Dayn would react to the truth of my recent illness.

Dayn mumbled my name; he lacked still the ability to speak easily in my presence. Our reunion was predictably stilted: a formal exchange of the most minimal of greetings. It was Abbot Medwyn who told me that Dayn had married Lady Liya dur Cam not long after I had left Tyntagel. I had not even been informed of the engagement, though it had been formalized months before my leaving.

I told Dayn no more regarding my own immediate past than he had already heard from Abbot Medwyn, and Dayn certainly did not press me for further information. He made only one disapproving reference to my precipitous departure, muttering dully, "You never could make anything easy, could you?" Dayn had always been the most tolerant of my kin.

Chapter 2

We left Benthen Abbey the next morning. I relinquished to the abbey my share of the Venture reward and the few belongings, save Varina's stone, which I had carried for so many leagues. Dayn had brought me a trunk of clothing packed for me by his wife. I ought to have felt appreciative of her consideration, but I could not even summon enough emotion to regret deeply my leaving the abbey.

I spent the next few days bouncing uncomfortably in a carriage, while my brother rode freely beside the cumbersome entourage which confined me. The only gladness of my state was solitude; my father had not seen fit to equip the company with any female escort. I had resolved to wallow in self-pity, but I could not sufficiently overcome my feeling of resignation.

Tyntagel Keep was just as I remembered. The oak which I had healed before my flight sported new leaves and added stature. I wanted to reach it, but I had strayed too far, and I feared to examine the extent of the metamorphosis. Not one of my family appeared to greet my return. A servant took my trunk but made no offer to assist me from the carriage. Dayn vanished toward the stables, leaving his sour lackey to ensure my cooperation in returning to my ancestors' home.

The second housemaid of the east wing met us in the entry hall and led me to my room. Her name was Rosal. She was very young and often forgetful of her position's proper restraint, even with the Tyntagel sorceress. She had frequently spoken to me in the past, and I had enjoyed her unconscious trespasses. She acknowledged me now only as much as minimally necessary.

My room had not been touched. Dust covered it thickly, and the familiar musty smell had gained in measure. I shook the counterpane, dislodging a spider which scampered under the door. The spider's escape came more easily than would mine; Rosal had locked the door as she left, taking the room's only key.

I counted the folds on the heavy curtains, pressing them with my fingers to feel their familiar texture of soft velvet worn in irregular patches. My window overlooked the narrow road which wove through the village by a route which darted erratically from dwelling to dwelling. Tiny figures traveled it, proceeding with their daily affairs as they had always done. I could name them by their places and paths without need to see their features. They did not change. Each knew his role and followed it from birth.

My own role had been molded tightly around me,

and my liege-father would hold me to it. A year's delay had been requested for the propriety of Lord Grisk's bereavement; my intermediate absence could have been kept unnoticed beyond Tyntagel Keep. Any inquiries henceforth could be countered by the vague account of illness and a time of religious retreat. I felt much like the toy which returns invariably to its initial position, no matter how many tumbles it takes.

I had returned to incarceration. Even if I did escape again, I had no practical goal. My horror of espousal to Lord Grisk dur Niveal had not wavered, but my impulsive endeavor to elude it had brought me only greater anguish.

I felt another compulsion now: to seek him whom I had known as Master Kaedric. I dreaded another encounter, fearing to revitalize that terrible fire which my mind could barely contain, but I needed to find him. I needed explanations which only Lord Venkarel could supply, and I needed to understand the change he had wrought in me. Master Kaedric—Lord Venkarel—would not seek me; he had left me to Benthen Abbey. I could not expect another chance meeting, since the Infortiare was generally a most inaccessible personage. The Tower of the Infortiare adjoined the King's castle in Tulea; a Tyntagellian lady inhabiting a hall of that castle stood a much better chance of meeting the Infortiare than would a Tyntagellian runaway. If my father still wished me to travel to Tulea for Lord Grisk's inspection, I would comply.

Rosal brought my meals to my room, removed the remains, and never spoke or relented enough to smile. The punishment did not disturb me. The silence of Benthen Abbey had been deeper, and I knew that the present confinement would pass. I was far too haunted by misplaced, spinning thoughts to fret at the flow of a few days. I was haunted by the shades of another's life. I tatted careful laces and waited while the sun cycled and my mind's fragmentary memories firmed.

* * *

"You were careless, Fylla," said the plump woman, a blowsy blossom rank with the attendant smell of stale roses. "You should have come to me before you had the child."

The woman thus addressed was badly worn, her face was pinched, and the smoldering beauty she had always owned had paled with recent abuse. She was ravaged, this woman who had been known as ageless among her peers in a career of notoriously short tenure. She looked a curse at the child, the spindly boy of three or four or five, who had vanquished her. She hated him. She pleaded, "Ora, I can still bring in customers. I was your best draw. You told me that."

"Look at yourself, Fylla. My customers want more than a worn-out skeleton."

"Ora," cried the desperate Fylla, "Just let me stay a week. It'll be worth your while. If not, you can still send me out."

"No more, Fylla," declared Mistress Ora with impatience. She patted her stiffly curled, yellow hair. "Go to Doshk. He may take you."

Fylla's wide blue eyes shone contempt. "Me in Doshk's sty? I'd as soon bed a maggot's meal as the slime he caters to."

"Don't be so choosy, Fylla. You can't afford it. Get out."

The black-haired whore, who had once commanded the highest prices on Ven's waterfront, faced Mistress Ora with pathetic dignity. Ora prospered, but she was old, and Fylla felt a sneering pride at being young. Youth was all that remained to Fylla, and even it was a fostered self-deception; Fylla's birth had preceded Mistress Ora's by thirty years.

Pushing her slight, dark-haired son roughly before her, Fylla emerged onto the foggy street. Her heel caught on a wooden plank rougher than the rest, and she stumbled. Tears stung her eyes, for she used never to trip; she had been beautiful and dancer-graceful and far too fine for the wretches who now comprised her dwindling clientele. Her son regarded her with sorrow from eyes of startling blue.

"Damn you, Kaedric," she muttered, but the boy continued to trail her steps dutifully. She had always been careful, but still the boy had come. She had wanted to abort him, but the burning fever had come to her each time she tried, and then it was too late. He was born, and his eyes were clear and knowing, and she could not leave him, though she despised herself for the weakness.

Her steps slowed at a grimy inn. Two men who entered it eyed her with initial interest, until the fog broke enough to show how weak and colorless she had grown. They veered away; she would have scorned them and their diseased bodies, but their rejection hurt. She stared at the inn for several minutes. The child seated himself placidly at her feet.

A man very fat but strong and cruel appeared at the doorway of the inn. He searched the fog, and he saw the woman. He bared stained teeth. "Why, Mistress Fylla, have you come to pay your respects to me? You're not so haughty now, are you?"

Fylla stiffened, but she smiled in shadow of her old enticements, a stretching of lips which had been seared dry and cracked by her long fevers. "I was wrong about you, Doshk. You have established yourself well."

"Better than you've done," he answered.

"I've had some hard times of late, I admit, but I could still bring you more profits and than you have ever seen."

"You're done, Fylla, and you know it." He smeared greasy hands across his apron. An outburst of shouts rocked the inn, and Doshk turned to the door with a snarl.

"Doshk," called the woman, her pride defeated by long strain and hunger. Doshk yelled through his inn, and the fracas quieted to the normal, steady roar. "Doshk," repeated Fylla, "You'll want to replace Gella."

"I can buy a bony carcass from the butcher, Fylla. I don't need to hire one."

Growing frantic, Fylla said, "Then buy the boy,

Doshk. He's strong, and he'll have my looks. He'll fetch you good prices in a few years."

With a snicker begun, Doshk paused. Fylla had commanded great prices before the boy's birth, and the child did have the promise of his mother's remarkable coloring and fine features. "He's no use to me yet," muttered Doshk. "Bring him back in a few years, and we'll talk again."

"Keep your worthless bargains, Doshk," said the woman cuttingly, but she knew a breath's relief.

Doshk had not done with her. "Five kesni for him, Fylla. It's a fair offer, and you need it."

"Fifteen, Doshk, and a night's room and board," said the woman starkly. She would not look at her son.

"Five or nothing, Fylla. I don't need another mouth to feed, and the boy is useless as yet."

Fylla wrung her slender hands and felt the bite of hunger. "I can sell the boy elsewhere, Doshk." She wished she could believe it. Even as she spoke, she waited with dread for the fever to start. It had not troubled her since that outflow of fury in which she had actually struck the boy, but she continually expected its return. Fylla did not know how well she had wrought the binding of her son's Power.

Doshk delved into a deep pocket, fumbling with the coins therein. He withdraw seven small pieces of iron and displayed them on his pasty palm. "You can eat for a week on this, Fylla, and maybe you'll get some customers if you're not half-starved."

Fylla snatched at the coins. Doshk let them fall and laughed at the woman's desperate scramble to claim them. One coin rolled to the boy; he gathered it carefully and offered it to his mother. She hesitated only an instant before she jerked the coin from the boy's hand. She left him with his hand outstretched. Doshk kicked him roughly, and the boy struck the gravelly gutter with a soft whimper. Doshk kicked him again.

A weasel-faced young man detached himself from the inn's shadow and pursued the diminished Fylla.

She was unwary with distraction and perceived the man only when his scabbed arm encircled her. She screamed as the knife flashed. The man pried the seven coins from her clenched fingers, while blood pooled at her throat.

Fylla's son shuddered. Doshk grabbed his arm and dragged him within the inn.

I dreamed of Fylla for fourteen nights, and every dream ended in a pool of her seeping blood and her son's unshed tears. I was bitterly weary when the fifteenth sun enflamed the morning sky. A tentative knock rattled a bit of broken gilt-work on my chamber door. I folded away the laces which would never be completed within my somber, steadfast once-home. I was glad that Lady Altha still shunned me; hers was not a face I should ever miss. Lady Liya was much pleasanter company, and I craved distraction from the vivid death of a waterfront whore.

I had met Liya once when her family passed some days with us during an excursion they made to Tulea. She still resembled a diminutive doll, tiny and energetic, though maturity had endowed her generously. She could not have been more than nineteen, but I could anticipate Lady Altha's reaction to the potential usurper. Liya would not be dominated as easily as Balev's wife, Nadira.

"Good morning, Rhianna," she announced brightly. "I bring you a gift," she added, handing me the key to my room with a conspiratorial grin. She surveyed my shadowy room with distaste. "What a ghastly way to welcome you home after your illness. Dear me, has anyone even told you that we are now sisters?"

"Dayn did mention your marriage. I do apologize for my inability to attend," I said wryly.

"Well, you are hardly responsible for your illness, are you?" she asked with a touch of authentic curiosity. She would have been unobservant indeed if she had not found flaw in the ruse of long indisposition.

I digressed deliberately. "Have you been acquainted with the prospective disposition of my future?"

"I have been told to advise you in the selection of gowns which will suitably impress your future husband. I am officially ignorant of any specific arrangements," she intoned very seriously. "However," she continued with a wink, "Lord Baerod and Lord Brant dur Niveal have exchanged a number of recent communiques, and some members of the Tyntagel household will travel to the King's court very soon; regrettably, I am not yet listed among those fortunates. I believe Lord Grisk dur Niveal, Niveal's court representative, currently requires a wife."

I laughed with her, genuinely light of heart as I had not been for far too long. I had retained more uncertainty of my journey to Tulea than I had acknowledged to myself. I could consider my next steps when I reached King Astorn's court.

Liya said dreamily, "Of course, there are a great many eligible young men at court other than Lord Grisk. With such a cache from which to choose, one might possibly discover some more appealing alternatives. You would not actually consider Lord Grisk, would you, Rhianna?" she asked with sudden concern. She blushed as she said, "I realize he is your father's choice, but he has been connected with some rather unpleasant rumors."

"If Lord Grisk found me too unappealing for consideration, I should not feel greatly slighted."

Liya's smile reappeared. "I *am* glad, but you should not rely too heavily on displeasing him. You are quite attractive in an ethereal way. I do wish I had your trick of looking at a person as if you saw all sorts of things the rest of us could never comprehend. It gives you such an elusive, mysterious quality. Everything I think or feel is plain for the world to see. I am afraid Dayn will grow bored with my predictability."

"I certainly should not recommend emulating me if you wish to retain Dayn's favor," I disclaimed fervently.

"Oh, come, Dayn does not dislike you so. He may find you a little daunting, but then you are very like your father." Privately I disagreed with appalled incredulity but made no comment. With a rush of remembrance, Liya reached the purpose of her visit. "Your father!" she exclaimed, clapping her delicate hands. "Your father has ordered the dressmaker here this noon. I was told to fetch you for the fitting. We had best hurry, or we shall both reap a wainload of trouble."

Chapter 3

Fabrics finer than any I had ever worn, flurries of conferring seamstresses turning and twisting me like a mindless doll, and Liya coordinating the gradual amassment of an astonishing assortment of laden trunks: the elaborate preparations for my journey to Tulea contrasted sharply with my previous, spontaneous departure. I was assigned a very elegant and opinionated personal maid named Tamar, who experimented endlessly with arrangements of my hair and various ensembles of jewels and other accessories. Her dispassionate attention made me feel more than ever an inanimate object. When Liya and Tamar deemed me suitable, I was paraded before the elders of the Tyntagel household, none of whom I had seen in nearly a year. My father nodded curtly.

The travel caravan began assembling the subsequent day. Liya gushed with delight when told that she and Dayn would join the caravan, which, I learned to greater puzzlement and disquiet, would include my father as well. Liya bubbled with the gaiety of projected activity. Dayn regarded his wife with the tolerance of devotion, but he did not echo her enthusiasm. Some cause beyond a daughter's betrothal spurred my father's decision to travel to Tulea, and it had sobered Dayn to a point even Liya could not reach.

"Rani," I heard, and the name stirred fear and hope, but it was Evram who called me. He seemed paler and plumper than I had seen him last, or perhaps it was only by comparison with a handsome scoundrel/thief and a man whose gaze was ice and flame.

"My father will be displeased if he observes you with me, Evram," I said with a slightly forced smile. "But I am glad to see you well."

"Rani, how could you leave without telling me? I worried for you."

"You would not have allowed me to go, as I thought I must."

Evram bobbed his head nervously, trying to conceal the glances of concern he threw at my father, as yet absorbed in issuing final orders to Balev before our departure. "You ought to have come to me, Rani. I would gladly have taken you to Benthen Abbey if you had asked it. I shall take you from here now if you wish it. I know the guards. They will help us to escape."

"Dear Evram," I sighed sadly. I was certain that Evram did not actually believe that his influence over the Tyntagellian guard outweighed my father's, but it was an offer the more gallant for the uncharacteristic lie. "Please forget me, Evram. I am less than ever what you wish to believe me."

Evram interrupted me, a thing he had never done before. "Rani, I dislike to see anyone treated this way. I offer to help you as a friend." He looked again toward my father, and he shuffled nervously. "I suppose no one told you. I married Mistress Terrell, your niece's governess, last month."

Evram's expression was woebegone and embarrassed. I was relieved and sorry, gladful and hurt. I hardly knew Evram, I realized. I had discounted him as no more than infatuation's foolish victim. He had been my friend, perhaps my only human friend, and I had not repaid his friendship well. My realization came late. "I am pleased for you, Evram. Mistress Terrell is a fine and intelligent woman."

"And a suitable choice for a shopkeeper's son," said Evram with the grin I remembered fondly. He sobered quickly. "Terrell will meet us at my father's shop. I have a cousin in Amlach who will help me start anew. We can smuggle you from the coach as you pass through the oak wood. It is dark there, and we are less likely to be observed. I can take you to Benthen or to another abbey where you are not known, if that is what you wish."

"Evram, I could not allow you to make such sacrifice for me, and there is no need for it. I travel to Tulea of my own volition. I am done with fleeing. Go back to your wife, Evram, and tell her that she need not follow you into exile."

Evram hesitated, and I pressed his hand, fleetingly ruing the loss of old dreams. "You are a kind and good man, Evram."

"We shall always be here if you need us," promised Evram slowly. "We are not important people, my lady, but we are your friends."

"Friends are always important, Evram." But there are deeper, less tangible bonds, Evram, and they demand precedence. They steal me from this gentle world of yours which I have only begun to appreciate, now that I must lose it.

We journeyed slowly, encumbered by a ridiculous train of wagons and carriages. Since Liya rode with Dayn, I was left with the dismal company of Tamar. I offered no objection to the arrangements, since I had resolved to maintain my passive role as far as possible, but the exchange of poor company for the solitude to which I had become accustomed did not improve my temper. Tamar doubtless reciprocated my sentiments, but she at least received payment for her trouble. I gazed sightlessly out the carriage window at the mountains we circled, lost in hurtful memories not my own, and many days vanished.

The road to Tulea stretched wide and well tended, but steep downgrades on either side betrayed the city's origins as a citadel of defense. Traffic thronged along the Seriin capital's single formal access, and our massive caravan congested the street to an inconceivable degree. Since the road had been carved from the ridge of Tul Mountain specifically to confine traffickers to a limited stream, such an unexpected addition to the normal wayfarers as a noble's entourage brought travel to a virtual halt. We spent a full two hours in the final approach to the city's gates; only within a furlong from the gates did the city come into view, sheltered as it was in the arms of Tul Mountain.

Tulea surpassed the most fluent descriptions. She was the heart-jewel of Serii and the home of kings. Gazing down at the distant glint of silver sea, the city rose in tiers to the white crown which dominated the view, the castle of the heirs of Tul. No solemn gray Tyntagellian walls served Tulea; pastel circles faded to pale tints as the buildings progressed up the mountain. In the narrow streets vendors crowed, gay in brightly colored stalls. Wealthy nobles in sea-silk and gold, merchants of countless wares, and tattered, tired travelers from every Seriin city mingled in Tulea's terraces. Wily young rascals darted everywhere underfoot, testing the attention and the patience of their elders. The chaos and the clamor fascinated me, but the castle drew my attention above all else: reminder of the central force of the Seriin realm, King Astorn, the heir of Tul.

I did not at first observe the edifice which loomed above the castle. It was a tower carved from the dark mountain stone, and the grander dwelling of the King made the tower seem stark and insignificant. The base of the tower clung to the mountain; the mountain wall retreated from the tower's continuing height, and a black bar seemed to bind the tower to the castle's upper floor. I had read the tower's description; it was Ceallagh's Tower, the tower of the Infortiare of Serii. I rubbed at the muscles of my neck; they were tight and aching.

We passed through the terraces of the commoners with their layered homes of abutting walls. We continued through the lower terrace of the lesser nobles with its grand manors and elaborate formal gardens carved in green and red and yellow. The bulk of the caravan left us as we reached the level of the royal terrace;

baggage was carried along the servants' path to the Halls of Serii's First Houses. We drove through the finely wrought gates, and the lines of liveried guards parted to let us pass.

Miraculous as it appeared as a diadem above the Tulean populace, the King's castle did not reveal its true enormity and overwhelming opulence until viewed from the King's terrace itself. Fanciful forms, each intricately carved and inlaid with precious ores, adorned the facades of the various Halls as well as the central castle proper. Spires, deceptively delicate, pirouetted and rose from vast gardens to the hub of Tulea, the home of Tul and his many generations of descendants. In Tyntagel, I had never felt the impact of a First House kinship; the King's castle burdened me with a sudden sense of awe that I belonged to a House of such history. I wondered how the royal family members withstood the formidable rivalry of their own edifice, the stunning culmination of inspired centuries.

The individual Halls belonged externally to the overall castle theme of magnificence; within, they bore the imprint of the families to which they owed title. In the Hall of Tyntagel, tapestries and heavy velvet hangings created a familiar stifling sensation, defying the silver and light of the Hall's exterior. The entry was smaller, the stair rose straight instead of curving as in Tyntagel Keep, the salon opened onto a dim inner courtyard, but it was withal the home of my family. I wondered if the same oppressive atmosphere pervaded much of the castle's inner realm; it would be a bitterly disappointing irony.

My uncle, Lord Dhavod, greeted us. He was a solid man of middling years who had never learned to smile. His wife, the Lady Ezirae, fluttered at his side. Ezirae invariably fluttered. Though in her fluffy and frivolous way, Ezirae at times projected the charm of utterly naive simplicity, she was a tediously silly woman. I often wondered how my humorless uncle tolerated her at all.

An excruciatingly correct maidservant entered the hall to announce Lady Yldana duri Amlach with a rigid curtsy. Yldana swept into the room in a wave of pale green silk, immediately commanding the attention of everyone present, eclipsing even the flurry of fuss attending the arrival of Tyntagel's liege lord. Even Liya seemed dimmed by my sister, who had not changed from my memory's glistening picture. Yldana needed no sorcery to bewitch; she drew adulation as irresistibly and implacably as a magnet draws iron.

"I do wish you had given me greater warning of your coming, Father," she cooed sweetly. "I should have prepared a more fitting reception."

"You are a worthy daughter," said our father, his dark eyes softening and his brow for the moment smooth. He bent to kiss Yldana's proffered cheek. "My business in Tulea, however, will allow me little time for social indulgence."

"Nonetheless, Father, you must not expect to devote all of your time to work. I simply will not allow it. Dayn's new wife will label us slavish." Yldana smiled enchantingly at Liya. Liya beamed, and I observed ruefully that my sister had made yet another conquest. "Of course, we must all strive diligently to impress the young lord of Niveal. We do not want our Rhianna to die a spinster." I winced inwardly; Yldana had retained her taste for mockery. I had truly come home.

Chapter 4

We were not spared even a day's reprieve to recover from our journey. My first evening in Tulea included as honored guests both Lord Brant dur Niveal and his son, Lord Grisk. I submitted to Tamar's ministrations, acutely disinterested in the prospect of meeting the man intended as my husband. I was far more intent upon the view from my chamber window of the Infortiare's Tower. I shivered when I looked upon it, but my eyes would not leave it.

My father had never before watched me with such concern nor scrutinized me so carefully as he did that evening. I welcomed Lord Brant politely and nodded a correct acknowledgment at the introduction of his son. I allowed myself a secret smile, for Lord Grisk barely glanced at me before turning his attention to Yldana, whose husband had remained conveniently absent.

Less openly dissolute than my prejudicial antipathy had led me to expect, Lord Grisk might have appeared well-favored to one more receptive than I. He was a strongly muscled man of a type which appeals to many women. The years had not yet displayed the stain of dissipation on his features, and the faint vulgar imprint which I descried could well have been due to my own bias. The only appeal he held for me was his total disdain of my existence.

Supper, always an uncomfortable meal, was rife with schemes and crossed purposes. Yldana deftly directed Lord Grisk toward me, to the obvious approval of both our father and Lord Brant, but Yldana's condescending efforts merely effected a transferral of Grisk's attentions to a discomfited Liya. Lacking Yldana's sophisticated defenses, Liya cast pleading glances at Dayn, who was occupied in a heated discussion with Uncle Dhavod regarding the Infortiare's recent edict against nobles who refused cooperation with required Ixaxin testing. No rescue came for Liya, since only she and I realized her plight; Lord Grisk included me marginally in the conversation, enough to satisfy the peripheral interest of the other members of the party without actually deigning to notice me. As the evening progressed, Liya suffered so obviously that I almost regretted my inability (and lamentable unwillingness) to distract Lord Grisk. One whispered comment from Lord Grisk upset her particularly; I could not hear it, but Liya blushed furiously and excused herself from the table on a hurried pretext of malaise.

Lord Grisk did not appear displeased with himself, though Liya had escaped him. He turned to me, the poor third choice, as he chortled, "Your sister-in-law has led a sheltered life, Lady Rhianna, but she is pert enough that a short time in Tulea should serve to educate her. You had best learn by her example."

"Since I shall not be troubled by personal experience with amorous suitors," I finished for him coldly. "Vows of marital fidelity do not concern you, I gather."

"A pretty woman unattended is an invitation, Rhianna. Fools like Dayn and Amgor marry the enticers but neglect to watch them; they should expect the consequences."

"Whereas you intend to marry a dull wife and enjoy illicitly the more enticing wives of others."

Grisk rubbed the ruddy fringe of his moustache. "You will learn to curb that sharp tongue, Rhianna, but I think we understand each other. You will get a husband—a good catch at that—and I will get heirs I know are mine."

"We are not formally betrothed, Lord Grisk. You are presumptuous."

"I am practical. The formalities await us, but I see no reason to pretend that we shall not eventually wed."

"You discount my own opinion of the matter."

Incredulity stole across Grisk's features before he laughed. "Play coy, if it amuses you. We both know that agreements between our domains have already been made."

"Agreements change."

"That is for our liege-fathers to decide."

His words silenced me, for that I could not dispute.

Liya remained unwontedly subdued the next morning. Dayn's humor seemed no grimmer than it had been since our arrival; I decided that Liya had not told him of Lord Grisk's offense. Fatigue etched hollows beneath her eyes, and I thought the aftermath of journeying alone could not account for it. Liya had enjoyed the privilege of riding much of the way, and she had shown no signs of strain on the previous day. I mentally berated Dayn for his insensitive obliviousness, but I did not feel able to intervene actively.

Yldana waltzed into our midst, the morning sunshine catching fire in her dark hair. "It really is too fortunate," she announced airily. "My dear friend, the Lady Veiga duri Sandoral, has agreed to invite Tyntagel Hall to a little gathering in the castle gardens this very afternoon. It will all be very rustic and informal, you understand, but it will be a terrifically important event. Veiga is the wife of the King's Adjutant, after all." Liya brightened at the news, and Ezirae positively oozed enthusiasm, but Liya's happiness ebbed when Yldana told me pointedly that Lord Grisk would also attend.

My father greeted Yldana's invitation by cordially and firmly declining on behalf of the men of our family, alluding to various urgent matters of nebulous nature. Dayn showed some trace of disappointment, but he pressed his wife to enjoy herself in his absence, a bit of generosity which poor Liya could not graciously refuse. Since Amgor also occupied himself in less frivolous pastimes, the party which Yldana eventually led in her gauzy gaiety consisted of Liya, Ezirae and myself.

Extending across the shady lawns which formed one of the castle's numerous parks, Lady Veiga's elaborately catered event bore little of the rustic feeling which Yldana had described, but I was still eager to participate. I had savored little sunshine since Benthen Abbey. Restored recollections had dimmed the days of gold in those gardens, and I gladly revived memories of the time in that haven to supplant the dark visions which I now more clearly recalled.

Seated demurely between Ezirae and Liya, I pretended to a fascination with Ezirae's embroidery of a blossom which the living flora wholly eclipsed. The dreadful Grisk had appeared all too promptly. He fawned alternately upon Yldana and Liya, uttering coarse drolleries with an impertinent familiarity which

Yldana carelessly disregarded while Liya stammered uncertain replies. I think Liya barely understood half of his references; I recognized only a little more by observing my sister's amused responses. Ezirae embroidered in apparently blithe ignorance of the scandalous behavior enacted beside her.

Glowing in sheer coral, Yldana made less effort to discourage Grisk than she had done the previous night. "Lord Grisk," she teased, "you should not squander your attentions on respectable married ladies. Rhianna's finer qualities will become evident to you only if you apply yourself diligently to the study."

"Married ladies can be most educational," said Grisk slyly.

Yldana's perfect lips formed a response, but her lazy glance sharpened abruptly on a point somewhere behind me. Both Ezirae and Liya turned in a blatant show of curiosity which I refused to emulate, but I was equally intrigued by the focus of my sister's rapt gaze. Ezirae fairly squeaked with excitement as she whispered effusively across me to Liya. "Yldana must be absolutely seething. I am sure she did not know Lord Arineuil had returned. It was quite bad enough that he left without a word to her, but now he shows up after a year or more without a bit of notice." The name teased me, but Ezirae's avid interest in the progress of one of Yldana's conquests disconcerted me. I had not thought Ezirae so careless of propriety—even for the sake of the thrilling gossip on which she thrived. "We heard he left on family business," she continued, "But there is little enough family left in the line of Ven, and Lord Arineuil never showed any interest in business before. It was undoubtedly," nodded Ezirae knowingly, "a Woman."

"Lord Arineuil has a simply scandalous reputation, Rhianna," explained Liya needlessly, her own eyes alight with intrigue, and my sluggish recognition coalesced.

"Hush, Rhianna," said Ezirae, though I had yet to speak a word. "He is coming near."

Lord Grisk halted his unheeded flirtations and scowled glumly at the man who approached. Yldana smiled bewitchingly and lowered her voice to its sultriest pitch. If she were angry—as Ezirae's ruminations made seem likely—she contained it well. "My dear Lord Arineuil," she drawled. "The ladies of Ven must be indeed enticing to have occupied you so long."

"Not one is so enticing as you, Yldana," answered the gentleman smoothly. He saw me then, and I stifled a nervous laugh at his quickly covered startlement.

Yldana regarded him from lowered lashes. "My brother's new bride, Lady Liya, will be visiting us for a brief while," she said, misjudging the cause of Lord Arineuil's stare. My sister added, as an afterthought meant, I suspected, to distract Lord Arineuil from Liya's charming blush, "My sister, Rhianna, will remain longer—if Lord Grisk has his way." Yldana beamed at Grisk consolingly.

Ineuil had recovered his wit; he turned an innocent gaze to me as if he had not previously observed my silent presence. "Must your sister depend on such grievous company?" he asked. Grisk's fists tightened. Ineuil prattled, "You are still mourning Tilla, are you not, Grisk? I should not like Lady Rhianna to meet Tulea from such an odious perspective." Ineuil bowed to me with a faint, conspiratorial grin.

"You are not in a position to cast aspersions, Arineuil," growled Grisk.

"Nor should I ever do so," answered Ineuil, guilelessly hurt, but his green eyes danced. "Especially toward someone of such scintillating refinement as yourself, Lord Grisk. I congratulate you on your excellent taste in brides once again. I did congratulate you the last time, did I not?"

"Arineuil," chided Yldana without particular fervor, "You ought not to remind Lord Grisk of his tragic loss."

"Have I done?" asked Ineuil. "I am sorry, Grisk. I do keep transgressing. Perhaps that little parlor maid—Nora?—can console you. She did so well the day Tilla died. Not a soul could have guessed of your bereavement that very afternoon. It was an inspirational display of fortitude, Grisk." Grisk had risen, and Ineuil gave the Niveallan's shoulder a hearty pat. Grisk jerked his heavy arm and swung it with violent intent, but Ineuil dodged nimbly aside. "Yldana," declared Ineuil gleefully, "it was too unkind of you to have kept your lovely sister hidden all these years." Yldana's gaze hardened. I experienced a fervent wish to box Ineuil's ears. Yldana would never forgive me for attracting the attention of one of her interests, and I could hardly explain my prior acquaintance with Lord Arineuil without aggravating a very delicate situation further.

"Rhianna does not frequent your circles, Lord Arineuil," said Yldana with a petulant turn of her lips. "She does not understand your foolish persiflage. If you must break new hearts, please constrain yourself to more worthy opponents than my unfortunate little sister. Your protracted absence from court cannot have deprived you so quickly of selective discernment."

"To the distress of my revered family, my appreciation of the finer things never wanes, nor does my diligence in the pursuit of such treasures as I espy. I could hardly neglect a sister of yours, Yldana. You will excuse us, Grisk? I should not like to interrupt your conversation further. Yldana and Lady Liya appeared so engrossed when I arrived. Lady Ezirae, your embroidery skill never falters." Ineuil gripped my reluctant hand implacably, pulled me to my feet, and removed me from the party before the astonished eyes of every nearby participant. I winced at the flurry of whispers which followed us to the stand of trees that rimmed the park.

"Do you realize how much trouble you are bestowing upon me, Lord Arineuil?" I sighed when we had escaped the range of curious observers.

"You once doubted the sincerity of my suit, dear Rani, implying that I attended you only for lack of other female company. I could not permit your misapprehension to continue."

"You choose an awkward way of proving your point."

"Nonsense! I shall have you know that my attention is considered a commodity of exceptional value. You will be the most celebrated lady of the court for days to come."

"Notoriety is not on my list of desirable attributes."

"You are not very appreciative of my discretion. I could have supplied you with a far more interesting reputation by mentioning our lengthy liaison. How would Lord Grisk react to that information, I wonder? He is a very jealous man, your future husband."

"Our common journey, Lord Arineuil, was scarcely a romantic frolic."

"The truth would incriminate us both with far more serious consequences, my dear sorceress."

"Then please forbear to address me by that ridiculous title," I countered sharply.

Ineuil answered more contritely than I might have expected. "Forgive my thoughtless tongue, Rani. I am not really so free with secrets as you may believe."

My spurt of sincere panic assuaged, I returned calmly, "You evidently keep your own well enough. Do the ladies of Ven never communicate with those of Tulea?"

"Ven women are legendary for their discretion," he said seriously; then he grinned openly. "A gift exceeded only in Tyntagel, I surmise."

"You are a rogue, Lord Arineuil, albeit less irresponsible than you pretend."

Laughing, he draped his arm about my shoulders. "My Lady Rhianna, you know me far too well, which is a humbling admission for a man of my repute. It is a pity to waste you on Grisk."

"I did not come to Tulea to wed Lord Grisk."

"Yldana seems to differ with you." We had wandered near to the upper edge of the wooded glen, and the windowless mass of Ceallagh's Tower loomed starkly before us. "Have you seen him yet?" asked Ineuil, markedly casual.

I did not bother to dissemble. "I have just barely arrived. In any case, the youngest daughter of Tyntagel does not frequent the Infortiare's circle."

"You will be presented to the royal family and its chief adviser soon enough; you are the daughter of a First House." He added with deliberation, "I rather thought, however, that Kaedric might have sought you."

"I served Lord Venkarel's purpose for a brief time, but he has no cause to seek me."

Ineuil took my shoulders to turn me, and he studied me closely. I met his gaze, wondering how much he had descried of the Taormin's tricks. "You did come to Tulea to find him?" demanded Ineuil with abrupt insistence.

I answered tersely, "Yes."

A moment's pause: Ineuil continued lightly, "I know of a very romantic villa where we can together watch the sun set into the Seriin Sea."

I smiled and responded without rancor, "You do spout the most ridiculous nonsense at times, Lord Arineuil." Ineuil was still the most handsome and charming man of my acquaintance, but I knew in that moment that I was immune to his unquestionable attractions. The realization made me feel vaguely invincible and obviated any regret I had at rediscovering the ease I felt in Ineuil's company, despite the trouble which the association would likely cost me. "I am nearly minded to accept your offer just to watch the agility of your retraction."

"Cruel Rhianna, your honesty wounds me. Your acceptance would delight me immeasurably, though I admit that the villa must wait upon the completion of certain business transactions which bind me to Tulea at present."

"Your unflagging devotion to duty is inspirational, my Lord Arineuil. I am sure that my sister appreciates your constant diligence as well."

"Yldana is a luscious vixen," mused Ineuil with a self-deprecating smile, "But the first time I find myself envying Amgor, I shall flee the vicinity until sanity returns."

"Amgor considers himself remarkably blessed."

"Amgor is a weak fool, and Yldana drives him to distraction. He spends so much time suffering pangs of jealous anguish that he has lost any semblance of intelligence that he may once have possessed." Ineuil squarely faced the distant sea. "Serii suffers such a surplus of his kind these days that even such an irresponsible rascal as I must exert himself against the consequences. We are sinking into the sort of self-destructive madness which claimed Hrgh."

I spilled a portion of my troubled thoughts. "Lord Hrgh has wrought such calamity as few could match."

"I am not unaware of the magnitude of the force which Hrgh released," answered Ineuil grimly. "The ramifications of Hrgh's folly may be more pervasive, but the ignorant conceits of Hrgh's counterparts can as easily destroy us. Kaedric's battles have not ended. Consider that before you seek him."

His vehemence startled me, recalling me from my fire-shrined phantasms. "Surely King Astorn must be aware of such an epidemic among Serii's noble Houses," I said tentatively.

"King Astorn manages well such civil cases and trade agreements as have promoted our prosperity for so long, but the line of Tul is as afflicted by indolence as the rest of Serii."

"A trait from which the House of Ven is immune?"

"Very far from it. My uncle advanced in the forefront of ineffectiveness, which is why my cousin rules a decimated domain." He plucked a leaf and began to shred it meticulously. "If my uncle had enforced his laws, there would have been no abused slave-child to ignite a city."

"Kaedric," I whispered.

"Lord Venkarel," amended Ineuil icily. He tossed the leaf's shorn skeleton to the draft which fell from the mountains. "The Infortiare who makes us choose now between himself and a deathless Sorcerer King." Ineuil sighed. "King Astorn still supports the traditional rights of Ixaxis, but he is not strong in spreading that loyalty. The movement against Ixaxis and the

Infortiare's influence mounts daily, now that we can least afford it. The fools have even begun to gather at court."

"My father has come to Tulea after an absence of at least a dozen years," I admitted.

"And Lord Baerod dur Tyntagel is vociferous in his hatred of wizardry. He must find your abilities awkward to explain."

"He has never acknowledged them."

"Typical. Lord Grisk incidentally shares your father's antipathies." Ineuil issued a sudden, wicked grin. "I must say to your father's credit, however, that he excels in his production of daughters. He named you aptly, as well."

"My mother named me," I said absently. "How long has this movement against Ixaxis been brewing?"

"Since the first sorcerer exercised his Power. Envy builds hatred, and even those who care nothing for magic and its consequences jealously observe the wizards' longevity. Why should Ixaxins live five times longer than those of us without the Power of wizardry? Because it is their nature; because they are superiorly designed, and the price they pay is not commonly recognized beyond Ixaxis' cliffs; because they are not entirely human: the best of the reasons do not sit well with Seriin nobles, who consider themselves more individually important than any Ixaxin. The less educated Seriins rely on basic superstition for their hatred of wizardry."

"Serii has survived that sort of prejudice since its inception. My father's father hated Ixaxis, but he never tried to overthrow the Infortiare."

"Lord Alobar was an inoffensive little man who never exercised the Infortiare's authority. Hrgh had a popular appeal despite his Power. Perhaps it is merely Kaedric whom the anti-Ixaxins especially hate; he does not have a particularly warm and winning personality. You know how grudgingly I serve his cause, and I know far more of the pertinent facts than do most. You want to know why matters foment more severely now than they have in all the millennia since Serii's birth, and I have no better answer than: Kaedric himself. It is an incomplete answer at best."

We walked silently then, following a winding path against the mountain. A clear and icy stream leaped in and out of a stone bound passage to feed the ponds and fountains of the royal gardens. We stopped beside a waterfall, a narrow splash of silver against the mossy emerald and black-veined ferns. The pool at its base mirrored soft fanned fronds and sheer heights, which glistened with damp slivers of light and violet shadow.

"This path continues to the vale of Tul's forked peaks," said Ineuil, "But the way is rough and seldom used. The wind through the pass is fierce, and the rewards of braving it are meager. Ceallagh's tomb lies there, but it is a simple monument eroded by the years and rather disappointing on the whole."

I cupped cold water in my hand and watched it trickle through my fingers. Another mote of sunlight was lost to shadow. A light blinked to brightness atop the wizard's dark tower. I stared fixedly at the glow. "I must return," I said.

"This makes an admirably secluded location for an evening tryst," suggested Ineuil with a resurgence of his courtier's flippancy.

"Then we had best leave before we interrupt one. I have committed enough improprieties for one day. Yldana will be furious as it is, and I left the party without even meeting the hostess, let alone thanking her."

"Veiga rarely bothers to attend these things. She will not hold your omission against you. You know, I suppose, that she is Hrgh's sister," he added with a sidelong glance.

"No, I did not know," I answered soberly. "She must strongly support Lord Venkarel's foes."

"Veiga's sympathies are difficult to fathom. The Dolr'hans are a clannish lot, but Veiga at one time cultivated Kaedric quite openly. She is a very shrewd and ambitious woman."

"You sound disapproving. Is she so very unattractive?" I asked sardonically, shrugging off my very genuine curiosity.

"How shallow you make me sound. In point of fact, Lady Rhianna, Veiga Dolr'han is an exceptionally beautiful woman whose brother was once my greatest friend, but I have never been able to overcome an intense dislike for her."

"She spurned you?"

Ineuil scowled at me terribly before he laughed. "I confess that may have been a factor. I am too unimportant for Veiga's ambition, and I am not sufficiently exotic for her prurient tastes."

"You make me glad to miss her acquaintance."

"Not miss it—merely delay it a while."

The sun sang a final, amber chord, heightening textures and shedding shadows on Ineuil's silken finery. There were new creases in his brow imperceptible in kinder light. "You appear very healthy for a man recalled from death," I said with a memory of his figure tossed limply in Horlach's hall.

"Abbot Medwyn is an effective medic, and my injuries, unlike yours, resulted from the weak, incidental chaff of that Power struggle. When last I saw you, even Medwyn doubted your survival."

"As you say, Abbot Medwyn's cures are effective," I concurred wistfully.

"The abbot serves body and soul, but it requires wizardry to bring back the mind from where you walked."

"How fortunate for me that such aid was available," I said uncertainly.

"Yes, very fortunate," stated Ineuil flatly.

The garden party had ended in twilight by the time we returned, and I never learned whether or not Lady Veiga had attended it. I reached the castle spoke which formed Tyntagel Hall and found fortune had favored me: the men of the household remained absent and were not expected to return until very late.

Ezirae had retired for the evening, which left only Liya to fend off with my imperfect explanations.

Liya's somber introspection over Lord Grisk had yielded to her natural ebullience. She arrived at my room almost as I did, plopped herself upon my bed, and beseeched me in a breathless rush for the details of my afternoon. Liya made my answer easy; she did not wait to hear it.

"It is just so romantic," she gushed. "Imagine captivating Lord Arineuil himself. Rhianna, I am so happy for you."

"We only walked about the park, Liya."

"Well, I did not suppose he had proposed yet. But he is interested, and that is what counts at this stage. It is just so romantic," she repeated. Thoughtfully, she added, "Yldana was not pleased, though. I should have thought she would be."

I restrained a cynical retort. I would not contribute to Liya's disillusionment by dispelling her notions of Yldana's generosity. Liya's precious innocence seemed destined to suffer enough without my help.

"Liya, my dear sister-in-law, Lord Arineuil is a very charming man and very pleasant company, but we are not the least bit romantically inclined toward one another." Liya smiled knowingly. She did not believe my protestations, but I did at last manage to send her to her own chamber. She remained certain that I had not revealed all that had transpired with Ineuil, which was quite true, but her substitute suppositions seemed so harmlessly preposterous that I gave them little more thought. I did not take into account Ezirae's position of authority among the ranks of court gossip mongers.

My first inkling of the impact of my imprudent excursion came two mornings later. Two of Ezirae's nieces, Ziva and Flava, had been consigned to their aunt's care; Ezirae's own children were grown and gone, and the halls of Hamley overflowed with any willing relations. Neither Ziva nor Flava displayed particular interest in Ezirae's strained attempts at youthful rapport, but giggling animation sparked in them at my entrance. Their excitement in their private exchange of thoughts trebled and Ezirae's eyes brightened attentively, as a manservant announced both luncheon and Lord Grisk, an unfortunate combination.

The unpalatable Lord Grisk swaggered into view upon the servant's heels. Bowing minimally to Ezirae, he greeted me with a disconcerting enthusiasm. "Good day to you, my Lady Rhianna. That is a very becoming color you wear. Green, is it?"

"So I have heard it called," I answered dryly. I decided that Lord Grisk grew more repellent with every meeting.

Lord Grisk looked at me uncertainly, resolved his dilemma of reaction by a hesitant laugh, and then patted my arm as if I had uttered a witticism of astonishing cleverness. I suppressed a shudder as Grisk's spatulate thumb rubbed my sleeve. "Let me lead you inside, my lady. So much sun cannot be comfortable for a delicate complexion."

I regarded my unfashionably browned hands critically, but I could not escape Grisk's proffered escort from the courtyard. He minced his steps awkwardly, as if suspecting me of partial paralysis. My father displayed rare emotion in his surprise at Lord Grisk's sudden attachment to me. I could see the calculating reappraisal of my worth in bride price.

It was a ghastly luncheon. Grisk attempted charm with bludgeoning tact. Ziva and Flava tittered constantly. Liya shrank against Dayn and would not speak a word. Ezirae injected my attributes into the general conversation at inopportune intervals. My father and Uncle Dhavod conspired in speculative undertones. I toyed with a bit of fish and counted minutes.

A fortuitously timed message summoned Lord Grisk soon after the meal's completion. He made much of the secrecy of the cause which claimed him, hinting broadly at lofty matters of vital importance to King Astorn and Serii. He found me disappointingly devoid of awe. Undaunted, he managed a few more words between us.

"I hope you did not take my teasing seriously, Rhianna. I never meant to imply that I found you undesirable. You obviously wished to make the point clear by your little demonstration with Lord Arineuil, but now that we understand each other better, I am sure that you will not feel the need to repeat such unsuitable antics. We shall speak more of this when I am free of my duties, and I am sure you will find my apology most acceptable." I snatched my hand from his with a disgust which I tried, for diplomacy's sake, to conceal.

I had not recovered from my distress at Lord Grisk's sudden change in attitude when a liveried messenger brought me a missive sealed with the gull-wing crest of Esmar. Across fully seven sheets of vellum spread a singular outpouring of amorous avowals. The signature of Lord Joret dur Esmar conveyed nothing to me, save for a dubious image of a rather ardent young man who had briefly spoken to Yldana at the garden party. Lord Joret had obviously never seen me, since his flowing paeans to my beauty displayed exceptional inaccuracy in every specific. He closed with a windy sentence to the effect that he would never have risked my reputation by whisking me away as had Lord Arineuil, however great the temptation. I found the letter unspeakably funny, even as I rued the validity of Ineuil's prophecy of my notoriety.

Liya delighted in the ensuing plague of pleas for my company over the next few days, while I retired to the depths of Tyntagel Hall lest I actually encounter one of the prolific gallants. Liya chided me for my timidity, Ezirae speculated gleefully, and my father stared at me as if I had sprouted leaves. I personally suspected, despite my hesitation to put the matter to test, that my admirers would be universally disillusioned if any ever met me; even blessed by Lord Arineuil's tacit approval, ardor could not easily withstand the reality of a rather aloof and unremarkable young woman.

I held to my room and its window's view. I enjoyed the sun only in the inner courtyards. I withstood the sporadic company of Grisk by adopting the full measure of Tyntagellian puritanism, ensuring that we were never without chaperon. He accepted my prudery grudgingly, invariably recalling to me an afternoon with Lord Arineuil, but I gradually mitigated Grisk's suspicions of my deception by currying the belief that my refusal to emerge from Tyntagel Hall was due to my wish to avoid the scandalous lord of Ven. Neaped by events, I awaited the returning tide.

Chapter 5

Heat grows. The yellow crackle of a consuming energy snarls at my flesh. There is a spiderweb of light, and it is blue-hot and deadly. There is dark emptiness gaping where the fires clash. I am caught by the fire. It carries me, and it sears my mind. There is only fire, and I am lost.

My nights were uneasy. The dreams which the abbey had partially stilled were returned to me in their fullest measure. I awoke in the night too frightened to scream. I felt my arms, expecting to find the skin shriveled and hard. I opened my eyes to test the world, and I lay motionless in the fragile relief from horror, counting heart's beats of peace and normalcy.

My eyes traveled the white-walled room, clung to the heavy gold drapes, and slid to the window relentlessly. There was no light by which to see the Tower. There had been no light in the Anxian tavern.

Day's glow took hold, and I lived in the world of my family: a Seriin lady of no obligations save duty to her liege. Liya had begun to love the social pattern, or at least she emulated the enjoyment of it well. She was ever with Yldana or Ezirae's gossipy friends. Dayn was seldom with his wife; he journeyed much on missions of which he would not speak. My father and uncle spent many hours locked in conference with messengers. Lord Brant joined them often, as did Amgor. There was a grim air to all these proceedings except when Yldana appeared. She would laugh and tease, and all their faces would brighten. Then she would flit to another party, another excursion, and Tyntagel Hall would become solemn again, save for Ezirae's chattering.

Grisk visited us too frequently for my taste, but he vanished on unspoken errands as often as did Dayn. My own days were so filled with the inconsequential essentials of my gender and class that I at times forgot that I had once escaped, lived another life and learned a darker history. Even glimpses of Ineuil (we had not spoken again) did not suffice to make real the Venture and that time of hardness. My memories seemed surreal, but when the dreams came in the night, I knew that I was entrapped.

It was inevitable that I would see him eventually: the Infortiare. One who lived in the King's castle must eventually encounter those others who shared that privilege. There would come some festive foolishness of my rank at which my nightmares would invade my saner life. I would meet him again and learn if I could bear his presence.

"Are you not the least bit excited, Rhianna?" asked Liya with such wistfulness that I regretted my inability to empathize with her enjoyment. Having been too young for formal presentation to King Astorn and Queen Alamai of Serii on her previous visit to Tulea, Liya's eagerness now was an obsession of anxiety. My own nerves tingled but not with delight.

"I shall be as pleased as anyone here to see Their Majesties arrive." We had been waiting for over an hour, standing uncomfortably motionless in tightly molded shoes, endeavoring to maintain the requisite illusion of perfection. Though I had been interested when we arrived, now I merely chafed to see the discomforts of protocol ended. I twisted my head very slightly, just enough to see the line of other newcomers to King Astorn's court. One young boy fidgeted cautiously; several pairs of shoulders had sagged from their earlier upright postures.

A large and plump man with black eyes and pasty complexion waddled into view from the curtained recess behind the dais. A steward loudly announced the man's name: Lord Borgor dur Sandoral, Adjutant to His Majesty, King Astorn. The husband of the elusive Lady Veiga ambled gracelessly past the line awaiting presentation. I had expected a more prepossessing figure for the Lady Veiga's husband, but Liin's arrogance had an obvious price; Liin's elitism made selectivity difficult. Lord Borgor paused once, briefly inspecting a blushing Liya, and took a seat near the edge of the dais. A taboret similiar to Lord Borgor's remained empty; it was placed on the opposite side of the royal dais, slightly higher than that of the Adjutant.

We waited several minutes more before the symbolic clash of stone against silver heralded the royal family of Serii. King Astorn and Queen Alamai grandly preceded their children, the heirs following in order of rank. Prince Orlin, a tall, handsome boy who greatly favored his father, beamed with the confidence of his assured place as future ruler of a vast and prosperous kingdom. The Princess Joli, who followed Prince Orlin, marred the procession's dignity with an innocent stumble. The princess recovered quickly but her lapse sent her four young sisters into a fit of muffled snickers and giggles; the Princesses Henzela, Alza, Phoebe and Leytia lost their composure to such an extent that Queen Alamai gestured peremptorily, and a gray-haired governess ushered the four youngest children from the room.

The King and Queen of Serii made an attractive couple, impressive in their costly finery, but I could not deny feeling a hint of disappointment. By the time the royal pair had progressed down the line of their subjects to me, the lovely Queen Alamai's attention had obviously tired of the whole proceedings; she contemplated an emerald which her fine finger hefted awkwardly. King Astorn greeted each individual with a remarkable cordiality, but I could not honestly assess him as a forceful or particularly intelligent man. I dropped a curtsy of respect, recalling even as I did the concern Ineuil had expressed over the present state of Seriin authority.

I could feel no more sanguine over the prospect of Serii's royal heirs. Prince Orlin looked the part of a regal scion with his wavy brown hair and gold-flecked eyes, but I thought my own brothers displayed more signs of the leader's gift than he. I watched as the prince waited petulantly for a servitor to adjust the royal chair to a new position. The four youngest daughters were not so young that they should have abandoned discipline for so slight and unworthy a cause as their sister's distress. Princess Joli glared sullenly throughout the remainder of the proceedings, disfiguring herself far more severely than did the scarlet birthmark which crossed her face. Only Princess Joli lacked the perfection of royal features, and her attitude was devoid of the most marginal civility; it disheartened me that her truculence provided the only evidence of spirit among the royal lot.

The King and Queen of Serii, flanked by their eldest children, took their places on the dais. Lord Borgor offered some preliminary paeans to the heirs of Tul. King Astorn spoke some inconsequential words of welcome, which apparently held his audience enthralled. My own attention was diverted as a tall, spare figure appeared from the recess through which the royal family had emerged. King Astorn himself glanced distractedly at the newcomer, aborted his speech with an absent wave, and yielded the proceedings to Lord Borgor.

I never heard Lord Borgor's speech. Lord Venkarel departed after only a moment of converse with the king, but he remained in my thoughts throughout the rest of the ceremony. The emblem of his office had hung from the fine gold chain around his neck, the gold starkly prominent against the formal black silk of the Infortiare. The man was so familiar to me that I could bring memories from his past into my mind, but the Infortiare of Serii stirred awed humility in me, as my King did not. I saw the clear ice of well-remembered eyes, but Lord Venkarel did not look beyond the royal dais.

I stood as one entranced through the exit of the royal family. Liya nudged me ungently, else I would not have filed out as required. She fortunately mistook my abstraction for deep emotion at my presentation to the king. When we had escaped the King's Hall, she linked her arm in mine as if we were sisters in truth. She gave me the silence for contemplation I wished, and I mentally applauded my brother's choice of bride.

Dayn and Ezirae met us upon our return to Tyntagel Hall. Dayn frowned slightly at sight of his wife's friendliness toward me, but Liya ran to him gaily and his expression cleared. Ezirae burst forth with questions, asking about every detail of pomp and attire. Her own life had been spent almost exclusively at the king's court, yet she never tired of further stories.

"Then His Majesty suddenly stopped speaking," recounted Liya, "and Lord Borgor continued, while King Astorn conversed with the tall man in private."

"Lord Venkarel," asserted Ezirae, bobbing her head up and down decisively.

"The Infortiare," breathed Liya. "Do you really think it was he? Imagine, Rhianna, the King and the Infortiare could have been deciding the fate of Serii as we watched."

"Lord Venkarel had no business interrupting His Majesty," mumbled Dayn.

Sensitive to her husband's mood, Liya swerved to a less controversial topic. "Now that we have been presented, Rhianna, we are eligible to attend the royal ball next week. Shall I wear the pink satin, Dayn, with the Bethiin pearls you gave me? Or does the pink make me look too childish?" Dayn touched his wife's hair fondly, and I retreated, glad to escape.

* * *

There were plots and counterplots around us. A man who could destroy Tulea with a thought lived among us, and he had deadly enemies. I wondered how many of the bright courtiers around me recognized the falseness of court life, how many believed it; how many merely played the game. Certainly the promise of a royal ball featured prominently in every conversation I heard for a week of days.

Most of the castle's inhabitants had been planning for the king's ball for several weeks, and Liya seemed determined to compensate for lost time by going into a whirlwind of preparation. My influx of cards and missives began to include pleas for dances, as well as requests for more substantial favors; the line of court gossip still celebrated me unreasonably. From Ineuil I received no word; after plunging me into the role of fashionable desirability, my notorious acquaintance had remained conspicuously absent.

Tyntagel Hall seethed with such frenzied activity that I took to escaping the social madness at dawn, exploring the castle gardens from rill to rocky peak in glorious solitude. The enjoyment which I derived from those stolen hours mingled with an ache for the rapport I had felt with my Tyntagel woodlands. I could hear the trees as clearly as I had ever been able to do but they would not welcome me freely. More than mere strangeness of unknown gardens, I suspected the cause stemmed from the changes I had undergone in the maze of the Taormin. I had lost the easy intimacy with the wild which had long been my solace, and the realization hurt me. I added to my list another claim against the Infortiare of Serii.

I climbed through a tangle of undergrowth, which betrayed the disuse of the path I trod, and found myself again at the waterfall glade to which Ineuil had brought me by a more orthodox route. Around the bole of a white pine were wrapped the arms of a spindly-limbed girl weeping heavily into the mossy bark. On the verge of retreat, I saw her push away from the tree and beat against it blindly. She lifted her face, and the violent stain of the birthmark from cheek to chin confirmed her identity. "Stupid tree," she cried, "you probably hate me too."

I hesitated, torn by her despair, and the young princess saw me. She scrambled to her feet, shouting imperiously, "How dare you spy on me? I shall order you thrown into the castle dungeons." She stood even shorter than I did. Her eyes red with tears and with a twig dangling from her chaotic brown hair, she could not achieve a very intimidating pose, despite the blazoned emblem of Tul upon her wrinkled frock.

"Forgive me, Your Royal Highness," I answered solemnly. "I did not mean to interrupt you. I came to speak with my friend."

"Is someone else coming?" shouted the princess wildly.

Tentatively, I tried to soothe her as if she were a trapped bird or a frightened flower. Aloud, I answered as reassuringly as I could, "It seems most unlikely, Your Royal Highness. The friend to whom I referred is the pine beside you. He really is a fine, stout fellow, though he does tend to be a trifle stuffy and self-important at times. He certainly does not hate you."

The disheveled Princess Joli regarded me suspiciously. "How would you know?" she asked. At least she did not again threaten me with imprisonment in a dungeon which did not exist.

"I asked him," I returned calmly. "He sorrows for you and would comfort you more if you would accept him."

She sniffed contemptuously. "I suppose you think I am stupid because I am ugly. Do you know who I am?"

"You are the Princess Joli an Astorn yn Alamai dur Tulea y Serii. I consider Your Royal Highness to be neither ugly nor stupid."

"You are a liar. Everyone knows about the stupid, ugly Princess Joli. I shame my family. Princesses ought to be beautiful. My sisters are beautiful: even Leytia, who is only seven, and my brother is handsome. I am the misfit. I am also impossible."

"Then we have much in common, Your Royal Highness. I also have a very beautiful sister, and my two brothers are quite handsome. I am generally considered to be entirely impossible."

Princess Joli dropped to the ground ungracefully. "Are you impossible?"

"I never thought so."

"I am," she declared proudly. "I never do anything I am told, and I never see anyone I dislike."

"Does not constant rebellion grow rather tiresome, Your Royal Highness?"

"If you try to lecture me, I shall banish you. Why do they think you are impossible?"

"I tend to talk to trees. It is considered an unsuitable pastime."

Wide eyes of amber peered at me intently. "Are you a wizardess?" demanded Princess Joli.

"No, Your Royal Highness." I equivocated. "My mother was a sorceress of Alvenhame, and I inherited a few small skills from her."

"I thought all Tyntagellians disapproved of sorcery." She congratulated herself with a smile, saying, "You thought I did not recognize you. You are the Lady Rhianna dur Tyntagel, and you were presented to me last week. You are going to marry Lord Grisk dur Niveal, though the betrothal has not yet been formalized. Servants know everything that happens in the castle, and I can hear everything from my room if I hold my ear against the wall in just the right place. You also had a scandalous rendezvous with Lord Arineuil. What is the pine saying now?"

"He is pleased to see you smile," I answered, disconcerted by the princess' rendition of my life.

"Can you understand any tree?"

"I have not found an exception as yet."

She rose with exuberant alacrity, grabbed my hand, and began to pull me with her. "You will tell me what all the trees in the park are thinking, or I shall tell everyone that you are a sorceress."

"Your Royal Highness, the park contains a great many trees," I protested, astonished by the princess' transformation of mood.

She considered, absently prying the twig free of her tangled hair. "We shall start with the special ones. What is that one thinking?" She pointed to a gnarled spruce.

"She thinks you are an outrageous imp."

Princess Joli gave me a scathing look. "It is no good at all unless you tell me the truth."

"The spruce revels in your joy; it is a tonic to her weathered soul. *I* think you are an outrageous imp."

Princess Joli gleamed, and her elation did fill the trees as surely as had her earlier depression. She drew me in an undignified run from tree to tree of the garden's less frequented regions, and we stopped only when the encroaching afternoon sun wilted even Princess Joli's enthusiastic energy. She said no good-bye but threw her arms around me, then dashed away in an unladylike scramble. She stopped for just a moment and called back to me, "I really never meant to banish you or anything like that." She disappeared into the royal enclave. I shook my head, exhausted but oddly charmed by the princess with a capacity for trouble worthy of an army of pestilent demons. I did not mention my morning excursion to my family. Though my tardy return elicited some initial questions, the more enticing subject of the incipient ball maintained its sway and spared me.

Chapter 6

I finally achieved the grudging approval of Mistress Tamar, though the accolades of Liya tended to accord the credit to Tamar's artistic touch. In sapphire sea-silk and silver, I felt foolishly self-pleased by a reflection almost as fair as the imaginary subject of Lord Joret's fanciful prose. I actually partook of sufficient eagerness to satisfy Liya's impatient anticipation of the ball, as we awaited Ezirae in my room.

"What a lovely pendant, Rhianna!" said Ezirae, appearing at last as Tamar adjusted about my neck the chain on which I had hung the Lady Varina's gift.

"It is lovely," said Liya, herself exquisite in rose silk and gold lace. "What is it, Rhianna? I think I have never seen such a stone before."

The stone, my sole contribution to my attire, did seem to glow more brightly than I had remembered. It recalled the stars of Nimal's crafting. I began to regret my impulsive choice of jewelry, despite its loveliness. "I really have no idea what it is," I answered vaguely. "I have had it for some time. We ought to go downstairs before father sends a search party for us."

We were very late, and the men of the household had begun a predictable discussion of our lack of punctuality. Lord Grisk had arrived; the widening of his eyes as he beheld me disturbed me, though it did in some measure please my vanity. I had not expected his escort to begin to Tyntagel Hall, and my hopes of eluding him in the crush of the ball vanished. I accepted his arm grudgingly. Liya refused to look at him; she clung determinedly to Dayn.

Painfully self-conscious, I approached the royal ballroom with Grisk still at my side. Before we had even left the arched entry to the King's Hall, Lord Brant met us, along with Grisk's brother, Egar, a brusque and bearded bear who towed along a timid wife. My father greeted the Niveallans with a hearty clasp of arms.

I distrusted this gathering of Niveal, an atavistic fear of conspiring predators rising within me. My distress mounted when Liya wheedled Dayn away to the ballroom proper, and Ezirae deserted us for a clutch of her Hamley cousins.

Amgor came to us through the crowd of gilded celebrants, his black hair sleek and his waistcoat scarlet satin. "My Lord Baerod," he said tensely, giving me no notice, "Master Ruy has been awaiting your arrival."

"Then direct him to us, Amgor," ordered my father impatiently. Tyntagel's ruling lord presented an imposing air in his finery, and the chronically nervous Amgor shuffled his finely shod feet. "Lords of Serii do not dance attendance on Caruillan message-boys," added my father with ill humor.

"Arku Ruy represents King Cor himself, Baerod," interposed Lord Brant. "We do not want to offend him by arguing points of etiquette."

"The man assumes too much," retorted my father, tapping his fingers together ominously.

"He is less presumptuous—and far more palatable—than that common villain, Venkarel," growled Grisk, gaining nods from his kin and from my uncle. Amgor glanced guiltily about the room and its indifferent throngs.

A lovely vision in amber tissue floated over to us with chiding words. "My incorrigible father," said Yldana, "you are corrupting my husband by working him at a royal gala. I will not have it."

Amgor gazed at his wife pitiably. His shy uncertainty toward the woman he had wed reduced the lord of Amlach to a figure of ridiculous weakness. I saw Amgor's desperate expression when Ineuil joined us. Amgor was a handsome man, but his wife overshadowed him and made him insignificant. Ineuil was rare, for he held his own share of attention, complemented by my sister and enhancing her. Ineuil placed his arm around Yldana's waist quite naturally, and he beamed innocently at Amgor. "You are a sly man, Amgor, to have captured this woman before the rest of us could come to our senses from shock at her beauty and charm. And you, Grisk, appear determined to repeat the crime against those of us less quick to act. Lady Rhianna, you do look exceptionally lovely this evening."

"You are most gracious, my lord," I answered with an effort at proper sobriety. My father was frowning intensely, and Ineuil's bland indifference amused me disproportionately.

"It is amazing, is it not," purred Yldana, "How a few formal trappings can transform even the plainest of women? Your maid, Rhianna, truly has worked wonders today."

"She spent long enough at it," grumbled Dhavod, for Ezirae had embellished the account of my preparations so as to excuse her own tardiness.

"I find the merit of frills and furbelows seriously overrated," answered Ineuil with overly emphatic solemnity. "A beautiful woman shines in any setting—to the eye of a connoisseur."

"It is good to know that the lord of Ven had honed his skills in some respect," said Lord Brant with little grace.

"Lord Arineuil certainly strives to ensure an ampleness of experience," sneered Grisk.

"Even irresponsible fools must occupy themselves somehow," added my father with a contemptuous stare which would have withered most men. Ineuil smiled broadly and brought my hand to his lips, his other arm still around Yldana.

"So long as Lord Arineuil does not occupy himself with my future wife," warned Grisk, jerking me ungently away from Ineuil.

Yldana interrupted with ominously oozing sweetness. "Why Rhianna, how *very* naughty of you not to have told me. I am so pleased for you. And I must commend you as well, Grisk. Have you begun the wedding plans, father? You *will* let me help? I can *hardly* wait to tell simply everyone that my own little sister is going to marry the handsome Lord Grisk dur Niveal. Rhianna, you should be proclaiming the wonderful news to all of Tulea instead of standing here with these gloomy folk." Yldana clucked and cast lidded glances at our father and Lord Brant, inviting them to join her cheerful censure. "I, at least, shall see to it that the news is spread sufficiently to forestall unwelcome interruptions of the two of you tonight. I am hopelessly jealous, Rhianna, and my dear Amgor is too devoted to his other duties to be able to comfort me." Amgor essayed a denial, but Yldana waved away his protestations. "It is quite all right, Amgor. I understand that Amlach and Serii must take precedence over your silly wife's fancies. I am sure that Lord Arineuil will take pity on a poor, respectable matron and accompany her in a waltz."

Ineuil had been watching me with peculiar abstraction, but he answered Yldana quickly and brightly. "If the other matrons of Serii looked like you, Yldana, the incidents of marital infidelity would diminish by half. Or perhaps they would double. It rather depends on one's perspective. You have considerable experience in infidelity, Grisk. What do you think?"

Grisk had begun to seethe anew, but a look from his father stopped his nearly violent response. "The opinion of a dandy who can forget his family's murder does not merit notice, Grisk," stated Lord Brant with contempt.

Ineuil's facile grin hardened, but he spoke almost merrily. "You would have me call out the Infortiare? A fascinating notion, Lord Brant. If I won, I should hang for treason. But why should I allow that eventuality to concern me, since I assuredly would not win?"

"There is such a thing as family honor," pronounced my father coldly.

Ineuil's arm tightened around Yldana. I marveled

anew at my sister's infallible ability to avoid censure; had I stood as near Ineuil as she did before our father's face, I would have paid for the impropriety for many months. Ineuil murmured, "I am sorry to disappoint you, gentlemen, but suicide holds no appeal for me. If the matter of Ven's honor concerns you so deeply, I should be delighted to relinquish the privilege of vengeance to you."

"Please excuse us, Lord Baerod," said Grisk, ignoring Ineuil with an effort. "Rhianna will dance with me now."

My father and Lord Brant nodded in joint approval, stiffly disregarding Ineuil's taunt as deliberately as Grisk had. Ineuil shrugged, grinned at me crookedly, and took Yldana's arm to lead her to the floor of the ballroom. I followed unwillingly with Lord Grisk.

I did thereafter achieve better opportunity to observe the king's ballroom than I had in the press at the entrance. Tiered crystal crowns of candles hung from a high vaulted ceiling set with golden mosaic, and the walls mirrored the flames to infinity. The gilded royal dais loomed dimly at the far end of the polished floor of ebony-dark marble. A colonnade of alabaster lined the length of the hall; beyond it the moon glinted on fountains of diamond and light. The patrons of the gala clustered and whirled like bright butterflies.

That which had appeared to be a chaotic throng displayed on closer inspection the full, segregated structure of Seriin snobberies and suballiances. No First House member associated with the lesser ranks of nobles, and the Houses of Liin and Sandoral were gathered nearest to the royal family. I could see Lord Borgor speaking to Queen Alamai. A beautiful titian-haired woman laughed with King Astorn. Better matched to the king than to the plain and portly Borgor, the woman fulfilled Ezirae's most glowing descriptions of the Lady Veiga dur Liin duri Sandoral. Another man joined them, and his chilling resemblance to Lord Hrgh snatched at my throat in a constricting grasp. Then I realized that the man was Hrgh's brother, Lord

Gorng Dolr'han, heir to Liin since Lord Hrgh's abdication.

My father stood glumly sour, arrogantly upright. He defied the general gaiety to affect him or those he ruled; Grisk at least spared me that sorry company. I later saw my father sequestered in a curtained alcove with Brant, Amgor and an oily little man in barbaric garb whom I took to be Arku Ruy of Caruil. I only glimpsed them, but the Caruillan unsettled me; I realized that he exuded a low aura of sorcerous Power. On consideration, the revelation was not extraordinary. Minor sorcerers were not so very uncommon. I watched the man, however, as best I could without revealing my interest to Grisk, and I regretted my inability to hear the conversation which transpired in the alcove. After a few minutes a pass of the dance revealed the alcove empty. Arku Ruy and the representatives of my extended family had left, and I did not espy any of them again that evening.

I was left with the inauspicious prospect of an entire evening of Grisk's dismal anecdotes and crude innuendo. I glimpsed Liya and Dayn occasionally, but they were completely engrossed in one another. Arm firmly entwined with Ineuil's, Yldana apparently fulfilled her intent to dispense news of my supposed betrothal, discouraging any possible savior. I saw her whisper confidingly to many; those few who missed or disregarded the warning drew no nearer than the reach of Grisk's threatening glare.

After more than an hour of incessant dancing, I began to despair that Lord Grisk would ever release me. I had lost any hope in the courage of my supposedly enamored swains. Ineuil had not again approached; Yldana occupied his full interest. Grisk persistently drew me closer, and the reek of stale liquor banished any lingering illusion of Niveallan gentility. I bore his touch by a mental withdrawal which left him partnered with a witless mannequin. My inattention passed unnoticed amid his tales of hunting's bloody fervor, with which recounted escapades he apparently thought to impress me.

I actually sighed aloud with relief when Grisk edged me toward the colonnade and freed me from the dance. I paid little heed to where he led me, glad only to escape from the noise and chaos inside, until we reached an untenanted portico near the rugged bones of Tul mountain, which the castle abutted. The enclosed passage from the king's castle to Ceallagh's Tower gaped and shimmered at the end of the walkway we trod.

I mustered my voice with difficulty. "I think we ought to return to the ballroom, my Lord Grisk. This is not a fit place for light conversation." I could feel the power of the Tower's shielded entry, and I could feel the greater Power beyond it. I blinked rapidly; tongues of fire crossed my vision.

"It is not for conversation that I brought you here, Rhianna," sneered Grisk. "As we are to be married, it is fitting that you learn to please me. I have given you the mincing dances you women enjoy. Now the night is mine to dictate."

I pulled my eyes from the Tower entrance to this new danger. "I am not yours to command, Grisk," I answered hotly.

"You must learn first to drop these pretenses, Rhianna. You are not so innocent as to have withheld your favors from Arineuil."

"You are an unbelievable fool, Grisk," I said in disgust.

Grisk gripped me, and he was strong. I tried to pull away; he shook me viciously. I clenched my teeth, but with each jarring impact, the sight of Grisk's unwholesome gloat mingled more ineluctably with my fiery nightmares. The scream I tried to suppress tore with fire from my mind.

Chapter 7

Varina's stone throbbed achingly cool against my breast. Ten paces from where I stood, Lord Grisk struggled to rise from the tiled flooring. A lengthy shadow stretched across him.

Grisk cursed profusely; blood trickled from his mouth. His most civilized words amounted to, "Bastard son of a whore—Venkarel, you will regret this."

"You are scarcely in a position to cast either threats or aspersions, Lord Grisk. You have intruded upon His Majesty's private quarters." The precise voice of the Infortiare, my erstwhile Venture Leader, rang scornfully against the cold stone.

Grisk regained his feet inelegantly. He tugged his coat into sorry order; it had been ripped in his fall. He glared. "Come with me, Rhianna," he demanded with confident disdain.

"Lady Rhianna will remain," countered Lord Venkarel calmly.

Grisk snarled, "Do you expect me to leave my betrothed wife with *you?*"

Musingly, Lord Venkarel said, "You really are a detestable slug, Grisk. I strongly recommend that you leave my sight before my regret at sparing you mounts further."

Fear wrestled visibly with arrogance, and Grisk wisely reconsidered the danger of arguing with the Infortiare. The Infortiare began to walk toward the lord of Niveal; Grisk scurried into the dark without another glance at me, running with panic's haste not to the ballroom but into the shadowy gardens. I closed my eyes to stifle the nausea roiling within me.

When my eyes reopened, the view I faced had drastically altered. Before me curved a wall: the lower half was paneled in polished burl, the upper portion paned in exceptionally clear glass, beyond which the dark expanse of Tulea spread a flickering tapestry to the lower valleys and the sea beyond. To my left and slightly downward, the castle shone with candle glow, and the lilt of distant music could be heard. It occurred to me that I was developing a habit of leaving court functions abruptly. I shifted in the chair of well-worn fleece.

The wall opposite the windows stretched straight between a pair of heavy wooden doors. Books lined the wall entirely; as the room was large, the number of volumes was considerable, and many were fragile tomes of great antiquity. What furniture the room boasted showed the craftsmanship of quality worn smooth and haggard through an age of usage. Motley manuscripts, maps and missives were strewn on every desk and table and on every chair save two.

The chair which my Lord Venkarel occupied appeared to have once matched the one in which I sat, but a haphazard application of velvet to its upholstered parts had defaced it. The sorry chairs struck me as inordinately mundane and unimpressive attributes to Ceallagh's Tower. History surrounded me, but it was tired.

"Do you often dissuade unwelcome suitors by attempting murder, Lady Rhianna?' asked Kaedric sardonically. Legs stretched before him, he lounged at ease, as remote as he had been in the Anxian tavern.

"I attempted nothing of the sort," I protested indignantly. My head wanted to crack into a score of splinters.

"You not only attempted it, you very nearly succeeded." Blue eyes narrowed. "I expected the wretched Grisk to attribute the attack to me, but you should be capable of distinguishing your own handiwork."

"Thank you for your intervention," I murmured ungraciously, belatedly adding, "my lord." I had forgotten how coldly he attacked, whether with Power or word. The Taormin had distorted my perspective, giving me memories of the child's vulnerability, which the man had destroyed. I wished desperately that my head would clear and that Kaedric would not badger me. I had felt such a compulsion to seek him. I knew the gladness of achieving the necessary, but I could not recollect the questions which had seemed so vital. I pressed my fingers to my temples. "Why did you stop me?"

"I could hardly allow you to fling Power indiscriminately on His Majesty's doorstep, though curtailing a lovers' quarrel is a novel application of the Infortiare's authority." A trifle less harshly, he added, "I also rather suspected that you did not intend to kill."

"How should I have thought to intend the impossible?" I asked bitterly.

Kaedric considered me over tented fingers. "You blame me for the destructive turn of your Power. I seem to recall warning you repeatedly against my company for fear that something of the sort would occur. Since you patently disregarded my advice, I cannot feel excessively guilty about your current plight."

I shook my head, too weary to spar. "My lord, I wish only to learn if the change can be reversed."

"Not by any method I know."

"Then I must live with the risk of destroying those around me at any moment?"

"I trust you have more sense than that. Power can be controlled by mental discipline; you must learn the techniques."

My senses had begun to return. I smoothed my sapphire skirts, shyly feeling again the wonder which had touched me at the royal presentation: this man was the legatee of Ceallagh, the Infortiare of Serii and every land in the Alliance. I had traveled with him for many leagues, but I had not known him then. Tardily, I assumed the formal deference due the Lord Venkarel dur Ixaxis. "My lord, I shall obey such commands as you see fit to give me." I lifted my eyes to his cool regard. "But my father would never permit me Ixaxin training."

"Tyntagel has yet to secede from Serii. As it happens, my lady, I outrank your father."

"My father has many allies, my lord, and he acquiesces easily to no one."

"I recognize Lord Baerod's influence, Lady Rhianna, but I think you know that I could counter it. However, I do not intend to press the lords of Serii for the sake of your education." Blue eyes flickered. "In point: you must learn sufficient safeguards of Power; such learning must transpire without your father's knowledge. I presume you intend to remain in Tulea with your affianced husband."

I did not bother to deny commitment to Grisk. "I shall remain in Tulea as long as cause exists."

"Then I shall teach you myself."

I stiffened, unsure of my reaction. I could exercise a certain freedom within the castle enclave, so the suggestion was reasonably practical. I argued weakly, "My lord, I am unworthy of your time." The lamp flared, and the windows revealed our reflections: a frightened lady in blue silk and silver, attired for a frivolous court occasion and not a wizard's study; the man of dark adamant who watched her. The lamp grew ordinary and dim; the world beyond the glass returned.

"My lady, you preserved my life," answered Kaedric with a grim smile. "It is a dubious honor but a singular one."

"I deserve no credit for the outcome, my lord. It was a reaction not of my planning."

"Whatever your intentions may have been, you did supply the necessary margin to counter Horlach for the nonce. Horlach has awakened now and is gathering forces from every corner of the Alliance and even stirring the old troubles with Caruil, but you prevented the war from ending with the first battle."

"There was a Caruillan named Arku Ruy at the ball," I said, embarrassed by thanks I did not merit. "He was a sorcerer, but my father met with him."

Kaedric cocked his head. The Infortiare's medallion gleamed. He studied me. "Arku Ruy's Power is insignificant, but he has mastered the rudiments of disguising it more effectively than most of his ilk. With some training, my lady, your empathic capabilities should make you a most efficient monitor."

"I am not so gifted at rapport as I once was, my lord," I answered with a careful dearth of emotion. I remembered with hurt the remoteness which had restricted my level of contact with the trees of the King's gardens.

"And I am more so. The Taormin seems to effect interesting exchanges. The polarities have shifted, while we have each gained in total Power. The ramifications would make a fascinating study." He elaborated dryly, "You surely realized that the 'contamination' was not one-sided." He paused, but I gave no response; the past had ensnared me.

"Keep the kid in your sight tonight, Pru. I have important customers coming who need my attention," warned the fat man. He pushed a very small boy at a youngish woman, insufficiently covered by a tawdry robe of yellow chintz.

"Do I look like a nanny to you, Doshk?" complained the woman peevishly.

"You work for me. You do as I say," shouted Doshk. "I paid for the boy, and I don't let go of what is mine. Which you'd best remember, Pru," he added significantly. The woman rolled her eyes at a stale but sincere threat. The boy watched the two adults from a cautious corner of the dingy room.

"I earn my way, Doshk," said the woman crossly, "And I can earn it in other quarters as well as yours." Doshk's florid features reddened, and Pru wisely recanted, "I'll keep him, but you'll pay me a full night for this, Doshk."

"Where's your charity, Pru?" sneered Doshk.

"In the sewer with yours, Doshk," snapped the woman. "You only want the boy because you couldn't have the mother."

"He'll bring good money in a few years," retorted Doshk.

"If he lives, and if he takes after Fylla. You're going head-soft, Doshk. He's a rotten risk."

"Shut up, you worthless slut," snarled Doshk. "You've not been bringing them in so fast lately. If the kid runs, it's from your pretty hide I'll take the price." He slammed the door behind him, and the thin walls shuddered.

Giving Doshk's back a rude gesture, Pru squatted inelegantly before the boy. "You won't give any trouble now, will you, Kaed?" she said assertively. "Because you'll be as sorry as your dead ma if you do." The child continued to stare blankly from his very blue eyes. Pru snorted, "You don't understand a word, do you? Well, at least you won't be telling stories about Pru's little vices." Pru withdrew a vial from her ample bodice and waved it before the child. "Doshk wouldn't much care to know I had this out of his own supply." She giggled ridiculously, as she contemplated her cleverness in stealing the drug. She reached for the boy's hand, and he pressed himself against the paint-peeled wall, unable to retreat further. Pru smiled. The boy relaxed, and Pru slapped him, grabbing him and shoving him into the room's tiny wardrobe. She locked the wardrobe door, thumped herself onto the lumpy mattress, and extracted the stopper from the vial.

The child in the closet cried very quietly.

I reached for the child who suffered, snatching back my hand as I recognized the man whom my hand had nearly touched. "We ought to begin your training immediately," said the Infortiare slowly, "But your thinking is muddled tonight. I suggest you avoid your enchanting Grisk for the moment. I shall expect you here in the morning." He rose abruptly and strode to the far door.

"My lord," I called, needing to detain him whom I wished I had never known. "My lord, I cannot command my time reliably," I whispered, a weak excuse for halting the Infortiare.

Kaedric answered with acrid irony, "I shall trust your ingenuity to overcome the obstacles of a Seriin lady's burdensome existence."

Feeling ridiculous, I interrupted his exit once more. "My lord, might you direct my return to the castle before you leave?"

"First lesson, my Lady Rhianna," he said distinctly and dangerously. "It is better to pursue your instincts than to question a wizard over nonessentials. Take any path you like, so long as you do not enter *this* door." So saying, he closed the forbidden portal behind him with resounding emphasis.

"My Lord Venkarel, you are not a gentleman," I said to myself, contemplating the room in which I found myself alone, reluctant to depart. The room bore the blurred imprint of many owners, no one most dominant, as if the current tenant had kept his own personality carefully absent. I idly perused a few of the myriad documents which covered the furnishings beside me. Most bore the angular scratches of a hasty and purposeful hand. The languages varied, and unfamiliar symbols covered several sheaves.

I turned to the nearest door, that which Kaedric had obliquely recommended. I found behind it a descending stair; I was very near the Tower's summit. I closed the door carefully and gathered my skirts above my ankles.

Two levels down I found the passage to the king's halls. The moon still dusted the loggia, but moonlight's shadows had shifted with the hour. I bypassed the obvious exit, too appalled by the prospect of returning to the ball. Another five flights of stairs: a door opened onto the lower gardens.

From the castle rang the merry laughter and dizzy whirls of music. Against my heated pulse, the cacophony pounded imperiously. I heard each whisper of night wind, each breath of grass and leaf as if it were a raucous shout. I began to run, heedless of my fragile attire. I shadowed to reach my room unseen, bolted my door, and crumpled, shaking, against the flimsy barricade. I could not say what I feared just then: the force of Kaedric, the dark, impending fury of Horlach, or the fire in my own veins. I sobbed silently, weeping in huddled despair. I fell to sleep clenched in midnight's black solitude.

Chapter 8

The lesser gray of dawn roused me. My twisted muscles ached a peevish protest, and I stretched them painfully. A hound whined in the distance, but no other creature-sound marred the stillness. The revels of the royal ball had delayed the castle's morning.

The clear, cool light revived me, and cold water restored me to some coherence. I had survived my dreaded reunion with the Lord of Ixaxis, and he had offered me, in his dauntingly impersonal manner, an anchor of hope. I put aside my tears and my rumpled silks, donned a smock of coarse cotton, and slipped down the stairs. I hastened, for my family might well question me when they arose, and they could thereby curtail my freedom to depart. My Lord Venkarel had commanded me to return in the morning; I intended to comply.

I crossed the dew-decked lawns and climbed the wooded slopes below the Tower. I opened the gate in the low stone wall which encircled the Infortiare's residence, an obstacle which I had penetrated blindly during the night. The Tower seemed to rise unbroken from the hills, polished basalt etched unnaturally straight against velvet blue and lilac mountain shadows. I could not see the windows which encircled it, nor the portal through which I had left it. I closed my eyes and reached for the door, hoping my actions were not as absurd as they seemed. My hand met the latch; the door was unlocked. I grimaced and entered the smoothly paneled circular vestibule.

I climbed the seven levels, wishing at about the third that Lord Venkarel had selected a lower floor for his study. Carved doors of intricate design hid the Tower's lower regions from view. Curiosity nearly bid me open one, though most displayed the dust of long disuse. I had been effectively granted permission the previous night, but I decided not to risk a needless offense.

The door to the study stood open. The daylight view sprawled spectacularly. Distance made orderly the teeming of Tulea's streets, and the circles and spokes of the city's planning showed clearly. To the west lay thick forests; the eastern slopes rippled in bands of ocher crags. The sea, rimmed by the cloudless sky, painted the distance dark and bright; inlets etched deep blue streaks. Intervening hills hid the nearer shores, but the isolated island of Ixaxis stood freely visible.

"From the standpoint of wizardry," greeted Kaedric without preamble, "three classes of elements exist: matter, energy and infinity. That which distinguishes wizards and sorcerers—the appellations are interchangeable for theoretical purposes—from the so-called mortals is the ability to manipulate energies as well as matter." He spoke from behind the most heavily laden desk, addressing me without raising his head from the documents before him. I whispered a sigh, recalling my legions of tutors. The latest was certainly the most daunting. "If a mortal wishes to access energy," he continued, "he must do so by material means; he strikes a flint to light a fire. A wizard handles the energy directly." The candle near his hand tossed sudden blue fire from its wick. "As the mortal uses energy, so the wizard can use infinity, but any form of indirect usage entails a degree of hazard concomitant with the magnitude of desired effect, making infinity a very intimidating tool. That is an oversimplification of a very intricate subject, but it should suffice to introduce you to Zerus." He stood and handed me a faded tome which I could barely heft. "Zerus covers the basic operations of action, conversion and commutation along with their properties and essential postulates. You may use Lord Amberle's desk: the enameled monstrosity beside the denuded plinth." He left me, withdrawing through the door I had entered, and the room felt of ghosts and not of life.

I toted the book to the indicated desk, an object of craft inordinately detailed and ghastly. It had been newly cleared; the dust drew imprints of the literary stacks now settled on the floor beside it. I brushed at the dust with my kerchief, which brightened the desk's designs but did not improve their character.

As morning strengthened into day, I studied alone in the Infortiare's library. It was my familiar life returned, and I cared little that I might be missed and less that Zerus' symbolisms and derivations seemed to offer minimal practical significance. It required no depth of wizards' lore to accept that action could affect a book or a table. That Lord Venkarel could spin fire from air appeared evident; if Master Zerus wished to call the operation "conversion" and name the result "commutation," I felt no inclination to quibble. It was more difficult to accept the mortal actions which impacted energy. The cited examples did not accord with any mortal effects I recognized, making the correlations to infinity's manipulation largely unreadable. I could, however, tolerate Master Zerus cheerfully, because he distracted me from a world quite as complex but all too real.

I returned to Tyntagel Hall just short of midday. I had assumed a substantial delay of normal activity after the night's festivities. My prediction proved well founded. I reached my room and changed to a luncheon gown before the chambermaid appeared. Yielding my room to her ministrations, I joined my family in the dining hall.

Only my Uncle Dhavod had preceded me. He greeted me solemnly, inquiring after my enjoyment of the ball with courteous disinterest. "It is perhaps unfortunate," he continued, "that the announcement of your engagement occurred so informally, but it does save considerable bother." He added more generously, "Though I suppose you women like that sort of fuss. I am sure your father will ensure you a substantial wedding ceremony. Ezirae can provide you with considerable advice on the subject. She personally supervised the weddings of each of our five daughters." I murmured a noncommittal response, having altogether forgotten Yldana's carefully fomented acknowledgment of my betrothal. My uncle and I sat in awkward silence until Liya joined us, her eyes as shiningly bright as her buttercup dress.

"Good morning, Lord Dhavod," said Liya cheerfully. "Good morning, Rhianna. Is no one else to take luncheon? But of course," she recalled, dramatically clapping her hand to her brow, "Lord Baerod is with Dayn. It is so unfair that they should have to rise early after such a lovely evening. Will Lady Ezirae join us at least?"

"Ezirae is indisposed," contributed Dhavod stiltedly. "She will take her meals in her chamber."

"The poor dear," said Liya contritely, though I could not imagine why Liya should feel apologetic over Ezirae's condition, an infallible result of the Hamley tendency to overindulge. Lord Dhavod strongly disapproved of his wife's weakness, but he had never succeeded in curtailing her habit. The result was a tacitly acknowledged family secret known throughout Tulea's social enclave.

"Rhianna, I nearly forgot," bubbled Liya suddenly. "Yldana has invited us to join her afternoon gatherings. All of her closest friends attend, even the Lady Veiga duri Sandoral. It is quite a social honor. We would have told you last night, but we could not find you." Liya's sentence trailed uncertainly at the end. More firmly, she added, "We could attend in Amlach Hall this very day. You will come?"

I looked at Liya's eager face, hating to disappoint her, but the thought of enduring Yldana's taunts weighed more heavily. "Perhaps tomorrow I shall feel more ready for witty converse," I temporized. "The excitement of the ball has quite fatigued me. Indeed, I think I shall retire to my room as soon as luncheon ends. Do you mind very much, Liya?"

She did, but she answered bravely, "Certainly not."

"You might go yourself," I tried.

"Nonsense. Court society will just have to await us a little longer."

Feeling wretchedly guilty for my lie to Liya, I locked my chamber door and left Tyntagel Hall for Ceallagh's Tower by the window of my room and a helpful elm outside it. I had stubbornly determined to master the text which Kaedric had given me, however useless its contents might seem, and my luncheon had been only an impatient interlude. I did not know how to study by half measures.

I blithely intended to regain the mood of secure unreality which had warmly enwrapped my morning, but the door to the Infortiare's study was firmly closed. I could feel Kaedric's Power beyond it, and I knocked tentatively, regretting my haste in returning. I found the Infortiare again at his desk, inspecting a document on which the ostentatious seal of Caruil showed prominently. "Your devotion to study is laudable," he remarked and continued working.

I moved slowly to the desk he had allotted to me. I opened the text of Master Zerus carefully. It was essentially a mathematical treatise, fine for distracting mind-games but insufficient to compete with the intense occupant of the room. Head bowed over the vellum on which he wrote, Kaedric frowned and impatiently brushed an errant black lock from his eyes. Memory taxed me remorselessly. I concentrated on Zerus' postulates. The page blurred; I reread it, achieving no greater understanding the second time or the third. I pressed my nails into my hands, cutting the skin. The freezing winds of Ven intensified the hurt.

"I don't pay you boys to loll," said the fat man, lending emphasis to his words with a kick at the nearest of the three children. The boys quickened their strokes, chopping the wood for the inn with frenzied energy. The innkeeper was fat and lazy but strong and quick with a blade, and the boys feared him utterly. They knew by the reek of the man's filthy tunic that he watched them still, though they dared not face him. After a critical moment, the man moved inside to escape the bitter cold.

"You don't pay us at all," muttered one boy, taller and broader than the other two. He dropped the axe into the snow with disgust. "But you'll pay me one day, Master Doshk, or greet the Ven-Lord's gallows."

"You do talk grand, Deev," mocked the red-haired boy beside him. "Are you going to tell your story to the constable personal? Or maybe you're minded to talk to the Ven-Lord himself? He'd be mighty pleased to talk with a flea-wracked piece like you."

Deev snorted and gestured rudely. "There's plenty who'd like a glimpse at Doshk's private larder."

"And I suppose Doshk is going to tell you where it is because he likes you so much," said the red-haired boy. Only the third boy, black-haired and thin to emaciation, continued to work.

"Maybe Doshk doesn't have to tell me," said Deev mysteriously.

The redhead leaped at Deev and grappled for the larger boy's throat. "You slimy beggar, if you know where it is, you'll tell me or wish you had." The redhead tightened his fingers around Deev's neck.

"All right," croaked Deev. The redhead eased his grip slightly, and Deev struck hard. The red-haired boy doubled in anguish. Deev kicked him, an unconscious imitation of Master Doshk.

"You little nothing, Ag. I'd as soon tell garbage boy there." Deev threw a heavy piece of kindling at the black-haired boy, who ducked it indifferently and persisted in hewing the wood.

The wayward stick struck a burly man just entering the inn. Cursing, he spotted the three boys at the woodpile. Deev and Ag ran behind the inn, shoving the black-haired boy to the snow in the process. The stick's angry victim grabbed the fallen boy and beat him into unconsciousness.

The impact of snow thrown into his face and a rough nudge brought the black-haired boy to his feet in practiced haste. Arms akimbo, the blubbery Doshk glared at the boy. "You're a worthless brat," said Doshk disgustedly. "I'd give you to a Caruillan slaver for an iron kesne. Your mother knew what she was about when she sold you, you lazy runt. Get back to work." Doshk hit the boy hard with the flat of a hefty knife.

Moving stiffly, the boy regained the axe he had dropped. Deev and Ag were making a great show of effort for Doshk's benefit. The black-haired boy winced as he resumed his labor; the angry man had cracked three of his ribs.

"What's the matter, Kaed?" sneered Deev, after Doshk had left. "Don't you like honest work?"

"That sailor who came today isn't going to admire those bruises, Kaed," said Ag. "You'd better cover them by tonight, or Doshk will cook you for sure."

"That's right, Kaed. You know how Doshk likes to satisfy his paying customers, and you've not been too popular anyhow since you shivved old Brodae."

The black-haired boy did not answer. He raised the axe and brought it down on the log with vicious deliberation. His blue eyes burned.

The snatch of vision hurt and embarrassed me. I suffered very personally for the boy, Kaed, but I could not equate him with the Ixaxin liege who stared at me so arrogantly. "You are not going to master the laws of wizardry by watching me, Lady Rhianna," said Kaedric coldly.

"No, my lord. With your permission, my lord, I shall take my leave now."

"That was a remarkably short lesson."

"I have recalled a conflicting appointment."

Kaedric knew that I lied, but he waved his arm

indifferently. I closed Zerus' text firmly. It would beckon me again, but escape comprised my present need. Memory's flood rebuilds old sorrow if the memory is sharp and anguished; if the memory comes newly to the mind, it has no cushion of familiarity to soften its pain. For now, I could not hold myself free of Kaed so long as Kaedric faced me. Whether it was my mood or simply fatigue, it was inexorable. A sharp rap on the door made me jump.

"Your taste in company has certainly improved, Kaedric," announced Ineuil grandly. He bowed to me, his fair hair gleaming. "Lady Rhianna, I assumed you had forsaken the realm of sorcery in favor of a more traditional role as lady of Niveal." Ineuil intoned the title with the pomposity of Lord Borgor. "You have heard, O Great Infortiare, that our fair sorceress is to be the next bride of that infamous paragon, Lord Grisk?"

Kaedric had raised his head. He fingered a slim red leather volume lettered in faded gold. He answered, "If that is all you came to tell me, Lord Arineuil, you may return the way you came."

"It is not, but I thought the tidbit interesting." Ineuil considered me thoughtfully. "I should not personally have considered Grisk a likely choice for any sorceress."

"I must be going," I murmured swiftly, still eager to escape Kaedric, more eager now to escape Ineuil's scrutiny and the chance that he would discover my infernal binding to the Infortiare. Neither man stopped me.

I did not at once return to Tyntagel Hall. I sought the garden corner farthest removed from the Tower of the Infortiare, hoping to discover some measure of the tranquility that had once been mine with my Tyntagel oaks. The touch of tree and earth did soothe me, but it could not erase the truth of what I had seen.

I could not escape my own mind, and there was a canker in it. Whether I faced the Infortiare or fled to far Ardasia, his Power would taunt me; the memories which had twisted him would follow me. The fractured images of a life not mine would continue to coalesce, filling me, until I should be in memory's darkness the murderer of Ven.

Selfishly and fervently, I rued the creation of the Taormin in that hour. I hated the Sorcerer King Horlach quite personally with a recognition of the wrong his tool had inflicted upon me. I rubbed Varina's stone and hated the pain he had given that lady's world. I thought of Hamar and Lord Hrgh Dolr'han and the miserable dead-alive creatures who still guarded the castle of their ancient tormentor: victims, along with many others whose names in the history tomes had never greatly affected me. I railed against fate's instruments: Lord Brant, Lord Grisk, and my liege-father who had driven me to a desperate decision in a tavern in Anx. Perhaps I was unjustly bitter, but I was growing to doubt my ability to survive Kaedric's resurging past.

By eventide, I had grown calmer. I could not alter that which had been done; anger bought me nothing. My father had not sent me to Anx. Lord Grisk had not forced me to a mad attempt at healing the Infortiare of Serii. If any cure for my sorcerous ailment could be derived, it was the Infortiare who must lead me to it. I would return to Zerus, because the alternative was madness.

Chapter 9

My days assumed a pattern, and the mastery of the wizardry I had previously shunned grew to occupy my mind if not my heart. I had become slightly less apprehensive around Kaedric, for I had experienced no recurrence of involuntary, empathic memory. In truth, I saw him seldom, considering how many hours I spent in his library; the king and the cares of Serii occupied him, taking him beyond the Tower confines. Never did he fail, however, to anticipate my need for further materials to study.

History lessons had joined the theoretical material, and the history taught by Ixaxis did not always agree with the legends I had learned in Tyntagel. The practice of wizardry I still regarded with ambivalence, but I could no longer question the superiority of Ixaxin scholarship. Their histories, their philosophies formed cohesive wholes. Most important, Ixaxis remembered.

I had mastered the symbolic machinations of Zerus by forcing my mind along new pathways of thought and perception. After several texts of a similiar nature, the strange mode of thought which they promoted no longer seemed so unnatural, but I tried to curtail its intrusion into my other life. My mind kept a precarious balance. Even my vaguely projected wedding, which only I considered less than inevitable, demanded little of my time. Having presumably assured himself of his bride, Grisk appeared content to defer the marriage for as long as Lord Brant would condone. Grisk cited frequent business in Sandoral, but I privately considered the cause to be a combination of pride still pained by sorcerous encounter, the obvious ebb of Lord Arineuil's attentions to me, and the rumored addition of a comely young parlormaid to the staff of Niveal Hall.

I was uneasy but too occupied to be ill-content. It was Liya whom I began to pity, for she had not ceased to seek the rarefied social sphere of her imagination. It did not exist; the castle inhabitants were men and women, as good or bad as any others. Liya had coerced me to attend a very few of Yldana's afternoon confabulations, and each had bored me to distraction.

"Worm-silk lasts to a tedium, Ritsa."

"But sea-silk simply will not take the range of colors."

"*I* could never want for any hue more pure than sea-silk's natural gold."

"I found the most perfect lavender silk the other day."

I could not comprehend how the noblewomen of Serii could devote so much time to debating the relative merits of silk from a worm or a mollusk. The other conversations to which I had marginally attended lacked any greater substance. I had come to Yldana's little gathering to appease Liya, who was animatedly expounding about lacquerwork dolls to a portly lady of Esmar. Yldana was displaying her latest gem acquisitions, and I was endeavoring to find a quiet corner in which to retreat.

I sidled through the clusters of shrill gossipers toward the salon's ornate doors and the library beyond them. I blessed the silence as I slipped through the doors, but I was not the first to escape. The woman at the library window stood motionless and remote. She was exquisitely gowned, and rubies coiled in her titian hair. She turned suddenly, and she was as beautiful as my sister, but her manner was icy cold.

"Even the library is crowded," she remarked caustically.

"I did not intend to interrupt your privacy, my lady," I returned, appalled by her rudeness. "My sister's guests seldom frequent the library."

A faint smile curled her lips. "So you are Yldana's little sister," she murmured. "The sorceress' child."

I recognized the oddness about her then: she has Power, I thought with shock, and she knows the use of it. "I did not realize that my sister included wizardesses among her acquaintances."

"I am not an Ixaxin," retorted the woman with cutting disdain. "A Dolr'han does not bow to a Venkarel. A Venkarel serves only to amuse us."

Her attitude frightened me, recalling to me the calamity which her brother's arrogance had wrought. "I meant no offense, Lady Veiga," I said with all the contrition I could feign.

"You are merely inept, then. How common." She left without further comment. I could hear my sister greet her with an enthusiasm undiminished by Lady

Veiga's haughty responses. I could not remember ever meeting a woman I liked less than the Lady Veiga dur Liin duri Sandoral, though she did fulfill Ezirae's ebullient descriptions of elite, sophisticated perfection. Despite the prestige and influence of Lady Veiga's heritage, I could not comprehend her popularity among court circles, unless it was her Power which gained it. Lady Veiga had the Power of a wizardess—I had begun to appreciate the distinctions by which Ixaxins measured their fellows—but her Power was difficult to perceive clearly. Even Ineuil, who was otherwise so well-informed, seemed unaware that Veiga shared her brother's ability. I wondered how Lady Veiga had come to befriend my sister, a lady merely of Tyntagel and Amlach, and I remembered with peculiar distaste Ineuil's linking of Lady Veiga with the Infortiare. I began to develop an unwise curiosity about the sister of Lord Hrgh Dolr'han, but it was days before I humored it.

"You are late today, Lady Rhianna," said the Infortiare as I entered.

I had slowed at sight of him, though I had run much of the way from Tyntagel Hall. "I was detained, my lord. My family begins to wonder why I am so often absent of late."

"Does your Niveallan lord suspect you of illicit trysts?" asked Kaedric with crisp sarcasm.

"Lord Grisk has been much away from Tulea," I answered stiffly. "My kindred are concerned lest I disappear from them as I once did."

"That would be notably difficult from the king's castle without recourse to your Power, which your family denies exists."

"That is why I have been allowed such unprecedented freedom, my lord. My family believes that my time is spent in the king's gardens, and they consider me both well betrothed and well guarded against departure."

He answered acidly, "Then you should have no difficulty in attending your studies promptly."

"They still question me, my lord," I retorted defensively.

"Discourage their questions. You have sufficient Power."

"I am not accustomed to the use of Power as a weapon, my lord," I said sharply. I lamented the words as I spoke them.

"As I am?" asked Kaedric with biting precision. "The Infortiare does not attack without provocation, my lady, nor does he otherwise defy Ceallagh's laws. I suggest you reread those laws if you cannot recognize the difference between 'discouragement' and 'aggression.' "

"Yes, my lord," I answered meekly.

"Lady Rhianna, I distrust you most when you are so dutifully humble and compliant. You have honed that particular illusion too well."

I regarded him with genuine surprise, but I flushed before his mocking gaze. "Perhaps you would prefer that I emulate Dolr'han hauteur, my lord," I said.

"It would not suit you, and it would be equally transparent."

"A Dolr'han's qualities *are* doubtless too rarefied for a lowly lady of Tyntagel," I returned.

"As I am only a Venkarel," responded Kaedric in like tone, "I am doubtless too inferior to appreciate either noble species."

"Including the Lady Veiga? She has Power."

"Veiga prefers to turn her talents in other directions than wizardry." He blocked me from a rush of his recollections before I could even see their general form. He cannot prevent my sharing his memories of Ven any more than I can, I thought wonderingly, but Ixaxis is shielded from me save for fleeting and irrelevant images.

"I am pleased to know that a choice is given to some," I said tartly.

"But not to us, my lady." I regretted my sharpness for that instant of unexpected sympathy, but he proceeded with irritatingly obscure irony. "I doubt, in any event, that you share Veiga's tastes. What prompts this sudden interest in Veiga Dolr'han?"

"She is my sister's friend," I answered diffidently.

"Do all of your sister's friends incur such fascination on your part?"

"No, my lord," His ice-blue eyes had narrowed. He distrusts me, I realized with shock; he tests me for motives and schemes against him. What does he think I could possibly do that he could not easily counter?

"My lord," I began, trying to convey something of my curiosity's motives, because I loathed being suspected unjustly. "I never truly met Lord Hrgh Dolr'han. I thought his sister might be like him."

Kaedric nodded very slightly, a grudging admission that my explanation was tenable. He answered me with deliberation, "Veiga is more ambitious and possibly more intelligent than Hrgh, but she has less Power. Veiga allowed Ixaxis to bind her Power a number of years ago, when she opted for the mortal path and Lord Borgor."

"How could she be more ambitious than a brother who would steal the Taormin?"

"Hrgh's bane was arrogance. He believed he could master the Taormin, and that belief opened him to Horlach's influence. Hrgh would not have awakened Horlach intentionally."

"Whereas Lady Veiga would have done so deliberately?" I asked incredulously.

"In like circumstances, presuming the perfect Power which Hrgh believed himself to possess, Veiga would use any means to further her personal goals—including the awakening of Horlach." He spoke with detachment, but he measured his words carefully.

"You state your suppositions, my lord, with great assurance. You must know the Dolr'hans well." I felt cautiously for his reaction.

"My own history will not further enlighten you regarding Lord Hrgh Dolr'han. I suggest you resume your studies and permit me to continue mine." He spoke to me no more, and I did not try to question him again that day, but several times I found him observing me as I read. It was an expressionless regard which I could not fathom, for he had retreated entirely from my mind's awareness. He understands only distrust, I thought, because he has never himself been trusted. But how could anyone trust such Power as his?

Chapter 10

"Rhianna!" called Liya, excitedly waving a sea-tossed find for my inspection. With her skirts tied above her knees and her hair flying free, Liya looked no older than Ziva and Flava. The three of them ran across the sand with bubbling laughter, daring the waves to catch them. Liya paused to steal another shell from the churning water; she raced to regain the dry dunes before the waves could drench her.

I had resisted the outing, grudging a day of idle shopping and meaningless chatter. Protests disregarded, I had been summarily sent forth with Ezirae, Liya, Ziva and Flava. We had indeed passed most of the day in pursuits as tedious as I had anticipated; lengthy discussions with sea-silk purveyors over the weave suitable for my bridal gown struck me as singularly fatuous, since I privately intended that no marriage would occur. Our day's excursion had led us, however, to the edge of Tulea, and the young Hamley sisters had pressed for permission to visit the shore. Ezirae had clucked about the encroachment of twilight, but Liya's added blandishments had overcome objections.

I had seldom visited the sea, and I had never before trod the warmth-washed southern beaches. The inlet which approaches Tulea is largely protected, and the waves which reach that far lose most of their force and majesty in the effort. We none of us minded the lack. Even Ezirae removed her stockings and stepped a few gingerly paces across the sand. Liya and the giggling sisters explored the length of the cove, discovering caves and corners with the supreme delight of innocence. I laughed with them, but though I did not, like Ezirae, sit sedately on the safer heights, I could not find the freedom of joy which the young trio showed. I lingered near the water's edge, gazed at the glimmering sea, and studied the distant island in its midst.

Ixaxis did not draw me. The force which held me to the wizards' path dwelt not on that island. I could feel Ixaxis, nonetheless, through its shields of strength more formidable than its looming cliffs. I could visualize the path which climbed to the school itself. I could see the columned buildings and the twisted pines which, clinging to precipitous rock, gave shelter from the cutting winds. I could see the gray-robed students, the scholars in white and gold, members all of a guild whose origins stretched back to time's beginning. By its own accounts, the Ixaxin guild predated the rise of sorcery, stemming from a time of magics more remote from my concepts than the wizardry of the Infortiare. Those very ancient histories bewildered me more than any feat of a Sorcerer King. The records of Ixaxis, though more complete than any others, acknowledged their own inadequacy regarding the lives and events predating the rise of Horlach.

The people of that early time, having attained both plenty and leisure, had refined all energies into the single goal of personal longevity. Some experimenter finally derived a successful means of prolonging life, but the price of the gift was sanity. The first "Immortals" were destroyed, for they were murderous in their violent outbursts. Those few who proved controllable were confined and allowed to exist for the purpose of further experiments. By the time the creators of these aberrations realized the extent of the change which had been wrought, the Immortals had used their new Power to effect escape.

Naming themselves Sorcerers, the immortals destroyed the civilization which had reared them and began to remold the world to their own liking. They bred and raised children to take from the world as they pleased. They fought among themselves, and many died violently whom the passing years could not otherwise touch.

Of the first Immortals, none survived to verify their natural longevity. Rhianna of Dwaelin was believed to be of the third generation. Horlach may have been son or grandson of the first; his lifespan appeared never to have been matched or fully measured, but he had exerted absolute rule for at least ten millennia. He destroyed his most potent foes, thus weakening the Immortal strain. The blood of mortals further diluted the sorcerous gifts over generations, but the loss brought forth the tempering of sorcery with compassion.

After ages of sorcerous reign, many of the Immortals' heirs still sought their kingdoms of tyranny, but some began to seek a restoration of justice and knowledge. Those few began to gather at Ixaxis, an isolated school which had preserved some meager part of presorcerous lore by maintaining a constant aura of insignificance. This final bastion of mortal science became the womb from which formalized wizardry was born.

It was a quelling thought: much of the world I knew had been molded by lunacy. The heir of Power was the heir of madness. The scions of Power stood sentinel against themselves.

I heard Ezirae call a reminder of the passing time. Liya returned reluctantly with Ziva and Flava. We restored our skirts and our hair to a reasonably presentable state, but a trail of sand and our dangling slippers betrayed us. Master Stev, the coachman, resumed his post lazily; the footman helped us into the carriage with a somewhat scandalized air.

We bounced over rough roads for some miles, the road smoothing only as we regained more civilized routes. We were admiring Liya's trove of flotsam and a fisherman's float found by Flava, when the carriage jerked and then settled askew. Ezirae fainted with a melodramatic flair. Ziva and Flava promptly began to scream.

"Hush, sillies," chided Liya. "We have only tilted into a ditch. Rhianna, can you see what has happened?" I left to Liya the unenviable task of calming the Hamley contingent, while I clambered from the vehicle.

"There has been an accident, my lady," apologized the footman, a burly fellow who seemed overly mature for his occupation.

"Obviously," I answered dryly. The left front wheel of the carriage had half vanished in thick mud at the road's edge. Master Stev was staring at it as if it might at any moment leap free of its own accord. "I assume, Master Stev, that you would like the carriage emptied so as to clear the wheel," I prompted. "We would like to reach the castle before nightfall."

Master Stev pursed his thin lips and shook his head slowly. He looked at the wide road, the horses and the carriage wheel. He straightened his hat, and I thought I would shake him if he did not speak soon. Just as my patience was failing me completely, Master Stev decided to answer me. "There is an inn just beyond the far hedge, my lady. We cannot leave before morning."

"Master Stev, if you require assistance from the inn, by all means obtain it. The suggestion of remaining here until morning is not at all satisfactory."

"It is a very pleasant inn, my lady," offered the footman helpfully.

"It may be a veritable palace, but I have no intention of staying there because of a misguided carriage. A wheel in the mud cannot be so complicated as to require more than an hour's effort. Place a plank beneath the wheel and let the horses draw us free," I concluded in exasperation.

Liya asked from the coach, "What is the trouble, Rhianna?" Disgusted by Master Stev and his cohort, I stalked to the side of the carriage from which Liya leaned. Irritably, I said to her, "Master Stev seems determined to afflict us with a night at the local inn, an establishment most probably operated by his relatives, judging by his insistence."

"Is the carriage damaged?" asked Ezirae, who had revived on her own when sympathy was not forthcoming.

"Not a whit," I returned. "I find it incredibly convenient for our previously competent driver that the one intractable ditch in Serii should coincide with such a well-favored inn."

"Rhianna, you are too suspicious," rebuked Liya mildly. "We are not in such a hurry. A country inn might make for a very pleasant evening. Your father even suggested that we stay away for the night. It really is rather exciting."

"It really is too thrilling," said Flava in a poor imitation of Liya's enthusiastic style. Ziva tossed her braids and forgot her hysteria with a giggle. Outnumbered again, I abandoned any further objections. I could hardly admit that the return for which I chafed was to Ceallagh's Tower and not to Tyntagel Hall.

The inn was indeed a pleasant establishment, clean and prosperous and well-trafficked. The innkeeper welcomed us, and his effusive wife cooed with all the sympathy even Ezirae could desire. They managed to find three choice rooms for us and a space in the rear for our servants. Had I been the affluent merchant turned away for lack of quarters just as we arrived, I should have protested the injustice heartily. I made no mention of my observation that our arrival seemed to have been anticipated, deeming further protest pointless.

"Just wait until you see the new bonnet Stev bought me, Ylath," said Inda proudly. The second floor chambermaid of Tyntagel Hall had few opportunities to boast to her third floor counterpart. Ylath was well wed, and Inda still waited for Stev to decide himself.

"It cannot have cost more than a copper kelne if Stev gave it to you," retorted Ylath with a disparaging wag of her white-capped head. "He has not had more than that in his pocket since his old ma quit keeping him away from the taverns."

Inda preened and crowed, "It happens Stev did a bit of service for His Lordship lately. His Lordship can be very generous when he has a mind."

A skeptical Ylath laughed. "What could Stev do that His Lordship much cares about?"

Inda answered mysteriously, "That, Mistress Ylath, is none of your concern!"

Chapter 11

I wandered in the garden near the walls of Tul a moon after the protracted shopping excursion. A queer, nostalgic notion had bidden me don an approximation of my old travel garb and imagine myself again the hopeful suppliant of the Dwaelin Wood. Of late I had grown too far apart from my old friends due to more than my changed Power. I still could not merge with them as once I had, but I no longer minded so keenly that slim distinction. I could speak to them still and heal their sorrows. I coaxed a sapling to survive that afternoon, and the effort gladdened my own heart as well.

When first I heard the woman calling, I was too far removed from human speech to understand her. Her persistence led me finally to focus on her words. "Your Royal Highness," she cried plaintively. "You must present yourself before the Caruillan emissary. Your Royal Highness!"

I let my awareness explore, and I followed it to a tangled thicket. "You are being summoned, Your Royal Highness," I whispered to the princess hidden in its midst.

I heard a startled rustle. "Lady Rhianna? Please do not tell her where I am," pleaded Princess Joli. "Caruillans always remind me of bloated spiders, and they are worse now that Liin and Sandoral have supported their suit to join the Alliance. I will not smile and simper for another one of them."

The approach of the governess silenced Joli. Espying me, the harried woman began, "Have you seen. . . ." I might have revealed the errant princess if the question had been completed. The governess, however, assessed my unprepossessing attire, categorized me, and assumed a pompous manner. "Her Royal Highness may be in this vicinity. You will search for her," she demanded firmly.

The governess' self-important manners irritated me. Even if I had been the servant for whom she mistook me, I should have expected some element of courtesy. I drew on my loftiest demeanor as I retorted, "Mistress, if Her Royal Highness were nearby, she would undoubtedly censure your insolence. Your incompetence in assuring Her Royal Highness' familiarity with significant appointments is solely your responsibility to remedy. Your arrogance offends me."

I evidently spoke to better effect than I anticipated. Quite deflated, the governess mouthed a servile, "Forgive me, my lady. I did not recognize you. I was distraught." She fussed nervously and hastily retreated toward the castle with another muttered apology.

The princess' voice rose again from the thicket when the governess had gone. "Lady Rhianna, that was wonderful," Her Royal Highness whispered. "I knew that you would not betray me."

"Your Royal Highness, I shall remain pleased to have aided you if you justify my trust by appearing before the Caruillan emissary. However much you may dislike Caruillans, you can hardly avoid official functions on the basis of prejudice." I filled the final word with distaste, feeling somewhat hypocritical, since my own uncharitable feelings toward the people of Caruil were largely unsupported by personal encounter. I had known only one Caruillan, a bitter warrior-Venturer who had been unpleasant but not without honor.

"I do not trust Arku Ruy," sulked Joli.

"Your distrust may serve Serii," I answered impulsively.

The thicket rustled, and a tousled head appeared. "I could help if anyone would listen to me," said Princess Joli seriously.

"Then prove yourself. Accept the responsibilities of your position. Show that you are the heiress of Tul, who alone of mortals dared join Ceallagh against King Horlach."

Princess Joli neither moved nor spoke. I scarcely breathed, sensing great import in the moment. A bird warbled evensong.

The princess cocked her head and grinned impishly. "Mistress Amila will look foolish when I appear of my own accord," she said with ungenerous relish.

"I suppose she might," I responded. Assuming Mistress Amila to be the haughty governess, I could not help but sympathize with Joli's observation. I made a poor oracle of advice on duty and decorum.

In her hasty fashion, Princess Joli dashed to her father's castle. Disproportionately pleased with myself, I curtseyed to the thicket. "I think we have done well, my friend," I said and made my own way toward the castle.

On my return to Tyntagel Hall, I found Liya seeking me urgently. "Thank goodness. I thought you had vanished from the earth," she spewed in a breathless rush. "We are due at Amlach Hall within the hour."

"What social obligation besets us now?" I responded with no more anticipatory delight than Princess Joli had given to her Caruillan encounter.

"We are to spend the night as Yldana's guests."

"That is a cause for urgency?" I asked with a laugh.

"Your father ordered it, Rhianna," answered Liya, and my sister-in-law finally conveyed to me her sincere distress.

"Liya, what troubles you? Yldana's hospitality is not that grim."

"You and I are to stay with Yldana," said Liya with a threatening tear. "Ezirae has gone to Hamley Hall. That is all we need to know."

"Are those Dayn's words?"

"Yes," she returned as the tear fell. "It is only for a night."

Any quarrel with Dayn could set Liya crying, but a sudden coincidence struck me. "It was only a day's outing a month ago. Liya, in what have my father and Dayn become involved?"

"Rhianna, I vow I do not know anything about it. Please hurry."

"It pertains to the Caruillan to whom they spoke at the ball," I prompted unmercifully.

"Caruil wants to join the Alliance. It is natural that the emissary should speak to the members of a First House."

"In a secretive manner which upsets you so visibly?"

"I never learned to hide my feelings like you Tyntagellians," said Liya with a depth of bitterness that silenced me.

Ezirae entered propitiously, bubbling with delight at the prospect of a night amid her comfortable Hamley kin. Her chatter hid the stilted coolness of those of us doomed to an occasion of less blissful camaraderie. Liya's mood seemed likely to alienate any scion of Lord Baerod's House, and Yldana and I had never savored one another's company.

With Yldana, Liya and I spent an uncomfortable evening dwarfed by the exaggerated formality of Amlach Hall's ornate decor. Yldana may have even regretted the petty snobbery for the sake of which she and Amgor had segregated their portion of Amlach Hall from that of Amgor's score of cousins. Subdued by our solemnity, Yldana toyed idly with her supper. Liya might have been ages absent. Without even Amgor's attendance, the enjoyment of baiting me offered insufficient enticement to Yldana's denigrating wit. We three who ought to have shared the camaraderie of sisters found only discomfiture in common. I was least betrayed by fate, for I could find the joy in loneliness as well as the torture.

With the clearing of the last trace of the barely sampled meal, we ceased to feign the fondness of familial friends. Liya withdrew to the room allotted her. Yldana took to her own lavish chambers. I sought the Amlach library, though my memory linked it unpleasantly with the Lady Veiga Dolr'han.

The clan of Amlach took little stock in literary pursuits, and I had never been in accord with Yldana's taste for novels about exaggeratedly impassioned females. I selected a nonsensical romance of more promise than the bulk, but it proved too predictably mindless for distraction. After an hour of struggling, I yielded with a sigh of resignation to my dangerous curiosity. Shadowed against servants' eyes, I left the Amlach library for the dappled starlight and the ward of Tyntagel Hall.

The lawns were damply cold and soaked my slippers. I thought myself into a measure of warmth as I watched my father's Hall. I was not alone in surreptitious nocturnal wanderings. Cloaked and quiet figures converged, very gradually, very naturally. Only a steady, careful observation combined with preconceived suspicions would have questioned the influx. I observed Lord Brant with Grisk arrive openly; they were customary visitors. Others whom I could not identify were muffled and tended toward the lee of shrub and wall. The waddling strut of Lord Borgor betrayed him; I followed the king's adjutant, Lady Veiga's influential husband, into my father's assembly room.

I never learn the value of ignorance; I could have wished to witness less that night. It was Lord Borgor who nominally led them, these conspirators from every major House of Serii. I saw my father and Dayn, Dhavod and Amgor, Brant, Egar and Grisk: they heeded the words of Borgor; they lauded the Caruillan, Arku Ruy, who spoke fervently against the influence of Ixaxis. Arku Ruy curried favor for Caruil by denouncing the Ixaxins as the sole cause of Cariul's exclusion from the Alliance. He omitted any mention of Caruil's lawless approach to sorcery as the original source of the rift; Caruil had provided a haven to every renegade, sorcerous or otherwise, for uncounted years. Dayn, at least, ought to have recalled Caruil's history as well as I; we had learned it from the same stern tutor.

I winced at Arku Ruy's slippery platitudes and the murmurs of approval rising from the honorable lords of Serii. "As you know," said the Caruillan, "King Astorn has taken our plea into serious consideration. Hours ago, His Majesty informed me that he may soon undertake a journey to Bethii to discuss the matter with Queen Marylne and the other rulers of the Alliance. King Cor regards this as an auspicious sign for the unity of our peoples, but my king is concerned, as I am, that the Infortiare will not accept a decision in our favor. We must be vigilant in our defense against treachery. The time of proof against Ixaxis comes, and our long efforts will be vindicated!"

Cheers of fanatical zeal chorused his emotional words. Lord Borgor stilled the crowd with tolerant patience and proceeded to recite the chronicle of traitorous conspiracy. "An unfortunate lapse on the part of our Pithliin operative has been referred to Lord Morgh dur Liin for amendment. Lord Morgh assures us that the Ixaxin representative in Pithlii will be successfully eliminated by month's end.

"Regarding the Ixaxin agent discovered in Coru: it has become apparent that an elderly woman witnessed the execution and was permitted to survive on the basis of her age, gender and social insignificance. The situation is an expensive reminder of the folly of maudlin self-indulgence in a cause as dangerously vital as our own. The alcoholic drudge proved to be an englamored wizardess working with the dead agent. It became necessary to dispose of our own hireling so as to protect our operation against discovery. We cannot afford such incidents! The Infortiare is a cunning foe, who will use our every weakness. If we are to remove the evil canker from our society, we must proceed with caution and intelligence—and as little mercy as the Infortiare himself would show.

"A personal note: Arku Ruy informs us that King Cor recently welcomed to his court Lord Hrgh Dolr'han. I am sure that many of you join me in rejoicing at this news. We have all been deeply concerned for the worthy young man who first awakened us to that dangerous villain in our midst, the wizard who calls himself Lord Venkarel. Lord Hrgh is still troubled by the realization of Ixaxin duplicity, but he is well and establishing himself rapidly in Caruil as a man of influence and sound judgment."

I could not listen to further insanities. I moved to depart, thinking to exit through my father's office rather than the now-crowded portal by which I had entered. My mind turned toward my goal, and I felt the darkness.

It was the full burning pain of memory which I had thought vanquished by the gentle peace of Benthen Abbey. Serpents writhed in bleeding ribbons across my mind, opened charred fissures which my thoughts could not traverse. Careful walls of Ixaxin discipline, which I had not consciously realized I had built, crumbled helplessly, but recognition of the toppling barriers anchored my escape.

I coiled within a deep recess where oak trees grew and sunlight brushed the age from weathered stone. I breathed of a sculptor's love for his lady lost in a nacreous whorl. I recited Zerus' symbolic litanies, and I held to the image of a man of black hair and eyes of ice who had carried me from the flames once before.

The fire retreated to a waiting, deadly ember of dark menace. It searched for me still, hidden from my sight by the door of my father's office. The crowd at the outer door no longer daunted me. I brushed aside the blind fools of Seriin noblesse, eluding their notice with a thought. King Astorn himself could not have stopped my flight from the shade of the Sorcerer King.

I inhaled deeply of the garden's chill air, gratefully absorbing autumnal cold until I ached and shivered. I strove to expel all trace of the malignance which hovered unbearably near. I did not know the form it currently wore, but I knew that it and not Lord Borgor led the mad conspiracy. I was tormented by the knowledge that the illusory break from sorcerous dominance would be led by Horlach, the deathless Sorcerer King, and that my family served him.

An impractical impulse urged me to run and cower childishly within the shield of the Infortiare's will. I caviled at the impropriety of paying midnight visits to any man, but it was outright fear of further embroilment in the conflict of wizards which actually restrained me. I rationalized that the news I bore would be no more than Lord Venkarel already knew.

I reentered Amlach Hall in the bleak company of guilt and worry. Silence cast soft echoes from my slippered feet. Pale light fell from Yldana's door across the darkened hall. A diaphanous silken cloud haloed her silhouette as she slipped with the ease of practiced intimacy into the arms of the man she greeted. She drew him warmly into the candle glow of her room. That Yldana amused herself in Amgor's absence did not surprise me, though her openness when Liya slept across the passage annoyed me. Nor could I claim particular shock that Yldana's favor had enticed the profligate Lord Arineuil dur Ven. The assignation did shed a cynical light on Ineuil's disparagement of Amgor; while Amgor conspired with the other pawns of Horlach, Ineuil did not exactly occupy himself with the salvation of Serii. I was only surprised at how greatly the discovery aggravated my sepulchral mood.

Chapter 12

Dawn brought high clouds and frigid winds, signs of autumn's onset. Leaves, tenacious beyond their time, withered slowly. One stubborn rose still budded in the king's gardens, but the other canes were barren. Skeletal stalks became sere and brittle in the fields.

In Cuira, a man died, purportedly of a wizardess' theriac. A child of Esmar espied armed men in Caruillan colors entering her liege lord's hold. Fire claimed an inn in Malka; a stranger welcomed there the previous night had commented on the queer effect of moonlight on the chalky cliffs of Ixaxis.

I watched Yldana sweetly greet her husband, mocking him subtly with a hypocrisy which cloyed. Liya met Dayn with no less canting an embrace. With frozen distaste, I accepted Lord Grisk's encircling arm, and my father nodded righteous approval. I envied Ezirae's naive delight in the blithe social facade surrounding Tyntagel Hall, but Ezirae had indulged heavily in her own crutch; her reddened eyes were blurred. The essence of Horlach had left my father's House, but the taint remained in all of us.

Another full day elapsed before I enacted the inevitable betrayal of my family. My decision had progressed beyond choice when I felt Horlach stain Tyntagel Hall, but still I did not want to be Ixaxin, and I did not want to choose Ixaxis' Lord above my own.

I found him with the dusk amid a litter of texts and tattered documents. Kaedric met my eyes, demanding with a trace of exasperation, "Have you any idea how little information exists regarding Horlach, the man?

Legends abound of his evil reign. His victims are legion. But of substantiated personal history, virtually nothing can be found. The Taormin is worse. Horlach did not create it; he merely warped it to his own schemes. The Taormin's original purpose and the methods of its making are buried beneath an eon of superstition." He rubbed his brow wearily. "Forgive my pedantry, my lady. I have just spent a day reciting history to a king who will not heed the lessons of his ancestors. He prefers the patent nonsense of a Caruillan sycophant."

"Most of the lords of Serii echo His Majesty's sympathies, my lord. They conspire against you, and Horlach leads them."

Kaedric's compelling eyes narrowed slightly, and they held me. "My lady, you are become astonishingly well informed."

"The conspirators met in my father's Hall the night ere last," I answered, feeling traitorous myself, though it was treachery I betrayed. Kaedric had frowned, and I knew his mood. I burst forth unthinkingly, "I feel sufficiently wretched without you constantly distrusting me and examining my every word for subtle intentions against you. I have betrayed my liege and my family to you, my lord; you might at least *pretend* to believe me."

"Was Horlach among the conspirators?" demanded Kaedric after a pause.

"Yes, my lord, but I could not identify his host. I am sorry, my lord. I ought to have realized the importance of such an identification and probed farther."

Kaedric's expression had softened, though there was puzzlement in it. "I can hardly blame you for the omission, my lady. I have myself encountered Horlach twice of late, and neither time did I linger beyond necessity."

"I evidently bring you no new information," I responded glumly. My agonizing decision had not even been necessary.

Faint humor touched Kaedric's eyes. "In fact, my

lady, your 'betrayal,' as you call it, is itself a most astonishing disclosure." He touched the sorry velvet of his chair. "I have given you little but grief and trouble, Lady Rhianna," he said hesitantly. "I merit neither your loyalty nor your trust, but if you are willing, I should like to hear a more detailed account of this conspiratorial meeting."

I recounted the scene I had witnessed, hiding the embarrassment which invariably beset me on the rare occasions of Kaedric's gentler moods. He listened to me intently, nodding occasionally and clenching his right hand tightly as I told of the Ixaxin murdered in Coru. He continued to watch me for some moments after I had finished. "Thank you, Lady Rhianna," he said at last.

"I hope the information is of use, my lord." I could feel his memories pull at me. I spoke to break their grasp. "Shall I resume my studies, my lord?"

"Only if you are irredeemably enthralled by Telmar's *Treatise on Metaphysical Foundations*. Personally, I have had quite enough for one day both of scholarship and intrigues of state. I am even tired of this room, inconceivable as I should once have found such a thought."

I looked at the vast room with its limitless view. "With Ceallagh's Tower at your disposal, my lord, you hardly seem constrained in your surroundings."

"The exploration of my immediate domain is an indulgence vanquished by a sea of ceaseless crises. When I was named Infortiare, I thought the function's sole redeeming feature was the opportunity it provided to leisurely excavate the Tower's recesses. Ceallagh himself lived here, as well as every succeeding Infortiare, and a great many of their possessions have never been removed. The historical wealth never interested Alobar. I had grandiose ideas about the forgotten secrets I might uncover among the dusty relics of my predecessors. I have lived here for five years, my lady, and I have yet to enter any room beneath this floor." He laughed in self-mockery.

"You did not wish to be Infortiare," I said, bemused by his sudden communicativeness.

"I have no heroic ambitions, Lady Rhianna. The choice of the Ixaxin Council devastated me as much as it did Hrgh."

"Could you not have refused the honor?"

"I was persuaded, reluctantly, that Lord Hrgh was too unpredictable for the post. I could not name another candidate who would accept. Every other significant Power of my acquaintance sat on the Council which had chosen me! I still wonder whether Hrgh would have been a better choice."

"Lord Hrgh surely demonstrated his unsuitability by taking the Taormin. Even Lord Arineuil, who was Lord Hrgh's friend, recognized that act for madness."

"Yes, Hrgh Dolr'han is quite unsuitable now, if he even lives (which I doubt, despite Lord Borgor's pretty story). I ensured that Hrgh could never be Infortiare when I defeated him in his formal challenge. In a perverse way, I am responsible for the awakening of Horlach."

"Lord Hrgh ought never to have challenged you at all. He should have respected the Council's decision, whatever his private misgivings."

"The Infortiare should be, by Ceallagh's decree, the member of the Ixaxin Guild who holds the greatest Power at the time of selection. The Council's choice is not infallible, since few of us ever exercise the limits of our Powers. Hrgh sincerely believed himself to be best qualified, and I would never have willingly told him otherwise."

"You defend Lord Hrgh more fervently than does Ineuil," I observed.

"And Ineuil, as we all know, despises me for destroying most of his family and his domain. Did he tell you that he actually tried to kill me once? I defeated him, of course, but not with wizardry or even blade. I suggested to him that his family's indolent neglect of their duties had produced me and the miserable hole which I finally purged. I reminded him that as my liege lord, his uncle had been legally responsible for my enslavement and its unsavory conditions. Ineuil's sporadic allegiance to me owes as much to misplaced guilt as to anything."

Diffidently, I asked, "Did your mother actually sell you?"

Kaedric appeared not to object, though he did start perceptibly. "I must remember that the Taormin exchanges more than talents: how much of my history did you acquire? No," he said firmly, halting my response. "Perhaps you had best not answer that.

"As far as I know," he continued, "my mother sold me shortly before one of her less satisfied customers slit her delicate throat. Having no conscious recollection of the event myself, I can only trust to the dubious word of Master Doshk, who thereafter owned me."

The clear depths of dangerous eyes met mine, and my own gaze fell. "You did not know that you were a sorcerer?" I asked softly.

"The only sorcerers I knew were charlatans and potion peddlers. I never realized that Power actually existed, until Doshk and circumstances pushed me that inch too far. I incinerated him and nearly everything else within reach, and I spent the next few days staring at the horror of ash and rubble I had created. I was not particularly repentant, but Doshk's world I had at least understood."

"How old were you, my lord?" I did not tell him that I knew he had regretted his unintentional act of retribution deeply and immediately.

"Fourteen or fifteen, I suppose. My age is one of those many uncertainties in my life. Is your curiosity satisfied, my lady?"

I answered hurriedly, "I did not mean to pry, my lord."

"Obviously no one informed you that Lord Venkarel does not discuss his past," said Kaedric dryly. "Since I have said so much, however, I shall add one more note. I do not merit your sympathy for my childhood misfortunes. If that is the basis of your choice to serve my cause, then return to Tyntagel before you are disappointed. My detractors do not apply their vivid epithets without a measure of justification. The pretentious mask of an Ixaxin scholar does not eradicate my unsavory origins, and the slums of Ven do not yield men of gentlemanly honor."

He spoke with sarcastic indifference, but the words hurt him and I felt his pain. I said nothing, fearing to injure further this man whom I had thought invincible. "Blast your empathy," he said suddenly, rising and turning away from me.

Indecisive, I remained as I stood. The depths of long-held bitterness stirred in me the need to heal, and I ached to touch the dark sorrow away. I would have gone to him at a breath of acceptance.

When the gray-robed woman spoke, both Kaedric and I must have whirled to her with the speed of guilt. "Dear me," she murmured mildly, combing knotted fingers through unruly white hair. "I thought the ghost of Lady Erian had surely claimed you both." She extended her hand to me and announced bluntly, "My name is Marga. You are not what I expected to find in this stolid hive." She projected her focus beyond me. "You have been keeping secrets from me, Kaedric."

"The Lady Rhianna dur Tyntagel is my student, Marga."

"You teach unusual classes," she retorted, stepping back to appraise me critically.

"I learned the art from you, Mistress Marga," answered Kaedric. "I do not, however, recall a lesson on impugning one's host after an uninvited entrance."

"I could not have my student surpass me in everything," grumbled Marga indignantly.

"An eventuality which you need never fear. If your donning of student gray is a subtle attempt to prod my humility, rest assured: my pride has suffered several setbacks already tonight."

Marga raised an eyebrow. "Perhaps I ought to have insisted that you take a student years ago. Teaching can be a humbling experience." Mistress Marga winked at me, but I found her frightening. "In fact," she explained to me, "I wear gray because the white robes of a scholar are so confoundedly impractical. I formed the habit of entering here unannounced because it used to shock Alobar, and Kaedric has never reformed me of the practice. Dear Alobar always reacted to my arrival as if he suspected me of the most indiscreet ulterior motives. I hope you give Kaedric a great deal of trouble, Rhianna. He was by far the most difficult student Ixaxis ever suffered."

"Must you disillusion her completely, Marga?"

"It is only just. You caused me enough inconvenience. Are you going to welcome me properly, Kaedric, or are you too addled by your lovely student to remember courtesy?" Kaedric bent and solemnly kissed Marga's proffered cheek, while I wished myself in farthest Ardasia. Mistress Marga might sound disarmingly direct, but she conveyed unsettling insinuations.

"With your permission, my lord," I said a trifle stiffly, "I shall take my leave." Mistress Marga smiled with irritating complacency. Kaedric started to speak but, instead, nodded curtly.

Chapter 13

When next we met, Kaedric accorded me a careful formality which I did nothing to dispel. I adhered to my lesson rigidly and exchanged with the Infortiare only minimal conversation. I did not see Mistress Marga again; I assumed that she had departed as abruptly as she had appeared.

The days were growing colder, and inclement weather curtailed my garden visits, making my absences from my family more difficult to explain. Tyntagel Hall had become increasingly dismal. Liya and Dayn bickered constantly. My father's temper had deteriorated to such a point that even the servants avoided him: Arku Ruy had departed for Bethii, and King Astorn's promise to follow had yet to be enacted. Lord Grisk had become a frequent visitor, and Dhavod and Ezirae could speak in accord of nothing but my impending marriage.

When Abbot Medwyn arrived at Tyntagel Hall, my delight nearly overwhelmed him, and I did not even pause to question his unlikely appearance in my family's vestibule. He clucked mirthfully as I hugged him. "The lot of an elderly priest has certainly improved, Rhianna, when he merits such a welcome."

"I am so pleased to see you, Abbot," I responded sincerely.

"And I you, Rhianna, but you need not strangle me to prove it. The exhibition is delightful but most undignified," he added with a wink which creased his whole face.

"Is all well at the Abbey?"

Abbot Medwyn frowned fleetingly, and my warmth of pleasure froze. Grisk, from whose tedious company I had been summoned to greet the abbot, approached us, and Abbot Medwyn inquired politely, "Is this one of your kin, Rhianna?"

I tried to suppress a grimace as Grisk placed his hand on my shoulder possessively. I responded with restrained distaste, "Abbot Medwyn, this is Lord Grisk dur Niveal."

"Lady Rhianna is to be my wife," announced Grisk firmly, eying the abbot with suspicion.

Abbot Medwyn nodded once. "My congratulations, Lord Grisk. I know you will forgive an old man for his dearth of social grace, but it is so seldom I can discuss old friends when I leave the Abbey. The conversation would bore you, so I shall briefly steal your intended bride. May we stroll in the garden, Rhianna? These noble manors rather daunt me." Abbot Medwyn smiled like a cherubim as he maneuvered me to the door.

Grisk let us go with little grace. Having been told the acknowledged story of my lengthy stay at Benthen Abbey, Lord Grisk quite thoroughly disapproved of my association with Benthen's abbot. Grisk would have liked the truth far less. I sighed with relief when we had left him.

"You do not seem to have gained any fondness for your betrothed, Rhianna," said Abbot Medwyn gently.

"I wish I could tell you otherwise, Abbot Medwyn."

"A wizardess cannot be coerced into marriage, Rhianna."

My glance dropped guiltily, and I countered the accusation with a query. "You did not answer my question about the Abbey. Is something wrong? I am sure you did not journey to Tulea to visit a Tyntagellian lady who once burdened your charity."

"You were not a burden, Rhianna," said the abbot kindly. He frowned. "A great many things are wrong these days, Rhianna. Benthen Abbey is not immune." Our footsteps fell on sand. "Kaedric tells me that you have been studying wizardry."

"You came to Tulea to speak with Lord Venkarel?" I asked, already certain of the answer.

"Another attempt was made to steal the Taormin, Rhianna."

"But it failed," I insisted urgently.

Abbot Medwyn agreed hesitantly. "It failed," he answered carefully. "Master Gart was slightly injured, but no other harm was done." I started; I had nearly suppressed all recollection of Master Gart, inextricably linked as he was with Hamar and Horlach's undying guardians. "Master Gart agreed to remain with the Abbey after the Venture," explained the abbot, "though he holds generally to himself. Kaedric suspected another attack would be forthcoming, and he deemed the protection of a warrior's steel an advisable precaution. Master Gart was a compromise between a contingent of the Seriin army and the Abbey's traditional reliance on faith and peace."

"I am glad that Master Gart has found a place of refuge," I returned truthfully.

"Yes, age does not make the loss of friends any easier: Hamar and Gart traveled together for many years." We walked some minutes in easy silence, which made me rather wistfully recall the secure sanctity of Benthen Abbey. I walked with the holy man rather than the Venturer; with the holy man I felt at peace.

"In many ways, Abbot Medwyn, I envy you your calling."

"It would not suit you, Rhianna, even were you not possessed of that other Power. Your faith lies in the creatures of the earth and not in Him who made them."

"Is the difference so great?"

"Perhaps not." Abbot Medwyn smiled. "Let not my fellow clergymen hear me say that. They already consider me quite eccentric because of my dealings with Ixaxins." He added suddenly, "Your family—and Lord Grisk—support the movement against Ixaxis."

It was not a question, but I responded with acerbic precision, "The attitude of my kin regarding wizardry is not well hidden."

"When are you going to make your choice, Rhianna?"

I looked at Abbot Medwyn in surprise. "Having already betrayed my own father's plotting to Lord Venkarel, I should think my decision clear," I answered defensively, "but I suppose Lord Venkarel did not mention the incident; I told him little he did not already know."

"Kaedric told me of the meeting in your father's Hall. He has made good use of the information. My question, however, remains. You have assuredly served the Infortiare more than once, but you still regard your father as your liege lord. You are also promised in marriage to Lord Grisk, who would hardly approve of your association with Kaedric. Lord Grisk does not even approve of a harmless old abbot. You cannot forever maintain such contradictory allegiances, Rhianna."

"I am not eager to dissolve all ties with my family, Abbot. That does not mean that I agree with their politics."

"You do not agree with them, but it is easier to acquiesce to the dictates of your heritage. Thus far, you have accepted the easy route: running from a family decision you disliked, appeasing your family by apparent agreement when flight proved an unpalatable alternative. You have helped the Infortiare when it was convenient for you or you had no other option. If I asked you to take a deliberate step in this battle we wage, would you take it despite the possible cost?"

I disliked the truth of his words. I answered gravely, "I have no great fount of courage or strength, Abbot Medwyn. I should like to say I would not hesitate before the wrath of Horlach: we have so very much at stake." I could not face him as I finished, "I am neither Ceallagh nor Tul. I am the very unimportant daughter of Lord Baerod and a wife he despised. I do not know what answer I should give you."

"Rhianna," said Abbot Medwyn with deliberation, "the Taormin was not taken from the Abbey, because it was not there to be found. Kaedric did not return it to us."

I turned to him with deeply felt dread. A shaft of sunlight blinded me. "Abbot Medwyn, what do you imply?"

"Rhianna, I think perhaps you alone, save Kaedric himself, know truly what transpired in Horlach's castle last winter. I have tried to discuss it with Kaedric." At my expression of protest, Abbot Medwyn continued quickly, "Kaedric has ever been reticent. Perhaps it is only that which keeps him silent, but he will not reveal the Taormin's whereabouts to me or to the Ixaxin Council."

"He would not conceal the Taormin without cause, Abbot Medwyn, and he would not take it for his own use," I insisted with less assurance than I would have wished.

"So I believe, also, but I feel some responsibility for it and for Kaedric as well. Talk to him, Rhianna. You were with him when he used it first. You have the best chance of learning from him whether he has used it again."

"Abbot Medwyn, I have not the right to question the Infortiare."

"You defied him openly to join a Venture."

"I did not know whom I defied, Abbot Medwyn."

Abbot Medwyn smiled at me sorrowfully. "I know, Rhianna." He did not need to add that he had strongly dissuaded me from that defiance at the time.

"Surely the Ixaxin Council would be better suited to such a task as you suggest."

"I have already spoken to the representative of the Ixaxin Council. Mistress Marga agrees with me that you are best qualified to approach the subject."

I thought of the forceful little woman who had taught wizardry to the Infortiare. The absurdity of Abbot Medwyn's suggestion struck me fully even as I caviled, "If Lord Venkarel refuses to answer both you and Mistress Marga, he will consign my questions to ridicule."

"We ask only that you try, Rhianna."

"He would not take the Taormin for himself."

"I would believe him if he said it. In his own way, Kaedric is as stubbornly proud as a Dolr'han."

We had nearly circled back to Tyntagel Hall. Grisk watched us from the entryway. "I make you no promise, Abbot. Lord Venkarel frightens me nearly as much as does Horlach."

Abbot Medwyn merely nodded thoughtfully.

Chapter 14

I waited in the Tower library, unable to concentrate on any task but the confrontation which Abbot Medwyn had beseeched of me. I paced the room nervously, touched the gilt and leather spines of carefully tended volumes, and realized that the books were the only items in the room that had seen any significant recent attention. I brushed a corner chair and rubbed a cobweb from my fingers with distaste.

"Traditional dread of Ceallagh's Tower makes housekeepers an elusive commodity," commented Kaedric from the door. "One of my predecessors, a Lord Pareth, grew so desperately offended by the pervading grime that he devoted the better part of his tenure to a search for a dust-cure. His contributions to Seriin government lapsed accordingly."

"It is a pity that he failed," I murmured uncertainly. Kaedric wore the formal black silk and gold of the Infortiare, and I thought it unfair that he should so resemble the ageless Sorcerer Kings of legend. He began to examine the stack of letters on his desk. He had already spared me more converse than he had done in a fortnight.

I began tentatively, "I spoke with Abbot Medwyn this morning."

The Infortiare answered absently, "He mentioned an intention to see you."

"Is he staying in the Tower, my lord?" I asked, though I knew the answer.

"He prefers the local manse of Parul," responded Kaedric, still studying the papers he held.

With headlong decisiveness, I embarked. "Abbot Medwyn said that an attempt was made to steal the Taormin. He also said that the attempt failed, because you had never returned the Taormin to the Abbey."

I had gained the Infortiare's attention. His eyes had hardened. He enunciated dangerously, "What further bits of wisdom did the good abbot impart?"

"He is concerned for you, my lord."

"Ergo, he announces my business to the world. Medwyn's tongue has grown heedless."

"Mistress Marga shares his concern, my lord." Slowly, Kaedric straightened the letters in their stack. "Do you have the Taormin, my lord?" I pleaded.

"You presume too much, Lady Rhianna," he responded tightly.

Privately I agreed with him. I moved nearer to him; I sat on the edge of the too-cluttered chair facing his. His muscles were tensed, his hands' slight motions exhaustively controlled. "Lord Venkarel, I have walked with you in the Taormin's world. I am afflicted by it with some shade of your Power and your memories. If you use it, I shall know."

With a rapid movement, his hand gripped mine across the wood desk. His fingers were hard, and they pressed into my bones.

He could have touched the walls on any side: the flat, gray planes which did not end. The prison above was the bloated face of Doshk, a drunken, drug-mad Doshk from whom prosperity had turned her favor. Doshk giggled, an obscene sound spilling from an evil humor. The boy wanted to cry, but he had forgotten the way of it.

Doshk was large, too strong and tall. The boy was very thin, stretched by recent, undernourished growth; he was still small for his age, but he was not quite as much a child as he had been a month before. Doshk reached a huge, rough hand toward the boy, and there was no escape.

Doshk simpered, "You're not going anywhere, Kaed." Doshk rubbed his hand across the boy's chest, and the boy stiffened, assessing the chances of survival if he struck at the offending hand. Deev never had retreated from the intrusive touching of Master Doshk, but Deev had died of greed. Ag had finally struck, and Ag lay downstairs in a pool of blood widening from his crushed red head.

"You're growing, Kaed," said Doshk with a rough, abusive caress. "You'll favor your mother. I've told you about Fylla, haven't I, Kaed? She was a slut, your mother, who thought she was too good for Doshk. You're not too good, are you, Kaed? You'll do just as Doshk says, won't you?"

The boy knew: what Doshk wanted of him; what Doshk could do to him; that Doshk would kill if defied; that a sober Doshk was difficult to elude, and a drunken Doshk was relentlessly powerful. The boy wished for the knife which had been taken from him a year ago, when Doshk had realized that the boy's skill had begun to compensate for physical weakness. The boy tried to stand immobile as Doshk ran heavy hands across him, but pain and disgust made him gag and jerk free of his owner. Doshk glared from reddened eyes. Doshk hit the boy, the heavy metal studs at Doshk's wrist raising oozing welts across the boy's back.

The boy relaxed determinedly, and Doshk bared his yellowed teeth in approval. "That's better. Be smarter than your mother and maybe you'll live to a happier age." Doshk giggled again and began to wheeze. "She sold you, Fylla did, and only Doshk would take you." A clatter sounded through the floorboards.

"You've a customer, Master Doshk," answered the boy. He spoke so rarely that even Doshk was startled, but the words made no impact. Doshk was entirely focused on his drug-spawned dreams. He fondled; he struck. The boy bled and hated. The thief below the stairs found the body of Ag, stepped around it indifferently, and proceeded with his petty pilfering of the little that remained in Doshk's crumbling inn.

With deft and practiced fingers, the boy lifted a key from Doshk's waistband. The boy submitted to Doshk's painful touches, but he patiently worked toward the door. The key turned. The boy tensed, and Doshk's suspicious eyes squinted. The boy moved quickly, pressing open the catch of the door and pushing against Doshk. The big man fell; the boy clambered past him, through the door, down lightless stairs. Doshk sprang on him with a leap, crushing the boy to the grimy floor.

The sharp, sallow face of the thief appeared against the kitchen's yellow light. Distracted from the boy, Doshk eased to a crouch. The boy rolled clear, but he could not stand, for his head throbbed unmercifully. The two men grappled now; their knives were too sullied to shine. The thief's knife gouged Doshk's heavy thigh, but the thief stumbled, tripping over Ag's body and cursing it. Doshk kicked the knife from the thief's grasping hand, and the boy snatched it eagerly.

The boy tasted hope. He sidled carefully around the dark room, avoiding the clutter of tables and limping chairs which might betray him by a sound. The door would open to him soon, and he would be away. Ag and Deev—even Pru—were dead. Doshk's hirelings had deserted when the pay fell short. There remained none to stop the boy but Doshk, and Doshk was methodically hacking the body of the thief to bloody strips.

The door opened. A black-browed mongrel filled the entry. He saw his partner beneath Doshk's butchery; he saw the boy who sought escape. With arms of steel strength, he grasped the boy's neck in a deadly hold, and the boy saw hope depart, as it had always done.

The boy had always been weak in a world which honored only strength and cruelty. He had paid and suffered for his weakness and for his mother's pride. His back was crossed with scars, for he had not fulfilled Doshk's hopes; the boy had been too determinedly cold to bring money to Doshk's larder. The boy had fought to survive, driving himself beyond strength to outlast his fellows. He had absorbed every trick of duplicity, every crumb of knowledge which might help to free him. He had given nothing of himself save the labor which Doshk had beaten from him. He had hoarded hope, and it ate at him from within.

The thief tightened his grip, and the boy choked. The thief would kill him in another instant. It would be easier to acquiesce, thought the boy wistfully, easier than being weak among the strong. The thought angered him, because if he died now, he would never know what it was to be strong. The boy gave a death's-edge scream, and the world caught fire.

The fire spread rapidly. Doshk died in a searing burst. The thief who thought to kill a spindly boy gawked at fires springing wildly from the stale wood room and the bodies on its floor. The black-browed thief felt his arm burn crisp, though the young throat which it encircled did not blister. The thief stepped backward in horror and agony. He watched the boy's still figure, alone in a circle of flame. Like Ag's red blood, the circle widened. The thief beat at his own burning body as he ran; he would be among the few in Ven to survive that day, but he had lost his arm from shoulder down.

The fire, now started, would not stop. It was anger and hatred from years of abuse, bitterness against a mother who had sold her son; it was fueled by memory of all the cruel haranguers who had beaten and used the son of a too-arrogant whore. It was the fear of a child, raised to iniquity, of the lawgiving enemy—the liege—whom he did not know and of the lawless whom he knew too well. He had found a key more potent than Doshk's. Kaed felt the dark and callous minds as he reached through the city, and he purged them, hating them, wanting them gone. He chanted it like a desperate litany, "I hate them. I hate them. I hate them." He trembled from exertion and the terror which pounded from his own mind. "I hate them. I hate them. I hate them." He intended to destroy them all, not knowing that there was kindness or a world beyond Ven's underbelly. "I hate them." His voice trailed into silence.

His mind cooled. He was only a child; he grew tired. He had stricken to fiery death five thousand men and women; each scream stayed screeching in his mind. Some three thousand more would die of the ancillary mortal flames. Tomorrow's dawn would weep.

He freed my hand, and the visions stopped. His eyes defied me to speak again. "You have the Taormin, my lord," I said. I hated his memories and his guilt, for it was mine now, and I would not let it rule me.

He shot stark words at me. "I am the Infortiare, Lady Rhianna."

"I can find the Taormin without your permission if I wish, my lord."

"You could offer it to His Late Majesty, King Horlach, as well," retorted Kaedric sharply. He stood now, and his ice-laden eyes delved within me. "But if Horlach did not destroy you, I would. My lady, you live by my sufferance," he hissed, dropping the shields by which he had learned since Ven to protect those around him from his Power. No more than a selected easing of those perpetual barriers had sent death to a band of brigands in a mountain crevasse. Only once had I seen him actively attack: in the hall of Horlach with a focus of power so narrow that the impact had barely touched my awareness. The Infortiare did not need to attack me; his blatant Power blinded, and I bit my lip to hold to my sanity with the distraction of a physical hurt. I shuddered for the benighted citizens of Ven, even as I ached with personal guilt over their murder.

"By what right," prodded the Infortiare relentlessly, "do you question me, Lady Rhianna dur Tyntagel? If I take the Taormin, or if I choose to use it—have you the knowledge, the wisdom to judge my decision? Would you send the Taormin to your wizard-hating Tyntagellian hypocrites? The very name of Tyntagel was enwrapped with sorcerous legend long before your ancestors took it for their *sorcerous* domain. Did you think your heritage of Power came solely from a woman too frail to survive her twentieth year? Your father is a sorcerer, Lady Rhianna, though he blocks his Power even from himself. You never observed that simple fact, did you? You cannot recognize your own father's Power, you have never realized that the first Lord of Tyntagel was a Sorcerer King, yet you consider yourself qualified to judge me?"

I repeated obdurately, "I entered the Taormin with you, Lord Venkarel."

"By right of which accident you dare dictate to me?" He stood perilously near to me, blazing down at me with the blue of ice and fire. "Return to your

Niveallan lord, Lady Rhianna. Raise children to the glory of Grisk! You have learned controls enough to emulate your father in denial. Expect no more of me."

He compelled me to leave, pressing me with his Power down the long flights of stairs. I left the Tower by the garden door; I knew the door would be locked to me if I tried to return. I think I wept like the silent rains of Ven.

Chapter 15

I had succeeded, after a fashion, in attaining Abbot Medwyn's answer: I knew that Lord Venkarel held the Taormin still, and I knew that he intended to use it. I had scant cause for the certainty I felt; for that reason alone, I told myself, I hesitated to reveal my story to the abbot. Abbot Medwyn visited me twice more in the next week, but he did not press to know whether I had acceded to his request. I volunteered no syllable of reference to the Infortiare. If the abbot knew of our argument, he did not speak of it.

I had grown very accustomed to my hours in Ceallagh's Tower, and the days seemed long without them. I greeted the news of King Astorn's departure for Bethii with an approval which nearly matched my father's though my reasons differed vastly from his. The festivities attendant to the event would mitigate the boredom. I was become no better than any jaded courtier, ignoring the scheming which I knew transpired. I had made my try at bravery for Abbot Medwyn's sake and had failed miserably.

On the day of King Astorn's departure for Bethii, solemnity vanished from Tulea. Curricles and carriages denied encroaching clouds, as the parade circled the castle grounds, collecting its bright array of Seriin nobility. The youngest members of various households (most especially the numerous Hamleys) dashed and darted everywhere underfoot. I glimpsed among them Ziva and Flava; hair ribbons streaming, they blithely disregarded the dignities of self-proclaimed maturity. They grinned at me as they whirled past in mock flight from an assortment of friends and cousins. I waved at them and thought it a pity that Liya still sequestered herself.

"This is not a day for genteelly observing from afar, Lady Rhianna," mocked Ineuil. He had appeared with Ydlana glowing radiantly at his side, her husband not in sight.

"Ezirae and Dhavod have claimed Tyntagel's right to participate in the parade. I am not so privileged," I responded lightly, but I felt uncomfortable with the knowledge of my sister's illicit affair. That her partner was my sometime comrade, Ineuil, made me even more uneasy.

With more friendliness than I should ever have expected from my sister, Yldana said, "Carriages are for old dowagers who have forgotten how to enjoy a festival day, Rhianna. Walk with us to the town and learn what they miss." She bestowed on me one of the enchanting smiles which she used to such advantage. I cynically suspected that she invited me only for the sake of public propriety, but the mere unlikeliness of the offer swayed me.

Somewhat to my surprise, neither Ineuil nor Yldana pierced my chimerical contentment. The two maintained a patter of sharp observations, but their barbs did not cut deeply, and Ineuil firmly encouraged me to join in their laughter. "Your sister is too solemn, Yldana," he twitted. "We must try to corrupt her."

"So long as the efforts stop at a touch of frivolity, Lord Arineuil," returned Yldana admonishingly, but her smile betrayed unlikely confidence in Ineuil's affections. I should not have trusted Ineuil's fidelity to any woman, but I obviously lacked Yldana's perspective.

We sampled sticky buns and meat pasties from colorful stalls. We cast encouraging coins at dancers and minstrels and poets who recited slyly humorous lays. We watched King Astorn, proud and distinguished, ride past us on a horse of pale gold. The fair and fragile Queen Alamai, who would accompany her husband to Bethii, followed him in a golden carriage. Prince Orlin, the young heir who would be regent in his father's absence, rode beside a carriage laden with his brightly bobbing sisters. Princess Joli sat rigidly pressed against the carriage seat between the golden, soft-eyed twins, Alza and Henzela.

A rude jest from the crowd brought the haughty Prince Orlin to a protective stance before his sisters. He flourished his shiny sword ineffectively under the tolerant watch of the official royal guards. I could feel Joli shake her head with disgust, and I could appreciate the uncharitable comment. Prince Orlin was a handsome boy who might one day mature into an acceptable king, but he seemed an insubstantial leader for a troubled Serii. I shivered, recalling the forces who would not cease their scheming while the regent ruled.

"If you are moping over our king's propensity for producing ineffectual heirs," whispered Ineuil mischievously, "At least credit him with proving more prolific than his own sire."

Yldana actually giggled. "King Astorn has not stinted of himself in the servants' halls either," she said in an undertone.

"Do not offend your sister's delicate sensibilities, Yldana," chided Ineuil with sententious sternness belied when he grabbed her wrists and pulled them to his chest.

"Better my influence than yours, rogue," teased Yldana, breaking free of Ineuil's grasp. With a laugh, she took my hand and drew me with her in a dash through the crowded streets, disregarding equally spattered mud and indignant victims of our careening race. Yladna ensured that Ineuil did not lose sight of us, and he took care not to catch us too soon, but I could not help enjoying their delight in the game.

"A fine spectacle we make," said Yldana when, breathless, we stopped. She raised her fine wool skirt enough to reveal the sodden stockings clinging to her ankles. "I shall be taxed even to convince Amgor of my impeccable propriety this day."

"Your persuasive gifts more than equal the task, Yldana," said Ineuil as he joined us. "To enjoy a festival day is a patriotic duty, and we know how highly Amgor regards a duty."

Yldana grimaced, comically twisting her fine-featured face. "Amgor can be such a pompous bore. Now, quit your disapproving glances, Rhianna. Your thoughts regarding Grisk are not so loyal."

"I am not married to Grisk," I answered defensively.

"You are promised to him. It amounts to the same thing," returned my sister.

"My opinion was never requested," I said.

"Do you think mine was?" asked Yldana. "It is the lot of a Seriin lady to wed as her liege commands. We may turn into suffering slaves like Nadira or mope like Liya because our pretty dreams grow sour, or we may find enjoyment as it comes." She exchanged a look with Ineuil which made me suspect that my presence would soon become burdensome. Yldana's words rankled, because I wanted to condemn her, but I could no longer quite manage it. On my own hypocrisy, Yldana and Abbot Medwyn agreed.

"My lovely ladies," said Ineuil, draping an arm around each of us, "This talk grows depressingly familiar. I have a friend nearby who pressures no one to the dismal task of upholding tradition and family honor. He stocks the most tantalizing vintages this side of Mahl, and his rooftop boasts a sensational view of King's Street."

"Your friend doubtless happens to await us?" asked Yldana coyly.

"Master Caylin has keen insight and an even keener sense of profit," intoned Ineuil seriously. "I may have mentioned my possible arrival with Serii's two most exquisite pearls."

"Does Master Caylin flirt as outrageously as you do, Lord Arineuil?" taunted Yldana.

"He practices, but his technique requires some polishing. I thought perhaps Rhianna could lend him some literate quotes from young Joret dur Esmar's outpourings."

"You are remarkably well informed, Lord Arineuil," I answered. Of all my spate of admirers, Lord Joret alone had persisted beyond the official announcement of my betrothal. I had yet to meet him; Lord Joret seemed to thrive on contemplating the unattainable unknown.

Yldana laughed prettily. "Since Arineuil's attention to you at Veiga's little party gained you the admirers, it is unsurprising that Arineuil should be aware of their existence. The reaction is as inevitable as it is fleeting."

"Have you seen Veiga of late?" asked Ineuil too casually.

"I should be jealous of your interest, Lord Arineuil, save that Veiga is too busy manipulating her beastly husband to find time for someone of your frivolous temperament," said Yldana. "Veiga scarcely appears in public anymore." My sister spoke lightly, but she was not pleased with the turn of discussion.

"Borgor never impressed me as such a captivating fellow," remarked Ineuil. "Perhaps I shall have to cultivate the Adjutant more carefully to learn his secret attraction."

"My dear Arineuil, you know quite well that Lord Borgor associates with no one less than the king or the Dolr'hans." Yldana's voice was tight. "He has barely acknowledged his own family since he became Adjutant, and that honor stemmed solely from Veiga's efforts. You may as well try to cultivate the Venkarel."

I listened with care, curious to know the cause of Ineuil's questions regarding Sandoral's loftiest pair, but Ineuil terminated the conversation with a timely arrival at Master Caylin's touted establishment. I had, for a moment, pondered a careful question to the Infortiare as to whether Lord Arineuil served Ixaxin interests with his probes. I recalled with a painful jounce that Lord Venkarel would not hear me. I might have questioned Ineuil directly, but the trouble of seeking him out for private conversation outweighed the dubious rewards.

I had lost some of my defiantly buoyant humor, but Master Caylin proved as fine a host as promised and did his best to please us. He was an unimpressive man of middle age, beset by a myopic squint and stooped shoulders, but he served a savory lunch in simple but substantial style. From the rooftop aerie, we watched the merry folk at holiday below us, while we enjoyed privacy from disapproving peers. As the afternoon progressed, Master Caylin brought forth his colorless wife and two rather unprepossessing children. I feared we might pay for our pleasant meal with a tedium of family tales, but the gifts of Caylin's brood extended beyond the obviously well-stocked cupboard. An adept lutenist, Master Caylin played while his wife's vibrant contralto gave counterpoint to the clear soprano voices of the ungainly boy and his angular little sister. We lingered until shadows overtook the city, and though Yldana leaned indiscreetly close to Ineuil, I might not approve, but I no longer greatly minded.

I wore a strangely surreal mood upon my return to Tyntagel Hall. The festive air of the day had infected even my father, who was as nearly cheerful as his nature allowed. I refused to seek in him the stain of Power with which my Lord Venkarel had derided me.

Though Dayn and Liya remained conspicuously silent, the evening passed easily until the arrival of Lord Brant and Lord Grisk. "Perhaps we have been selfish, Baerod," said Lord Brant with a sly wink at my father, "in delaying the wedding of our children. Eager young lovers should not be forced to bide for the sake of political convenience. We could yet arrange the ceremony for year's end as originally planned."

Ezirae's protest covered my own horror. "Lord Brant," she said primly, "two weeks will not suffice to prepare for a Young Lady's wedding."

"We are not altogether unprepared," said my father. He nodded thoughtfully to Lord Brant. "I shall consider the matter."

To escape such talk, even Grisk's suggested stroll in the courtyard appeared palatable. I let him escort me beneath the cirrus-speckled sky of near-winter Tulea. I stepped away as he reached for me. "Do not paw me, Lord Grisk," I said absently.

"I am losing patience with you, Rhianna."

"Have you tired of your parlormaid?"

"You have not been so chary of your favors yourself."

"You are worse than Joret dur Esmar, building a world upon a conversation I once had with the lord of Ven," I returned with scorn.

"I suppose you just conversed with Lord Venkarel as well. Credit me with some sense, Rhianna. I never mentioned that little incident, but I did not forget it."

"Then you should recall that my favors did not seem to agree with you," I said with sudden fury.

"That meddling bastard, Venkarel, is not here tonight. You are not very selective in your lovers, Rhianna."

I raised my hand to slap him, but Grisk struck my arm. He hit me once more, knocking me back a pace, with a blow that would leave a blue, mottled imprint on my shoulder. Wickedly, Grisk snarled, "You may give more pleasure as a wife than I expected."

I glared at him, holding tight rein on my anger. "I have no intention of marrying you, Grisk." He grabbed at me, but I shook him off with a wisp of Power. He reentered the salon in my wake, docile with puzzlement. Our kin regarded our quick return with surprise.

"My Lord Father, Lord Brant," I announced clearly, "You suffer under the impression that I intend to marry Lord Grisk. I regret that I have not previously made my position clear, but I remedy that remission now: I shall not marry Lord Grisk."

I had shocked them, and I did not await their recovery. I heard my father calling to me angrily, as I took the stairs to my room with deliberate haste. I could hear incoherent snatches of Lord Brant exchanging abuse with his son. Ezirae shrieked pathetic apologies, and the chaos set Liya and Dayn to arguing.

The most disquieting feature of the following morning was its utter normalcy. Tamar awoke me with a firm knock and a piece of new brocade which she consideringly draped across me. She had no sooner departed than Ezirae arrived requesting her. "She promised to do something with Ziva and Flava," said Ezirae fussily. "I do hope she has not forgotten." I began to wonder if I had only dreamed the events of the previous night.

"Good morning, Rhianna," said Liya to me in the hall. "Do you know that Prince Orlin has already planned a dance? It will be small, of course; only the First Houses and the prince's favorites will be invited. But it will be all the better for being exclusive. I am so tired of hearing about nothing but whether or not King Astorn will go to Bethii and whether the Caruillans will join the Alliance! It will be wonderful to have the court normal again. I think I shall wear the silver tissue." She sprinted to her room as gaily as if she had not just spent the last month in sullen withdrawal and bristling defensiveness.

"Good morning, Rhianna," said Dayn courteously as I entered the small dining room reserved for the break of fast. My father nodded curtly and continued to talk to Dhavod of the news that my brother Balev's wife would soon bear another child. Liya and Ezirae joined us, and the atmosphere was nearly cordial.

"I hope you need not leave Tulea until after the dance, Dayn," said Liya.

"I must speak with Lord Morgh before he departs Liin for Caruil. We must agree upon the spring shipments. I would delay it if I could, Liya," said Dayn sincerely. It was the first civil exchange I had heard between the two of them in weeks.

"Dayn will be gone no more than a month, Liya," offered Dhavod as consolation. "The negotiations should proceed quite quickly, since nullification of the Niveallan agreement virtually demands acceptance of Lord Morgh's terms." My father made no comment, and the conversation strayed to other topics. It was the only reference made to any change of status effected by my declaration of the previous night.

Chapter 16

As Liya predicted, the Solstice Dance of Prince Orlin was a much less extravagant affair than the king's ball. Held in the same enormous hall, the ranks of attendees seemed even smaller than the scant two hundred of Ezirae's estimate, despite the extending illusion of the mirrored walls. The effect apparently satisfied His Royal Highness, who enjoyed the company of the prettiest Seriin ladies of his age. In contrast to the remote splendor of the royal dais the night of King Astorn's gala, the vivacious swarm around Orlin had the impact of a young boy's birthday party supervised from a discreet distance by his elders.

As a result of the youthful takeover of the positions of highest traditional rank, many of the more exalted members of the Seriin court mingled freely among the multitudes. Liya tallied the aristocracy of her dance partners by a ratio involving the number of times she had previously met them and the occasions of their fame; since she had never before met Lord Gorng Dolr'han dur Liin, that gentleman apparently achieved the highest rating. She berated me, during a moment of private discussion, for my inability to name more than three of my own partners. I had danced with

Ineuil, Amgor, and Ezirae's brother, Lord Zam; I had danced with a few others, but their faces had faded as well as their names.

"You are hopeless, Rhianna," sighed Liya with a hint of condescending humor.

"And I hoped she might be improving," said Yldana, appearing with the illustrious Veiga. "Perhaps we can endeavor a cure. How has Rhianna failed us, Liya?"

The sight of Lady Veiga had Liya speechlessly entranced by virtue of an astonishing display of rubies, as much as by the lady's own mystique. Lady Veiga obviously enjoyed her effect on the gaping girl. Liya's eyes widened farther as a subtle movement brought the chandeliers' fire to ignite the stones around Veiga's neck.

"Lady Liya seems rather hopelessly uncommunicative," drawled Veiga. "Is the failing congenital among your kin, Yldana?"

Liya blushed in embarrassment. "Rhianna and I were discussing dance partners," said Liya, belatedly answering Yldana's query.

Veiga raised her topaz eyes to the ceiling, commenting, "What a fascinating subject. Tell me, Lady Liya, have you actually discovered anyone of interest in this prepubescent assortment of our regent's delight?"

Yldana responded diplomatically, "Not all of us are so difficult to please, Veiga. Even I have found a few intriguing opportunities tonight."

Lady Veiga scanned the room with blatant boredom, but her inspection narrowed upon a late entrant. "Possibly you are correct, Yldana," she murmured. "Not every interesting man kept to his own Hall tonight."

Following Veiga's gaze, Liya proffered doubtfully, "I suppose he is handsome."

"So are many statues," retorted Yldana in a brittle voice.

Lady Veiga's lips twisted in an arrogant smile. "You disappoint me, Yldana. There is fire beneath that ice for the lady who dares to rouse it."

"Lady Veiga!" remonstrated Liya, shocked into rebuking her idol. "He is the Infortiare!"

"Lady Liya!" mimicked Veiga. "I am a Dolr'han!"

Yldana was uncomfortable. "Veiga, I am sure Liya meant no insult."

"Really, Yldana," sneered the beautiful Veiga, caressing her burning rubies with a spidery hand. "The affair was no great secret. If it offends you less, Lady Liya, you may console yourself in knowing that Lord Venkarel was only an insignificant Ixaxin student when I knew him. At the time, my association with him was considered quite demeaning to *me,* but I happened to be very bored that particular summer."

Liya having been effectively horrified, Veiga left us with an airy smirk. Not quite able to conceal her own dismay, Yldana said brightly, "Veiga enjoys her little jests, Liya. If I am not mistaken, Lord Ghren is trying desperately to attract your attention. Be merciful to the poor man and dance with him." She shooed Liya across the room, then stood immobile and expressionless, watching Lady Veiga stop to bespeak Lord Venkarel.

"It was not a jest, was it, Yldana?" I asked with studied calm.

Yldana had quite forgotten me, and she started when I spoke. "No, of course not," she answered impatiently. "Veiga often amused herself with Hrgh's classmates." Almost angrily, she snapped, "What does it matter to you? You are a sorceress. What a pity for Tyntagel that Father never offered *you* to Hrgh!" Tears gathered in her eyes.

"Yldana," I began, bewildered by this vulnerability from my unassailable sister at a moment when I was myself none too steady. Yldana pushed away from me and fled toward the ladies' chambers. I started to follow, but Yldana would not welcome my sympathy. I made my own escape to the deserted patio in the shadow of the colonnades. Yldana's collapse distressed me—more since I deemed its cause was largely the golden Lord Hrgh. With Lady Veiga I was infuriated;

I refused to examine the cause of my excessive ire. I forced myself to unthinking calm as I listened to the nightsong of the trees, merging with the music and the murmurs from the ballroom.

I did not hear his approach, but I felt his presence. "Does a contrite wizard merit a waltz with a lady of Tyntagel?" asked Kaedric softly from behind me. I paused before turning, trying to still a torrent of conflicting reactions. I would not meet his eyes, but I accepted his hand with a silent curtsy.

He held me gently, in his arms and his Power. "You spoke to me truly, my lady. I grow as dangerously arrogant as Hrgh."

"I ought not to have spoken as I did, my lord."

He grinned at me. "It was incautious," he admitted. "I ought to flay Medwyn and Marga for putting you up to it."

"Please do not blame them, my lord," I said with some concern.

"Worry not, my lady of the Dwaelin. I have not allowed my temper to exceed the capacity of my antagonist since Ven." I must have looked doubtful. Kaedric laughed a trifle shamefacedly. "As you so pointedly observed, my lady, we did use the Taormin together. I have a rather good idea of the extent of your Power."

"That is not a particularly comforting thought," I answered dryly, but a part of me exulted.

"It should be; it is the reason Marga supported Medwyn's choice of you as the voice of sanity. If I seriously tried to harm you, my lady, I should be opening myself to equal injury. Marga knows that I am far too selfish to risk that contingency."

I could not credit his words, though he voiced them sincerely. "The only person I seem able to injure is myself, my lord."

"Lord Grisk might differ with that statement, if he were privy to the pertinent facts." After a moment's silence, Kaedric added, "Would it be injudicious to applaud the termination of your engagement?"

"Is there such a thing as a secret in Tulea?" I asked rhetorically, but his innocuous comment affected me disproportionately. For no good reason, I felt it incumbent upon me to explain, "My lord, I never acknowledged my supposed betrothal. I was simply slow in informing my family of their mistake. I expected them to be furious."

"They are not?" asked Kaedric with an intonation between statement and question.

"By appearance at least, they are not," I agreed.

"Lord Baerod finally realizes how foolish it would be to waste you on that Niveallan catastrophe. It may be the first time your father and I are in accord."

"More likely, my father found a better trade agreement and was glad of an excuse to break with Lord Brant." I attempted a lightness I did not feel. The touch of the Infortiare's devastating Power disturbed me less than the unexpected, deep awareness of the dance we shared. I collected my unruly emotions. "But you have certainly analyzed my father's motives in this as in any other act of potential political import."

"Suspicion is a bad habit of mine," conceded Kaedric in a self-deprecating whisper. His fingers gripped mine. He had gathered me against him: I was not sure when we had moved so close; I did not know how long my cheek had brushed his. A tremble would bring my lips to his. I stepped back, fiercely flustered, until only my fingers lay still within Kaedric's.

"May I expect you at the Tower tomorrow, my lady?" asked Kaedric, watching me intensely with his blue crystalline eyes. I drew my hand quickly from his grasp, regretting my panicked retreat as his eyes returned to frost. "Since you have apparently taken an interest in the Taormin, Lady Rhianna, I would discuss it with you. Come or not, as you please. I thank you for the dance."

"Rhianna?" came Liya's tentative whisper. Warily, she glanced from side to side of the desolate patio before joining me. "We are preparing to leave, Rhianna.

Your father is looking for you." Hurriedly, she added, "I did not tell him where you were. I was so afraid *he* would still be here."

"You are muddling your pronouns, Liya," I commented.

"I looked for you earlier, Rhianna," said Liya. "I saw you with Lord Venkarel."

"You wanted me to find interesting dance partners."

"He is the Infortiare."

"That obviously did not concern Lady Veiga," I remarked wryly, "whom I thought you so fervently wished to emulate."

"A Dolr'han may do things that are questionable, but you are not a Dolr'han, Rhianna."

I smiled at her a little sadly. "I only danced with the man, Liya. Even my father would not consider that a crime."

She sniffed disapprovingly. "I should not care to be seen dancing that way even with Dayn. You were virtually embracing."

"What nonsense," I answered crisply. "You let the shadows delude you. Even if I were as brazen as you imply, why would the Infortiare take an interest in me? Ixaxis and Tyntagel are not notoriously compatible." I laughed at her crestfallen face. "I believe you are so desperate for a scandal that you have begun concocting them. Ezirae is influencing you badly, Liya." By the time we returned to our family, I had convinced her that her imagination and Lady Veiga's jest had conspired to create delusions.

I nearly persuaded myself as well.

We met not in the Tower library but in a small adjacent room furnished with a single large table and the five mismatched chairs we occupied: Kaedric, Marga, Medwyn, Ineuil and myself. I felt out of place. The feeling mounted as Kaedric explained his reason for summoning us.

"You are each in some sense integrally involved in this decision. My own vote has been made, but I have been reminded that even the Infortiare—or especially the Infortiare—must not make the choice alone. Obviously, I could consult His Royal Highness, Prince Orlin, and the King's Council: they would debate the question, if they considered it at all, for so many months that the point would lose all relevance. We shall not need to locate Horlach via the Taormin once he has begun his attack in earnest."

"Since you have chosen the electors," suggested Ineuil, "it seems that you intend still to make the decision yourself."

"Ineuil's point is well taken, Kaedric," said Abbot Medwyn.

Marga interposed, "Kaedric has been accused at one time or another of nearly everything but stupidity and overwhelming concern for the opinions of others. Be grateful he consults us at all, gentlemen." With a flash of potent spirit, she proceeded, "If either of you considers *me* a spineless syncophant, let me reassure you: I vote against the use of the Taormin." Only Kaedric did not visibly react to Mistress Marga's announcement; he had withdrawn from the discussion to observe. "The rest of you may discuss it as long as it amuses you, but you either agree with Kaedric or not. This business of weighing factors is a procrastinator's pretense."

"Not all of us understand the subject as well as might a member of the Ixaxin Council, Mistress Marga," said Abbot Medwyn. It struck me that the charitable abbot did not much care for Mistress Marga.

"It would be helpful if we at least understood the feasibility of using the Taormin to any advantage," suggested Ineuil carelessly, tilting his chair to a precarious angle.

"Very well," said Marga irritably, "I shall apprise. Kaedric is perfectly capable of using the Taormin."

"I thought Ixaxis considered the Taormin impossible to utilize in these days of diminished Power," inserted Ineuil.

"Do not interrupt me, Lord Arineuil. However, you

have made a relevant comment. On the occasion of your brash, youthful masquerade as a latent sorcerer, you apparently absorbed some small amount of sense. At that time, we did teach that the Taormin's secrets were beyond the capacity of current wizardry. Circumstances forced us to amend our assessment as we realized that Kaedric's Power exceeded anything referenced in the annals of Ixaxis since Ceallagh contained Horlach initially. Kaedric can use the Taormin, which is precisely why he must not. We cannot be sure whether Horlach originally warped the Taormin to his schemes or whether it corrupted him."

Ineuil summarized with incongruous jocularity, "All hail, King Venkarel!"

"Horlach knew that the Power of a Sorcerer King was reborn," I said slowly, without thinking. Even Kaedric displayed a flicker of surprise at my words. I had suddenly become the reluctant cynosure.

Pensively, Marga nodded and said with a trace of wonder, "What a thought that is. Hrgh did not awaken Horlach. Horlach was never fully bound; he used Hrgh to draw Kaedric into activating the Taormin."

Abbot Medwyn sighed with regret, "I wish I could disbelieve it. I am sorry, Kaedric. I must vote with Mistress Marga."

"Then the deciding vote belongs to Rhianna," declared Ineuil unexpectedly. "I prefer the possibility of King Venkarel to the certainty of King Horlach." With a shrug, he yielded attention to me.

I had wanted no part of this conference, agreeing to attend only under the combined blandishments of Abbot Medwyn and Kaedric. Uselessly, I wished that Ineuil had not this once opted to concur with the Infortiare's choice of method. I directed my answer to Kaedric, for the decision had been made and he alone mattered. "My lord, if you will accept my presence when you use the Taormin, I shall give my sanction."

With a slight smirk, Marga observed, "Under the circumstances, Rhianna is uniquely qualified to monitor. Your lady appears to be a suitable match for you, Kaedric."

Kaedric did not answer for a moment. "Are you prepared to begin immediately, Lady Rhianna?"

"As you will, my lord."

Chapter 17

The stairs leading upward from the Tower library were much narrower and more tightly coiled than those with which I had grown familiar in the Tower's lower realms. They were paneled in the same dark wood, giving them a claustrophobic impact which chilled me. Kaedric had taken me alone through that door which I had never yet passed. Marga, Medwyn and Ineuil had left us; Marga had agreed with Kaedric that the dangers inherent in the experiment with the Taormin made non-participating observers an inadvisable luxury.

We climbed the stairs to the highest room of Ceallagh's Tower, a room so small in girth that I suspected it had been intended as no more than an observatory. It was a spartan chamber, that which Kaedric had made his own. Despite sense and the weighty cause which brought us, I halted at the threshold in prudish reluctance. Kaedric remarked with some amusement, "Since you intend to enter my mind, Lady Rhianna, entering my chamber ought not to daunt you."

He was quite correct, but Tyntagellian custom had conditioned me. I focused on our goal and its import. "The Taormin is not here," I observed in puzzlement.

"It is accessible from here." Kaedric nodded toward a high window which framed the vale of Ceallagh's tomb. "This is the only window in the Tower from which Tul's peaks are clearly visible."

"The Taormin is unguarded?" I asked incredulously.

"I entrusted it to him most qualified to hold it: Lord

Ceallagh. It is far safer than keeping it here or at Benthen Abbey." He moved a fawn rug, which might once have been fine, to an area of the floor from which the tomb could be seen, and he seated himself cross-legged upon it. "For our present purpose, a certain distance from the Taormin itself is desirable. I merely feel more comfortable knowing the thing is in some sense before my eyes. It is probably an unnecessary conceit."

He gestured, and I sat opposite him on the rug, my wine-colored skirts spilling across the smooth wood floor. Kaedric studied the base of the mountain cleft, but I was certain he beheld a thing of amber filigree. I watched his eyes grow distant. With a fatalistic sigh, I reached for him with my mind.

Images of images: the Taormin shed impersonal perspective on a child of Ven, a child of Tyntagel. I saw Master Doshk and the dying Fylla. I saw Mistress Ericka and a gardener's son whom I had not known I knew. I heard words which I could never have consciously recalled to comprehension.

This was not the chaotic scramble fostered by Lord Hrgh. Kaedric drew on the Taormin lightly, probing its intricate tangles with a delicate respect for the patterns' potentials. I could not alone have found any method in the tortuous weave, but I followed Kaedric, and my surety of Power grew with the design.

Kaedric pressed a twist of tangled filament: anger, fear, confusion, and a bitter depth of loathing abetted by shattered pride. It was the larger part of Lord Hrgh Dolr'han, the part which knew that Horlach had condemned him to be a pawn in the struggle for an ill-born, once-slave of Ven. Kaedric smoothed the binding knot of darkness.

"You are as damned as I, Venkarel," stated Hrgh clearly. "Horlach will use you, but it will be your name, not his, that is cursed through the coming ages. You and your infernal Power will live forever, more surely enslaved than you were when you were born."

"I can free you, Hrgh," sighed Kaedric with rending pity for the paragon of whom only hatred remained.

"I want none of your mercy, whoreson," countered Hrgh furiously.

Kaedric stayed the releasing touch. "Have you not paid enough for the sake of pride, Hrgh?" I marveled that the remorseless Infortiare could find such sympathy for a man who returned only disdain. Hrgh suffered terribly, but I could feel no compassion for the lord of Liin, bound as much by his own superciliousness as by King Horlach.

It was murder, in a sense, which I contemplated. As such, I would rue it, but Hrgh had already lost the form of man, and he lacked the strength of Power to walk the Taormin freely. The bindings wracked him. "Lord Hrgh," I said coldly, "you shame the First Houses of Serii. But my sister loved you." Hrgh stiffened, for he perceived and knew me then, though we had never truly met. Arrogance poured from him, and he would not bespeak me, but he raised no will to stop me, for I was a lady of his own rank. I completed the gesture which Kaedric had begun, and Lord Hrgh an Morgh yn Elga Dolr'han dur Liin received such peace as death could give him.

Kaedric touched me gently, and we sat again in the Tower room, the burnished sun of Tulean winter patterning our shadows. "When first I arrived at Ixaxis," explained Kaedric pensively, "I considered Hrgh Dolr'han the epitome of everything I had never known: honor, erudition, refinement. I emulated him, and he tolerated me because I amused his vanity. His patronage eased a time of very difficult transition for me." Kaedric stood and, offering his hand, drew me to my feet. "If I attempt any more today," he said with a slight, regretful smile, "My head will throb for a week. The Taormin apparently requires the exercise of some neglected mental sinew. Will you forgive me, my lady, if I neglect to escort you out?"

I withheld a faint smile of my own, for such genteel courtesies had never concerned him previously. "Of course, my lord," I responded very formally. I turned to leave, but Kaedric restrained me briefly.

"My lady, if you continue to assist me, Horlach will no longer need me to regain his material life."

"Is that what he seeks of you?" I asked slowly.

"He wants a host able to hold his Power. I doubt the question of gender will seriously concern him. Be very cautious, my lady."

Ineuil had lingered at the garden access, and he hailed me as I emerged. "I feared I might be waiting here a day and night or, worse, that the earth might shatter while I watched. Since neither calamity transpired, shall I assume the experiment proved uneventful?"

I felt little urge to speak of the past hour, especially to Ineuil. Since I had just sent his erstwhile friend to death, I found answering his cheerful query grimly awkward. Unable to gentle the news, I said directly, "Ineuil, Lord Hrgh is dead."

"I suppose I expected that," he responded soberly. "Still, I kept hoping for some miraculous resurrection of the friend of my youth. Fate is seldom kind to foolish hopes."

"I am sorry," I murmured sincerely.

"It is not of your doing," he said with forced brightness, and I did not correct him. The truth held too much complexity to convey. "Were there any other discoveries of note?" When I shook my head negatively, he continued, "Well, we shall see stirrings soon enough, I warrant. Horlach will not rest idly while Kaedric masters the Taormin. I assume that Horlach knows when the Taormin is used?"

I shrugged my ignorance. "It seems likely. We may only hope that he has no means of reaching it for the present."

Ineuil stared at me strangely. "I wish I could shirk the eerie feeling that I am talking to Kaedric."

I looked at Ineuil with surprise which yielded to disquiet. "Was I quoting him?" I asked brittlely. "I suppose in matters of wizardry I have few other references."

"You have become a model wizardess, infinitely loyal to her Infortiare. I regret to say that I preferred the shy sorceress."

Having accustomed myself to Ineuil's meaningless praise, I found his earnest criticism a stinging reversal. "I serve the Infortiare as you do, Lord Arineuil. That does not make me an Ixaxin."

"You have changed, Rhianna. Even your sister sees it."

"You know my sister far better than I do," I returned caustically.

"I am not the one to blame for your lack of sibling understanding. Yldana envies you devilishly. I once thought she had some cause, but I can only pity a woman who loves Kaedric. Good day to you, Lady Rhianna."

"Good day to you, Lord Arineuil," I responded mechanically, benumbed. The Taormin could mold me to Kaedric's contour if I were incautious, a fact which I had allowed myself to forget. As for the rest, I concluded that Ineuil had devoted himself too long to the pursuit of romantic interludes, shook my head, and followed the path to Tyntagel Hall.

Year of Serii—9008
Liin Keep, Liin, Serii

How like Morgh, thought Dayn uncharitably, to give better to Caruillan syncophants than to a fellow member of a First House. Since I arrived, I have been managing Liin for him virtually unaided, and not a whit of appreciation does he give me; he does not even give solid answer on the trade agreement. This is the first state dinner to which he has invited me, and I only serve here to fill the odd corner by the kitchen.

Dayn stared glumly at the half-naked backs of two bulky Caruillan officers, wondering how the Caruillans kept from freezing in the Seriin climate. The two soldiers comprised Dayn's view of the dining hall. When one of the officers moved to another table, Dayn decided that the expanded view was yet worse. The room seemed a sea of Caruillans, grabbing food indiscriminately and seldom resorting to any proper utensil. The soldiers (Dayn had yet to discern any Caruillan whose function was not primarily military) seemed to spend remarkably little time actually eating; they occupied themselves mainly in pulling at and pinching the comelier serving maids. The result was a chaotic failure of the usual Liin staff efficiency and a great deal of grumbling from the kitchen.

In his neglected corner, Dayn, receiving barely a third of the dinner's courses, retreated farther toward the wall in a vain attempt to avoid the crush of distraught servants, and began to feel even more miserable than he had during the last few depressing days. He tried a gingerly sip of wine, grimaced and settled for another roll. Dry bread seemed more palatable than the richly sauced comestibles. Unhappiness and worry had always tended to take a toll on Dayn's stomach.

Dayn watched the noble men and women of Liin, while his vague feeling of nausea grew. These selfsame silken sophisticates had no use for a younger son of the Tyntagel Lord, but they toasted the king of Caruil and cheered his pirates, because Lord Morgh commanded and Lord Morgh knew where advantage lay. All hail King Cor of Caruil, for he has eradicated a great, terrible hold of schoolchildren. All hail Blood-Talon Cor, who has conquered for us, because he does not share our shrinking cowardice.

Morgh is going to toast Caruil again, decided Dayn, as Liin's liege rose and commanded silence with an imperious gesture, which most of the Caruillans ignored and most of Liin's nobility were too sated and stupefied to comprehend. "To new friends!" declared

Morgh grandly. Insipid, thought Dayn; Morgh looks his age and more, despite his tailor's talent for hiding Dolr'han paunch, but need he act so feeble-witted? It is a wonder even these Caruillan savages can abide him.

"To the expansion of the Alliance, and to the strengthening of our united cause!" cried some Dolr'han scion.

"To the death of Ixaxis!" added another Liinite thickly. Do they ever tire of hearing themselves prate, wondered Dayn sourly, and an extra hint of guilt gnawed at his pained internals.

King Cor rose rather slowly, pausing to adjust the gilt scabbard of Caruillan formal wear. The Caruillan men, so far as Dayn had been able to determine, never changed their peculiar attire, nor did each own more than a single set of leather breeches and soiled silk vest. For state occasions, Caruillan dignitaries simply doffed steel arms in favor of painted tin, as Cor had made a great show of explaining on first arriving.

Cor was a swarthy, surprisingly little man with a shrewd eye, a ruthless sense of humor, and a fine instinct for opportunism. "My good friends," announced Cor with such deliberation that Dayn straightened and forgot his discomfort. "The welcome you have shown us is deeply heartening. We are pleased by your city, which makes my next remarks sincerely sorrowful to me." Every Caruillan in the room had grown quiet and attentive. The oblivious voices of Liin arrogance sputtered over incoherent sounds from the city beyond the keep walls, while Blood-Talon Cor displayed his stained and broken teeth in a feral smile.

"When your emissary first approached me, Lord Morgh," continued Cor cheerfully, "I must confess that I thought your ideas of cooperation absurd. We of Caruil are warriors, who take and rule by strength. I had doubt of any benefit you soft-living Seriins could offer us." Morgh's finely pleased expression did not waver, carved from either political practice or too much wine, even when Cor draped his glance appreciatively across the Lady Galea Dolr'han, Morgh's second cousin and reputed mistress. "We have come to see, however, that your city holds more treasure than we ever realized. It is fortunate, this," said Cor heartily, "for otherwise we might be very unhappy with you for misleading us."

Those nobles of Liin who remained capable of any comprehension began to look puzzled. Dayn struggled to push the clouds from his own senses, for an illogical suspicion had occurred to him. He eyed the wine from which he had briefly sipped and wondered if he imagined the trace of cloudiness in its midst.

Three staccato screams seemed suddenly to drive into Dayn's brain. The bulky soldier in front of him drove his ornamental dagger into the neck of Lord Okhren Dolr'han. Through the nobleman's spurting blood, Dayn watched a ghastly play of treachery begin, and yet he did nothing.

"You promised us the 'unimaginable wealth' of Ixaxis," shouted Cor to a bewildered Morgh, "so we fought the stinking rocks of Ixaxin waters to take the accursed island, and we found nothing! There are no wizards there, and the only treasure is a load of chalk and lies. I do not know what game you thought to play, Morgh, or if you could really be so simple as to believe in the godhood of your damned Infortiare, but I am not a fool to humor you longer. I conquered your dreaded island for you, even if the winds and reefs alone fought back, and I will be paid." Cor had taken a sound sword from his tinseled scabbard, and he sliced Lord Morgh's still bemused head from its neck.

Dayn had risen, but the door from the kitchen had been flung open, pressing his back against the cold, mirrored wall. He heard the shrieking slaughter, and he feared to move. It was his old, deep fear and doubts made real: that in true battle he would be unable to function and would so bring shame upon his father. He had served in the king's army for five years and found no certain answer; he had guarded Serii's vague northern borders diligently, earned (what he considered) unmerited praise for so well securing the northern cities and townships of his jurisdiction, captured and successfully intimidated many of the thugs and robbers who frequented the more desolate lands, but he had never fought a battle that was not wholly weighted in his favor.

Dayn believed himself a coward. The notion had grown in him over the years since he first ran in panic from his sister's sorcery. He had clung to his older brother's side and opinions, trying to emulate one who did not know this terror of being found weak. His frail baby sister had exploded into an ogre before the eyes of his imagination, and he had never again felt secure in his own abilities.

The sounds of bloodshed retreated from Liin's Great Dining Hall, and Dayn emerged cautiously from his dim corner. He would not look at the carnage which was all that remained of Dolr'han nobility. He would not face the fabulous rooms and passageways which Dolr'han feet had for centuries proudly trod. Dayn slipped around the door and into the kitchen, taking the servants' way, for he felt it suited his shame.

The servants had fared no better than their masters, and bodies slumped against the once spotless white tiles. A woman was crying, and Dayn saw a grinning Caruillan complete the act of rape by stabbing her to death. The Caruillan spotted Dayn and lunged at him with bloodied sword. Dayn dodged and kicked instinctively, knocking the Caruillan against the kitchen's marble table. Dayn ran blindly into the unfamiliar corridors of the servants' wing, but the Caruillan followed in an instant.

It took only a pause before a latched door for Dayn to lose his previous lead. The Caruillan was as huge as most of his countrymen; he slammed Dayn against the door with an effortless force. Dayn tasted warm blood and did not know whether it flowed from the sharp pain in his lip or the ache of a smashed nose. He waited for the searing sharpness of steel to cut his spine. He could only turn around dumbly when the Caruillan's weight sagged and slipped from him.

"That is for what you did to Leisa," cursed a rather pudgy man to his victim; he pulled a hefty knife from the dead Caruillan's back. The man wore servants' clothes, and they had been torn and spattered. "I never butchered anything but dinner before this," added the man a little apologetically, now addressing Dayn. "My name is Targar. Can you use one of these?" he asked, offering Dayn the Caruillan's sword.

Dayn's voice caught, and he could not answer. He settled for a nervous nod and accepted the weapon from Targar's rough hand. Dayn fit his fingers around the sword's hilt with loathing; only a few traces of the deceptive gold paint still clung to the sword's pommel.

Dayn helped Targar to drag the Caruillan away from the door, then meekly followed Targar through the portal. They picked their way through dead men and women who had been dragged from work, ease or slumber. The bodies of the Keep guards had already stiffened, and their cloaks had been stripped from them. All of the bodies were nameless to Dayn, but Targar acknowledged each with a nod of stoic respect.

"There is a stair to the cellars along here," offered Targar. "We can take the cellar route clear to the gate house."

"I cannot leave the keep undefended," said Dayn automatically, though he continued to follow.

"You want to die?" demanded Targar. "You will if you stay here."

"I am a lord of Serii," argued Dayn unreasonably.

Targar cast Dayn a look of utter disgust. "The whole bloody Caruillan army is in Liin, and you lords of Serii brought them here. I am not blaming you personally, mind, but if I were you, I think I might trust to someone else's judgment for a while. Maybe you have not been seeing too clearly who your friends are."

Dayn stared at the plump and very ugly Targar, realizing that he owed his life to a menial from the Liin Keep kitchens. "Mayhap you are correct," conceded Dayn with a sudden sympathy for Targar's resentment. Targar had extended the first generosity

Dayn had witnessed in Liin. It irked Dayn, for it forced on him unpalatable ideas.

A pair of Caruillans lurched from a side passage, espied Dayn and Targar, and spilled the bounty of their looting across the floor. Dayn rushed at the larger of the pair, driving his borrowed sword upward through the man's viscera. Targar had tackled the other Caruillan, before the pirate could free himself of his plunder. Dayn hacked off the Caruillan's foot, and Targar's knife found its way into the Caruillan's tattooed hide.

Dayn offered a sword to Targar, who shook his head. "I would as soon use a tool I know," insisted Targar fervently. Dayn nodded; he could understand a need for the familiar, even when the familiar served less well. A clamor echoed from the hall from which the Caruillan attackers had come. Dayn and Targar rose wordlessly and made their way through narrow, less frequented passages. They could hear the Caruillan plague spread loudly around them. The cellar door was locked, but Targar drew a key from his waist-ring. Targar entered the dark cellar and found candles by touch. Dayn closed and locked the door behind them, softening the growing sounds of the Caruillan raiders.

As they descended into the cool recesses beneath the servants' wing, the sounds ebbed further, until Dayn could almost persuade himself that the whispering cries were the sounds of a normal, busy Keep. The acres of stored goods astonished him. Dayn thought he could never alone have found passage through the maze of root cellars, wine cellars, fur closets, and granaries. Targar led unerringly and only broke the silence after many minutes: "I wonder how long it will take Cor to find his way down here?"

He was answered by a roar which shook the ground, and the dark room they were on the brink of entering became bright before them. Dayn and Targar retreated hurriedly as a portion of the ceiling crashed to the floor in flames. "They have set the Keep on fire," exclaimed Targar wonderingly. The fact seemed to dismay him more visibly than the horrors of the carnage they had already observed.

"Is there another exit on this side of the Keep?" asked Dayn sharply.

"There is a loading access, but we could never reach the gate from there."

"We shall certainly never reach the gate from here," countered Dayn, shouting to be heard over the flames and cracking timbers.

They were forced to retrace their steps through four rooms. They hastened through four more rooms as the sounds of fire raced behind them; the greater part of Liin Keep had been carved from layered stone, but the servants' wing had been built primarily of wood. When Dayn and Targar had climbed the last stair, Targar hesitated, fumbling overlong with his keys, before opening the door. Dayn did not press him, for he, too, feared to face the certainty of enemies in the courtyard; Dayn did cast uneasy glances at the glow of spreading fire. The flames expanded into fury as they reached the kegs of ale in the next room, and Targar flung open the door with a burst of desperation.

Liin Keep burned spectacularly, though the marble and gold facade of the Dolr'han quarters resisted the assault. In the yard the army of Liin fought, taking better toll of Caruil than Cor might have expected, but the effort could be called no more than feeble. Liin's army had been outfitted for parades and trained in protocol; even Dayn knew more of tactics than Liin's generals. Dayn and Targar shoved themselves through the fray, clinging to each other's company, though they barely knew whether those at whom they slashed were foe or ally. The bright banners, which had been hung in honor of Caruil and Cor, curled and smoked overhead; they would carry the sparks through the city, and the finely carved woods and tapestried walls would shrivel to cinder and ash. Like a wizard's fury, thought Dayn bitterly.

Dayn shut his ears to screams and lingering moans, to the crackle of a city afire, and to the cries of incredulous Liin. He and Targar ran when they could, pressed relentlessly through mobs of fleeing citizens, killed when some persistent Caruillan could not be dodged, and gradually neared the city's edge. There is no honor in survival, thought Dayn, when so many who are innocent die. He wanted to stop, yield to the massacre, but Targar tugged at him and he continued.

Did hours pass? Years could have come and gone, and Dayn would not have known. The mighty Pontneun gate of Liin had crumbled by the time Dayn and Targar reached it; it had been clawed and torn by its own desperate citizenry. With Cor's fleet occupying the harbor, and the eastern half of the city aflame, only a few of the great gates offered exit. Cor's legions had secured the wall early, knowing its strategic advantage, and they held it comfortably, sending Liin's own arrows into the frantic crowds below.

It had become a Caruillan game to let most of those who neared the gate stand safely. The Caruillans rained arrows only on those who sought to pass. The game did allow a few escapes, but the Caruillans enjoyed the sport of baiting still more than easy slaughter. They watched closely the folk who hesitated: it was hard to leave a sanctuary, however temporary and artificial, to face such unpromising odds of survival as awaited those who braved the gateway. Shopkeepers, who had never thought to face such certain danger, wavered, debating their chances. Scrubs and harlots huddled with merchant's wives, united by indecision. Occasionally one figure would start to run, hoping to catch the Caruillan archers unaware, and a flurry of frightened people might follow.

A tow-headed girl ran out the gate alone and died a pace from the wall. A young boy ran next and died a handspan away from her, but a dozen of his comrades continued fleeing. Arrows pursued them, but at least two men kept running, and one survived beyond the archers' range, his example encouraging another rush. Dayn and Targar joined the dash, though Dayn berated himself fiercely; he was quite probably the only lord of Serii left alive in wretched Liin, and duty whispered cruelly that her defeat belonged to his cowardice. Dayn also knew that Targar had been right to counsel escape; Liin, the great, golden hub of Seriin elitism, could not be salvaged by any resource left within her.

Dayn did not see Targar fall, but the serving man with his brave butcher's knife did not reach the haphazard cluster of survivors, who had gathered in exhaustion at the nearest edge of safety. Dayn sat with the others upon the bare earth, watching the smoke of the city hide the stars. The cries were muted from here, indistinguishable if one did not know the source. The tired little knot of survivors shared the silence. Most had lost home and family. All had lost a measure of innocence and hope. All feared that morning would renew the horror, bringing the Caruillan horde spilling across the valley like a spreading disease. Most recognized that the nightmare which had so abruptly shattered their complacent lives had only begun its work.

Chapter 18

Year of Serii—9008
Tyntagel Hall, Tulea

"Have you received any word from Dayn, Liya dear?" asked Ezirae across the table. My father looked at Ezirae irritably, for her supper conversations with Liya invariably managed to cut across his with Dhavod.

Liya did not quite succeed at smiling. "There has been nothing since the first letter, Aunt Ezirae," she said patiently, as she had done each day of the past week. "Dayn told me that he would have little time for writing. Lord Morgh asked him to assist in entertaining the Caruillan guests."

"Caruillans," tutted Ezirae predictably. "My father, may his soul rest freely, always maintained that the only thing less trustworthy than a drycat was a Caruillan. He always maintained that."

"I am sure he did," responded Liya gravely.

"I simply cannot understand it," continued Ezirae heedlessly. "Everyone is treating the Caruillans like honored guests these days. Lord Morgh dur Liin caters to them, and King Astorn has gone off to Bethii to discuss giving them trade privileges. A year ago, Caruillans were raiding our coasts. It is all so bewildering."

My father had heard Ezirae make similar comments many times before, but he had disregarded them as he disregarded nearly everything Ezirae said or did. His mood was less charitable tonight. "You need not parade your ignorance for us constantly, Ezirae," he said cuttingly. "We are well aware of your indomitable biases. What is it now?" he demanded impatiently as a commotion arose in the hall.

A stained and disheveled version of my usually impeccable brother pushed past startled servants. With a little cry of horror, Liya ran to him and stopped a pace away, not quite touching his rent and blackened coat. "My Lord Father," said Dayn with the stiffness of exhaustion. Dayn swayed, and Dhavod moved to steady him, guiding my brother with Liya's help to the chair which Liya had occupied. Dayn raised his head slowly, and I could not believe that the bitterness contorting his features belonged to my brother.

"What has happened to you?" demanded our father accusingly. Liya shook her head in protest, but Dayn straightened defensively.

"I failed you, Father," said Dayn with forced tightness. "I did not gain your precious trade exchange with Liin. Lord Morgh is dead, and the Caruillans have taken the city."

"What madness is this?" asked my father irritably.

"An ugly man with a knife told me that the madness

was ours, my Lord Father. The lords of Serii are all mad." Dayn's voice trailed, then surged harshly. "I thought to spend no more than a few idle days in Liin, merely formalizing a trade agreement on which all interested parties had already concurred, but Lord Morgh requested my assistance in a matter of 'local diplomacy.' Lord Morgh intimated that I could alleviate the painful vacancy left by the banishment of his son. Lord Morgh needed me to manage Liin's mundane affairs, while the Dolr'hans celebrated their Caruillan guests."

"Why ever would Lord Morgh associate with such barbarians?" asked Ezirae. "I really cannot understand what the Caruillans have to offer which could possibly outweigh their disgusting personal habits."

Dayn laughed acidly. "They offered to attack Ixaxis for us, Aunt Ezirae. We lacked the stomach to do it ourselves."

Our father interposed with a quick frown, "Dayn, you are rambling."

Dayn struck the table an impatient blow which rattled the crystal. "It is not a secret any longer, Father. By the morrow, the word will have spread all over Tulea, and the rest of Serii will know before the week ends. It is the Caruillan battle cry; they laugh it in our faces." Dayn turned to Liya, who gazed at him possessively. "We have kept the secret overlong, alienating even those we love for the sake of conspiracy. Lord Morgh was not the only Seriin Lord bewitched by Caruil." Dayn looked meaningfully at our iron-willed father, who only fractionally dropped his gaze before my bedraggled brother's censure. "The result of the Caruillan foray against Ixaxis is not altogether clear, Father, since we have only King Cor's rendition on which to rely. The Caruillans claim that they took Ixaxis unchallenged. They fought the island's natural defenses, scaled the chalky cliffs, and found nothing: no treasures, no pillage for their coffers, and not a wizard, scholar, or beardless boy.

" 'You offered us a city, Lord Morgh,' said Cor, 'but your choice did not impress us. We have decided, however, to be generous and accept as substitute the city of Liin.'

"I am not sure Lord Morgh ever really comprehended Cor's words. Cor drew a very genuine sword from his decorative scabbard and decapitated the Lord of Liin."

Dhavod had turned ashen; Ezirae stared without comprehension. Liya had buried her face against Dayn's trembling knee. My father had closed his eyes and bowed his head toward the goblet in his hand. "How many others escaped?" asked my father with the faintest trace of a quaver.

Dayn shook his head. "From Liin Keep, perhaps a few servants. There were more survivors from the city itself, but not as many as there should have been." Dayn's voice cracked. Liya's hand crept into that of her husband, and his fingers tightened around hers.

"You are free of it now, Dayn," she reassured him quietly.

"You never saw Liin, did you, Liya? One could deride the Dolr'han snobbery, but they were right to be proud of their domain." Dayn stared beyond us. "A serving man named Targar used a butcher's knife to save my life. We fought our way free together through the whole accursed city, and Targar died at the gate." Dayn choked at the memory.

"Did the Caruillans use sorcery?" I asked fearfully. My own mind echoed Dayn's account with the chaotic horror of a dying Ven.

Dayn explained to me with care, as if I had no wit to understand, "It was to abolish wizardry that we approached Caruil initially. Caruillans do use minor sorcery, but they are not wizards to fight with Power." Dayn twisted around toward our grim-faced father. "I think now that such wizards do not exist at all. We have sacrificed Liin, Father, out of fear of a phantasm."

"Venkarel exists," returned our father thinly.

"He is one man," countered Dayn, almost shouting. "We have dreaded to act openly against him for fear of what his guild might do to retaliate. We have listened to Cor and Arku Ruy and Borgor, but what miracle have we ever seen an Ixaxin do? The wizards we fear do not exist. The Ixaxins are a handful of men and women who have built their influence out of myths, and Caruil has made good use of our credulity."

Dhavod answered, "I saw Lord Hrgh fall before Venkarel, Dayn."

"But Hrgh was not harmed," argued Dayn.

"Venkarel destroyed most of Ven," insisted my uncle.

"So the rumors would have us believe," said my brother in response, "but fires start in many ways, and no special Power is needed for their making. The Ixaxins are expert at implying enormous capability without providing any real evidence. They manipulate us! We pour our resources against them, and we achieve nothing. Our supposed allies turn against us, and Venkarel sits in his damnable Tower and laughs at our naiveté."

"Venkarel must have paid Cor richly to betray us," mused our father, unshaken in his confidence. Lord Baerod dur Tyntagel did not show the strain of shock which suddenly painted Dhavod with age. Dhavod lacked the strength of a sorcerous heritage.

"The name of your enemy is not Venkarel," I asserted scornfully. Dayn and my father fastened their attention on me. There was an element almost of contrition in Dayn's eyes, but my father showed suspicion and open loathing. I said firmly, "You have been hurt, Dayn. Take him upstairs, Liya. I shall come shortly to tend him."

Liya obeyed without question, and Dayn was too weary to object. Ezirae hovered helplessly, but a glance at her liege lord's set expression made her decide to follow Liya. My father issued an order to Dhavod with all the natural authority of Tyntagel's Lord: "Bear word to His Royal Highness. The Council must convene." Dhavod bowed and complied, patently relieved to yield to his brother's command. I awaited the confrontation I knew must come.

"What do you know of this matter, Rhianna?" demanded my father. His voice condemned me, blaming me unquestioningly.

"Caruil has started war upon us, and you accuse me?" I asked incredulously.

"I am not altogether blind to your acquaintance with Lord Venkarel, Rhianna. If you know something of his involvement in the attack on Liin, I demand that you reveal it."

"Are you not confusing the names of Caruil's conspiratorial allies, my Lord Father?" I asked, wondering whether Grisk had spoken or my father himself had actually discovered my visits to Ceallagh's Tower.

"The Caruillans have proven their own treachery; they have not exonerated the Infortiare. The story of a deserted Ixaxis is patently absurd. It is far more likely that the Infortiare merely offered the Caruillans a substantial incentive to alter their target to Liin." He reiterated his theory to himself more than to me. "How does one fight the devil?" he growled.

"Why would Lord Venkarel wish to destroy Liin?" I prompted, desolately impressed by my father's unfailing faith in his prejudices.

"Attend your brother, Rhianna. You clearly know nothing of import."

I responded with the meekness expected, "Yes, my Lord Father," feeling helpless against his obduracy. I could not combat my liege. Abbot Medwyn was correct: I could not chose definitively.

Chapter 19

Dayn's physical hurts were not deep. I cleansed them and gave him an infusion of valerian, which would heal Dayn's ragged nerves more than it would his rent skin. I left him to Liya's solicitous care and sped to Ceallagh's Tower, but my delay had given others time to act; Prince Orlin had indeed convened the King's Council, and Kaedric had been summoned to it.

I waited in the Infortiare's library, reading, studying and pacing. My Ixaxin lord would come eventually. Kaedric would not give me comfort, but he would understand my fears. He would recognize the specter which I dreaded more than any Caruillan.

"Your father does have a flair for narrative, my lady," remarked Kaedric as he entered, accepting my presence without question, "but I could wish he had expounded less on his peripheral theories regarding the sack of Liin. Is your brother faring well?"

"Only exhaustion seriously plagues him, my lord. I think Dayn has slept little since fleeing Liin."

"I shouldn't wonder; the death of a city is a nightmarish business. I suppose you await my report," he added with a rather twisted smile. I wanted to tell him that I sought reassurance rather than uncomfortable truths, but I held silent. "And you need not bother with the protest that you have no right to question the Infortiare, since that is presumably why you are here in despite of your Tyntagel proprieties. Very well, I report: Prince Orlin convened the King's Council at your father's behest. After a prolonged dissection of your brother's story, with which I assume you are already acquainted, Prince Orlin has decided to ride forth with a detachment of the Tulean guard to rout King Cor and the Caruillan scavengers. The members of His Royal Highness' select troop will be young gallants who know nothing of actual warfare, but enthusiasm recognizes no damping logic."

"His Royal Highness will not listen to you," I observed resignedly.

"His Royal Highness quakes like an aspen when I address him. In any case, the Adjutant presides over decisions of soldiery, and Lord Borgor encourages His Royal Highness to take immediate military retribution. Since the Caruillans used no obvious sorcery in their attack, I have no lawful jurisdiction save what the regent allows me."

"What of King Cor's allegations regarding Ixaxis?"

"His Royal Highness has been 'persuaded to disbelieve the Caruillan account, but the matter is of secondary importance.' In point of fact, Lord Borgor has convinced His Royal Highness to accept your father's theories, but Prince Orlin is not about to tackle me with an outright accusation. Hence, he shelves the subject and pursues his vision of glorious combat."

"Is the Caruillan account true, my lord?" I persisted.

"I suspect King Cor is incapable of telling the complete truth on any subject."

"My lord, you have a most provoking way of eluding questions."

"My lady, I have had a great deal of practice." I met his mocking glance. The Taormin had made him a part of me, yet I agreed with Ineuil that the woman who loved Lord Venkarel would earn no envy. With more irritation than I had a right to feel, I rose to leave. Kaedric stopped me with a gesture. "By my order, Lady Rhianna, the island of Ixaxis was evacuated over a month ago. I so informed the Council, but the Seriin lords devoted themselves to doubting me rather than assessing the implications of my statement. I did not inform the Council that the Ixaxin Guild members are now dispersed throughout Serii, while most of the Ixaxin artifacts remain concealed on the island."

"Ixaxis had become an obvious target," I mused, focusing on the dark patch amid the phosphorescent sea.

"And a demonstration of wizardly defense, while effective, would only heighten the animosity which we wish to dispel. Unfortunately, I did not account for the Caruillans' peculiar persistence; otherwise, I should not have left Liin so vulnerable, despite Lord Morgh's efforts to counter me."

"Did Horlach direct the Caruillans?"

"I wish I knew the answer to that conundrum, my lady. Horlach certainly merits a share of the blame, but the degree of his involvement is as elusive as his precise location. I spend each Council session inspecting the Seriin lords for Horlach's taint, but I find no madness but their own. Have I assuaged your curiosity sufficiently?"

I had received more information than I had anticipated. "I have been presumptuous again," I said apologetically.

"Where should I find so sympathetic an audience if you were not?" Kaedric rubbed his neck and grimaced. "With the lords of Serii and a Sorcerer King intent upon my demise, words from anyone not bent on my immediate destruction are warmly welcome. I begin to wish that Medwyn had left me in the ashes of Ven. It would have made for a much simpler life."

My mind moved involuntarily to soothe him. It was a reflex as direct as a shift to ease a cramped position. It was the habit of an empath enhanced by the Taormin's patterning. In my mind, Kaedric met me, touched me and withdrew. I recalled that I had feared his touch; I had more cause now, for I comprehended his Power and its ability to change me.

"My lady, I recommend that you depart summarily, lest I harm you more than I have already done." It was a superfluous warning. I had run to the stairs in spontaneous retreat, and his caveat sounded only to my Power.

Chapter 20

Prince Orlin led a brave, bright troop. In crisp crimson, they rode forth proudly; the golden horses, the famed breed raised in Viste, stepped daintily. It was a fine parade: young men well-favored and eager, personally selected by His Royal Highness, the prince regent. His Royal Highness scorned to note the occasional jibe which followed him through Tulea's streets. His troop shone too boldly to be diminished by a few soured soldiers whose scarred maturity did not accord with His Royal Highness' concept of a suitable army of vengeance. When the genial troop had passed, Tulea seemed betrayed into unkindly age and cynicism. The citizens placidly resumed routine, but unwonted stillness created a mournful pall.

Winter held us: Tulean winter, made mild by ocean gentling but gray and somber, nonetheless. Whispers rose: that Ixaxin wizards had joined the legions of Blood-Talon Cor, and they wrung from Liin such despair as would cry to the winds for eternity. The threads of unrest twisted around Tulea and caught in her heart. In the marketplace in full daylight, a merchant fell upon the impoverished carcass of a self-styled witch for the thieving of a skin of spirits from his stall. The witch's comrade in poverty intervened to spare the woman from the bane of imprisonment, but mischance struck the merchant to his death upon the cobbles. The cry arose against sorcerous intrusion: the bewildered witch in her grimy rags became a conniving wizardess, her comrade a Caruillan spy. By the time the Tulean guard arrived to suppress the riotous mob, the conflagration of irrationality had claimed some thirty lives. Sanity returned with the timidity of shame, but the specter of distrust had been raised.

Ezirae's nieces had been returned to Hamley amid protesting squeals of social deprivation. Ziva and Flava were not alone among the noble young to find themselves suddenly banished from their accustomed court haunts. The growing exodus exceeded any usual seasonal variations in Tulea's castle populace and left a hollow dearth of joyful chatter. Even the most stalwart supporters of Prince Orlin's foray did not expect quick redemption from Serii's troubles.

With the diminishing population of the castle, the Hall of my father lost something of the excessive gloom engendered by unfavorable comparison. Tyntagel's meager contingent among court nobility had not dwindled; indeed, Amgor and Yldana now joined us as often as not, for the despised Amlach cousins all had fled, and Amlach Hall echoed dolefully. Little gaiety could be found among us, but stiff and leaded silence grasped

Tyntagel Hall no more firmly than it did the larger part of Tulea.

Kaedric had essayed the Taormin a ten of times, discerning with each effort new strata of complexity, but Horlach had made no overt, betraying move. Orlin had been gone a tenday, and rumors that the prince regent had liberated Liin met with skeptical indifference. "I have an uneasy suspicion that Lord Borgor's couriers bear us biased news," said Kaedric. "I have neglected His Royal Highness in searching for Horlach. Let us see whether the Taormin can serve to bring us more reliable reports."

Kaedric turned inward, transitioning smoothly to the Taormin's webs, and I accompanied him, more certain of my own path than I could have anticipated a week before. Kaedric had not warned me idly; I could have used the Taormin alone now, and I knew how precariously I should exist were that realization to extend beyond Kaedric and myself. I disliked considering how far the Infortiare's own Power had expanded.

Liin had indeed burned, leaving only a pitiful shell of the once-great city. I had never seen her glory, and it was gone now. Little about her lived, though some survivors had begun to rebuild. Caruil had left proud Liin sacked and shorn of every beauty. I thought I felt a relict of Dolr'han conceit amid the wrack, but the scion of Tul drew us along another path. Kaedric touched the threads of many minds and many memories, and he took from them a single fading strand. At Kaedric's touch the pale filament glowed and shivered like taut wire. We wrapped ourselves around it and absorbed it.

Prince Orlin observed with a frown that the flag of Tul had slipped; a gust had pulled it from the column, and dew had plastered its silk against the charred ledge where it had caught. The sight depressed him, but the whole of Liin looked very grim now that dawn revealed the sum of her ravages. In the dusky light of yesterday's fog, the city had somehow still seemed glorious to him. And the skirmish at the gate: that had been grand.

Orlin gazed at his injured hand with a touch of pride. True, the nasty little creature who had wounded him had been a Seriin vulture rather than a Caruillan warrior, but the vulture had fought fiercely. When cornered, the awful parasite had actually bitten Orlin's hand, and Orlin had been forced to whack its head with the flat of his sword. It had seemed quite a marvelous battle at the time.

Really, this gray mood which was taking hold of him was most annoying. Victory had been wonderful: riding staunchly into Liin and watching the scavengers scatter before the crimson wave of Orlin's handsome troop. They had arrested quite a large number of looters, driven off many more, and rescued one screaming woman from a villain whom they had summarily executed. The only Caruillans they had seen had been dead or dying, but Orlin's men had quickly dispatched the few survivors. No doubt Blood-Talon Cor had observed Orlin's approach and launched his ships in hasty retreat. Perhaps Orlin would plan a retaliatory attack on Caruil.

It really was too maddening that he should feel so depressed. He had deliberately established camp in the quayside portion of the city, which had been thoroughly leveled by fire and lay upwind of all those dead citizens in the less devastated districts, so as to avoid the contaminating touch of disease; Orlin had been quite proud of that decision. Of course, thought Orlin sourly, I suppose we ought to effect some more permanent protection by disposing of the bodies altogether.

This was not turning out as Orlin had anticipated. Disposing of the dead and arresting looters were not the stuff of great sagas. The more Orlin considered his mood, the more he decided that it was all the fault of that man, Mots, who had spent a considerable portion of the night berating Orlin quite unjustly. Orlin's men had saved Mots' life, freeing him from beneath a timber Mots could never have budged alone, fed the man a hearty supper and made him welcome in their camp; all Mots could do was sneer just like the fools in Tulea, who were only jealous of Orlin's youth, after all. Orlin wished Lord Borgor were with him. Somehow Borgor always managed to explain things so clearly, eradicating Orlin's self-doubts with a deftly knowing gem of advice. Borgor would certainly dismiss Mots' theories that Cor only savored his conquest, tarrying on his ships until the next attack: the attack on Tulea.

It is strange that we have seen so few Caruillans, nor even a distant vessel on the sea. I assumed yesterday that the fog hid Cor's retreating fleet, but the fog has cleared, and the wind has been poor; no ship ought to have been able to travel yet so far in such weather. Maybe it is true that Caruillans use sorcery to speed their vessels. Orlin shunned that final thought.

When the day had lengthened, and Orlin's spirits had not improved, he gathered his officers around him. The prince thought their bright, patrician faces and good humor would cheer him, and he felt a vague need to plan something or do something now that his goal of reclaiming Liin had apparently been achieved. Orlin's officers displayed little enthusiasm for talk of scouring Liin into some sad respectability, but the hesitant suggestion of a foray against Caruil did excite them. Orlin felt no better than before.

The fog had returned: a thick, yellow cloud which Orlin found unsettling. If only Borgor were here, thought Orlin again. He would tell me that this pressure I feel constricting my lungs is only from sour smoke. Borgor would assure me that my head reels with victory and not with the echoes of the restless dead. Borgor would tell me that I feel cold and hot at once only because of a slight chill and fever, and he would send me immediately to bed.

Orlin's officers were laughing, building and rebuilding every story of capture or chase, comparing and concocting amusing anecdotes about this prisoner or that capture. Lord Joret's tales had a particularly imaginative flair. How can they be so carefree amid the rubble of so much ruined beauty, wondered Orlin enviously. Why can I not set aside Liin's tragedy and rejoice instead in my own good fortunes, as they do?

Orlin felt his head begin to pound. He noticed that several of his officers had fallen silent, their faces pinched and strained. Across the camp the horses had begun to whinny in an off-key tone which Orlin could have sworn held panic. Lord Chath dur Viste, Orlin's second-in-command, made a restless, awkward attempt to rise, but he fell back, choking horribly.

All the young officers tried simultaneously to reach him. They succeeded only in creating a scramble of utter confusion and incoherent apologies. Feeling absurdly sickened by his comrades' useless gentilities, Orlin took hard hold of Lord Drimon and ordered him very fiercely to fetch the medic. "Clear away, for lords' sake!" shouted Orlin roughly, and he did not care that they stared with more astonished concern at him than at pitiable Chath. Chath's coughing had grown deep, and the young officer's hands came blood-smeared away from his face. A terrible contortion racked the Viste lord, and he struck Orlin in a mindless spasm. Chath jerked violently on the ground, his back arched horribly and cracked, and Chath lay still and colorless.

Lord Joniax had started shaking heavily. Lord Rosh had turned pale, and he clutched at his throat. Orlin's own breath had grown more labored, and his tongue felt like fire. He looked across the camp, and the fog had parted. The ships of Caruil loomed in the harbor, and Blood-Talon Cor laughed from the nearest bow. At Cor's side, three spidery women in black veils and silver robes waved their arms and moaned.

Ixaxins spurn such melodrama, thought Orlin wildly. These are sorcerers not wizards, but, lords, they have Power. Relying on an instinct he had never tested, Orlin commanded, threatened, and physically pushed his men, coercing as many as could move to mount the horses. It was a nightmarish effort, for each of them was suffering from the attack, and no armor did they have against Power, no weapon with which to retaliate. A number of the horses had fallen, too, but somehow, some few of Orlin's troop struggled enough to mount and ride. Orlin headed his steed toward Tulea, following a figure who might have been Joret. It mattered only that they distance themselves from the harbor of Liin and the sorcerers of Cor. Orlin could not quite remember if distance greatly affected Power, but he knew no other escape to try. Orlin had never listened well to lessons of wizards' history.

The horses carried them, the bright young men who so recently had planned to conquer their world. No Seriin troop shall make foray without escort by a representative of the Infortiare, Orlin recalled with horror. No battle shall be waged without Ixaxis' aid. Precaution, said Ceallagh's laws, can forestall catastrophe, and only Power can defend against Power.

The sting of hot acid racked Orlin's throat and lungs. It spread to his eyes, and he could not see. All sound and sense, save pain, had failed him. The horse ran erratically, torn by its own demons until it dropped, its fine bones shattered. The prince regent landed heavily in the filth of a ditch, and he could only dimly suspect that the horse no longer bore him. *Venkarel,* cried Orlin in his failing mind, *why did I never listen?*

Then the Venkarel was there, like a vision of death. "Venkarel," croaked the young, dying prince. "Stop them," Orlin pleaded. A feeling had come upon Orlin that there was something that the Venkarel needed to know. It was a strange feeling, for it raised in Orlin an odd sense of kinship with the long dead Tul: not for Tul the warrior, whom Orlin had hoped to emulate in battle, but for the mortal Tul who had dared to defy a Sorcerer King. "What a pompous fool I have been," said Orlin to himself.

"You have served Serii honorably, Your Royal Highness," said the Venkarel with a gentleness of understanding which struck Orlin as remarkable. "That is a claim as great as any man should wish to make."

Tied to Kaedric's will, I could not recoil at the litter of shriveled skin and fallow pelts. I could not turn away from Prince Orlin's death. "Caruillan sorcerers do not have such Power," I protested to Kaedric alone.

"Evidently, their abilities have been altered," he answered, and he added, "they will turn toward us soon. Orlin's few surviving followers should reach the city by this evening. We ought to have a brace of days before the Caruillans reach us." Kaedric had grown very grim, and hard lines of tension crossed his face. "I had best inform Lord Borgor that a siege is imminent and let the Council begin its panic gently."

"Prince Orlin was young to pay such a price for folly," I murmured.

"Horlach is no respecter of age or its lack."

"Benthen Abbey will despair of me soon if I continue to devote all my energies to laical issues," jested Abbot Medwyn. "Young priests are allowed to be vagabonds and meddlers in secular affairs, but an abbot is expected to tend his abbey."

"At least your vocation is not threatened with extinction," said Marga sourly. "Another day of playing stolid merchant's widow in a dingy Tulean flat will leave me as mad as Nimal. I am going to frizzle Wal Seris and plant myself on Kaedric's doorstep."

"You know that you are always welcome, Marga," said Kaedric as he entered, "though even Ceallagh's Tower cannot very well accommodate all the wizards of Ixaxis. Who is Wal Seris?"

"An oaf of a sea-silk merchant who thinks himself a very fine marital catch indeed."

Ineuil commented mischievously, "Perhaps you should not scorn your suitor, Mistress Marga, until the future of your profession grows brighter." Marga glared, and Abbot Medwyn choked back a laugh.

"I did not call this meeting to discuss Marga's marriage prospects," interrupted Kaedric, though he had also suppressed a fleeting grin at Marga's indignant ire. "We are about to be attacked by the forces of Caruil, led ostensibly by Blood-Talon Cor but certainly abetted by Horlach. And, Prince Orlin is dead."

"That little monster Joli is regent?" exclaimed Marga. "Lords help us, Orlin was bad enough."

"His Majesty's Council was not pleased either,"

said Kaedric, "though Borgor already schemes to seize another puppet. Borgor will manipulate himself into control of a realm that will no longer exist."

"I hope King Astorn is enjoying Bethii," observed Ineuil morosely.

"Did Prince Orlin's troop share his fate?" asked Medwyn.

"Some few were permitted to escape," said Kaedric in answer. "Once they reach Tulea with their tale, anarchy will ensue, and that miserable witch in the marketplace will not want for company. King Cor did not exercise mercy in allowing survivors."

"So we must prepare to keep discipline now," said Ineuil. "If we start conscripting our defenders against Caruil immediately, they will be too busy grumbling at mortal troubles to think about distant sorcery."

"You may have trouble convincing Borgor to authorize official mobilization," suggested Kaedric doubtfully. "Whether or not Borgor has become Horlach's direct tool, Serii's Adjutant appears intent upon serving Horlach's interests."

"By the time Borgor realizes that I am using his name in vain, we shall have the persuasive presence of Cor on our doorstep. My tavern acquaintance with Tulean soldiery will give me credence—as will the talent of an excellent forger I know." Ineuil smiled wanly. "I was trained for the military role; it is the part tradition dictates for lesser noblemen. I have avoided its official bonds for years, and now I tie the noose myself."

"Console yourself with your forged authority," recommended Kaedric dryly.

"I fully intend to do so. You just keep me clear of sorcerous interference, O Infortiare, and I shall remind King Cor of the justifiable renown of Tulean—and Seriin—indomitability."

"There ought to be enough of us in Tulea to form an effective Wizards' Circle," mused Marga. "That would leave Lord Arineuil free to form his army. I do wish you had allowed more of us to come to Tulea, Kaedric."

"The first business of Ixaxis is education, Marga," returned Kaedric wearily. "We must not destroy the seeds of future hope in our focus on the present war."

"I am certainly not going to call on you to inspire our army, Lord Venkarel," reproved Ineuil with black humor.

"I should rather hope not!" agreed Marga fervently. "Really Kaedric, we are not defeated yet. We are, in fact, quite a formidable group."

"You are not alone in this battle, Kaedric," added Abbot Medwyn carefully.

"I am simply another cog," rejoined Kaedric with light mockery. "Well enough—I am assuredly no warrior. Lord Arineuil, the army is yours to command. Mistress Marga's Circle should be able to counter the Caruillan sorcerers to a large degree. Abbot Medwyn, the cares of the inevitable wounded are yours. Lady Rhianna and I shall do what we can to mitigate Horlach's meddling. Let fortune favor us if she will."

Chapter 21

"My lady," said Kaedric when the others had gone, "I am going to seal the Taormin against remote usage. I should like to seal it altogether, but I suspect that can only be done from within, and I am not so noble as to imprison myself in amber filigree on the chance."

"You no longer think it can be used against Horlach."

"I think it cannot be used further to find Horlach. Our searching has in a sense served its purpose; it has pressed Horlach into action at a time not altogether of his choosing. Beyond that, the Taormin's aid becomes double-edged. Horlach knows it too well."

"That has ever been true."

"Yes." Kaedric laughed shortly. "Perhaps my nerve

is weakening." He shrugged. "My decision is not irrevocable. We know where the Taormin lies, and physical proximity will release it to us again."

"You implied to the others that we would continue to search for Horlach's presence."

"You and I have formed our own Wizards' Circle, my lady. We no longer need the Taormin for work at the monitors' level."

"How much more effectively could Mistress Marga's Circle operate if its members were enhanced by the Taormin?"

"If any of them survived the experience, they could probably shake Serii to the bone. The qualifying question is significant, however."

"I survived it, my lord, and I am no wizardess."

"Hrgh was a full wizard, and he did not survive." Kaedric grinned ruefully as he added, "And no matter what you may once have been, you are quite decidedly a wizardess now. You have the Infortiare's word on it."

The ragged, wounded remnants of Prince Orlin's glorious troop limped into Tulea on half-dead horses in a silent hour of the night. Abbot Medwyn met them and, as silently as the city, he gathered them into the ward of Parul Church. A young cleric was dispatched to the king's castle: to summon the Infortiare and to inform the princess regent that her brother's death had been confirmed by his erstwile followers.

I awakened to the distant ring of matins and a flustered Tamar shaking me urgently. She wore a flannel wrap, and curling papers twisted her hair alarmingly. "You would never allow me to leave my room looking like that, Mistress Tamar," I commented sleepily.

"My lady, there is a royal messenger demanding you," persisted Tamar. "You must get dressed, my lady."

"A royal messenger?" I asked, honestly bewildered. "His Majesty does not even know me," I began. But King Astorn was in far Bethii, and the regent in his stead was an impulsive girl with whom I did, after a fashion, share an acquaintance. "Tell the messenger that I shall come presently, Tamar."

Princess Joli appeared singularly humble for the titular head of Serii, dwarfed by her magnificent room and lacking the bravado she had occasionally shown. Princess Joli dismissed her attendants when I arrived, and they departed reluctantly, awkwardly bemused by the elevated status of their royal charge. Mistress Amila, the governess against whom I had unintentionally conspired with Her Royal Highness, eyed me suspiciously as she left.

"They all blame me for everything," lamented Joli without preamble. "I never asked to be regent. How could papa leave us like this? How could he leave Orlin in charge of anything? Orlin had to show how great and brave and clever he was, and all he did was make a mess of everything. What am I going to do, Rhianna?"

I could sympathize with Joli's confusion. I found her beseeching plea for my advice more than a little daunting. Having thoroughly embroiled myself in the Infortiare's concerns, I knew what answer I must give, but the giving of it immured me with the guilt of my own partisanship. I compromised. "Your Royal Highness must seek the counsel of those best qualified to give it."

"Lord Borgor is a weasely toad," responded Her Royal Highness. "Look what his advice did for stupid Orlin," she added disparagingly, but her voice caught on her brother's name.

"The chief adviser to the sovereign of Serii is the Infortiare, not the Adjutant," I returned.

"Everyone tells me to depose Lord Venkarel. He even makes papa nervous. Lord Borgor says that Lord Venkarel has made a pact with King Cor and is just waiting to take Serii for himself."

"As Your Royal Highness mentioned, Lord Borgor's advice has not proven very sound."

"Lord Borgor is not the only one to say it," grumbled Joli, but she watched me keenly. "Do you recommend the Infortiare because you are a sorceress?"

With impulsive honesty, I replied, "I am a wizardess, Your Royal Highness, and I serve the Infortiare, but I also serve you and Serii. You are an intelligent observer, Your Royal Highness. Do you believe it is Lord Venkarel who conspires with Caruil?"

"Arku Ruy could have been pretending to conspire with Lord Borgor as a diplomatic artifice to cover Ixaxin intrigues. Arku Ruy did not *like* Lord Venkarel, but neither does anybody else."

I blinked at Joli's unexpectedly intricate analysis. "As it happens, Your Royal Highness, I like Lord Venkarel very much, though he does not exert himself to acquire friends. I also trust him. I cannot expect you to share that trust on my testament, when our own acquaintance is scarcely substantial. I submit, however, that Lord Venkarel has no cause to make pacts with King Cor. If Lord Venkarel wished to control Serii or Caruil or the entire Alliance, he could reach and take his desire unaided."

The princess regent hugged herself in tight contemplation. She wore a pale pink robe trimmed with pink and white flowers. Her hair hung lankly. "I was only nine when Lord Alobar died," said Joli slowly. "He was a nice old man who used to tell me stories and make me paper stars that glowed yellow when I held them." I failed completely in an attempt to visualize saturnine Lord Venkarel similarly entertaining a little girl with paper baubles. "He told me he was going to die," said Joli with retrospective sadness. "He was not very old for a wizard. He told me not to be afraid of Lord Venkarel, because Lord Venkarel could not help being Powerful any more than I could help being a princess." Joli raised her head. "Will you bring Lord Venkarel to me, Rhianna?"

"I believe he is at the Parul Church, Your Royal Highness. I shall bear your summons to him," I answered, aching for both the princess and the Ven slave whom fate had laden with responsibilities neither could eschew.

* * *

I had not traversed Tulea or any other burg unescorted since my Venturing sojourn and an almost forgotten sense of liberty stirred in me. The temptation to stray from my errand grew, but I could not give in to it. I knew the location of Parul only vaguely; it was Kaedric's presence there which marked it unmistakably.

The tiny hospital which the Parul priests maintained had been overburdened. Abbot Medwyn had converted a wing of the Parul parish classrooms into added wards, and such physicians were gathered as could be recruited to the cause. Most of the cots in these rooms were still empty (filled only by Orlin's few survivors), but their number held a gloomy promise. A solemn Sister directed me through the waiting rows of starkly linened pallets. A half-dozen beds held muffled forms; a low whimper drew me to a boy whose delicately featured face had escaped the ravages which marred those of his comrades. The Sister who tended him brushed his fine, dark hair from his feverish brow and teased him with a smile.

"My handsome young lord," she said cheerfully, "if you must toss about and disturb those dressings over which I labored so carefully, you should not be surprised by a little discomfort."

"I only wanted to see how badly scarred I shall be," apologized the lordling with great contrition. "I could never face my lady if I were maimed."

"Your lady will be nothing but proud of you, my lord. Is she your betrothed?"

"Oh, no!" responded the young man. A fit of deep coughing wracked him, and it was a few moments before he continued. "She is the finest, the most beautiful lady of Serii. She does not know that I exist," he finished despondently.

"Come, she probably thinks you the finest, handsomest man in Serii and just bides in hope that you will bespeak her."

"Do you think she might?" asked the boy with almost religious awe. "I shall be healed soon, shall I not? I must defeat the Caruillans for my lady."

"You will have time enough to think of battle after you nap."

"I am not a child," complained the young lord. The Sister gazed at him sternly, and he continued meekly, "At least bring me some paper that I might write to my lady first."

"You have already written her a score of pages," laughed the Sister, but at the boy's crestfallen expression, she relented. "One more sheet of vellum, my lord. Our supplies are not infinite, and you need your rest."

"One more sheet, and I promise I shall behave. Thank you, Sister," gushed the boy.

The Sister espied me. "I am here to see Abbot Medwyn," I said, unwilling to advertise Kaedric's presence more than necessary.

The Sister smiled. "Of course, my lady. I am headed that way myself. I shall be pleased to guide you."

She led me into a warren of cells, and I commented idly, "You seem to have conquered that young lord's intransigence easily. You have nursed before."

"I have had some experience," she agreed. "A religious must tend the folk too poor or too wise to trust an untried medic's filthy leeches." She sighed heavily. "Not that anyone can likely help or hinder that poor boy you saw."

"He suffered no great pain," I asserted with troubled surety.

"He has been very heavily drugged. It is unlikely he will live to serve his adored lady in battle or anything else. Abbot Medwyn," said the Sister in curt announcement, "there is a lady here to see you."

"Thank you, Sister Adri," answered the abbot, and the Sister left us. "Rhianna, I would feel more sanguine about this visit if you did not look so woeful."

"Forgive me, Abbot Medwyn. Sister Adri and I were discussing one of your patients. I actually bear a summons for Lord Venkarel from Her Royal Highness, Princess Joli."

"You reveal the most unlikely connections, my lady,"

said Kaedric, emerging from shadow. "When did you become Princess Joli's emissary?"

"Her Royal Highness asked for me this morning. We share a common interest in trees. My lord, I am not sure how long her resolve to trust me will persist."

"If it lasts long enough to gain me an exclusive audience with the regent, I shall throw the wealth of the Infortiare at your feet. Medwyn," he said with a shrug, "You know better than I how to administer a hospital." Kaedric ushered me from the room, remarking as we walked, "Lady Rhianna, it might be best if you were not seen accompanying me back to the castle."

"It might be best if I did not wander Tulea at all, my lord, but I must obey the princess regent's orders. I promised to bring, not send, you to Her Royal Highness."

"Are you supposed to guard Her Royal Highness from the evil machinations of the Infortiare?"

"Princess Joli does not blindly oppose wizardry, my lord. She was very fond of Lord Alobar."

"Lord Alobar was a poor wizard but a good man." We had reached the occupied ward, and Kaedric grew silent. Sister Adri had returned to the young, besotted lord, but she drew the linen pall over his face. "How many will die before we are done?" asked Kaedric with a sigh.

"I wonder who he was," I said sorrowfully.

Kaedric answered absently, "Lord Joret dur Esmar," and I closed my eyes, willing denial. In one of those ridiculous, effusive paeans to which I had paid so little heed, Lord Joret had written that he would make himself worthy of me. He had not specified how, and I had not until now missed the daily letters which had ceased with Prince Orlin's celebrated, sorry foray. The tragic, wasted death roiled in my heart: another dram of guilt.

Chapter 22

The most influential gathering in Serii, the King's Council, numbered nearly half a hundred of the most prestigious representatives of Serii's nobility. I felt woefully misplaced and exceptionally conspicuous entering at Princess Joli's side, but Her Royal Highness had pleaded with me, and her desperation had persuaded me more than a direct command would have done. I think few of the councillors actually gave me notice, intent as they were on observing the previously disregarded princess who had imperiously summoned them. I saw my father start at sight of me, but he betrayed by no other sign that he recognized my existence. The less impenetrable Lord Brant dur Niveal scowled openly and often.

Lord Borgor spared me a brief, unflattering glance before convening the assembly. Joli proceeded to the chair of Tul with laudable dignity in light of her shaky condition moments before entering. Kaedric already occupied the place at her right. I stood behind Joli's chair in the region between the regent and the Infortiare.

Lord Borgor took his position on Joli's left, saying to her in a placating voice which managed to carry across the room, "It is customary for your father to state the purpose of the meeting at this juncture. If Your Royal Highness will inform me of the cause of your concern, I shall be pleased to announce it to the members of His Majesty's Council."

"I am quite able to speak for myself, Lord Borgor," said Joli regally. "Please recall that I am the regent, and you serve me." She continued more loudly, "It would be well if each of you recalled that Lord Borgor's is not the voice of Tul and Serii." She did not quaver now. "Serii has stood firm against many tides of trouble and dishonor since Ceallagh crowned my great-sire. Serii is the first and the greatest member of that Alliance which restored peace and prosperity to the tortured world shaped by the Sorcerer Kings. We are a single kingdom in that Alliance, but we are much more, for it was from Serii that freedom spread through the aid of the Ixaxin wizards, who give us allegiance.

"My lords, Serii is beset. The pirates of King Cor of Caruil have committed heinous treachery, defiling the fair city of Liin where they were welcomed, and even now they approach Tulea. The might of Serii can counter Cor's barbaric brigands, unless we allow our own self-seeking elements to overcome us. Serii's strength is the unity of Tul and Ceallagh, the cohesion of mortal sinew and wizard's Power. I have called you here to demand of you an answer: do you, the lords of the Seriin domains, support the realm of Tul and Ceallagh? If you affirm your faith, then we shall fight the battle before us with the sure strength of millennia. If you will not trust to the heirs of Tul and Ceallagh, then the battle is already ended in defeat, for Serii exists no more. Let those who believe still in Serii pledge their loyalty aloud: to the Regent of Tul and to the Infortiare of Ixaxis.

"Lord Sieg dur Aesir, what is your answer?"

I had heard Joli's speech before, the joint product of Kaedric, Ineuil and Joli herself, but Joli was a surprisingly compelling orator. The initial spatter of poorly suppressed laughter among the councillors had faded quickly in face of Her Royal Highness' persuasive determination to exert her proper authority. The hapless Lord Sieg dur Aesir, whom alphabetical honors afflicted, shifted nervously, helplessly beseeching Lord Borgor with an eloquent glance for some guidance in handling the recalcitrant child who presently held the crown of Serii.

"Your Royal Highness," said Lord Borgor smoothly, as clearly pleased by Lord Sieg's deference as he was disgruntled by his intended puppet's refusal to be tied to his strings. "Surely you cannot doubt that every rightful," he smiled in a superior manner at Kaedric, "Lord of Serii supports your father, King Astorn, unequivocably." Kaedric returned Borgor's scathing sneers with cool austerity. Encouraged by a lack of argument, Lord Borgor turned a patronizing tone against Joli. "We understand, Your Royal Highness, that your brother's tragic death has upset you overwhelmingly. Naturally, you seek reassurance at this time of distress, but the Council Hall is perhaps inappropriate for personal pleas. Your handmaiden," he said with a slight gesture toward me, "can doubtless reassure you more effectively than a room full of dour old men. With your permission, Your Royal Highness, the Council will proceed to the topics which press us. Lord Sieg, you may be seated."

"Lord Sieg," announced Princess Joli indomitably, "you have not yet given your response to me, and you shall stand until I declare the answer satisfactorily clear." Lord Sieg halted in an awkward half-seated position. "As for you, Lord Borgor, I understand and acknowledge your refusal to pledge your loyalty to me and to the Infortiare. Your resignation is accepted. Lord Arineuil dur Ven, you are the new Adjutant. Lord Borgor, please relinquish your position to Lord Arineuil and depart this Council."

It was difficult to equate this assured young regent with the hysterical girl who had hidden in a shrub from her governess and berated an inoffensive pine. Even Lord Borgor was shaken. He began to splutter an incredulous protest, echoes of which flickered through the hall, but Kaedric's piercing attention quickly cured Lord Borgor's hesitation: Lord Borgor blanched and obeyed Her Royal Highness' dictate without another word. With admirable calm considering the derogatory whispers which followed him, Ineuil assumed the Adjutant's vacated place of honor. He looked a query at Joli, and she nodded her very royal permission. "Lord Sieg dur Aesir," demanded Ineuil, "how do you vote?"

With an uncertain quaver, Lord Sieg replied, "I support the Princess Joli dur Tulea, regent of His Majesty, King Astorn."

"And the Infortiare, Lord Venkarel dur Ixaxis," insisted Ineuil.

Lord Sieg looked coldly at Kaedric but bowed his head and affirmed, "And I support the Infortiare, Lord Venkarel dur Ixaxis."

There were no refusals to comply with Joli's ultimatum after the example of Lord Borgor. The sincerity of the pledges could be termed dubious under the circumstances, but the circuitous ethics of the nobility would be stalled in rebellion by the tether of a witnessed oath. My father's compliance was not gracious, but the stiffest response of all issued from Lord Gorng dur Liin, the younger brother of Hrgh and Veiga, the man on whom Cor's treachery had just bestowed liegedom. I could not altogether blame the councillors for their grudging acceptance. Not one of them doubted that Lord Venkarel had just assumed virtually unfettered control of Serii.

"Do you think they will really obey me, Rhianna?" asked the princess regent of Serii, shivering with reaction now that her councillors had left to perform the tasks of defense allotted them by the Infortiare and the new Adjutant.

I answered briskly, hoping that I sounded reassuringly confident, "They will at least cooperate for the moment and weigh carefully any thought of rebellion. They will respect your leadership, Your Royal Highness, because you give it, and for all their gesturing, very few of them know how to issue a decisive command."

"Your Royal Highness," said Ineuil with enchanting fervor, "If you will speak to your soldiers as eloquently as you have favored your Council, you will have an army of such loyalty as you have never seen."

Joli's amber eyes sparked with shy delight, and I reflected that Ineuil would some day regret his habit of instinctive conquest. The princess regent of Serii was both vulnerable and tempestuous, and Ineuil's flirtation in that quarter could garner him some severe repercussions. If it gave Joli the moment's confidence which she needed, I was forced to admit that the deception might profit us all; I resolved to ensure, however, that Princess Joli suffer no whit of anguish over Ineuil's transient attentions, even if it cost Serii the services of her Adjutant. Before Ineuil could whisk the princess to the fore of her burgeoning troops, I whispered to him sharply, "If you cause Her Royal Highness any sorrow by your intemperate flattery, Ineuil, my sister will lack for a lover."

"Rhianna, I am quite reformed of frivolous pastimes," he scolded with an unrepentant grin. "I am the Adjutant now." He turned to Joli and very respectfully offered his arm. She accepted it timidly, almost lustrous with pleasure. I left them to pursue their plans for proselytizing and departed the castle.

Late afternoon sun washed the terrace; Kaedric stood at the balustrade, surveying the city which still held an illusory peace. Prince Orlin had died, as had absurd, idealistic Lord Joret. A war was almost upon us, but it still felt quite remote. Kaedric had sealed the Taormin, and the curbing of its turbulent force in my awareness increased in me the deceptive sense of calm. Even the Infortiare himself no longer gave me terror; I had lost somewhere in the Taormin's coils that dread of him to which I had clung so long. I had told Princess Joli that I liked him, unapproachable though he strove to be. I had spoken truly.

Attuned by the Taormin and with no mist of fear and awe to blind me, I could see uncertainty in him. The harsh stain of slavery had left him hard and unnaturally lean, as scarred by sorrow as by the lash of Master Doshk across his back. I knew he stretched the physical scars into deliberate pain as he clenched his long fingers upon the unyielding rail. He was worn, though he wore the indefinably ageless youth which was the purest legacy of Power. I thought how fair he was with his startling eyes and black hair; even that gift had cost him by making him appealing to the merciless clients of Doshk. He was a man inconceivably gifted with all the inherent attributes which men desire, and by his gifts he was accursed. Ineuil had accused me rightly: I had grown to love the Infortiare of Serii.

I did not bespeak him, leery of his ridicule if he recognized the most honest source of my devotion to his cause. At the least, the perception would disconcert him, and he had enough serious concerns to occupy him without my contribution to confound him. I left the terrace, girding myself to confront my father instead.

Chapter 23

I was destined to discover quickly that my presence at Princess Joli's side had attracted greater notice than I had realized. Lord Artos dur Endor made a point of greeting me whom he had never deigned to observe before. Lord Misch dur Vedma acknowledged me with a nod, Lord Gorng dur Liin with a glare of withering vitriol. Yldana intercepted me before I reached Tyntagel Hall.

"You have made rather a sensation, Rhianna dear," said my sister with aloof grandeur. "You have been a very busy girl to make such influential friends in five months." Yldana's mood was not the best, and I suspected that I would be wise to escape her before her evident strain of temper erupted into venom. I shrugged noncommittally, unable to devise any safer response.

As Yldana continued, I gleaned a glimmer of the envious cause for her irritation. "Veiga would like you to join us at a small supper this evening." She added very sweetly, "Do bring an escort, if you can find one."

An intimate dinner with Lord Borgor and Lady Veiga did not rank high on my roster of desirable occupations, however covetous a prize my sister might find it. I thought cynically that Lord Borgor wasted no time in seeking substitute puppets. "I am sorry, Yldana," I murmured insincerely. "Could you convey my regret to Lady Veiga? I am otherwise committed."

With gratuitous relief, Yldana replied, "Of course, Rhianna." She added with a knowing smile, "Do give my love to father when you see him." I returned her smile blandly, realizing as well as she did that my reception at Tyntagel Hall threatened to be a stormy one.

My father had left word with the staff to escort me to his office immediately upon my arrival. Liya watched me gravely from the stair as I passed; she retreated quickly when she discerned my glance upon her. My father awaited me, enthroned in a tapestried chair and drumming his desk with impatient fingers.

"You wished to see me, father."

His eyes beneath his menacing brows sought to pierce me. His signet winked rhythmically. "What is your part in this Ixaxin contrivance?" he demanded sternly, and I did tremble inwardly through the conditioning of long habit. My father's neglect in punishing me for my denial of Grisk had given me a baseless hope of his softening.

I answered with apparent poise, "Ixaxis did not contrive Her Royal Highness' Council meeting, father, if that is the subject to which you refer."

My father snapped, "You know quite well to what subject I refer."

"Princess Joli determined the content of the meeting, father. She chose to support the Infortiare and Ixaxis without coercion of any kind. I applaud her decision, and I am very proud that the Princess Joli considers me her friend."

"It is interesting to note that Her Royal Highness'

choice of Adjutant should coincide with a name unfortunately linked with yours."

"Lord Arineuil dur Ven brings to the post of Adjutant much more substantial military experience than his recent predecessors."

"He is an amoral wastrel," said my father with disgust.

"He is an educated and intelligent man, who may possibly preserve Serii from the attempted assassination abetted by men whom you have professed to admire."

My father stared at me coldly through the whole of a minute. "You insinuate to me, your liege lord, that I am a traitor. You laud Her Royal Highness for demanding fealty of her rightful subjects. I give you then the selfsame opportunity: affirm to me your loyalty, or confess yourself Tyntagellian no longer and leave my House."

"My lord father," I said woodenly, wounded by the formal ostracism I ought to have expected and had always felt, "I esteem you as my sire, but I shall not serve you more." I had finally freed my father of his responsibility to me, and I think it was the only gladness I had ever given him.

I devoted my evening to consoling Joli over her newly discovered potentials and listening to her issue infatuated sighs over her new Adjutant. The occupation kept me from my own distress and so served us both. I had strayed from her once only in mind: a flare of brutal fire in Tulean outlands met the reassuring control of Marga's Circle. Cor's army approached.

Joli recounted her quavering apprehension as she beseeched the people of her city to unite with her against the Caruillans. Later, in the Infortiare's library, Ineuil described to me the remarkable effectiveness of her entreaties. "She has the full charisma of the line of Tul when she elects to use it," he told me, and he sounded sincerely impressed. "Who would ever have expected it from the ghastly little delinquent? She even had the Tulean rabble cheering the Infortiare! We have had volunteers flocking to us; most are not experienced soldiers, but they know of their city's natural defenses, and they are inspired. If we parade Her Royal Highness before them periodically, we may actually be able to keep them in patriotic fervor."

"It is a terrible burden for her, Ineuil," I said. "Do not push her to the point of snapping."

"My lovely wizardess, I shall accord Her Royal Highness all the delicate handling possible. She is one of our most valuable assets!"

"Can she keep the lords of the Council in tow?"

"Not on the basis of an emotional appeal. They are a cold lot, His Majesty's councillors."

"You number among them, I believe."

"A result of unkind fate and insufficient brethren, not to mention the thoroughness of Our Infortiare's revenge on my improvident kin." Kaedric, who was intently composing for Ineuil various (authentic) letters of authority by which to enlist Tulea-dwelling Ixaxins, gave no sign of having heard the taunt, but I wished it unsaid, nonetheless. I gave Ineuil a quelling look; he proceeded glibly, "Has war erupted yet in Tyntagel Hall?"

I forced a careless smile. "Erupted and ended: exit one Lady Rhianna. I am banished."

"Awkward for you," clucked Ineuil.

Without raising his head from his scribing, Kaedric offered distantly, "Ceallagh's Tower suffers no dearth of lodging."

"Thank you, my lord," I answered, caught by the knowledge that Kaedric was fully aware of our conversation. I caught Ineuil's amused glance and decided that increased responsibility made Lord Arineuil increasingly annoying.

Chapter 24

The army of Cor flung itself against Tulean battlements five nights after the death of Orlin. They had tarried, reckoning the defense they faced, but they had the might and the insidious guidance of Horlach to drive them. Marga's Circle, augmented now by independent wizards whose bonds with Ixaxis had otherwise ebbed, gripped Tulea and cradled her from the sorcerous onslaught.

Against those unversed in the workings of arcane Power, the Caruillans poured forth a legion of murderers and mercenaries. Their ships occupied every inlet, and the vessels spewed forth hordes. Such farms and settlements as surrounded the borders of Tulea proper had been ordered vacated, but the Caruillans destroyed wantonly, defiling against future use and slaughtering those who had refused to leave their family homes. Tulea was fully besieged; the flux of trade and travel which sustained her ceased.

Ineuil's hastily gathered army struck intermittently at the legions of Cor, attacking under the command of Tulea's few experienced warriors and retreating again to the city before the Caruillans could fully organize their might. In discipline, both forces suffered equal inadequacies. Tulea held the more strategic position (so long as her ample storehouses did not fail), and the brief clashes had so far taken a slightly greater toll from Caruil. Still, Abbot Medwyn's improvised hospital filled, as did the Parul gravesites, and King Cor held the advantage of time. Not only would Tulean supplies ebb, but the enhanced sorcerers of Caruil would not tire as quickly as Marga's woefully small Circle.

One of Marga's number, a wizened wizard, Achmyr, who had schooled in Ixaxis with Lord Alobar, had already taken his death blow. He had grown fatigued, and the Caruillans had focused upon him to destroy him. Lesser sorcerers, whom Marga had lately recruited, could battle for only the shortest of durations before becoming too weak for useful contribution to the sorcerous defense; they could not replace Achmyr. Kaedric fed his Power to the whole of the Circle, sustaining every member far beyond normal endurance, but he had battles of his own besides the general defense. I think he never rested in those days, for Horlach had begun a sourceless, wearing attack against the Infortiare. I had been recruited for Marga's Circle and so did not realize for some time how severely Kaedric was beleaguered.

Much of the individual mischief which Cor's sorcerers wrought gave more inconvenience than serious tribulation, but the number of loci of the disturbances began to exceed the level of minor irritation. Thatch and timber in the heart of the city suddenly caught fire; Abbot Medwyn's supply of medicinal potions attracted an untoward number of destructive accidents. Abraded tempers began to erode Tulean unity, and it became incumbent upon Joli to appeal incessantly to her subjects merely to maintain a shadow of their initial spirit. Joli's own frame of mind remained remarkably firm. The afflictions which wearied the rest of us seemed to give her a strength of purpose, which carried her far beyond anticipated measure.

Marga's Circle lacked the clarity of individual identity which I had felt with Kaedric in the Taormin, but like Joli, the Circle had a strength yielded by cohesion of purpose. Horlach expended energy holding the Caruillans together despite their innate distrust of one another; I could feel his filtered taint. The energies surged and swayed, Tulea and Caruil stirring the infinities, while mortal men spent blood, and their women wept.

The ruling Lords of Serii began at last to relent and lend their own resources to the battle, as the spur of personal hazard reached them. Some still demurred and debated, but others had sent word to their own domains. At least one message had successfully passed the Caruillan blockade, for a small troop from Elt appeared to taunt the Caruillans from the rear. The Elt contingent offered a reassuring hope that Serii had not forgotten her king's city, but the passing days brought no further forces, and the aid from Elt dwindled with death.

There was much death, and there was the hollow emptiness left by the parting of soul from frail flesh. There was pain and the ache of those tears which bleed into the heart. There was sorrow and ancient, bitter reckoning of dreams' glory lost, the end of hope and the beginning of futility. We died in the Circle with every thrust of sword, wept with every desolate, bereaved child. There was no dawn, no sun of clearer seasons; there was night and a dusky, darkling cloud of despair. There was nothing, and there was a heritage nearly forgotten yet newly restored. We should have lost, but failure was too hard a foe.

Horlach waited, watching, pulling at the weak and entwining the strong in webs of helplessness. Marga held her Circle firm, disciplined by her command. When Marga weakened, the sorcery of Caruil wrought horrors and havoc.

Though no more greatly gifted with Power than many lesser wizards, Mistress Marga had indomitably instructed Ixaxins for more than a century. She had the gift of great teachers to kindle the best in her charges. She brought that force to the Circle, pressing even the most unruly individuals into fruitful cooperation; as one of that errant number, I found Marga's lessons often humbling but cogent. Though others among us, both younger and more puissant, had failed before the steadiness of the Caruillan onslaught, Marga's collapse shocked us into a moment of blindness to the battle we waged. In that moment, Caruil took a toll from which Tulea would not recover, gaining holds in dangerous places due to our inattention. A double dozen of Blood Talon Cor's most aggressive partisans breached the Tulean gate, and we could not afterward ascertain how many of them escaped into the city to work their clandestine terrorism. The sorcerous holds they took were more subtle and more insidious still.

Medwyn ascribed Marga's condition to the inevitable result of protracted exhaustion and confined her to a room in the king's castle. Joli had provided both the chamber and the attendants, for Marga required care unavailable in Ceallagh's Tower. Marga would have rebelled vehemently over the fuss, but she did not rouse enough to realize her condition. The Ixaxin master who took her place as Circle leader was a skilled wizard named Macoll, but he lacked Marga's ability to unite our efforts, and the Caruillans tightened and took hold as sedulously as a bramble.

"How Rhianna?" asked the child of Tul, "How do I keep on being strong? I want to run away from all of it. I cannot keep pretending to be brave and sure of everyone. I have nothing left to give them."

"There is no one else, Your Royal Highness," I answered, my own heart aching in echo.

"I cannot keep on like this," quavered Joli.

"I know. But you will."

"How?"

I shook my head helplessly. "There is nothing else you can do.

Chapter 25

The winter mist covered me and set me shivering, but I had need of solitude and the comforting persistence of the trees. I had been sent from the Circle to seek a few hours' sleep; I suspected that troubled dreams would provide less of a restorative than imperturbable old friends. Having accepted at last that my Tyntagel oaks were as lost to me as Rhianna's Dwaelin Wood, the gardens of the castle had grown increasingly dear. I should never again know the trees as deeply, closely as I had done, but I savored these avidly. They were the trees of Tul, and Horlach threatened them.

I wandered near to Tyntagel Hall and espied Ezirae waving erratically from her parlor window. I returned the remote greeting, feeling more distanced from her than if I had not seen her at all. I had met Yldana a few times of late; she continually beseeched me to visit Lord Borgor and Lady Veiga, while maintaining ambivalent relief that I did not comply. I knew that Dayn had accepted a captaincy under Ineuil's command, but I had not seen my brother nor my other kin since my severance from my father's rule. When Ezirae came bobbing across the lawn to beckon me under the arbor, I felt as displaced from her in time as from the Lady Varina dur Castor whose stone I now wore.

Poor Ezirae stopped several paces away from me, plainly leery of too near an approach. She flicked her heavy cloak nervously, as if she could remove unpleasant circumstances with the drizzle of rain. "You should not walk about in this weather with your head uncovered, Rhianna," said my aunt automatically.

I hid a smile and answered demurely, "I am sorry, Aunt Ezirae."

"Your father would be most unhappy if he knew I spoke to you, Rhianna. He has given very specific orders."

"I did defy him very thoroughly this time," I answered, touched by Ezirae's own rare defiance.

Ezirae wagged her head assertively. "You must apologize to him, Rhianna. He will forgive you."

"I have other obligations now."

"It is not at all seemly, Rhianna," said my aunt with a worried cluck.

"We are at war, Ezirae," I responded gently.

"It is all so very distressing." Ezirae drew herself up primly. "What good will come out of defeating the barbaric Caruillans if we all become barbarians our selves in the process? Your behavior has been most improper, Rhianna. I must insist that you return to your family."

"Aunt Ezirae, I cannot."

With a blush of effort, my aunt persevered, "You cannot continue to defy convention without repercussions, Rhianna. You have a proud heritage, but you are making yourself quite unmarriageable. I have actually heard that you live in the Infortiare's Tower."

"I am a wizardess, Aunt Ezirae. Lord Venkarel is my liege lord."

Ezirae involuntarily stepped back another pace, but she was resolute in her well-meant intentions. She frowned and fretted, "It is so difficult. I simply do not understand Baerod, moping in his office and allowing a young girl to make these decisions for herself. First you and then Liya."

"Liya?" I asked, startled.

"Liya has gone to work with that abbot as some sort of a nurse, if you can imagine." Abbot Medwyn had gathered a number of volunteers, but he had not told me that my brother's wife was among them; we had neither of us had, of course, a great deal of time for idle chatter recently. I felt a pleasure of pride in my diminutive sister-in-law. Ezirae resumed her purposeful critique: "Lord Venkarel does not even keep a suitable retinue, and after all those dreadful stories about Lady Veiga—well, it is most improper." Ezirae paused as if an astonishing revelation had just come to her and mused, "Dear me, I wonder if that is why Lady Veiga has become so peculiarly interested in you recently. No wonder Lord Borgor is so displeased." The prospect of new gossip excited Ezirae into forgetting her careful distance and her disapproval. She said conspiratorially, "They have had nothing but troubles between them since he was replaced as Adjutant. One understands disappointment, naturally, but Lady Veiga is positively contemptuous when she even notices him or anything else." I did not point out that Lady Veiga appeared to share the Dolr'han failing of chronic contempt; I was sufficiently puzzled by the intimation that

Yldana's persistent conveyal of invitations had indeed been instigated by the lady of Sandoral and not the lord. I could not share Ezirae's belief that jealousy spurred the arrogant Lady Veiga.

A blow of discordant sorcery rippled through the Circle of wizards and very briefly disoriented me. Too much damage was wrought, and I reckoned my remaining respite would soon end. "What manner of interest in me does the Lady Veiga express?" I asked directly.

Ezirae opened her eyes very wide, bewildered as she always was when anyone attempted to redirect her from a scandalous speculation. She did gather her wits to form a reasonable answer without excessive delay. "She seems to ask about everything: what you studied as a child, where you have traveled, what you usually do for amusement. She has spent a simply outrageous amount of time with Lord Grisk. She has even been asking about your mother, though I do think she has had the sense not to speak of the subject to Baerod. Yldana is becoming quite irritated with Lady Veiga's obsessive conversation, and I must say I am beginning to agree. All of this war foolishness is bad enough without Lady Veiga duri Sandoral constantly hinting that you are somehow tied up in it. I wish these awful Caruillans would go away so we could get back to normal."

My head had begun to throb with fatigue and the echo of another Caruillan attack. The rain had begun to pound heavily. "I really must leave you now, Aunt Ezirae. I am very grateful for your concern about me." I kissed her cheek before she could jump away, and I think she was pleased, though it could have been only relief at surviving the experience of conversing with me. I could hear her tutting dolefully as I crossed the saturated lawns to Ceallagh's Tower.

I did sleep for several hours, spared the early Circle summons I had anticipated. The sun had fallen before I woke, and I could only vaguely guess the time as I studied the shadows shrouding the bedchamber I had borrowed from a long forgotten wizardess. The striving flux of Power was muted; evidently, even the Caruillans had begun to feel the need of rest. I climbed the stairs to the library, knowing I should find Kaedric there.

He occupied the worn velvet armchair, his eyes lidded, though his mind remained rigidly awake. He spoke to me lazily. "Your eccentric choice of conversational locales appears to be a Tyntagellian trait, though I should have thought Lady Ezirae's Hamley practicality would have proved stronger. The soldiers of Tulea and Caruil are daunted, but Tyntagellian ladies deem freezing rain ideally suited for an afternoon chat." Kaedric opened his clear blue eyes. "I saw you from Marga's window."

"Has Mistress Marga roused?"

"She has not stirred, but she is disquietingly busy on some level. Perhaps you could visit her later; you might have more success than I in reaching her."

Checking a selfish sigh at the omnipresent demands of duty, I offered meekly, "I have been remiss not to have visited her earlier. I shall go at once, my lord." My Power protested its weariness.

"At this hour, you would probably frighten her attendants into hysteria, and another night's delay will not disturb Marga. That, at least, is my rationalization for keeping you here instead. Tell me something simple and commonplace, my lady: something not weighted with the cares of the Infortiare. What occupies the Lady Ezirae duri Tyntagel? Is she ferreting new court scandals from the foundering fulcrum of our society?"

"She is concerned that Sandoral Hall suffers a lack of marital bliss," I said lightly but hesitantly, ambiguously motivated in discussing Lady Veiga with Lord Venkarel.

"That is very stale information. Veiga and Borgor share only a rapacious taste for power—of any kind. Your aunt's perspicacity wanes if she has only now discovered disharmony in Sandoral. Surely mere war cannot have caused Lady Ezirae's repertoire to grow so meager."

"Lady Ezirae is enormously upset by the state of her kindred. Lady Liya has begun to tend wounded soldiers in Abbot Medwyn's wards, I have forsworn my father for the Infortiare, and my father does nothing to stop either of us from such vastly improper behavior."

"Lady Ezirae suffers qualms for your moral character?" asked Kaedric with a cautious smile. "I suppose she dislikes your association with me nearly as much as does your father."

I replied with a trace of wistful humor for my aunt's particular perspective, "I believe my aunt considers the crime of wizardry less heinous than that of inhabiting Ceallagh's Tower."

"Alone with me," finished Kaedric wryly. "On the verge of calamity, your aunt quotes court etiquette." Meticulously, he traced with his finger the crease of velvet across the arm of his chair. "I doubt that Lord Baerod can be appeased by any act in which *I* am involved, but we might remedy the impropriety which so disturbs Lady Ezirae."

"I shall inquire of Her Royal Highness for other lodgings, my lord," I answered woodenly. Under less demanding external circumstances, I should not have expected the Infortiare to tolerate my precarious status as houseguest as long as he had. Mistress Marga had commented upon it slyly, for Kaedric's aversion to permanent visitors was well known by Ixaxins.

"That was not my meaning, but you might prefer it to the alternative." He was very firmly barriered, and I could read nothing from the stringent tone he took or the precise, expressionless set of his gaze. With extraordinary diffidence, he continued, "I thought you might consider marrying me, though I have an awful nerve to ask it under the circumstances," and I could not believe that I had heard him correctly. Kaedric proceeded in an uncharacteristic rush, which gave me no chance to speak, "Lords, I wish I had Ineuil's glib tongue just now. I should like to make some extravagant speech to tell you that you are the only meaning I have ever found in this world, you are become the faith which Medwyn despaired of ever instilling in me, and you have shown me the wizards' infinity, which I thought a theoretician's device until I felt you enter that unlikely Anxian tavern. Courtiers learn to say such things without sounding ridiculous, but I am not a courtier. I think you know what I am. I wish I could offer you better." Kaedric fell silent abruptly, and I caught my breath with an uncertain laugh.

"I shall be a difficult wife, my lord."

We were wed in the Parul chapel by Abbot Medwyn, while the cries of the wounded sang a strange marriage hymn. Kaedric had dragged Ineuil from the midst of a violent morning's skirmish by means which I preferred not to consider. Princess Joli had espied me leaving Mistress Marga's room in the castle and insisted on accompanying me, once she had by persistent badgering extracted my intent. Liya stood beside me also, though she had at first demurred from coming so near to the Infortiare, and her concession gave me much pleasure.

It was a very short and peculiar ceremony: Abbot Medwyn and Liya carrying the faint scent of the dying and the astringent odor of healers, Ineuil blood-stained and sporting a sword of battle, the princess regent of Serii acting as acolyte. Midway through the service, a messenger arrived from the castle with an urgent summons for Kaedric from Mistress Marga's nurse. We hastened through the final words, sealing the vows as Caruil hurled a virulent wave of destruction against Tulea, a blow which shattered irrevocably the Wizards' Circle which had been our chief defense.

"Go to Marga for me, my Rhianna," said Kaedric with a rueful sigh. "Ineuil, the Caruillans have breached the city gates; you and I had best see what we can do to stem the influx. Your Royal Highness should return to the castle before the fighting traverses the city."

"I can be more useful here," declared Joli determinedly, donning again her regal presence and certainty of command, "If only by aiding morale. Lady Liya, you will direct me, please." Liya smiled at me slightly without quite managing to look at Kaedric; then she followed Joli and a subdued Abbot Medwyn to the makeshift hospital. Ineuil coughed discreetly, Kaedric kissed me lightly, and both were gone.

Chapter 26

"Where is your sister, Yldana?" demanded Veiga fiercely. "We have asked you many times to bring her, and still you disappoint us."

"I have no influence with Rhianna," answered Yldana irritably. "I never did." Can Veiga talk to me of nothing else, she thought. And where has she been? I have awaited her for nearly an hour. "Did I misunderstand the hour of your invitation this morning, Veiga dear?"

Veiga withdrew her attention, and Yldana watched the change uncomfortably. This was the second time that Yldana had witnessed Veiga's shift into impossibly intense abstraction, and the last occasion had not ended well. Yldana had grown truly concerned that Veiga suffered a physical ailment, for Veiga's eyes were utterly distant and her skin was clammy and cold. Veiga had raved as well, and Yldana had sought Borgor's aid. Borgor had refused to come to his wife, and he would not speak of her. He had closed his study door in Yldana's face, and he had refused to emerge. When Yldana had returned to Veiga with a drafted servant, the lady of Sandoral had regained her normal aspect. She had derided Yldana, denying that the troubling incident had transpired. Now, it was recurring, and Yldana feared to an unreasonable degree.

The Lady Veiga dur Liin duri Sandoral laughed in private triumph. "He has kept it in our very reach, my

Liege, defying us to find it. Even the wizardess did not know how close to our hands it lay."

Yldana regarded her friend with growing disquiet. "Veiga, to whom do you speak? Borgor is in his chambers." The two women stood alone in the enclosed garden of Sandoral Hall. The heroic figures amid the formal plantings stared at Yldana with mocking, marble eyes.

"Borgor is a weak fool," said Lady Veiga, but she still gazed beyond the world in which Yldana stood trembling. "An insignificant threat from Venkarel made him crumble. The wizardess is stronger, but she is not the one. The one who took Hrgh, my King? Yes, the one who aided the Venkarel. It must be the other. The Lady Rhianna? Yes, we must see her dead."

"Veiga," cried a very frightened Yldana. "What are you saying?"

"Your sister must die as must the wizardess," responded Veiga in her own controlled, scornful tones. "She destroyed my brother, Yldana, and we cannot let her go unpunished."

"Rhianna never knew Hrgh," pleaded Yldana with bewildered dismay.

Veiga had returned to her inward sight. "But the Taormin is first. We have shattered the Ixaxin Circle and found it while the Venkarel's mind was elsewhere. Kill the wizardess who still fights us, Veiga, and it will be ours to claim. The Venkarel will be too besieged to stop us from taking it—and him. Then the tree-witch will be yours, Veiga, and your brother will be avenged. Yes, my King, I shall kill the Tyntagel witch, and my brother will be avenged." Lady Veiga's words trailed into silence, and the titian-haired sorceress stiffened into a death-image trance. Yldana touched her tentatively; Veiga did not react, and Veiga's flesh was as cold as the rubies around her neck. Yldana ran from Sandoral Hall, too horrified to care that servants watched her with dubious stares.

Marga was dying. Her distraught attendants reiterated their innocence of her failing condition until I nearly screamed at them to keep silent. The bewildered nurse was little better, apologizing endlessly for a situation she could not explain, and I finally dismissed them all in desperation for some peace. I had left Marga a few hours before, unawakened but at no apparent hazard for eventual recovery. I studied Marga's ashen face, as faded as her eternally uncooperative hair, and I knew that Kaedric would not see her alive again.

I tried to reach the obstinate spark of the wizardess which yet lingered. I could so nearly touch her mind; Marga strove to meet me. I ought not to have been so riven from her, but something had altered her in a fashion which frightened me. She was dying in body; in mind, she was already largely gone.

The forceful little wizardess died with my hand brushing her brow. Her passing shook me, and Kaedric would suffer it more keenly by far. I had failed to find the cause of Marga's unnatural decline, and I had failed to learn what activity Kaedric had felt her somnolently pursue. It was not pleasing news which I must bear unto my husband.

I felt impatient and aggravated by the nervous grief which had replaced my morning's precious euphoria. Yldana hailed me before I could escape the castle, and I met my sister with fractious asperity. "I am available for no luncheons, dinners, or other social functions in the foreseeable future, and you may so inform Veiga Dolr'han in whatever words please you. I am in rather a hurry, Yldana."

"Listen to me, Rhianna!" said my sister without any of her usual composure. She pressed my arm urgently. "The wizardess is dead, is it not so?"

I stopped abruptly and stared at my sister. Her jet hair was imperfectly coifed. Her brown eyes held worry rather than enticement. "If you mean Mistress Marga, yes; she died moments ago."

Yldana nodded nervously. "It was Veiga."

"What?"

"Veiga killed her. Veiga intends death for you as well," said Yldana fervently, and I could feel in her words the horror of truth. "Please believe me, Rhianna: I would never have helped her if I had realized what she planned. I knew she wanted vengeance against Lord Venkarel for Hrgh's sake, but she blames you also, though you never even met Hrgh. I think I no longer know Veiga. I think she is no longer sane."

"Yldana, what does she say of Hrgh?" I asked with the calm of unbearable dread.

Yldana wrung her restless hands and turned her eyes away from me. "Hrgh has been hidden in Tulea for the past year. He looks so much the same, but his mind is—gone."

"You have seen Hrgh?" I demanded, trying to persuade myself that I had not in fact killed the lord of Liin. I wanted to believe that Veiga could have learned of my part against her brother from the soulless husk, which was all that could now remain of Hrgh Dolr'han.

"Yes, I have seen him," burst my sister in despair, "And I thought I should do anything to see him avenged. I spied for her, Rhianna, on you, on Ineuil on anyone Veiga claimed would bring us closer to the Infortiare. I even stole private missives from father, though I never knew why Veiga wanted them. I thought I did it for Hrgh. I did love him, Rhianna. Veiga knew, and she used me."

"Where is she, Yldana?" I asked with cold certainty. I had set my mind to search already, and I had found Kaedric on the Mountain of Tul, while Cor's sorcerers wrought unchecked havoc at the city gate.

"I left her in Sandoral Hall an hour ago," answered my sister. "She was fey, speaking in two voices and two minds. She said she would see you dead, Rhianna. I never meant that you be harmed."

I stared at the path to Ceallagh's tomb, a pale and twisting snake against the mountain above us. A shaft of sun through angry clouds caught a crimson speck of shining. "Veiga wears the Dolr'han rubies," I said, and Yldana nodded a startled agreement. "Yldana," I insisted urgently, "send word to Ineuil and to Princess Joli at the Parul wards that we have found Horlach." Yldana regarded me dubiously, but my Power and near-panic united to persuade her. "Tell them that Kaedric goes to face him in the Taormin. Ineuil must use Horlach's distraction to destroy Cor's sorcerers by mortal means; we may have little time. Please, Yldana," I begged. My sister nodded rigidly; I fled to the trail of Tul.

I could feel the changing: we were losing the constancy of life and history which our world had known for so many ages. We had always known that there were other times. We had always known that there were other, turbulent forces locked beneath our rules and solid customs. Did I enact this rending upon myself? I did not rouse Horlach. I had run from gilt imprisonment, but I did not stir the fires which I found. I did not seek Kaedric; I did not know that he could exist. The fires would have burned without my intervention, but I felt guilt. I felt that I had overthrown more lives than mine with my small rebellion, and I felt my husband's guilt of rebellion against Ven. I wished deeply that the turmoil could be undone, that the rip could be repaired; but how could we two not have acted as we had done?

I ran the path as far as I was able, seeing nothing of the beauty or dizzying view. I felt the journey endless in my desperate haste. I drew heedlessly to myself the strength of the earth and trees, gathering such forces as I could muster, knowing I would spend the dearest of them for the cause of my lord and husband. My feet began to stumble and slow, but the inner vistas grew clear and close. When Kaedric furled his fingers around the Taormin's layered shell, I stood in sight of him, though my physical shell still labored up the rock-wracked incline.

They were three: my gaunt and perilous lord; the dim, avaricious image of the Lady Veiga Dolr'han; and a confusion of forms which rippled over a man of ordinary proportions, a man who wore the crown and barbed wreath of the Sorcerer King. "You must realize by now that you cannot defeat me, Venkarel," said Horlach. "We understand the laws of wizardry, you and I, better than the unimaginative Zerus who purported to codify them. Zerus neglected the orders of infinity shamefully: infinity commutes all things. You are merely matter and energy, while I am energy and infinity. You cannot overcome the basic laws of existence."

Kaedric answered with a comparable detachment, "You have not forsworn matter, Horlach. You persistently seek its restrictions; hence, you abrogate the advantage which you claim."

"You are an interesting foe, Venkarel. You make a point which I had not considered. Nonetheless, I shall take you now that I have found the Taormin again. You tricked me once, Venkarel, with your tree-witch, but I was not ready then. You will not repeat your small triumph. You have made the inevitable error of a relatively superior intellect in judging all others by the paltry standards to which you are accustomed. You try to use the Taormin against me, deeming yourself more exceptional than the multitude preceding you. You will fail as they did; I have held the Taormin longer than you even imagine."

"Yield to us, Kaedric," whispered Veiga seductively, "and you and I shall rule for eternity."

"With your chosen lord, Horlach, manipulating my every breath?" returned Kaedric grimly. "You were never that enticing, Veiga. Or do you forget that I refused such an offer even when you gave it to me honestly?" Veiga lashed out a coil of acid spite, which Kaedric blandly parried. Horlach chuckled indulgently, seemed to darken and coalesce, and exuded with a breath a throbbing wave of Power which pulsed into a semblance of the Taormin's whorls.

With a wand of inner light, Kaedric culled the angry nodes, smoothing the menacing webs. I moved beside him, lending my own will and Power as I had in less treacherous walks. He accepted me without pause, for we had become too closely bound to be distinguishable.

The sparks of baneful fire began to course. Kaedric moved to alter the weaving's pattern, and Veiga retreated in alarm, while Horlach implacably gathered the changes and rewarped them. The issuance from the Sorcerer King came faster, and there was no time for the care of certain study. We were well into the Taormin now, treading tortuous paths which I knew that Kaedric had not explored. We glimpsed souls caught within the twines, but they were lost, and we evaded them. Horlach did know his holding well, and it flexed and ebbed too easily to his command.

The fires stirred and sputtered into elusive furies. I knew peripherally that I had overtaken a foot-weary Veiga on Tul Mountain's merciless heights; Horlach's leaping essence had not needed of her the extra steps to Ceallagh's tomb. I continued to climb, and the stresses and taunts of Horlach and Kaedric waxed vaster, while the unwary and weak who stumbled in the path of the warring pair burned in acid and fire. Victims perished haphazardly in Tulea, Tyntagel, Ven, Caruil, Ardasia, and Mahl; the geography of the Taormin cared nothing for material rationality. Horlach's dead-alive were roused, and the gargoyles of his ancient gate spewed forth into innocent lands. Evil things stirred in the Dwaelin Wood, which had been stilled of any major sorcery for long ages, and the barrier-wall of Anx rippled and took flame. Horrors stirred lakes, and travesties of life crawled from forgotten crypts: the neglected toys of the Sorcerer Kings were revived in animus by the rending play of energies tearing magma from the Taormin. Horlach had taken his world thus; he had only to patiently persist, and any mortal would fall to him, who had no precious runnels of blood to protect.

"You never took the final step, Horlach," said Kaedric coldly, as he absorbed another spear of dark fire with a pain which he determinedly denied. "Despite your contrary contentions, you remained essentially energy and, so, mortal." The darkness which was Horlach hardened. He is alarmed, I thought; he fears my husband, whom he waited so long to use.

"You cannot go beyond me," insisted Horlach persuasively. Horlach paused and laughed cruelly. "You bluff well, Venkarel. You essay to push me into rashness. You would like to see me leave this domain to you, would you not?"

Kaedric responded slowly, "I shall not emulate you, Horlach. I do not wish to be a Sorcerer King."

Horlach emitted derisive fury. "You are a fool, after all," said the dark, undying king, as he wove destruction across the world. "What have your pathetic mortals given you that you should serve them so far?"

"They have given me fear and hatred, Horlach, and I have had a surfeit of both."

"I shall take you," promised Horlach. The darkness pressed against us with lethal skill.

"I cannot surrender to him, Rhianna," breathed my husband to me in his mortal voice; I had reached him at last in physical presence, and we stood alone to reasoning sight before the dull gray stone which marked the dusty bones of Ceallagh. Kaedric held the Taormin lightly, a strong and delicate grasp of a mechanical thing of twisting wires and mineral fragments. I could see its glow press light from his fingers; I could see the press of his fingers twisting light from Horlach's tangles. We stood in two worlds, and both were real and terrible.

The breeze carried the scent of rain. I touched my husband's hand and brushed his lips with tears. He held me softly, fiercely, and the beating fire of him filled me. "You shall not leave me, Kaedric," I whispered in return.

"We must lose this world, beloved."

"We have the other, and it will not end."

He parted from me slowly, and I had no recourse but to let him go. I watched him feverishly, remembering, though he would remain to me in mind. I recalled how cold I had thought his eyes, as the blue turned to gold with the fire which claimed his form.

Kaedric took the Taormin, wrenching it piecemeal from Horlach's grasp. Horlach's layered faces faded: a sallow, unimpressive little man remained. "You cannot defeat me," insisted Horlach.

"I can save Serii from you, Horlach, and from myself." Blue fire burst outward, and the darkness melted before it. "I release you, Horlach," whispered my husband, and the darkness died.

I stood alone atop Tul Mountain. I gathered the fallen Taormin from the hard ground and cradled it against my breast. The filigree was cloaked by ash, and I pressed it to me tightly.

I bit my lip, and the salt of blood mingled with silent weeping. "You had best return to the castle, beloved," said my husband gently. "Cor's forces will scatter without the insistent drive of Horlach, but there remains much work of recovery. You are the Infortiare now."

I shook my head, though the gesture had little meaning. "You are not dead, my husband."

With a sardonic humor which I well knew, Kaedric replied, "Even Ixaxis is unlikely to follow a ghost."

"I am little more without you. Let me join you now; I am your wife."

"And difficult, as you promised," said Kaedric with a shaken laugh. "We have unleashed years of turmoil this day, and we must effect a laborious remedy, my Rhianna. I can no longer act upon the world of matter save through you. I would I had not burdened you with this."

I essayed a smile and succeeded to a measure. "But I did bring it upon myself, my lord and love. Very well, I shall fulfill our obligations in this plane, but it is a delay only. You have accepted immortality, Kaedric; your wife must share it with you." I paused. "Kaedric, can you hear the trees?"

"Dimly, but as well as I ever could."

"I am glad," I said and turned my eyes and feet toward my city.

VI. THE EMBER

Year of Serii—9009
Tulea, Serii

King Astorn will return tomorrow, and Joli will relinquish the regency. Our king will not like what he finds, though word by now has reached him of the worst of it. His prized son is gone, and most of his councillors not dead have retired, like my father and my uncle, to domains which will not remember their traitorous follies. Joli has forged a new Council, and she has done well. I shall see that His Majesty heeds his daughter's words, for she has proven wiser than he; she will be a strong queen.

Horlach's futile war claimed so many: irascible, irreplaceable Mistress Marga of Ixaxis; the brash piratical king of Caruil, Blood-Talon Cor; the sadly unlamented scion of Niveal, Lord Grisk. Amgor is among the dead, victim of a festered wound. He failed steadily, despite Abbot Medwyn's efforts to save him. I think Amgor could not face the guilty truth of his part in conspiracy any more than he ever accepted the fact that his wife would never love him. Yldana was kind to him at the end at least; though grief has subdued her lustrous spirit, it has taught her mercy. Ineuil, I think, will wed her when her mourning time is done. He knows she worked with Veiga to use him, but Ineuil is not himself blameless of deceit. They seem to understand each other well, my sister and the errant lord of Ven.

Abbot Medwyn frets for me, delaying anew his return to Benthen Abbey, though Master Gart has come to escort him on a now uncertain journey. I have told

Medwyn vainly that he has no cause for his deep concern over me. I have Liya to attend me in Tulea, for Dayn has assumed Tyntagel's place on the Council. Joli comes also to see me, and there are ever visitors from Ixaxis. I do not try to explain that other sustaining presence; I should be adjudged as mad as the pitiable Veiga.

Abbot Medwyn knows that I bear Kaedric's child. The priest in him disapproves, for he realizes that Kaedric most truly wed me with the asking, but Medwyn remembers too clearly an intense young boy in a ruined, smoking city. Abbot Medwyn will welcome my son for Kaedric's sake.

I stand beside a sapling oak on the Mountain of Tul. The island which has made itself my domain catches sunset from its chalky walls. Dusk stains the castle below me, and the Tower is shadowed black. I feel the hearts of Serii, the throngs of Tulea, the bright glow of Ixaxis, and the solemn strength of Tyntagel oaks; I feel the lives across the seas and in the earth. There are more troubles in Serii now, and Ventures have been called to begin the healing of them.

I rub the stone of Varina of the bittersweet sorrow. He whom I love holds me next to him in that other world we share. I know that I must soon return to the castle, for Abbot Medwyn worries greatly when he deems me alone. He does not know.